City Wilds

Edited by Terrell F. Dixon

City Wilds

ESSAYS AND STORIES ABOUT URBAN NATURE

The University of Georgia Press ⤳ *Athens and London*

Acknowledgments for previously published works appear on pages vii–ix, which constitute an extension of the copyright page.

Athens, Georgia 30602

Designed by Louise OFarrell
Set in 10.5/14 Adobe Garamond by G&S Typesetters
Printed and bound by Maple-Vail
The paper in this book meets the guidelines for permanence and durability of the Committee on Production Guidelines for Book Longevity of the Council on Library Resources.

Printed in the United States of America
02 03 04 05 06 C 5 4 3 2 1
02 03 04 05 06 P 5 4 3 2 1

Library of Congress Cataloging in Publication Data

City Wilds : essays and stories about urban nature / edited by Terrell F. Dixon
p. cm.
ISBN 0-8203-2350-0 (alk. paper) — ISBN 0-8203-2339-X (pbk. : alk. paper)
1. Nature—Literary collections. 2. Urban ecology—Literary collections. 3. City and town life—Literary collections. 4. American prose literature—20th century. I. Dixon, Terrell
PS648.N32 C58 2002
810.8′036—dc21 2001037810

British Library Cataloging in Publication Data available

Contents

Acknowledgments vii

Introduction xi

1 · Reversing the Tides *Lisa Couturier* 1

2 · The Moss Rose *William Goyen* 8

3 · Where Have All the Animals Gone? The Lamentable Extinction of Zoos *Charles Siebert* 13

4 · Touching the Earth *bell hooks* 28

5 · Big City Waters *Michael Aaron Rockland* 34

6 · Bottles of Beaujolais *David Wong Louie* 47

7 · New Moon over Roxbury: Reflections on Urban Life and the Land *Rebecca Johnson* 61

8 · Zip-A-Dee-Do-Dah *Emily Hiestand* 73

9 · The Silence *Chet Raymo* 80

10 · A Paradise of Frogs *John Hanson Mitchell* 86

11 · The Girl Who Raised Pigeons *Edward P. Jones* 89

12 · Disturbing the Universe *Betsy Hilbert* 109

13 · Florida *Joy Williams* 114

14 · Paddling off the Edge of the Big Easy *Bob Marshall* 119

15 · Swamp Boy *Rick Bass* 132

16 · Conquistador *Wendell Mayo* 142

17 · The Soul of Treaty Oak *Stephen Harrigan* 154

18 · The Monkey Garden *Sandra Cisneros* 164

19 · Chicago Waters *Susan Power* 168

20 · Some Experiences with Insects *Leonard Dubkin* 174

21 · Thank God It Snowed *Ronald L. Fair* 182

22 · Minnehaha Creek *Jan Zita Grover* 186

23 · Feral Lasers *Gerald Vizenor* 195

24 · The Fabulous Sinkhole *Jesús Salvador Treviño* 204

25 · The Snake *Sergio Troncoso* 225

26 · Willow Game *Denise Chávez* 237

27 · Claiming the Yard *Alison Hawthorne Deming* 245

28 · From *Pieces of Light* *Susan J. Tweit* 250

29 · The Extinction of Experience *Robert Michael Pyle* 257

30 · The Dark Constable *David Wicinas* 268

31 · Nature Near *Leslie Dick* 278

32 · The Moths *Helena Maria Viramontes* 287

33 · Opossums and Thieving Pelicans *Paulino Lim Jr.* 293

34 · The Cleveland Wrecking Yard *Richard Brautigan* 299

35 · Plantswomen *Trish Maharam* 305

Acknowledgments

A number of colleagues in environmental literature have helped this project through their support for new directions in the field, and I want to thank Joni Adamson, Karla Armbruster, Mark Busby, Cheryl Glotfelty, Patrick Murphy, Don Scheese, Rachel Stein, Mikel Vause, Alison Wallace, and Alan Weltzien. Many colleagues across the country also have helped sustain a lively discussion about urban nature, and I am grateful to Tom Bailey, Michael Bennett, Ralph Black, Sue Ellen Campbell, Walter Isle, Katherine Joslin, Christopher Kokinos, Charles Mary Kubricht, Carol LaChappelle, Jennifer Price, Randall Roorda, John Tallmadge, David Teague, Lisa Slappey, and Adam Sweeting for good conversations over the years. I have also benefited from discussions about the specific shape this project might take, and I am thus especially grateful to Michael Branch, Betsy Hilbert, Elizabeth Rodriguez Kessler, James Langston, James H. Pickering, Barbara Ras, Will Riser, Scott Slovic, Kathleen Wallace, and Louise Westling. For the support and wisdom given by Linda Walsh, I am deeply grateful.

Permission to reprint Rebecca Johnson, "New Moon Over Roxbury: Reflections on Urban Life and the Land" granted by Continuum Press. From Adams, Carol J., ed., *Ecofeminism and the Sacred,* 1993. Reprinted by permission of the Continuum International Publishing Group.

Permission to reprint Emily Hiestand, "Zip-A-Dee-Do-Dah" granted by Beacon Press. From *Angela the Upside-Down Girl* by Emily Hiestand. Copyright © 1998 by Emily Hiestand. Reprinted by permission of Beacon Press, Boston.

Permission to reprint Chet Raymo, "The Silence" granted by Ruminator Books. Copyright © 1992 by Chet Raymo. Reprinted from *Soul of the Night: An Astronomical Pilgrimage* with the permission of Ruminator Books, St. Paul, Minnesota.

Permission to reprint John Hanson Mitchell, "A Paradise of Frogs" granted by the author.

"The Girl Who Raised Pigeons" from *Lost in the City* by Edward P. Jones, Copyright © 1992 by Edward P. Jones. Reprinted by permission of HarperCollins Publishers, Inc.

Permission to reprint Betsy Hilbert, "Disturbing the Universe" granted by The Orion Society. This essay was originally published in *Orion* magazine. 195 Main Street, Great Barrington, MA 01230; http://www.oriononline.org. Reprinted by permission of Betsy Hilbert and *Orion* magazine.

Joy Williams, "Florida" is reprinted by permission of International Creative Management, Inc., Copyright © 1997, Joy Williams.

Permission to reprint Bob Marshall, "Paddling Off the Edge of the Big Easy" granted by *New Orleans Times-Picayune.*

"Swamp Boy" from *In The Loyal Mountains.* Copyright © 1995 by Rick Bass. Reprinted by permission of Houghton Mifflin Company. All rights reserved.

"Conquistador" by Wendell Mayo is reprinted with permission from the publisher of *Centaur of the North* (Houston: Arte Publico Press, University of Houston, 1996).

Stephen Harrigan, "The Soul of Treaty Oak" reprinted with permission from the October 1989 issue of *Texas Monthly.*

Sandra Cisneros, "The Monkey Garden," is from *The House on Mango Street.* Copyright © 1984 by Sandra Cisneros. Published by Vintage Books, a division of Random House, Inc., and in hardcover by Alfred A. Knopf in 1994. Reprinted by permission of Susan Bergholz Literary Services, New York. All rights reserved.

Permission to reprint Susan Power, "Chicago Waters" (from *The Place Within,* 1997) granted by Henry Dunow and Associates.

Leonard Dubkin, "Some Experiences with Insects," is from *Enchanted Streets: The Unlikely Adventures of an Urban Naturalist.* Copyright © 1947 by Leonard Dubkin. By permission of Little, Brown and Company (Inc.).

Permission to reprint Ronald L. Fair, "Thank God It Snowed" (from his 1972 novel *We Can't Breathe*) granted by Ultramarine Publishers.

"Minnehaha Creek" copyright © 1999 by Jan Zita Grover. Reprinted from *Northern Waters* with the permission of Graywolf Press, Saint Paul, Minnesota.

Permission to reprint Gerald Vizenor, "Feral Lasers" (from his 1991 collection *Landfill Meditation*) granted by Wesleyan University Press.

"The Fabulous Sinkhole" by Jesús Salvador Treviño is reprinted with permission from the publisher of *The Fabulous Sinkhole and Other Stories* (Houston: Arte Publico Press, University of Houston, 1995).

"The Snake" from *The Last Tortilla and Other Stories,* by Sergio Troncoso. Reprinted by permission of the University of Arizona Press.

Denise Chávez, "Willow Game," copyright © 1996 by Denise Chávez. From *The Last of the Menu Girls.* Arte Publico Press, 1986. Reprinted by permission of Susan Bergholz Literary Services, New York. All rights reserved.

"Claiming the Yard" from *Temporary Homelands* copyright © by Alison Hawthorne Deming. Published by Mercury House, San Francisco, California. Reprinted by permission.

Permission to reprint Susan J. Tweit, sections of *Pieces of Light,* granted by the author.

Permission to reprint Robert Michael Pyle, "The Extinction of Experience" (from *The Thunder Tree*) granted by Lyons Press.

Permission to reprint David Wicinas, "The Dark Constable" (from *Sagebrush and Cappucino*) granted by iUniverse.com.

Permission to reprint Leslie Dick, "Nature Near" granted by the author. Permission to reproduce the Neutra drawing granted by Dion Neutra.

"The Moths" by Helena Maria Viramontes is reprinted with permission from the publisher of *The Moths and Other Stories* (Houston: Arte Publico Press, University of Houston, 1995).

Permission to reprint Paulino Lim Jr., "Opossums and Thieving Pelicans" granted by New Rivers Press.

"The Cleveland Wrecking Yard" from *Trout Fishing in America* by Richard Brautigan. Copyright © 1968 by Richard Brautigan. Reprinted by permission of Houghton Mifflin Company. All rights reserved.

Permission to reprint Trish Maharam, "Plantswomen" granted by the author.

Introduction

In *The Etiquette of Freedom* (1990), our foremost wilderness poet, Gary Snyder, observes that "wildness" is not limited to the 2 percent of U.S. territory that has been set aside as formal wilderness areas. "Shifting scales," he argues, "it is everywhere." So that we make no mistake, Snyder provides examples of wildlife in the city: "deer mice on the back porch, deer bounding across the freeway, pigeons in the park, spiders in the corners." Later in his book, Snyder comes back to the topic, providing a long catalogue of the nature found in towns and cities that includes, among other things, "old tree trunks," "paper-wasp nests," "rock-cleavage lines," "courting and strutting bowers," and "ground squirrel apartments."

Snyder's inclusive vision of what constitutes the wild has not always been widely shared. Even as interest in environmental literature has grown over the last four decades, urban nature has figured most often as an intriguing, if mostly marginal, oxymoron. As public attention in the environment has grown, discussions about urban nature have most often had a narrow focus on human health. While we have discussed urban toxic waste sites and landfills, city air and water pollution, little attention has been paid to the deeper origins of these and other environmental problems. We continue to act as if such urban ills can be seen as existing apart from our disregard of urban nature. While we assume that the city is apart from nature, we ignore how the absence of firsthand, place-based knowledge of urban nature has shaped a culture in which urban environmental degradation is the norm.

Since the last decade of the past century, however, the environmental community has begun to pay more attention to urban nature. As urban nature finally comes to the fore, it is helpful to look at why we have ignored it for so long and why our old attitudes are beginning to change.

In American culture wilderness has traditionally been seen as *the* site for wild nature, and in environmental thought and nature writing we have a long and deeply ingrained tradition that places the highest value on vast expanses of wilderness. This attitude can be traced to the earliest days of European settlement, when those who made the transatlantic migration often viewed their adopted homeland as a new Eden. Motivated by, among other factors, the desire to leave an older, established urban world for new, unspoiled landscapes, early American settlers saw nature and the city as separate. This dichotomy has been reinforced by the dominant tradition in American nature writing. Ralph Waldo Emerson and Henry David Thoreau, America's most influential nature writers, inherited a distaste for the city from European romanticism. As their work set forth the thematic framework that would shape most subsequent American nature writing, it continued and deepened the division between city and nature in the American psyche. Even as our country has undergone decade after decade of rapid urbanization, this split has continued to be a central feature in American environmental attitudes. Although there have been attempts at change—most notably the work of Frederick Law Olmstead in the nineteenth century and the City Beautiful movement in the first decades of the twentieth century, the dominant trend has remained the same. As American cities have multiplied in number and size, we have grown very adept—both in our lives and in our nature writing—at focusing our desire for contact with the natural world far away from where most of us live and work.

Another significant obstacle comes, surprisingly, from many of those who think and write about ways to improve the quality of urban life. Much recent and well-meaning commentary, such as that set forth in James Howard Kunstler's *The Geography of Nowhere* (1993), tends to focus on how our culture of chain store replication makes it hard to distinguish a fast-food restaurant or a strip mall or a suburb in Atlanta from one in Houston or Phoenix or Chicago. It is not so much that this type of analysis is wrong; on the contrary, it is usually and unfortunately accurate. The problem is, rather, that such attempts to improve our cities often argue for diversity in the *built* environment but fail to look directly at the need for urban nature. They do not do enough to counter the traditional belief that real nature stops at the city limits sign, that the value of urban nature is negligible.

Over and above any obstacles in our literary and intellectual traditions is another deeply embedded difficulty: finances. Urban land has monetary value, and in most American cities the developmental value of land is substantial and rapidly increasing. As population growth and urbanization have fueled the expansion of cities into ever more far-flung suburbs, the pressure to commodify and develop any "empty," i.e., natural, space also grows. New preservation opportunities and any expansion of existing urban natural areas are restricted. Room for nature diminishes. Our twentieth-century tradition of disinterest in urban nature has not helped with these urban land use issues. Although the threatened destruction of remote wildlands has provoked public outcry, debate, and resistance for decades, the continued development of open space in and around our cities has only recently begun to be a significant matter of public concern.

Despite these obstacles urban nature is emerging as an important environmental topic. This attitudinal shift seems to be dictated in part by demographics. With more than 80 percent of Americans now living in cities, it has become increasingly clear that any viable future environmentalism will need to be fostered within urban areas. This necessity is underscored by the aging of our population. The time is past when most city dwellers could draw on knowledge of nature gained during a youth spent in a small village or the countryside. For the increasing numbers of Americans born in cities, any first-hand, day-to day knowledge of nature comes from urban nature.

Ethnicity also plays an increasingly important role in the consideration of urban nature. As urban populations multiply, there is a steady increase in ethnic diversity within them. If environmental concerns are to gain and maintain the broad-based popular support necessary to prevail in the new century, they must garner support from citizens across the diverse ethnic groups that constitute American city life.

Underlying these factors is a growth in awareness. As our culture has begun to consider environmental issues with greater consistency and care, it has become clear that the traditional boundaries that identify only some kinds of nature as truly wild are beginning to give way, that the wild—once we choose to recognize it—inhabits the city as well as the country.

One key consequence of this shift is the growing realization that our cities are place-based. Knowing urban nature requires recognizing that Lake Michigan shapes human perception and experience in Chicago differently than does the East River in Manhattan, that the mountains and the geological fault-lines of Los Angeles affect that city's citizens differently than the bayous of Houston affect Houstonians. Although fast-food franchises, retail outlets, and subdivision architecture are alike from city to city, the varied locales of cities not only shape them differently but also provide different kinds of weather, flora, and fauna.

We are also beginning to realize that the act of knowing urban nature often differs from more traditional wilderness experiences. The changes that come with a focus on urban nature are many and substantial and some—those that help develop the crucial ability to cultivate an urban sense of place—should be emphasized here.

One such difference lies in accessibility. Although most American cities harbor less open space than their inhabitants need, urban nature, in its many forms, is more broadly accessible than rural nature and wilderness areas. Accessibility to urban nature is less limited, for example, by factors such as age, health, income, and distance than is wilderness access. Parks, trees, gardens, wild birds, and pets are often easily available to urban residents, and such nearby nature can be made a part of their lives without great physical effort, travel, or expense.

Another characteristic of the urban nature experience is what Gary Snyder refers to as "shifting scales." In place of the grandeur and sweep characteristic of the traditional wilderness experience, urban nature often exists on a much smaller scale. Such differences are not absolute, but in a city, acquaintance with a single tree, bird, or butterfly can be a connection with nature. Perhaps because urban nature is usually less grand, urban nature writing also seems to generate humor and comic awareness more frequently than its wilderness counterparts. In our experience with urban nature, there is also often less focus on the new and more focus on the kind of love for nature and place that comes with repeated acquaintance and familiarity.

Nature exploration also takes on different dimensions in an urban setting. Although there are—as several of the pieces in this collection will show—notable exceptions to this generality, the exploration of urban nature is often less heroic and less dependent on physical strength than is wilderness exploration. The emphasis is less on self-reliance as survival skill and as a measure of individual accomplishment than it is in American nature adventure narratives. In urban nature narratives, there is instead often an awareness of mutuality and interdependence. Solitude is also a less common feature. In fact, one defining difference in our relationship with urban nature may well be the frequency with which it connects to a sense of community such as working with neighbors in a community garden.

None of these differences are absolute. There are exceptions, degrees, and shades of similarity in all aspects of wilderness, rural, and urban nature experience, but as very general characteristics they help begin to define an identity for the urban nature experience.

Even as we note that the experience of urban nature has its own identity, we also must recognize that urban nature has much in common with other nature. Like other involvement with nature, watching and writing about urban nature depend upon and emphasize the ability to see. In city and country alike, the crucial act of vision includes not just the physical act of looking but also the critical choice to be aware of nature and the environment and the resolve to acknowledge the individual features of the non-human world around us. Urban nature appreciation also involves an aesthetic response. We are so accustomed to consigning our cities to the realm of the ugly that we often, even without realizing it, think that beauty resides only in more remote nature while we ignore the nature that can figure in our daily lives in the city. The beauty of a tree or a flower, a bayou or a lake, a cloud or a snowflake, a butterfly or a bird, once we choose to see it, can evoke an aesthetic response that connects us to nature. With such a response can come acceptance of the nonhuman world and the moral concern for its welfare that constitutes environmental consciousness.

Perhaps the best way to summarize where the experience of urban nature can take us is to realize that urban nature, like its wilderness and rural counterparts, can evoke in us that essential component of environmental awareness and commitment: a sense of place. The literary critic Thomas J. Lyon in an essay entitled "An Ethic of Place" provides an excellent summary of what happens as we attain this kind of relationship to place. There is, as he puts it, "a kind of enlightenment, a natural loosening of the boundaries of self" that connects us with "the life and flow of the universe realized in human terms." The key is to realize that such a sense of place can be evoked by and bind us to our city places as well as our wilderness areas and to know that a sense of reverence for one locale engenders a greater regard for all of nature.

Even as urban nature has begun to figure more heavily in discussions about literature and the environment, there has been the persistent, prevailing sense that nature writing has not yet really come to the city—that, although the subject of urban nature is becoming important, there is a severe shortage of literary texts devoted to urban nature.

This sense seems to be substantiated by the relatively few writers and books that came to the fore of literary environmental discussions during the nineteen eighties and the early nineteen nineties. As I, at that time, sought literary texts that would engage my students at a large urban university in the kinds of nature around us, the list was small. It included John Hanson Mitchell's *Living at the End of Time* (1990), Robert Michael Pyle's *The Thunder Tree: Lessons from an Urban Wildland* (1993), and Michael Pollan's *Second Nature: A Gardener's Education* (1991), along with a few short stories about urban nature by such well-known nature writers as Barry Lopez and Rick Bass.

Over time, however, it became clear that the literature of urban nature was more extensive than had been thought. With the help of colleagues and friends, I became acquainted with urban nature texts from earlier decades. Some earlier writers, such as Leonard Dubkin, were once rather well-known for their midcentury books about urban nature but have since faded into obscurity. It also became clear that some fiction writers of the sixties and seventies, writers such as Richard Brautigan, Ronald Fair, and William Goyen who had been recognized for other aspects of their work, also offered important perspectives on urban nature. Important new work also appeared. With the development of urban nature as a social and literary concern at the end of the previous century, more essays and books of literary nonfiction and more short stories and novels set out to explore city wilds. By the start of the new century it was clear that there was no shortage of literary texts and that the literature of urban nature constituted an important, although not yet widely recognized area of study within the field of literature and the environment.

This is not to suggest that there exists a body of urban nature literature comparable to that which focuses on wilderness and rural life, but rather to emphasize that there is, in fact, enough breadth and depth in existing material about urban nature to illuminate the subject. Moreover, this body of literature is destined to grow as more contemporary writers write about urban nature and as we recover more urban nature writing of earlier periods. The selections that follow thus represent a stage in our evolving knowledge about the literature of urban nature.

In choosing the final selections for this collection I used a variety of criteria. All of the pieces collected here were chosen because urban nature and the environment feature prominently in them; they treat urban nature not merely as a setting, background, or casual reference point but as a central subject. Short stories as well as essays are included here because American short fiction, with its diverse practitioners, ideological perspectives, and styles and its wide-ranging imaginative freedom, is essential to a full picture of how we see urban nature.

Since the intent is to provide a reasonably representative overview of urban nature writing in America, those very large cities that have traditions of urban nature writing—New York, Boston, Chicago, Los Angeles—have the largest representation in the anthology. There are also selections about other large cities such as Houston and Washington, D.C., midsized cities such as Minneapolis, Boulder, and Austin, and a few smaller cities such as Las Cruces and Key West.

The selections are generally grouped by city and clustered along geographical and regional lines. This arrangement is used (instead of organization by theme, genre, or narrative mode) to emphasize the fact that cities are specific places located within specific bioregions. The collection begins in the Northeast with a series of selections set in such older cities as New York, Boston, and Washington and moves to the South with pieces about Key West, New Orleans, Houston, and Austin. Midwest locales include Cincinnati, Chicago, and Minneapolis. The Southwest and West selections feature El Paso, Las Cruces, Tucson, Denver, San Francisco, Seattle, and Los Angeles.

The geographic, topographic, biological, and climatological diversity of these pieces is matched by the wide range of narrative types, styles, ideologies, and themes. These pieces were selected not only for variety in setting but also to illustrate the various ways that writers engage with the subject of urban nature. There is diversity also in the authorship of these selections, a richness that cuts across lines of ethnicity, gender, class, and age. The variety of voices include those of American Indian, African American, Asian American, European American, and Hispanic American writers. This ethnic diversity suggests that a focus on urban nature, with its capacity to engage writers and readers from many backgrounds and traditions, can help us move toward what we need in the new century: a richly multicultural environmentalism.

In the essays and short stories that follow, human contact with the rest of urban nature takes a number of forms and occurs in a variety of places. There are nature walks and hikes, trips to the zoo and to parks; community gardens, family gardens, and the cultivation of a single plant in a container on a fire escape; individual and community restoration projects; canoe expeditions on bayous and rivers, beach walks and lake swims; the raising of pigeons, bird watching, butterfly watching, and cricket watching; working in the yard and fly-fishing; individuals who study local flora and fauna and those who study the constellations as well as one whole neighborhood united by the mystery of a rare natural event. These experiences take place in yards, manicured parks, second-hand lands, greenbelts, and near downtown sidewalks, and on bayous, irrigation ditches, swamps, bays, canals, lakes, and seashores.

These places and these encounters highlight the plenitude and variety of urban nature. Sunshine and snow and desert rain appear along with human attempts to replicate and control climate. Spectacular sunsets occur and so do visions of the night sky's constellations, stars, and phases of the moon. The many different kinds of trees range from oaks and maples to willows and cottonwoods, Ponderosa pines, and apricot and apple trees, and there is an abundance of plants including sunflowers, wild iris, jasmine, tumbleweed, saguaro cactus, agave, aloe, lupine, clematis, sea moss, and saw grass. The variety of creatures includes ants, bees, spiders, worms, beetles, scorpions, and butterflies, and there are rats, squirrels, skunks, opossums, raccoons, feral cats, and snakes, as well as loggerhead turtles, ghost crabs, fiddler crabs, and Portuguese men-of-war. Birds such as starlings and sparrows, grackles and great-horned owls, belted kingfishers, dippers, seagulls, and Canadian geese inhabit these narratives and so do such other animals as deer, alligators, otters, crows, monkeys, and even a rhinoceros.

Although we seem to have discovered only recently this nature that has always been a part of our cities, we are now at a crucial point in our relationship to urban nature. If our growing awareness of urban nature recedes or if we fail to translate this awareness into protection for the open spaces and other places for urban nature that now exist, the attainment of more open space and nature access in urban areas, and place-based urban environmental education for city children, the future looks bleak. We could easily fall into that accelerating downward spiral in environmental concern that happens when each successive generation has diminished access to and, thus, diminished regard for nature, a phenomenon that Robert Michael Pyle in *The Thunder Tree* calls "the extinction of experience."

My hope is that the stories and essays collected in *City Wilds* will work against such extinction, that the explorations of urban nature in them will help us learn to see and cherish nature in the urban places where most of us now live.

City Wilds

I

Lisa Couturier was born in 1962 on the Jersey shore in Redbank, New Jersey, and she now lives with her husband and daughter in Bethesda, Maryland. Her B.A. in journalism and women's studies is from the University of Maryland, her M.A. is in environmental studies and creative writing from New York University, and she has published a number of essays on the environment. Her essay below, like the selection by Robert Michael Pyle toward the end of the collection, asks a crucial question: What kind of urban nature will exist for future generations? The essay, written when she lived in New York and first published in *The River Reader,* edited by John Murray, makes the point that when we look at urban landscapes we choose what we see: the built environment or the natural world, the skyscrapers or the river.

Reversing the Tides

Lisa Couturier

There was a child went forth every day,
And the first object he looked upon and received with wonder
or pity or love or dread, that object he became, . . .
The horizon's edge, the flying seacrow, the fragrance of salt-
marsh and shoremud . . .
—Walt Whitman, "Leaves of Grass"

The story is told in my family that when I was a year old my parents took me to the beach at Sandy Hook, New Jersey, which from the shoreline has a view of Manhattan. They took me out to the edge, where the sand meets the rocks, marking the intersection of Sandy Hook Bay, Lower New York Bay, and the

Atlantic Ocean. My father lifted me up on his shoulders and my parents pointed to New York City. They say I looked. They say I saw the city then, on a clear day.

I now live in Manhattan and every day I walk to the East River—which, although big and wide as most people might imagine a river to be, is technically a tidal strait and part of the larger Hudson estuary ecosystem that surrounds Manhattan.

On my walks to the river, the wind, carrying the water's salt scent, surrounds me; and I am pulled toward its estuarine currents. To get near the river's side I must walk along a tar path that begins at the end of my street and winds through a manicured park, around the mayor's mansion, and over a small grassy hill. Coming to the top of the hill, I anticipate what the water will be like at my favorite spot on the river—Hell's Gate, named so for the tangling of tides that mix here: the Atlantic tide travels up the Manhattan arm of the East River to collide with the tide of the Long Island Sound and the current of the Harlem River. Some days the tides look as though they're fighting. Dark olive-green waters hit and chop at each other and swirl and spiral all at once. Other times nothing, every drop of water seems to be just strolling along, friendly—as if water could sigh. I clear the hill, walk under an American basswood tree growing in a triangle of grass, and stop to let the wind blow over me. I take the air into my body, consciously swallow it, give my lungs—my entire being—a fix of the river's essence.

The smell of the water is as close as I will get to the river itself. There is no access, no great green shoreline. Looking at the river is more like looking at a mangy pound dog when you really want to see a shiny-furred, well-muscled purebred, its tail wagging. This body of water, like most of the waters around New York City, is for the most part surrounded by the dirty environment of the human world—fuel tanks, abandoned buildings, highways, skyscrapers, and such. But recently nature's presence has returned to the river: butterflies, seaweed swaying over rocks, seagulls laughing, Canada geese flying in their autumn V, striped bass passing through from the Long Island Sound to the Hudson River, snapping turtles who've survived the last four centuries in New York waters, American eels who swim to the Sargasso Sea to lay their eggs and whose young make the one-thousand-mile return trip to the city, peregrine falcons who nest twenty blocks down river but hunt and fly up my way, cormorants, herons, and egrets.

When I'm by the river, which itself has been so stripped—of its wetlands, of its shoreline, of its purity through pollution and abuse—I shed my own urban skin, a general impatience with things slow moving, to listen to the movement of the river and to its waves against the rocks. The rippling of the water soothes me, as though its sound fuses with my blood to calm me. Often, when the sun reflects pink and orange on the river in early evening, flocks of starlings or sparrows explode from the park's trees and circle out over the water as though they are riding an airborne roller coaster. They fly back over me, their wings beating against their bodies, and return to the park. As the sky darkens, the birds settle in for the night and I begin my walk home, envious that the birds, unlike me, are safe in the park at night by the river. If it is a summer evening, I leave the river's side during a concert of cricket song with a light show of fireflies—a performance worthy of Madison Square Garden.

It's been a while since I stopped being surprised by nature in New York City, which is, after all, simply a name we've given this landscape—a label meaningless to the birds, the turtles, the river. Besides, said James Hillman, the Jungian psychologist, the "Greek word for city, *polis,* . . . draws from a pool of meanings related to water . . . *polis* locates city in the wet regions of the soul . . . We need but remember that the city, the *metro-polis* means at root a streaming, flowing, thronging Mother. We are her children, and she can nourish our imaginations if we nourish hers."

Walking the river's promenade and looking across at Roosevelt Island, I think of a local legend, Thomas Maxey. He knew something about the wet regions of his soul, from whence his feelings and dreams informed his life and helped him nourish the riverscape. It is said he was a bit of a madman who was quite fond of birds. Shortly after the Civil War, Maxey built a fort at the tip of Roosevelt Island, just below Hell's Gate; and in front of the fort, he erected a gate that was somehow designed to be used as a nesting site for wild geese. On the gate he wrote this message: I INVITE THE FOWLS AND THE BIRDS OF THE AIR TO ENTER.

Could it be that Maxey wasn't mad, but just in love with birds and the river? Perhaps he simply sensed then what writer Thomas Moore says now: "Maybe one function of love is to cure us of an anemic imagination, a life emptied of romantic attachment and abandoned to reason."

Of course there must be biological reasons the animals have returned to the East River—a body of water that, according to some accounts, was so toxic it would burn a ship's hull clean by docking it here for a few days. Even as recently as the 1950s, sewage and pollutants from manufacturing plants were poured into the river. And it wasn't until the Clean Water Act of 1972 that New York finally stopped thinking of the river as its toilet. Until then we were dumping raw sewage into it daily. (Even now, when it rains more than an inch and a half, sewage treatment plants along the river overflow into it.) And today, although there are still PCBs and other toxins remaining in the river's sediments, the East River is staging a comeback, which, according to local news reports, has environmental officials somewhat mystified. Nevertheless, oxygen levels are up; coliform bacteria (indicating the level of sewage) is down; amphipods—food for fish—are back, as are the crabs and minnows herons feed on; apparently, biodiversity is on the rise.

The river is making enormous changes, as is the city. The New York City Department of Environmental Protection will soon invest over a billion dollars to research the contamination of the East River and other parts of the estuary.

Environmental science: What is it but a way to rationalize our longings for interdependence and interrelationship?

Environmental legislation: What is it if not a desire for deep change, a kind of compassion for the earth?

For years I thought of the East River as nothing more than a polluted, liquefied roadway on which rode huge foreign tankers, garbage barges, speedboats, the yachts of the rich, and a few sailboats. Now I stand alongside Hell's Gate, breathing the river into me, gazing at it, waiting for its turtles, geese, herons—the innocents we more often associate with Heaven's Gate. Thomas Berry, the eco-theologian, says that by pursuing what we love—our allurements—we help bind the universe together. Am I a madwoman now to think, like Maxey, that my allurement for the river might help her call in her creatures?

As a tugboat chugs down the river, I see a cormorant sitting on a dilapidated pier. It's not far from where I recently saw a snapping turtle swimming close to the surface of the water and almost mistook it for a deflated, discarded soccer ball. The cormorant extends his black wings to dry in the sunlight, and from the back looks much like the silhouette of Dracula. I watch him and remember the time I spent three years ago traveling through the underworld of the East River's sister waterway: the Arthur Kill. It is the place from whence the cormorant had flown, a place that most would agree is more deserving of the name Hell's Gate, and a place where all my ideas of nature as resplendent were abducted from me.

It is the faintest of sounds—a tiny tic, tic, tic—I hear as I hold to my ear an egg from which a seagull chick is pipping.

I am on the pebbly, scrubby, sandy shoreline of an island in the Arthur Kill—another large tidal strait in the Hudson estuary that runs through a polluted wetland along the western side of New York City's Staten Island, separating it from New Jersey. It is the end of my second summer as a volunteer assistant to two biologists for the Harbor Herons Project, and today we are searching for Canada goose nests. The search is a break in our usual routine of studying the more glamorous and elusive long-legged wading birds who, since the mid-seventies, have made a miraculous comeback in the wooded interiors of isolated islands in the East River and the Arthur Kill.

As I place the seagull chick back into its nest on the shore, I silently laugh at myself for missing the messy research we do in the heronry. Going into the birds' seasonal nesting area as quickly and quietly as possible, we gently lift the baby birds from their nests in gray birches and quaking aspens to weigh and measure them. We handle just a small sampling of the nestlings of the four thousand great egrets, snowy egrets, cattle egrets, little blue herons, black-crowned night herons, green-backed herons, yellow-crowned night herons, and glossy ibises who are living and raising their young quite invisibly within the boundaries of New York City. We count how many young are born and how many fledge. The birds are an indicator species—as they are at the top of the food chain in their environment, their health indicates the health of the estuary.

Across from the heronry and the seagull nest, on the New Jersey side of the Kill, the giants of the oil and chemical companies—Du Pont, Citgo, Cyanamid, Exxon, and others—make house. Their huge white storage tanks stand silent in the tall, lime-green salt-marsh grasses, while their smokestacks spew out EPA-approved amounts of waste into the air over the marsh.

The history of the Arthur Kill, like that of the East River, should render it essentially lifeless from centuries of oil spills, raw sewage, and chemical dumping. The soft turf of the salt marsh has absorbed (and will probably continue to absorb) so many oil spills—such as the several in 1990 that totaled 794,500 gallons (one hundred thousand gallons is considered a major spill) and caused the collapse of the fragile and already badly bruised ecosystem. Only recently has the Kill begun to bounce back. Still, when I glance down at my footprints in the sand I see oil that will persist for decades. It is buried but not benign.

I picture the mother herons fishing in the shallow depths of the Kill, their long bills poised to skewer fish, crab, shrimp: invertebrates who themselves have ingested the toxic and carcinogenic oils. The poison will be passed, and in part explains why many of our nestlings fail to survive.

Scattered along the shore and hidden in the marsh grasses is a veritable Wal-Mart of used plastic products: empty plastic containers of dishwashing detergent, shampoo, yogurt, toilet-bowl cleaner, and Chinese takeout, as well as balls, toys, kitchen sinks, anything and everything I could ever imagine having in my apartment. The trash has slipped off garbage barges that every day carry thirteen thousand tons of New York City's trash through the New York Harbor and down the Arthur Kill to be dumped in the world's largest landfill that, as it happens, sits next to the heronry.

Not far from the hatching seagull are children's baby dolls. They dot the shoreline. One is stranded in the stark sunlight, half-buried in the sand with a hand in the air. Another is missing its eyes and a leg. A third is just a head. We are several women on this island investigating the birth of birds, and we are of course acquainted with dolls, symbolic plastic bundles of the life within us—our own children, healthy, happy, living in a world abundant. But there is something sinister about the dolls' presence here, as though they are lost little ambassadors from the human world, living not in a foreign country but in humanity's damaged future.

When our work is finished, we emerge from the heronry carrying an assortment of dog ticks on our bodies and splattered with what we call "splooj" (our word for the large and liquid bowel movements of baby birds), bird pee, and regurgitant (which is often a concoction of undigested invertebrates or, if it's that of a cattle egret or black-crowned night heron, maybe a few pieces of Kentucky Fried Chicken or a small mouse or two that the mother bird picked from the landfill).

But I also carry a gift: an intimacy with the spirits, sounds, and touches of birds. The snowy egret nestlings, so fearful even as I try to calm them, wrap their long reptilian-skinned toes around my fingers in an effort, I guess, to feel safe. The excruciatingly shy glossy ibises lay limp in my lap while I stroke their dark brown feathers. And although the black-crowned night herons assertively nip at me, I admire their aggressiveness; it helps them survive. The colors, habits, feathers, pecks, personalities, smells, movements, eyes, and cries of these birds are inside of me. I, quite simply, love them.

"Tic, tic, tic." The seagull chick works tirelessly in the late morning sun to release itself. Using the powerful hatching muscles that run along the back of its neck and head, it is able to force a special egg tooth (a sort of temporary hatchet that has grown on the chick's upper mandible) against its beige and brown speckled shell to break it open—bit by bit by bit.

It is time to search for goose nests. As I gather up my binoculars and notebooks, I realize that after traveling through the Arthur Kill for two summers, I have given up trying to hate it. It both stuns and offends me. I cannot describe the chick's place of birth as ugly or beautiful: such labels seem too simple. I walk away from the chick knowing only that I feel deeply for this wasteland, where through the birth of birds I've witnessed a kind of magic.

The tugboat on the East River sounds a loud honk to a passing oil freighter and the cormorant flies off to animate the sky. Another day and still no snapping turtle. Tomorrow I will wait again.

My attachment to the East River has nothing to do with dipping my toes into it, with skipping stones over it, with riding it on an inner tube, with swimming in it, with cooling my face with a splash of it, with walking along its shores, with even sitting close to it the way I imagine rural folk might do on lazy summer afternoons.

I feel sympathy for the East River, for everything it has lost, but I love it for the same reason I love the Arthur Kill: for its magic. In all their woundedness, these resilient waterways are managing to give life. I can't accept the injuries New Yorkers have caused this estuary, but I feel there's a need to cherish what is left.

Who knows, maybe when my father lifted me up on his shoulders all those years ago, my eyes focused not on the city, but on its surrounding dark and damaged olive-green waters.

2

William Goyen was born in Trinity, Texas, in 1915 and died in Los Angeles in 1983. He graduated from Rice University and taught at Columbia, the University of Southern California, and the University of Houston. William Goyen's novels, especially *The House of Breath* (1950) and *Come, the Restorer* (1974), won him wide recognition, but he is best known for his short fiction, especially *The Collected Short Stories of William Goyen* (1975), which was nominated for the Pulitzer Prize. The multilayered complexity seen in "The Moss Rose" below is typical of his work, and this short story also embodies familiar themes of his: the persistent power of memory, especially memories of an earlier life in a rural setting, and the consequences of separating ourselves from the natural world.

The Moss Rose

William Goyen

For Elisabeth Schnack

"Portulaca," the Third Avenue man said to him at the door of his shop when he asked the name of what he thought was a box of moss rose plants for sale on the sidewalk.

"Aren't they moss roses?" he asked.

"Portulaca," the man said.

"Do they have orange and yellow and crimson blossoms?"

"That's right," the man said.

"And they aren't moss roses?"

"Portulaca," he said again.

He went on up Third Avenue saying the word to himself as he walked, so as not to forget it. *Portulaca.* "I guess that's what they call them up here," he said to himself.

He had grown up with them—*moss roses*—always in some flower bed, by a grave, by a pump where the ground was moist, in a hanging kettle on a porch. They were a part of another landscape, a flower illustration of many remembered scenes in another country. Here they were, on Third Avenue in New York City. Or were they the same—could they be? Oh, he thought, I guess people up here know and have this common little flower—why shouldn't they? But such a name as they've given it! *Portulaca.*

The El was quiet, the train was gone. Though the complicated and permanent-looking structure was there, soon it would be torn down. Third Avenue was quieter. People who had lived for years with the noise of the El interrupting their sleep and conversation and who had learned naturally to scream above it, still spoke in Third Avenue voices; but the train, the reason, was gone.

The children yelled in resounding voices on the sidewalks, though the noise over which they yelled had vanished; and he wondered if ever their voices would soften or modulate. No, they would go on through life yelling with powerful voices developed against the monster whose tracks they had been bred alongside. It would be the El going on through them; it was not really destroyed. They seemed the children of the El, and the tracks and platform had bred children who looked a little like them, curiously, as their parents did, so that their faces, bearing, physiognomy reflected the resisted force—as people who live in constant wind or on stony landscapes reflect the natural phenomenon which opposes them in daily life.

These Third Avenue people had the same vagabond, noisy air and quality that the ramshackle train and platform symbolized. The El had created a genus of humanity, almost as the plow had shaped his own; they looked as if they had performed some laborious job with the El, as an instrument of their daily bread, although it did not feed them or reward them with anything but noise and dirt. Still it shaped a style of life for them. Over the years a race had adapted itself to an inhuman presence and had learned, almost as if by imitating or mimicking it, a mode of life that enabled them to absorb it into their daily life, and to endure. They were a kind of grimly happy, sailorlike, reckless people, carefree, poor, tough and loud-mouthed, big-throated and hoarse-voiced. The old, who had lived so long with it, seemed very tired by it. They sat in their straight chairs on the sidewalks or on the steps of their buildings and conversed in loud voices—a gypsy breed with their Third Avenue dog, again his own special breed: a serene, somewhat sad, seasoned hound, resigned, fearless, and friendly.

Portulaca, he said, walking along. Little moss rose. Well, he was homesick. But wasn't everyone? he consoled himself. By a certain time something, some structure, in every life is gone, and becomes a memory. But it has caused something: a change, an attitude, an aspect. It is the effect of what was, he thought, going on, that is the long-lastingness in us.

Thinking this, he looked up at the sides of the buildings and saw that the "Portulaca" grew here and there on the Third Avenue people's fire escapes. It was a rather common summer flower on Third Avenue! Well, the moss rose belongs to them, too, as it did to the old guard back home, he thought. Somehow the little moss rose was a part of any old order, any old, passing bunch, and it clung to those who represented the loss of old fixtures of everyday life, it was that faithful a friend. Now it seemed right that it grow along Third Avenue in boxes and pots on rusty and cluttered and bedraggled fire escapes, as it had in a house he knew once that was inhabited by a flock of raggle-taggle kinfolks, full of joy and knowing trouble and taggling and scrabbling along, a day at a time, toward a better day, surely, they avowed. So, in that old home far away, the moss rose used to look out on a train track, though the scarce train was an event when it chose to pass that way, as if it might be some curious animal out of the woods that had taken a daring path by the house. Still, something of the same configuration was here.

Portulaca! Little moss rose! he thought. The same patterns do exist all over the world, in cities and towns, wherever people live and arrange life around themselves, a bridge over a creek or a tunnel under a river, there is a way to manage. And a sudden sight of this human pattern in one place restores a lost recognition of it in another, far away, through an eternal image of a simple flower, in the hands and care of both; and in a moment's illumination there was in him the certain knowledge of unity forever working to stitch and tie, like a quilt, the human world into a simple shape of repetition and variation of what seems a meaningless and haphazard design whose whole was hostile to its parts and seemed set on disordering them.

He went back to the shop and told the man he would like to try a Portulaca plant. On his fire escape, just off Third Avenue, it would grow and bloom the fragile starlike blossoms of the moss rose he had loved so deeply in another place and would love here as well, though it might be a little different from the old one—something in the leaf, slight but different. Yet, everything changes, he thought, slowly it all changes. Do we resign ourselves to that? Is youth passing when we see this—the fierce battle of youth that would not accept change and loss? But there is always the relationship of sameness, too, in all things, which identifies the old ancestor: the *relatedness;* we'll cling to that, to that continuous stem around which only the adornments change, he thought. What if the leaf is a little different? The family is the same . . . the bloom is akin—Portulaca or moss rose. Though the El was gone and the house of kinfolk vanished, two beings as different as man and woman, he would water and tend and foster the old moss-rose family that was still going on.

Sitting on his fire escape, after planting the moss rose in a discarded roasting pan, he looked out through the grillwork of the fire escape and saw the gaunt white-headed man who resembled so much his grandfather in his small room across the courtyard through the Trees of Heaven, where he sat night and day, serene and waiting. Where was his home? Did he know a land where the moss rose bloomed? In his waiting, in his drab, monotonous loneliness, there was a memory living, surely. Who knew, one day it might freshen in him at the sight of something that lingered in the world out of his past, right in the neighborhood, just out of his window, and gladden him for an hour.

Squatting on the fire escape, he thought of his own dreams and hopes. As he sat with the little plant, gazing at it for a long time, a memory rose from it like a vapor, eluded him, and sank back into it. He sat patiently, to catch the memory that glimmered over the petals. What hummingbird remembrance, elusive and darting from his mind, still took its flavor, its bit of sweetness, from the moss rose? And then it came up clear and simple to him, the memory in the moss rose.

It was in the back yard of The Place, as it was called by all who lived there, long ago, under a cool shade tree in Texas. A clump of moss roses grew, without anybody asking it to, in the moist ground around the pump like ringlets of hair wreathed with red and orange and yellow blossoms. He had hung the bucket by its handle over the neck of the pump, and Jessy his small sister held one of his hands while he jacked the pump with the other. The chinaberry trees were still fresh before the sun would make them limp, the chickens were pert, the dew was still on everything, even the woodpile, and the sand in the road still cool. Their old Cherokee rose, that his grandmother had planted when she was a young woman in this house, was gay and blooming at every leaf and thorn, and frolicking all over the fence, down and up and around, locking itself and freeing itself—it would quieten down in the hot afternoon.

Over the squeaking of the pump, he heard a voice and a word . . . "star . . . star." He turned to Jessy and saw that she had picked one of the moss roses and offered it to him, a tiny red star, on the palm of her hand. The bloom was so wonderous and the gift so sudden that he had thought, at that moment, that all life might be something like this twinkling offering. When they went in, the bucket filled, and their mother asked what they had been doing, Jessy had answered, "Picking stars . . ."

Now the place was gone, the water dried up, no doubt, the moss rose finished. Jessy was dead these many years; moss roses grew around her small grave—unless they had been overcome by weeds; he had not gone back to that graveyard for a long time. Here on his fire escape (the landlady had once advertised it as a "renovated terrace") was a fragile remnant of that vanished world; he would tend it; it would no doubt bloom, in time. To find that simple joy again, what could he do to recapture it, to recapture what had been, long ago in the moss rose and in himself—that ready acceptance, that instantaneous belief, in that pure joy of morning, in one sweet summer, long ago at the water pump, holding his sister's tiny hand? All that had followed, as he had grown, dimmed and tarnished that small blinking star: error and disenchantment and loss.

I used to dream of a little fresh sunrise town like that one where we stood once, at the water pump, he said to himself, where I would be, as fixed upon the ground as the moss rose round the pump, rising in the early morning in vigor to my work and moving and living round it, drawing more and more life to it, through me. Instead, work and life seem to have withdrawn from me more and more, to have pushed life back from where it began, into cities and stone buildings, onto pavements, to have impoverished me even of memories that would save me despair, in a huge grassless city where no flowers bloom on the ground.

When the moss rose bloomed again for him, this time on a fire escape in a great city where he sat with gray streaks in his hair, he would be grateful for that. There might even grow another star to pick. So he would watch, day by day, for the flowers to appear, speaking patiently to himself, and again for the hundredth time, that some change was imperative round which to rebuild, out of which to call back the fullness of forgotten signs of love and visions of hope. Believe that it is right ahead, he said to himself, sitting with the plant on the fire escape. Start with one little plain, going-on thing to live around and to take up an old beginning from. Until slowly, slowly, hope and new life will grow and leaf out from it to many places and to many old forgotten promises.

3

Charles Siebert lives and writes about urban nature in Brooklyn where he was born in 1954. His M.A. from the University of Houston is in Creative Writing, and he has published two books of literary non-fiction, *Angus: A Memoir* (2000) and *Wickerby: An Urban Pastoral* in 1998. *Wickerby* opposes the traditional pastoral narrative with its contrast of the city and the countryside and its willingness to ignore or discount urban nature. As the *Wickerby* narrative weaves back and forth between his home neighborhood in Brooklyn and a remote cabin in Canada where he stays for five months, Siebert discovers more similarities than differences in the nature of the two places. His essay "Where Have All the Animals Gone? The Lamentable Extinction of Zoos," first published in *Harper's* in 1989, is a meditation on the loss of his neighborhood zoo, on the nature of zoos, and on the nature of "cageless natural habitats."

Where Have All the Animals Gone?

The Lamentable Extinction of Zoos

Charles Siebert

I tried to visit my neighborhood zoo one afternoon last year but found it closed for renovations. According to a sign on the chain-link fence where the front gate used to be, Brooklyn's Prospect Park Zoo, first opened in 1935, is being converted into a "cageless natural habitat." This was a claim I at first thought a bit redundant and then preposterously bold, considering that most of the world's remaining natural habitats are, in fact, caged or fenced to keep us out and the animals in. Clearly, whatever was being planned here in Brooklyn was to be as unnatural as the previous arrangement of cages and pens; it would just be rendered more naturalistically, the animals more subtly contained—better, perhaps, for the animals and certainly for us, for our consciences. But for some reason, as I turned and headed back along Flatbush Avenue toward home, I was thinking only of the old black rhino, wondering whether he'd be back.

He used to be, if you turned left upon entering and walked up a brief hill, your very first encounter—standing there on his small, enclosed, grassless patch of park the way rhinos everywhere and for millennia have stood: two eyes wearily looking for some way out of that dirt-caked armor, the horned head heavily drifting an inch above the earth. Judging from my numerous visits (I live a few blocks away, on the other side of the Brooklyn Botanic Garden, along Eastern Parkway), he was never a very big draw, being, I suppose, entirely too unanimated, too much of what he was to look at for long. And yet I found him the most attractive, the most challenging to draw near to for that—a stillness to be outmatched by, a breathing part of prehistory, sensate stone.

I really think he knew me, might even remember me still: the figure on the periphery always making noises, waving, trying to take the measure of his ken—whether he heard the cars unraveling air from the trees along Flatbush Avenue and Empire Boulevard; whether sudden police sirens startled him or, like the distant, caged roars of the lions in the cat house on the other side of the zoo, he'd just come to take them for granted. I'd stand at the railing no more than ten or fifteen feet away and wonder if he could hear the sparrow's and the grackle's chirps and the differences between those and the songs of the African birds like his symbiotic sidekick, the oxpecker, who'd hitch rides on top of him in exchange for picking insects from his bristle-plated back. I'd imagine him holding to that same patch of earth years before I was ever brought to the zoo as a child in the late fifties, when this section of Brooklyn was one of high civilization's epicenters: a thriving zoo at the tip of a pastoral park that, in turn, was bordered not only by Grand Army Plaza and the Brooklyn Public Library, the Brooklyn Museum, and the Botanic Garden but by Ebbets Field as well, the former home of the Dodgers. And it was possible that on a given, still, summer afternoon, with a lull in the traffic and the zoogoers' chatter, this same rhino had the roar of a baseball crowd for a Duke Snider home run in his small, fur-tipped ears. I've even, I'll admit, thought about him standing out there alone long after closing hours, growing sleepy in the urban darkness, blinking slowly the domino-lighted buildings through the trees into sleep and whatever it is a displaced rhinoceros dreams.

His name, it turns out, is Rudy. The park administrator I phoned said that the new Brooklyn zoo will be primarily for children—interactive exhibits, walk-through prairies and aviaries, and smaller animals, more easily kept. As for the old animals, the big ones won't be back. They've been "placed" in more spacious, suburban, "safari-like" facilities. Rudy, I was told, is now living happily somewhere in Michigan.

It is quite possible that Rudy was pleased to leave a zoo that *Parade Magazine* had voted one of the ten worst in the country. In truth, the place had become a bit run down in a squalid, inner-city sort of way: a mere nine cement-laden acres of sooted Beaux Arts animal houses, heavily barred pens, and the inevitable enjambment of species within. Just inside the entrance, the polar bears' rocky, moated enclave gave way in a quick stroll to the brown bears', to the Asiatics', and then to the grizzlies'. Farther on were the ape and cat houses, barely distinguishable on the outside from the souvenir shop and snack bar—all set in a tight semicircle about a small acrid-smelling seal pool. Beyond these, already moving back around toward the front entrance again, were some zebras and llamas; a few gigantic replicas of Victorian-parlor bird cages; and, in a grouping more circus-minded than zoological, the iron-railinged roundlet of nature's thick-skinned, rotund oddities: the elephant on its plot, the hippos on theirs, and then Rudy.

With the big land-based animals disappearing now from all their homes on earth, it may seem selfish, small of me, to begrudge Rudy and the others their reprieve from an old zoo in Brooklyn. Yet I am not at all sure what one has to do with the other—why the zoo down the block gets dismantled because the animals' home in the wild has been; why Rudy and the others must be placed far from our view in a deep, suburban diorama because their free-roaming counterparts are disappearing altogether. Maybe Rudy disliked being displaced again. And how much difference will a bigger lawn in a cold clime make to him, to his happiness? Why not a few modifications of his old Brooklyn plot, a renovation that would have kept him, if not demonstrably happy or seemingly natural, at least close—close to people, close to me?

Rudy and the others are gone now, and with them a way of looking, literally and figuratively, at animals. They've passed so quickly from being curiosities to being scattered sympathies; from being the captive representatives in crude cages of an extant, flourishing wilderness to being the living memories of themselves in our artful re-creations of a vastly diminished one. If we once could keep them just down the block, it was, in part, because looking at them allowed us to travel in place a world away. But now we've discovered and displaced so much of that world that we feel only guilt about detaining them any longer in such a harsh rendition of ours.

The animals aren't any happier in the new natural habitats. These are places we've designed to make *ourselves* happier about our continued keeping of them. We are, in a sense, trying to eliminate zoos even as we go on designing and maintaining them. With our new habitats, we are trying to conceal from ourselves the zoo as living evidence of our natural antagonism toward nature; the zoo as manifestation of the fact that our slow, fitful progress toward understanding the animals has always been coterminus with conquering and containing them.

If the old zoos brought the animals here and asked us to imagine them *there,* the new natural habitats bring them here and leave us no choice but to imagine them here where we've always wanted them—in the suburbs of our attentions, safe at last from us and our cities. With all of them standing far from us, in their new habitats, we are no longer confronted with ourselves. We no longer have to look up close at who *we* are. Rudy and the others all have been placed now, and if we can't look at them, we can still see them in what's left of the wild—a habitat, a theme park we view like dismissive gods with a passing wave from the monorail.

Whether it's a woeful lack of imagination or a delusive surfeit of it that allows a person meaningful exchanges with a kept and compromised creature, I'll admit that I've always enjoyed my visits to our cities' old public zoos. It was their harsh juxtapositions, I think, the very characteristics that make them so sad, so unconscionable to some, that made them so compelling to me: the way Rudy's presence alone, so near a busy urban intersection, seemed to question the city's very makeup; or the fact that on a particularly slow writing day I could leave my apartment, take a short walk, and find some solace in a good long stare-down with a monkey.

I've had some memorable encounters in monkey houses. The two I remember best began typically enough with the vaguely comforting feeling I find I get when staring at animals too long, a feeling that they sense in me a kindred mental lethargy, a nearly equivalent blankness that invites them over, or at least out of themselves. Of course, it's also true that if you sit in a church and stare at a statue long enough, you'll swear it's motioning to you. But I didn't imagine the compelling exchange I had a few years ago with a chimp in the old Central Park Zoo. I'd been visiting with him for some time one afternoon, watching him watch disinterestedly from his corner shelf the steady stream of passersby. Then, with the first lull, he and I staring at each other, he climbed down, came forward to the bars, reached through to pick up a bag of peanuts someone had tried to toss in, and held it out to me. Looking to make sure we were still alone, I reached for it. He pulled it back. We repeated this routine a few more times, and then, seemingly disappointed with me, he dropped the bag and returned to his perch.

Only a month later, while staying with a friend in Oregon, I visited the old Portland city zoo and, the interlude with the Central Park chimp still fresh in my mind, made a point of spending some time with his West Coast counterpart. He too was hugging to one corner of his cage when I arrived. People would pause before him a minute and then pass along to the baboons next door while I stayed staring until we were alone, absolutely no one else in the ape house. He climbed down, came to the front, and stared back. At this point I no doubt believed myself to be on the verge of some out-of-body, cross-species, evolutionary experience. Suddenly he turned and went methodically to the back of his quarters, where he bent over and seemed to kiss the back wall before returning to the front bars again, very close this time, so that with his head stuck out he had no trouble at all getting me square in the forehead with a mouthful of water.

People do not go to zoos to learn about the imminent disappearance of species or to see habitats better viewed on public-television nature shows. People visit zoos, I think, to have some telling turn with the wild's otherworldliness; to look, on the most basic level, at ways we didn't end up being—at all the shapes that a nonreflective will can take. We are, by definition, such fleeting observers of evolution's slow-moving work that visiting a zoo and staring at animals can somehow stay us awhile, reinvolve us in the matter of existence. What the old city zoo did was to arrange such visits on completely civil terms—which is to say, our terms alone and unabashedly. Little effort was made to re-create natural habitats. We were to conjure up images of each animal's home by virtue of its starkly arrested presence in ours. Species of disparate regions and climates would all be kept in "houses," set a short stroll apart and given the most generic addresses: the Ape House or the Lion House, strangely provocative places because they were at once repositories of our ignorant disregard of the animals and monuments to our complete awe of them.

Noble statues of the beasts held within a house stood on either side of its front entrance, as action scenes of them unfolded in high relief along the frieze. Once inside we were struck immediately by that odor and the anomaly of our own harshly lit, echoing voices. Then we proceeded to take in the exhibits. They, too, were labeled in the most generic manner—GORILLA, the Latin name below, and a dot on a silhouette of Africa where it hailed from. It was as though the zookeepers did not want to muddle our experience of "gorillaness" with details. And sitting there, behind the bars in a small, spare, yellow tiled room that had, perhaps, one chained log in it, was the gorilla, looking both larger than life and yet, because of that preposterously anthropocentric frame, greatly reduced by it, like some guy who just got a bad evolutionary break.

The old city zoo was designed, as a visit to the art museum is, to invite our immersion in the works and have us be edified by them in some way. Indeed, the prototypical public city zoos—like Paris's Jardin des Plantes, which opened in 1793; or the London and Berlin zoos, which opened in 1828 and 1844, respectively—were all situated (as was my zoo in Brooklyn, years later) in close proximity of those cities' art and natural-history museums. Zoology was still a relatively crude science at that time (Darwin's *Origin of Species* didn't appear until 1859). But insofar as scientific inquiry was then governed by Francis Bacon's principle of understanding the world through strict and detailed observation of the objects in it (the very approach Darwin acknowledges employing for his research), the city zoo was arranged to be another step along the path to enlightenment.

The fact that the objects in this particular museum are living creatures and that most people's curiosity about them has always been less than scientific is part of what makes old city zoos so "public" and, in their way, profound. By pitting us so closely, one-on-one with the animals, they confronted us with our own strange need to look at them in the first place, to sidle up to their apparent blankness and project upon it, however divergent our projections might be. At the turn of the century the German poet Rainer Maria Rilke (one of many prominent zoogoing poets, Pablo Neruda and Marianne Moore among them) would sit for hours in the Jardin des Plantes watching animals, observing, for example, every movement of the panther, so that in his poem "The Panther" he describes even the motion of the cat's nictitating membrane—the film over its eye—as it sees an image through the bars (perhaps Rilke himself) that "fills/and glides through the quiet tension of the limbs/ into the heart and ceases and is still."

In a sense, the old zoo's arrangement was an open invitation for us to find in animals analogies to our own lives, there being so little detail about theirs to interfere. And yet the crudeness of their confines was, paradoxically, a reflection of the great regard we had for them, as though the keeping was enough, just getting them into safe view. Somehow, those old cages seemed to shout at us: "Hey, that's a goddamn lion in there, can you believe it?" And it wasn't just the lion, but that the lion—or any wild animal—was the envoy of an extant, limited wilderness, or at least our notion of that.

I made my last visit to the old Prospect Park Zoo nearly two years ago. I stopped by to see Rudy, spent most of my time in the lion house with the jaguar, and, on the way out, paused before the polar bears' old den—the scene of a bizarre incident in the spring of 1987. On a warm evening after closing hours three neighborhood kids snuck into the zoo; two of them went up over the curved spiked bars of the polar bears' home. According to the boy who managed to scramble back out in time, he and his friend were hot and wanted to swim in the bears' moat. By the time the police arrived, they found the bears pawing at the other boy's badly mauled body; not knowing whether there were other kids still somewhere in the lair and in danger, they killed the bears with repeated rounds of shotgun fire.

I remember the incident casting a strange spell over the neighborhood and people expressing confused emotions: sorrow for the boy who'd been killed, befuddlement over his and his friend's intentions, and, most vociferously, anger and remorse about the fate of the bears. It was never made clear what exactly those boys were thinking—there was talk of one of the boys making a dare—but it occurs to me now that when they climbed over those bars, they were, in a sense, stepping into the story of the bears, the idea and the aura of the old zoo animal. City kids in the summer will take the caps off hydrants, anything, to escape the heat, and if they sneak into a zoo for a swim, there are a number of less threatening moats—the seal pool, for one—in which to swim. They, however, sought out not the coldest pool but the pool of the *coldest animal,* the animal that *stands for* coldness: the ice bears in some children's book; or the ones who ride blocks of ice across soda-bottle labels and menthol cigarette packs; or those I've actually seen in southern city zoos in the summer, sitting on a giant block of rapidly melting ice that a zookeeper had dropped in there as a fleeting acknowledgment of the animal itself.

We weren't, in the old zoos, letting the animals be just animals yet—neither the ones with whom we were said to have once shared a peaceable kingdom, nor those whose fate, as the new habitat zoos keep reminding us, is now entirely in our hands. They were to us the curiously shaped and untamed aspects of ourselves. We thought of them, and still do—though zoological fact and the new habitats have tried to advance us beyond such notions—as the evolutionarily wayward remnants of those pieces that found their best, most "reasonable" alignment in humans, but that we like going to zoos to see in an attempt to discern ourselves in undiluted forms. At the zoo, they could only be either surprisingly like us at times or we, at times, surprisingly like them. (I will never forget the day some years ago when, walking in the old Guatemala City zoo, I happened upon, at the back of the ape house, the door to the city's local chapter of Alcoholics Anonymous.)

Somehow, the strangely affecting dynamic of a day at the old city zoo was that while it began with us standing starkly, face to face, with an animal, it always seemed to end with us confronting some slightly confining truth about ourselves. It's a curious mixture of emotions we feel standing that close to a wild animal: yearning, pity, embarrassment—for it and ourselves. There's an initial sense of exhilaration that allows us to forget our momentary overpowering of the animal in order to represent its power again, and then an incipient sadness that grows out of that moment and fills us with some vague measure of existential gloom about our need to spy on animals, to displace them in order to help place ourselves; about our one privilege over them, which at a zoo seems a curse—of being the only animal capable of looking back at all the others and calling them names. It's the same sadness Rilke expresses at the beginning of the *Duino Elegies* when he posits that "the shrewd animals/notice that we're not very much at home/in this world we've expounded," the same sadness that I've always thought compelled the original designers of old public city zoos to put the seal pool at the heart of things. It was the place to which we could report with our respective sadnesses, reflections, or just plain "zoo fatigue" and lighten our spirits, seals somehow being, with those quick, seamless, body-long presses of themselves through water—captivity's antidote.

On an unnaturally warm February afternoon this past winter, I stood beside the newly renovated seal pool at the now habitat-oriented Bronx Zoo, reading the question WHY CHANGE A GOOD THING? written in bold type across the top of a sign that had been placed there. The explanation given below was that whereas the old pool on this same spot had brought delight to eighty-seven years' worth of past zoogoers, the present pool is modeled after an actual seal rookery found on the northern coast of California, thus securing the comfort and delight of the seals here as well as our own, or so the presumption goes.

It's now a whole other sadness that we bring to the seal pool of a new zoo like this one in the Bronx. Aside from the urgent reminders about the animals' imminent oblivion, and the scolding tone of signs like those I passed along the walkway inside one entrance declaring that our INDIFFERENCE must now be replaced by our ONGOING CARE, there is everywhere this conceit about the animals' newfound happiness—the seals', for example, or the happiness Rudy is said to be feeling at this moment somewhere in Michigan. No one would argue that the cages and houses of old city zoos shouldn't be improved, expanded, modernized. But why abolish zoos and create habitats? If it's the animals we are really worried about, why have such places at all? As I watched a young pup ease onto a rock and then awkwardly fin itself from shade to Bronx sunlight, it occurred to me that Rudy might well hate the suburbs (many do). Once he'd settled in Brooklyn, who's to say that he didn't grow to like the so-called family of man, the daily blurred and squawking outline of us at the edge of his nearsightedness.

In fact, much of the reason for bringing him and the others into our sorry sphere of things in the first place was so that we could get a look at them and speculate about these matters. Somehow, by the end of a day of peering into deep, landscaped "natural habitats"—looking for the animals we've brought from so far away only to place too far away to really see—I'd decided that it was far less depressing to proceed, as one did in an old zoo, from the assumption of the animals' sadness in captivity than to have to constantly infer the happiness we've supposedly afforded them in our new pretend versions of their rightful homes. The former premise, at least, seems less of a lie about what a zoo is.

I spend most of my day at the new Bronx Zoo in the stately area known as Astor Court—the center of the old zoo which, with its now empty bird and lion houses along one side of the long grass mall leading from the seal pool, had the eerie air of a once thriving animal city that's suddenly been abandoned. The monkey house was open and considerably updated. It housed little ones—tamarins and squirrel monkeys, capuchins and marmosets—all set within a series of lit, glass-framed squares of deftly simulated habitat: soundless, odorless, like a wall of TVs tuned in to nature shows with the volume off. There were a couple of teenagers among the viewers who were behaving the way people often do in such places, mimicking the monkeys, reaching to get their attention, which in this instance meant tapping at the glass, something that suddenly seemed entirely out of place there, like museumgoers touching the paintings.

Out into daylight again, I walked across the mall to take a look at the lion house. On either side of the locked front entrance were the requisite sculpted, vigilant lions; a lazing lion couple stretched across the lintel; and a series of gnarled, roaring lion heads jutting out from the frieze. Along the entire back side of the building there's a narrow walkway bordered by a heavy stone balustrade where a garish middle-aged woman with teased silver hair was scolding a group of children who were waiting in pairs to use the rest rooms located down a flight of stone steps beneath the lion house. As I watched them, I was struck by what I realized must be one of my earliest childhood memories: my father leaving me to wait alone in bright sunlight by that balustrade as I watched him descending those stairs into a darkness of caged roars.

Nobody I saw bothered to see where the lions had gone. They'd approach the front door, mouth the first words on the sign there—THE LIONS ARE NOT HOME—and then walk off, not bothering with the stretched canvas sign that explained, in strolling increments, what had become of everything, ending with: "Gone natural . . . the big cats are now in wild habitats throughout the zoo . . . Lions in West Africa . . ." Wild Africa is a wide-open stretch of tree-dotted grassy plain with lions, gazelles, and peacocks. Imagine the newfound happiness of the lions, placed on a moated island of grass in sight of—but ever at a distance from—the gazelles, their natural prey.

I get the distinct feeling visiting such places that I am really being told to learn how not to go to zoos. It is true that the new habitats are a logical place to sound the environmental message, the alarm about the vanishing wildlife. But such places are also, like it or not, a manifestation of a human impulse: to have our civilized home and the wilderness in our backyard too. It's an impulse, moreover, that we've been acting upon ever since we began building *our* natural habitat: the city.

At this very moment, on two thin poles in a sudden clearing of tangled Central American jungle in southern Belize, stands a small wooden sign. The words burned across it designate the surroundings: THE COCKSCOMB FOREST RESERVE—JAGUAR PRESERVE. I remember the first time I stood before it, thinking how absurd it looked and, in turn, made all of us look: kind of the nether side of advertising, the declaration of a halt to ourselves, a small promise, to a vast, moiling jungle, of our absence. I was there about five years ago with a zoologist named Alan Rabinowitz, who—after two years of tracking jaguars through the brush and Belizean officials through the halls of government up north—had just succeeded in getting put aside for the jaguars of that region the minimum acreage of jungle they'd need to continue living naturally, without us. In return, Belize—a small, poor country desperate to develop its limited resources—gets to keep the tourist revenues generated by Cockscomb's visitors, those of us in the developed parts of the world who can afford a trip to a "cageless natural habitat" in order to walk where there are few apparent traces of ourselves and get perhaps a last guilt-free glimpse of *them* on, more or less, their terms.

In our two weeks of hiking through the jungles of Cockscomb, Alan and I didn't see any jaguars, they being secretive, primarily nocturnal cats. We were, however, twice very close on the trail of one: fresh tracks, the sound of faintly breaking brush, an edgeless, exhilarating fear (a feeling heightened by the fact that jaguars, as Alan explained to me, will often double back as you're plodding through the brush and trail you for a while). I'd known this feeling before of having the whole proposition turned inside out on you—you now the nameless, the observed one alone on their terms. I felt it once with just the passing, hot and malodorous, of a wild boar through the Terai jungles of Nepal, and once in a dugout canoe that, having made one too many turns down ever narrowing Amazon tributaries, came to a complete stop in the most alive dead end I'd ever known and the quietest noise because it had nothing to do with me. I believe at that moment I kept invoking the day of the week to myself and city traffic sounds—the parts of a day I knew to be elapsing elsewhere but that kept collapsing there into that silence. And then came this long, achy sigh and slip of a giant boa from a limb into water and, it seemed, my boat going down with it.

In his years at Cockscomb, Alan lost one of his assistants to the highly toxic bite of a pit viper known as a fer-de-lance, and nearly lost his own life when he crashed his tracking plane into the forest (we climbed around one day on the still dangling, rotted wreckage). He also saw all eight of the jaguars he'd managed to radio-collar and study succumb to the various perils jaguars in the wild face: natural perils such as disease, parasites, and infections; and those, like hunting and destruction of habitat, that accompany what some would say is just as natural, man's encroachment. He told me, as we sat up talking one night on the screened, lantern-lit porch of his jungle hut, that he knew jaguars didn't have much longer, nor did any of the large animals needing large acreage.

Still, Alan considered his jaguar reserve a qualified success, and in a month he'd be off to the Golden Triangle of Southeast Asia to work with an endangered species of tiger there, and then on to Taiwan to study the rapidly vanishing clouded leopard. He was spending his life this way for what we both acknowledged was a purpose so special as to be insignificant to much of the world: trying to preserve that feeling, what he described that night as a "sweetness," at the heart of a primeval fear he first felt in Belize the day he was walking a wide path through the jungle and, cresting a hill, came upon his first jaguar. He knew from the way it was just waiting there for him, fully aware of his approach, that it had never seen a human being before. It stayed, staring for a while, and then walked off silently into the brush.

The rest of the night, Alan kept talking about the incredible difference between walking into a forest that's informed by the presence of a top predator causing fear in everything below it and into one that's not, and I sat there imagining that—the world we're entering now, the world of fearless forests.

I next met up with Alan—it was a year later, and he was on his way to Taiwan—at the Bronx Zoo. He visits there occasionally to check in at the office of his sponsor, Wildlife Conservation International. We had lunch and then strolled around, talking, and looking, though very perfunctorily, at the animals. It's disquieting being at a zoo, old or new, with someone like Alan. I kept wanting to apologize for the inhabitants. We stopped briefly to stare at Wild Africa, and there passed a moment where I was, in fact, drawn in by the scene, believing it. Then a pigeon flew by, and drew my eye to some local shrubbery, then to an oak tree where a squirrel was sitting and unglimpsed starlings squeaked. And it was at this near seamless juncture of the habitat's evoked nature and the big city's local patch of it that my mind's eye snagged and the question arose: What's the difference?

The only answer, I was coming to understand, was none. The fact is, for us the "wild" has only ever been an idea. If too near, the wild has been a feared and unwished-for encounter; if too remote, it has been romanticized, coveted. The only meeting place the civilized world has negotiated between the absence and presence of the wild is the zoo.

Alan and I didn't discuss any of this. He had always struck me as at once resigned to and uninterested in zoos, though he was quite eager to show me the recently completed tropical-rain-forest pavilion for which he was a consultant. Once inside, I couldn't help thinking of those temple menageries of Montezuma or Kublai Khan, and it occurred to me that civilization had come at least this far now to have actualized for the public that basic impulse to have our safe home and our wilderness too. Everywhere water seemed to be splashing under sun-spliced palm fronds where colorful birds flitted in and out, birds you could go days before seeing in an actual rain forest. Walking over a small wooden footbridge connecting lower level and mountain rain forest, we passed a big pane of glass with a black panther behind it.

Alan led me to the trunk of a massive cypress made of some synthetic material or other and had me touch it, and he laughed about how authentic it looked, right down to the lichen and moss painted over the surfaces. Outside, there were big maps marking the world's belt of rain forests and, on a waist-high pedestal, a digital counter clicking off the acreage of rain forest being destroyed even as we stood there—me watching and Alan saying something about how he once hoped exhibits like this would inspire people to go to places like the Cockscomb preserve in Belize, but how he now thinks people will just keep visiting zoos.

I suspect he was also reminding me, and himself, that the wilderness needs to be represented before it can be considered. A good part of Alan's work in Belize, in fact, was getting different groups of people there to regard their own immediate surroundings. The Indians who live in the area of the reserve generally regard the jaguar with the same mythic reverence that their Mayan ancestors did, but they also will not hesitate to kill one should it wander too close to the village. As for those who live in Belize's large urban centers, Alan assisted in a campaign to get them to visit a crazy little zoo that had recently been opened there in the jungle about an hour outside Belize City. The two of us visited it together one day. There's not much allure to a zoo in the middle of the jungle: It looked as though someone had just dropped nets and cages into the trees and labeled whatever got trapped inside. Lizards were running in and out. Free birds and monkeys were stealing food from the pens of the captive ones. It was all very confusing.

With my local zoo closed now, I went to visit the one in Central Park the other day and found it open and fully renovated. From the brochure alone, I could see this would be a far different experience from the one I remembered. The map had none of the cartoonish aspects of the old zoo maps—giant smiling giraffe heads and those of growling lions sticking out from a clump of trees labeled something like Darkest Africa. I saw now instead a very clear, scientifically termed assortment of earthly climactic regions: a Tropic Zone, a Temperate Territory, a Polar Circle, and something called Edge of the Icepack (a really terrific penguin house), all set around, of course, the seal pool. Where I thought I remembered the lion and ape houses and my old chimp friend used to be, there was now something called the Intelligence Garden, described in the brochure as an orientation and resting area. Alongside it was the Wildlife Conservation Center, with the words "The Skin Trade" over the door.

I went in. It was a large, nearly empty room with world maps all around marking the places where killing animals for their skins has endangered their existence. In a far corner was a high counter with a woman sitting behind it and on the floor near the back wall a big pile of various animal-skin purses, high heels, belts, wallets, hats, boots. I wasn't quite sure if the zoo's curators had gathered them for the purpose of this exhibit or if this was some kind of drop-off center where guilty New Yorkers brought their personal items and then arranged their penance with the woman at the counter.

From there, I worked my way through the climates from hot to cold. The Tropic Zone was much like the rain-forest pavilion I'd visited in the Bronx with Alan, although here the birds were far more venturesome, flying all around me, landing on the walkways and railings, and there were fish in pools and salamanders, frogs, and lizards—kind of a primordial playground, The Garden without the big beasts, one of those fearless forests I'd been imagining.

Outside, a light, intermittent spring rain had begun falling, so I passed quickly through the Temperate area and stopped off to see the polar bears, whom I was surprised to find there, all the large, wide-roaming land animals having been, like the ones at Prospect Park, moved elsewhere. These bears, though, do have what seems to be a delightful den: a small, rocky sun deck and then all icy blue sea, so deep you can walk a steep wooden staircase all around the glass-bordered pool and watch from above or below the unlikely grace of them moving, so big, through water, their thick coats swaying slowly the other way like the wraiths of bears.

One bear never left the corner where glass, ocean, and stone merged, and, the entire time I watched her, she kept repeating the same sequence of movements: a short paddle forward from the glass to the rocks and then a massive, full-bodied flourish of a faint backward like . . . well, overacting in a silent movie. Over and over she went as I stood there watching, half hypnotized in the rain, thinking about all of those animals out there in the wild listening to us; and of all those we've been bringing up here in zoos and are now trying to teach their instincts to before perhaps putting them back there again; and thinking how there might not be one left anywhere on earth who hasn't heard it—that tapping, a footfall, a voice, a passing car or plane; who hasn't yet waited in some clearing to allow our image into its heart.

Behind me, in their cold room, the penguins were walking, and I remembered an afternoon I spent some years ago in a zoo aquarium, passing down its dark halls of diced and lighted ocean days—from one to the next—wondering if even a displaced fish knows that something's different or, like a zoo seal, just continues; whether it just drifts there in a smaller bliss or can hear all of us out here in the dim corridor like some faint gathering of gods behind the horizon.

The aquarium's penguins, when I arrived at their time-controlled day, seemed happy enough with it: bright and spacious, a giant papier-mâché cliff for their rookery behind them and a broad strolling area beside a cold, swimmable sea framed by the exhibit glass before me. And then, suddenly, it all came apart. Their sea began to drain and, as penguins hurried away from it to huddle against the back cliff, a door-shaped section of it shimmied and opened. They quickly came away from there—moving as one penguin now, with myriad shuffling feet and twitching heads—and, lost between a broken cliff and an emptied sea, they just stood and stared from the far side of their day toward that dark open door. A few minutes passed, and then one penguin—the smallest and youngest, it looked to me—decided to make a move. Working himself free of the others, he made his way slowly over to the door and, poking his head around while holding the rest of himself back—two wings like little elbows lifting slightly for balance—peeked into the darkness and took in a narrow hallway lined with mops, buckets, and brooms, and the tall shadow of the keeper receding, and a light clinking of his keys.

4

bell hooks was born Gloria Jean Watkins in rural Kentucky; she adopted her grandmother's name in order "to honor the unlettered wisdom of her foremothers." She now lives in New York where she teaches at City College. hooks has her B.A. in English from Stanford, an M.A. from Wisconsin, and her Ph.D. from the University of California, Santa Cruz. She has written cultural criticism from her perspective as a black feminist, including *Ain't I a Woman* (1981) and *Teaching to Transgress: Education as the Practice of Freedom* (1994). "Touching the Earth," an essay from her essay collection *Sisters of the Yam* (1993), contrasts her family's history working the land with her own life in a New York City apartment. It explores the relationship between caring for the earth and loving oneself, between loving the land and ending racism.

Touching the Earth

bell hooks

I wish to live because life has within it that which is good, that which is beautiful, and that which is love. Therefore, since I have known all these things, I have found them to be reason enough and—I wish to live. Moreover, because this is so, I wish others to live for generations and generations and generations and generations.

—Lorraine Hansberry, *To Be Young, Gifted, and Black*

When we love the earth, we are able to love ourselves more fully. I believe this. The ancestors taught me it was so. As a child I loved playing in dirt, in that rich Kentucky soil, that was a source of life. Before I understood anything about the pain and exploitation of the southern system of sharecropping, I understood that grown-up black folks loved the land. I could stand with my grandfather Daddy Jerry and look out at fields of growing vegetables, tomatoes, corn, collards, and know that this was his handiwork. I could see the look of pride on his face as I expressed wonder and awe at the magic of growing things. I knew that my grandmother Baba's backyard garden would yield beans, sweet potatoes, cabbage, and yellow squash, that she too would walk with pride among the rows and rows of growing vegetables showing us what the earth will give when tended lovingly.

From the moment of their first meeting, Native American and African people shared with one another a respect for the life-giving forces of nature, of the earth. African settlers in Florida taught the Creek Nation runaways, the "Seminoles," methods for rice cultivation. Native peoples taught recently arrived black folks all about the many uses of corn. (The hotwater cornbread we grew up eating came to our black southern diet from the world of the Indian.) Sharing the reverence for the earth, black and red people helped one another remember that, despite the white man's ways, the land belonged to everyone. Listen to these words attributed to Chief Seattle in 1854:

> How can you buy or sell the sky, the warmth of the land? The idea is strange to us. If we do not own the freshness of the air and the sparkle of the water, how can you buy them? Every part of this earth is sacred to my people. Every shining pine needle, every sandy shore, every mist in the dark woods, every clearing and humming insect is holy in the memory and experience of my people . . . We are part of the earth and it is part of us. The perfumed flowers are our sisters; the deer, the horse, the great eagle, these are our brothers. The rocky crests, the juices in the meadows, the body heat of the pony, and man—all belong to the same family.

The sense of union and harmony with nature expressed here is echoed in testimony by black people who found that even though life in the new world was "harsh, harsh," in relationship to the earth one could be at peace. In the oral autobiography of granny midwife Onnie Lee Logan, who lived all her life in Alabama, she talks about the richness of farm life—growing vegetables, raising chickens, and smoking meat. She reports:

> We lived a happy, comfortable life to be right outa slavery times. I didn't know nothin else but the farm so it was happy and we was happy . . . We couldn't do anything else but be happy. We accept the days as they come and as they were. Day by day until you couldn't say there was any great hard time. We overlooked

it. We didn't think nothin about it. We just went along. We had what it takes to make a good livin and go about it.

Living in modern society, without a sense of history, it has been easy for folks to forget that black people were first and foremost a people of the land, farmers. It is easy for folks to forget that at the first part of the twentieth century, the vast majority of black folks in the United States lived in the agrarian south.

Living close to nature, black folks were able to cultivate a spirit of wonder and reverence for life. Growing food to sustain life and flowers to please the soul, they were able to make a connection with the earth that was ongoing and life-affirming. They were witnesses to beauty. In Wendell Berry's important discussion of the relationship between agriculture and human spiritual well-being, *The Unsettling of America,* he reminds us that working the land provides a location where folks can experience a sense of personal power and well-being:

> We are working well when we use ourselves as the fellow creature of the plants, animals, material, and other people we are working with. Such work is unifying, healing. It brings us home from pride and despair, and places us responsibly within the human estate. It defines us as we are: not too good to work without our bodies, but too good to work poorly or joylessly or selfishly or alone.

There has been little or no work on the psychological impact of the "great migration" of black people from the agrarian south to the industrialized north. Toni Morrison's novel *The Bluest Eye* attempts to fictively document the way moving from the agrarian south to the industrialized north wounded the psyches of black folk. Estranged from a natural world, where there was time for silence and contemplation, one of the "displaced" black folks in Morrison's novel, Miss Pauline, loses her capacity to experience the sensual world around her when she leaves southern soil to live in a northern city. The South is associated in her mind with a world of sensual beauty most deeply expressed in the world of nature. Indeed, when she falls in love for the first time she can name that experience only by evoking images from nature, from an agrarian world and near wilderness of natural splendor:

> When I first seed Cholly, I want you to know it was like all the bits of color from that time down home when all us chil'ren went berry picking after a funeral and I put some in the pocket of my Sunday dress, and they mashed up and stained my hips. My whole dress was messed with purple, and it never did wash out. Not the dress nor me. I could feel that purple deep inside me. And

that lemonade Mama used to make when Pap came in out of the fields. It be cool and yellowish, with seeds floating near the bottom. And that streak of green them june bugs made on the trees that night we left from down home. All of them colors was in me. Just sitting there.

Certainly, it must have been a profound blow to the collective psyche of black people to find themselves struggling to make a living in the industrial north away from the land. Industrial capitalism was not simply changing the nature of black work life, it altered the communal practices that were so central to survival in the agrarian south. And it fundamentally altered black people's relationship to the body. It is the loss of any capacity to appreciate her body, despite its flaws, Miss Pauline suffers when she moves north.

The motivation for black folks to leave the South and move north was both material and psychological. Black folks wanted to be free of the overt racial harassment that was a constant in southern life and they wanted access to material goods—to a level of material well-being that was not available in the agrarian south where white folks limited access to the spheres of economic power. Of course, they found that life in the north had its own perverse hardships, that racism was just as virulent there, that it was much harder for black people to become landowners. Without the space to grow food, to commune with nature, or to mediate the starkness of poverty with the splendor of nature, black people experienced profound depression. Working in conditions where the body was regarded solely as a tool (as in slavery), a profound estrangement occurred between mind and body. The way the body was represented became more important than the body itself. It did not matter if the body was well, only that it appeared well.

Estrangement from nature and engagement in mind/body splits made it all the more possible for black people to internalize white-supremacist assumptions about black identity. Learning contempt for blackness, southerners transplanted in the north suffered both culture shock and soul loss. Contrasting the harshness of city life with an agrarian world, the poet Waring Cuney wrote this popular poem in the 1920s, testifying to lost connection:

She does not know her beauty
She thinks her brown body
has no glory.
If she could dance naked,
Under palm trees
And see her image in the river

She would know.
But there are no palm trees on the street,
And dishwater gives back no images.

For many years, and even now, generations of black folks who migrated north to escape life in the South, returned down home in search of a spiritual nourishment, a healing, that was fundamentally connected to reaffirming one's connection to nature, to a contemplative life where one could take time, sit on the porch, walk, fish, and catch lightning bugs. If we think of urban life as a location where black folks learned to accept a mind/body split that made it possible to abuse the body, we can better understand the growth of nihilism and despair in the black psyche. And we can know that when we talk about healing that psyche we must also speak about restoring our connection to the natural world.

Wherever black folks live we can restore our relationship to the natural world by taking the time to commune with nature, to appreciate the other creatures who share this planet with humans. Even in my small New York City apartment I can pause to listen to birds sing, find a tree and watch it. We can grow plants—herbs, flowers, vegetables. Those novels by African-American writers (women and men) that talk about black migration from the agrarian south to the industrialized north describe in detail the way folks created space to grow flowers and vegetables. Although I come from country people with serious green thumbs, I have always felt that I could not garden. In the past few years, I have found that I can do it—that many gardens will grow, that I feel connected to my ancestors when I can put a meal on the table of food I grew. I especially love to plant collard greens. They are hardy, and easy to grow.

In modern society, there is also a tendency to see no correlation between the struggle for collective black self-recovery and ecological movements that seek to restore balance to the planet by changing our relationship to nature and to natural resources. Unmindful of our history of living harmoniously on the land, many contemporary black folks see no value in supporting ecological movements, or see ecology and the struggle to end racism as competing concerns. Recalling the legacy of our ancestors who knew that the way we regard land and nature will determine the level of our self-regard, black people must reclaim a spiritual legacy where we connect our well-being to the well-being of the earth. This is a necessary dimension of healing. As Berry reminds us:

Only by restoring the broken connections can we be healed. Connection is health. And what our society does its best to disguise from us is how ordinary, how commonly attainable, health is. We lose our health—and create profitable diseases and dependencies—by failing to see the direct connections between living and eating, eating and working, working and loving. In gardening, for instance, one works with the body to feed the body. The work, if it is knowledgeable, makes for excellent food. And it makes one hungry. The work thus makes eating both nourishing and joyful, not consumptive, and keeps the eater from getting fat and weak. This health, wholeness, is a source of delight.

Collective black self-recovery takes place when we begin to renew our relationship to the earth, when we remember the way of our ancestors. When the earth is sacred to us, our bodies can also be sacred to us.

5

Michael Aaron Rockland has his B.A. from Hunter College and his M.A. and Ph.D. from the University of Minnesota. He is a professor of American Studies at Rutgers University. He has published one novel, *A Bliss Case* (1989), and a number of nonfiction books that include a translation of Domingo Faustino Sarmiento's *Travels in the United States in 1847* (1970), the *American Jewish Experience in Literature* (1973), *Homes on Wheels* (1980), *Looking for America on the New Jersey Turnpike* (with Angus Kress Gillespie, 1989), and the book from which the following essay is taken: *Snowshoeing through Sewers: Adventures in New York City, New Jersey, and Philadelphia* (1994). Mr. Rockland is a dedicated urban adventurer who takes delight in exploring the "nexus of nature and the built environment" and in finding beauty in what he terms "the haphazard landscape." He believes that "in the late twentieth century, a weed-and-trash-filled city lot or even a hillside above an interstate may be a better place than the wilderness to contemplate one's relationship to nature."

Big City Waters

Michael Aaron Rockland

Ah, what can ever be more stately and admirable to me than
mast-hemmed Manhattan?
River and sunset and scallop-edged waves of flood tide?
—Walt Whitman, "Crossing Brooklyn Ferry"

If one is intent on urban adventure, a natural place to begin might be New York City, the Big Apple, the mother of all urban adventure sites. New York's geography is endlessly fascinating. Four-fifths of the city is on islands surrounded by the ocean and great rivers; some thirty bridges angle across the waterways between the boroughs. As solid as it seems, New York is a liquid place, bearing more than a passing resemblance to Venice.

At the center of things, surrounded by water, the capital of the world but still an island, is Manhattan. Oblivious to its massive stone skyscrapers, waters rush by Manhattan's supine body on all sides—the Hudson on its western flank, the East and Harlem rivers along its eastern, with Spuyten Duyvil Creek rounding its head and New York Harbor, the beginnings of the Atlantic Ocean, resplendent at its feet. Like any island, Manhattan almost asks to be circumnavigated. I wondered: Could one circle Manhattan by canoe? More than once I had taken the tourist boat trip around the island, but now I fancied making the trip on my own.

Well, not entirely on my own. A canoe is a tricky enough proposition without attempting a solo expedition anywhere, much less when you're a rank amateur not entirely sure which end of the canoe is which and when you plan to travel through big city waters. If you sit at either end of a canoe, the other end lifts and catches every breeze like a sail; you're in constant danger of tipping over. And if you step into a canoe on one end, you're likely to fly right out of it into the water. This happened to me one summer on a Maine pond to the eternal delight of my watching children. The only safe way to pilot a canoe solo is by kneeling amidships, Indian-style, J-stroking all the while to keep yourself going straight, but that position and activity would precipitate knee surgery long before you made it around Manhattan.

Who then would go with me? My wife, Patricia, companion of choice in virtually all of life's other adventures, is an unrepentant antagonist of the great outdoors. She is a self-made woman—a lawyer by trade—and strong and tough-minded when she has to be, but she is the sworn enemy of all insects and variations of temperature greater than ten degrees. She encourages my adventures; she thought canoeing around Manhattan was "a fantastic idea." But it was the last thing in the world she wanted to do.

I asked Ralph Thompson, my next-door neighbor, if he was interested, and he fairly shouted, "Not a chance!" I was surprised by the vehemence of his reaction. I didn't know Ralph well, but he seemed a nice enough guy; our kids played together across the backyard fence.

Ralph said, "A canoe'll dissolve in those acid waters just like that. Phytttt! One minute there's you and the canoe. The next, just some green and purple bubbles. And if the toxic water doesn't get you, you'll get hit by a ship. Man, there's ocean liners in New York Harbor!"

Ralph, I recalled then, is an insurance agent with State Farm. When I first knew him, I would kid him by singing the State Farm commercial—"Like a good neighbor / State Farm is there"—but Ralph would say "That's right" and never crack a smile.

I next called Phil Herbert. Phil is a big admirer of tales of heroic adventure. His favorite book is James Dickey's *Deliverance.* "Look," he said, "canoeing around Manhattan could be a lot worse than *Deliverance.*"

"What are you talking about?" I said to Phil. "The Statue of Liberty will take good care of us."

"The Statue of Liberty?" Phil laughed. "She's standing up there like an advertisement for Right Guard. Those guys in *Deliverance* got buggered, and they were out in the woods. The Statue of Liberty won't do a thing when the muggers and buggers get us."

But I could tell that Phil was intrigued. And I was keen on Phil, because he's the kind of guy who will try anything. He's a survivalist without the right-wing politics; it's almost a religion with him. I also knew he had a yellow aluminum canoe stashed away under mountains of debris in his garage. Phil is the total out-of-doors freak. He has more outdoor gear than Hermann's sporting goods stores. "You got permission from anyone?" Phil asked.

This was a problem I had not anticipated. What if canoeing around Manhattan was against the law? Bikes aren't allowed on superhighways like the New Jersey Turnpike, so maybe canoes aren't allowed in the powerful waters around Manhattan. I began phoning various city agencies in the hope that, with permission granted, Phil would come with me.

But who you gonna call? The Parks Department suggested the Coast Guard. The Coast Guard suggested the police. The police referred me to the Port Authority. The Port Authority referred me back to the Coast Guard. This time the Coast Guard referred me to the offices of the several borough presidents through whose waters we would pass. I called the offices of the borough presidents of Manhattan, Brooklyn, Queens, and the Bronx. The first three referred me back to the Parks Department or the police, but a woman in the Bronx borough president's office said, "You need a permit."

"How do I get it?" I asked.

"You have to fill out a form."

"Can you send me the form, please?"

"The man who handles forms is on vacation," she said, stifling a yawn.

It was hopeless. If I persisted, I might eventually get a definitive answer from some city agency, and it would probably be no. The surer course was just to do it. If you want to do anything out of the ordinary in this world, don't ask permission, because there's always someone who will say no.

Let's face it, there are two kinds of people in this world: can-do people and can't-do people. Can't-do people usually work in government or for insurance companies, like my neighbor Ralph. Insurance people are the ultimate can't-do people because they don't want you doing anything, leastwise anything interesting or exciting. Not that they're truly interested in your health and safety; they just want to go on collecting premiums from you forever and never have to pay off. The one person I'm absolutely certain is glad I'm alive is a guy who sold me a life insurance policy twenty-five years ago. I've moved six times since then, but his annual birthday cards never fail to reach me. They're just like other birthday cards, but there's a covert message: "Glad you're alive; keep sending the premiums."

Insurance people will insure you against anything—poverty, bad marriages, meteors hitting your house. For a high enough premium I'll bet you can even get them to guarantee your immortality. An Argentine I wrote my first book on, D. F. Sarmiento, said in 1847 that the great thing about the United States was, if you wanted to do something dangerous, even kill yourself, nobody would stop you. Not anymore.

I phoned Phil Herbert and began to tell him of my travails gaining permission for the trip. Phil interrupted and said, "Why are you so uptight about a permit?"

"What?" I said.

"Let's just go. I've already got the canoe out of the garage."

"Right," I said, deciding on the instant not to mention who it was that sent me off on my adventures within the New York City bureaucracy.

One thing you should know about Phil and me: we're opposites—which is maybe why we get along so well. He's Irish-Catholic and I'm Jewish, and we have a kind of Abie's Irish Rose relationship. If Phil were a woman and I wasn't married to Patricia, I would marry him. I envy Phil his easy anticlericalism. He went through eight grades of parochial school, so he knows life is absurd and doesn't worry about it. Five thousand years of history and the Six Million keep me worrying about it.

Phil makes me laugh, which is the nicest thing I can say about anyone. We probably exaggerate our differences for the fun of it. Phil plays the hard-bitten misanthrope with me, and I the bright-eyed, bushy-tailed optimist with him. I told Phil this trip would make us the modern-day Lewis and Clark. "More like Mutt and Jeff," he responded.

Phil is a fireman, but he reads more books than anyone I know. His character incorporates both sides of the Irish stereotype: half responsible, serious FBI man with shiny black shoes, half falling-down-drunk poet.

I've always liked Phil's spur-of-the-moment approach to life. Me, I make lists. Sometimes, when consolidation would be too daunting a task, I even make a list list, a kind of concordance to my lists. It'll say something like: #1 list under magnet on refrigerator, #2 list on dresser, #3 list taped to bathroom mirror. Occasionally I can hear Patricia laughing somewhere in the house, and I know she's spotted one of my lists. She said to me once, "As long as your lists don't start to mate." I've even done something—and here I confess to the reader what I have never told another human being—that wasn't on a list and, afterward, when no one was watching, got credit for it by putting the item on the list and immediately crossing it off.

Phil and I met years ago at a reading I was giving from one of my works at the Old York bookstore in New Brunswick. His comments after my performance were so sharp and, frankly, so flattering I invited him for a beer and we became friends. It was a long time before he told me he was a fireman. It was as if he was ashamed of being a fireman around intellectuals. Of course, when I learned he was a fireman, I was glad. I had been afraid he was, like me, another professor.

The inside of Phil's house is even more full of books than his garage is full of sports gear. It looks like he's perpetually getting ready to have a garage sale. Books are stacked up everywhere—not just on shelves but spilling out of the closets and onto the floor. There are even bookcases in the kitchen.

The most extreme example of Phil's book obsession is his bedside table. There the books are stacked a yard high, no exaggeration. More than one girlfriend has threatened to leave him because of those books on the bedside table. I sympathize with them. Imagine lovemaking under such precarious conditions! I keep telling Phil that he and some lovely are going to die one night when an avalanche from the bedside table rolls down onto the bed. "What a way to go," he says.

Phil doesn't just buy these books and stand them around to impress people; he reads them. Reading is one reason he's a fireman. More than any other occupation it gives him time to read. Down at the firehouse they call Phil "Shakespeare." I'll phone him there and hear someone yell, "Hey, Shakespeare, it's for you." They give Phil a hard time because he's always carrying a book around and reading between fires instead of playing cards with the boys.

I also get a hard time at work. The professors at the university where I teach think I'm not sufficiently scholarly. In the academy, if your courses are popular you must be pandering to the ignorant student masses and couldn't be scholarly. My colleagues consider writing scholarly only when it's unintelligible to normal humans and appears in unread, obscure journals. The top third of each page is text, the bottom two-thirds footnotes. Even proud mothers of such scholars, when sent their publications, try to read them and give up.

If Henry David Thoreau appeared today and applied for a position at my university, *Walden* prominently listed in his curriculum vitae, he'd be turned down—seen as a ne'er-do-well camper and hiker, not sufficiently scholarly.

Maybe I should have been a forest ranger or a fireman, like Phil. No doubt Phil and I represent to each other what each of us partly wishes he was. I admire Phil's common sense and dogged bravery, and I guess he admires my ideas. Phil wishes he was an intellectual—which, of course, he *is*—and I'm his link to the academy. As for me, well, Phil is my ambassador to the "rednecks."

Our canoe trip began on a warm Saturday afternoon in August at the Battery, where we parked Phil's old Ford station wagon with the canoe lashed to the top and went to have a look at the water. We had decided to begin on the Hudson, which is so wide we'd have no trouble steering around any obstacle. There was no point tackling the narrower confines of the Harlem and East rivers right at the start.

At Phil's insistence, we had planned the trip to catch the tides. "Tides schmides," I had said, but Phil grimaced and pointed to his charts. As I would learn, it is impossible to make it up the Hudson in a canoe against the tides, which twice a day roll powerfully up the river 120 miles to Albany and then charge back down. "Try it," Phil said. "You'll end up in Africa."

We put the canoe in the water next to the fireboat house. Phil, being the stronger of us, got into the bow of the canoe. He pulled; I pushed and steered. The tide was coming in so strong you could see it and hear it smack against the wooden pilings. It barreled upriver and we went with it, moving up the Hudson with no more effort than it took to steer. You really believe in the moon's powers when you're in a tide. The Hudson was flowing upriver instead of down; that's all there was to it.

The water was also as choppy as the ocean, and wakes from passing garbage scows and tankers made it more so. But as long as we kept the prow of the canoe pointing into the waves, we did fine. It was scary though. Sometimes we went down so deep into a trough between swells we saw nothing but water; then, as we rose on the next wave, tall buildings popped up before us like great stone corks.

We passed the Circle Line pier, where a tourist boat was putting out from the wharf. Just upriver, the colossal proportions of the berthed aircraft carrier *Intrepid* loomed up out of the water. A sailor on the deck waved to us. At least I think he waved. He was so far above us, so tiny, it was hard to tell.

We kept rolling upriver. To our left were the high purple cliffs of the Jersey Palisades. To our right, block after block of Manhattan retreated behind us. Each time a bit of light flashed among the dense thickets of buildings on Riverside Drive, that was a block.

A police boat steamed past us downriver, and I hunkered down and tried to look inconspicuous. Phil shouted something to me over the wind, but his words rocketed before him upriver.

"Whadja say?" I asked.

Phil turned in his seat and repeated, "Maybe it's legal after all."

"Nah," I said. "They just don't know if it is or it isn't."

A minute later, the sound of diesels alerted us that the police boat was coming back. Uh oh.

It stopped two hundred feet away, and an amplified voice that nearly catapulted me out of the canoe said, "Put your life jacket on."

"We *have* . . . ," Phil started to yell, but then he turned and stared at me. My life jacket sat at my feet, in the bottom of the canoe. Sheepishly, under the full gaze of Phil and the police, I slipped the jacket on, and the police boat rumbled off downriver.

We passed Grant's grimy gray tomb high on the bluff. A strange place to stash a president; didn't Grant rate Washington, D.C.? Ten blocks farther north we spotted something white floating toward us on the surface of the water. As we got closer, I saw that it wasn't one object but a flotilla of hundreds of objects. "What's that?" Phil shouted.

"Looks like a school of jellyfish," I said. "Don't touch them. They sting."

As we came alongside the floating mass, Phil picked up one of the objects on his paddle. "Trojan, ribbed," he said. And now we were surrounded by a sea of condoms, each bobbing in the water and winking at us in the afternoon light. Had there been a safe-sex orgy in a community upriver? Was this a subliminal commercial for that then current movie, *Sea of Love?* I knew condoms were making a comeback in America, but this was ridiculous. "You and your urban adventure," Phil shouted.

"What's it mean?" I said to Phil.

"What?"

"The condoms. What's it mean?" All those condoms had to mean something, had to have some deep mythic significance. Some connection to Moby Dick?

"Why's it have to mean anything?" Phil said. "It's just a bunch of condoms. I thought you came on this trip to get *away* from the university."

The condoms floated away, and we continued upriver toward the towers of the George Washington Bridge, which, like everything else about the Hudson, is on a gigantic scale. Beneath the bridge, we examined the undersides of cars and trucks passing above us, a view you don't ordinarily have of them. The vehicles looked vulnerable, as if their private parts were exposed. It was like looking up the dresses of women on a staircase high above. I felt almost as if I should avert my eyes.

Soon after, the sun low over the Palisades, we reached the farthest limits of Manhattan. Making a right turn under the New York Central railroad bridge, which spans Manhattan and the Bronx just above the surface of the water, we passed into Spuyten Duyvil Creek.

Spuyten Duyvil brings Hudson River waters around the top of Manhattan, where they become the Harlem—not a separate river at all, but the branch of the Hudson that flows around the east side of the island. Some say the name Spuyten Duyvil is a corruption of the Dutch for Devil's Spout, but another interpretation is Spiting the Devil. In his *History of New York,* Washington Irving told of Anthony Van Corlear, who endeavored to swim across the fast-flowing waters to spite the devil but drowned in the attempt. A huge blue *C,* painted on the side of a gorge at a place called Split Rock, is near the spot where a Columbia University rowing team member also drowned in Spuyten Duyvil in 1976.

Spuyten Duyvil once flowed some blocks to the north, but in 1895 a new, enlarged ship canal was blasted through to replace it, the former Spuyten Duyvil was filled in, and Manhattan became shorter by two hundred yards. The Marble Hill neighborhood, named for its quarries, was now physically part of the Bronx—though it remained politically part of Manhattan, and its phone numbers appeared in the Manhattan directory, until only a few months ago.

Though Manhattan lost land in this instance, it has generally increased in size over time. Much of Lower Manhattan is filled-in land, including the recently created Battery Park City and World Financial Center, which were built on the fill from the nearby World Trade Center excavation. The propensity of the original Dutch settlers to push back the sea still seems to be carried in the genes of New Yorkers.

Luckily for us it was now slack tide in Spuyten Duyvil, as we needed quiet water to get out of the gorge. Luckily, too, there was a swampy spot on the Manhattan bank. We got out of the water there and, with our remaining strength, hauled the canoe up the cliff. Our plan was to camp overnight rather than chance descending the Harlem and East rivers in the dark. We could catch the next outgoing tide in the morning.

We put up the pup tent, wondering when someone had last pitched a tent in Manhattan. Quite possibly it was erected right where we were—Inwood Hill Park, the site of the last Native American settlement on the island and where arrowheads are still found. Phil wondered what the Indians would have thought of the New York City park sign that greeted us with its huge "No" followed by a long list of prohibited activities. Luckily, there was nothing on the list about stashing canoes in the bushes; the Parks Department hadn't reckoned on invasions from the sea. "Entering Park after Dusk" was, however, high on the list: number 3.

We had food with us but decided a fire would make us too easily detectable. Besides, we were both in the mood for a good meal and a little nightlife. As darkness closed in, we took a flashlight and, on unsteady land legs, made our way out of the park and onto Broadway, where Clancy's Bar & Grill stared us in the face.

Phil and I got a bottle of wine and some steaks. All the time we were in Clancy's I kept fancying myself a participant in that old TV show *I've Got a Secret.* I kept staring at the waitress's pantie line under her tight white uniform and wishing she would ask me something, anything at all. I wanted to tell her that Phil and I had just emerged from the waters of Spuyten Duyvil. But she never asked us anything about who we were or where we came from. I mean we could have been enemy spies or something. We could have been terrorists loaded with plastic explosives, put ashore by a submarine. Finally, I coudln't stand it anymore. "You may not believe this," I said, as she finished reciting the list of desserts, "but we're camping out in the park across the street."

"That's nice," she said.

"Nice?" I said to Phil when she had moved off to get our pies. "Couldn't she do better than *nice?*"

"Whadja want her to do, cheer?"

"Well, maybe a little appreciation."

"Forget it," Phil said. "On a river trip there's no point talking to anyone on the banks. Every time Huck and Jim talked to anyone on the banks they got into trouble."

But I was miffed the waitress hadn't admired our exploits. Shameful as it is to admit, there must still have been a part of me that equated canoeing around Manhattan with, say, leaping to catch the winning pass in the end zone, no time left on the clock, and all the women pouring out of the stands and jumping on me. The incident with the waitress suggested that women didn't care one hoot whether I caught passes or canoed around Manhattan. I knew Patricia didn't. But we men go on playing our little games.

After dinner, we took a cab downtown and saw a movie. It hardly mattered to us *which* movie. It was fun just to have snuck onto the land to see any kind of movie in the middle of a canoe trip.

"Where you going with that flashlight?" the blue-haired lady in the ticket booth wanted to know. Maybe she thought we intended to usurp the usher's job or disturb the other patrons by shining the flashlight around the darkened theater. "Oh, that?" I said. "Been shopping. Not to worry."

We really needed the flashlight when we returned uptown and walked into the park. It was so dark we couldn't find our tent and canoe. "Bastards stole them," Phil said. Someone must have seen us arrive and, the moment we quit the park, made off with our gear.

But we had been looking in the wrong place. Stumbling around in the dark almost an hour, we finally slid down a rock outcropping and tripped over our tent, which was pitched in the clearing at its base. What was it doing there, our canoe too? Things seemed so different in the night; I could have sworn our stuff had been moved.

Phil had some cigars, and we sat on a rock ledge overlooking Spuyten Duyvil and peacefully smoked them and looked at the water and the rising moon. Here we were in Manhattan, the most intense spot on the globe, but you couldn't know a more profound solitude. Night creatures moved in the bushes. An opossum—an animal I was familiar with only as a flattened highway object—ran into the clearing, looked at us, and darted out of sight again. Life seemed real good.

In the morning we had Pop Tarts and orange juice in cardboard containers and spooned up a whole jar of Smucker's Gooberjelly using plastic spoons. Gooberjelly is great stuff to take on a trip because you have the peanut butter and jelly together in the same jar and don't need anything else, not even bread.

But how I wished we'd saved some juice, because I had a gob of Gooberjelly stuck halfway down and nothing to wash it along unless I cared to suck up some of the PCBs floating on Spuyten Duyvil. My lungs felt like they were cemented together with Crazy Glue.

"Want me to do a Heimlich on you?" Phil asked.

"No," I croaked.

"How about a whack? Should I whack you a good one on the back?"

Before I could answer, Phil hit me hard on the back with the flat of his hand, and the Gooberjelly headed south.

"Where'd you learn to do that?" I asked Phil gratefully.

"Hey, man, I'm a fireman," he replied. "You call 911, you get 911."

We lowered the canoe into Spuyten Duyvil and continued on our way. Rounding the corner of Manhattan, we passed under the Broadway bridge, where a train was rattling overhead into the Bronx, and started down the Harlem River.

A short way down the Harlem the massive structure of George Washington High School rose up over my shoulder on the rocky promontory, inspiring one of my scale-the-nearest-cliff fantasies. I yelled to Phil about it, but he just turned and gave me a look. Across the river, on the Bronx bank, the massive Kingsbridge Veterans Hospital appeared and, soon after, Yankee Stadium.

Unlike the Hudson, the city crowds in from both banks on the Harlem and East rivers. Helicopters roar overhead down the rivers, and the water traffic is brisk. Tugboats and small tankers are thick in there, and we worked hard to stay out of their way. A guide on a Circle Line tourist boat must have said something about us over the loudspeakers, because the passengers cheered and waved wildly to us as we swept by.

But there was no time to bask in glory. The Harlem was about to join the East River at a place ominously called Hell Gate. We had been warned about this spot. There are whirlpools and vicious currents, and shipwrecks have taken place at Hell Gate. The East River, not a river at all but a tidal strait, drains Long Island Sound, and the confluence of its waters and those of the Harlem in such a narrow space creates great turbulence. It's as if the energy of Hell Gate exemplifies the spirit of New York—the collision of endless immigrants with the city's shores, the vast multitudes streaming through the streets.

We decided to hug the Manhattan bank, as far away from the swirling waters as we could get. With the added protection of Mill Rock, a tiny island that juts from the river offshore, we got through all right—though several times the canoe was tugged this way or that by an unseen hand.

Just ahead on the grassy bank was Gracie Mansion, the mayor's residence, a vestige of eighteenth-century New York. Distracted by this genteel sight, we inattentively entered the channel alongside Roosevelt Island. No one had mentioned the dangers of this channel, but it was here that all the turbulence we feared at Hell Gate became a reality. So narrowed was the river by the island that the water rushed through as if coming out of a hose. We rode the watery roller coaster, struggling desperately not to keel over or smack into the concrete bulwark. If anything got in our way here, a boat, a floating log, we were finished. For almost two miles we hung on, moving perilously fast, with the tides and current rushing us madly toward the sea.

Then, as we passed under the cable car and Roosevelt Island ended, the East River assumed its customary width and demeanor, and we breathed normally. We were able to enjoy the United Nations, which has a grace from the water one doesn't experience on First Avenue. Passersby on the walkways above Franklin Delano Roosevelt Drive yelled things at us, but the wind carried their words over our heads.

We passed under the baroque iron framework of the Manhattan Bridge, then under the gothic towers and finespun cables of the venerable Brooklyn Bridge. We could smell the Fulton Fish Market just ahead, so we knew the southern tip of Manhattan was fast approaching. We had to slow down. Otherwise, we would shoot past the end of the island and be dragged out to sea.

We decided to play it safe. Hugging the land, we painstakingly crawled from pier to pier, careful not to let the waves smack us against the barnacle-encrusted piles. In this manner, we crept around the wide foot of Manhattan and, after so many watery miles, were back at the Battery.

But the tides were rushing out as fast in the Hudson as in the East River, and now they were against us. Although we paddled our hardest to make it upriver the short distance to Phil's station wagon, we couldn't move. It took all our energy just to stay in place. Phil tried using the bow rope to lasso the huge bolts on the piles. Once he actually caught one of them and pulled us forward fifteen feet, but Phil was no cowboy and, after what seemed like fifty more tries, gave up. "Damn," I said. But I had no idea how to move the canoe upriver either.

We briefly considered tying on to a pier and waiting some hours for the tide to change, but the sun was frying us and, besides, we both needed a bathroom pronto. "Let's just say we did it," Phil said. "I won't tell if you don't." So we never did quite circumnavigate Manhattan; thirty-one miles and we couldn't make the last hundred yards because of the tides.

While Phil found this amusing, I felt like a failure. "You are one goal-oriented son of a bitch," Phil said. "Lighten up. Someday you'll think the most interesting thing about this trip is that we didn't quite make it."

This has proven to be true. Failures, disasters even, make the best stories, and I know that whenever I tell anyone about the trip around Manhattan I never fail to mention, with great good humor, missing our goal by only one hundred yards. But back then, as I climbed the fifteen-foot rock seawall behind Phil, with my share of our gear in one arm and the bow rope tied to my belt, I was depressed.

We were up now, but how to get our vessel up the wall? Even without the tides tugging at the canoe, it was a straight up, eighty-pound lift. While we cogitated on this problem, I held tight to the bow rope; if I let go for a second, that canoe was history.

After several fancy and failed attempts, employing what we remembered from high school physics (much discussion about fulcrums and pulleys and block and tackle), we simply grasped the bow rope and pulled the canoe straight up the wall on its keel, oblivious to the indignant shrieks of the aluminum. Phil's canoe bears the scars to this day.

Getting the canoe up had been such a challenge that I forgot my disappointment over missing our goal and cheered up. We loaded our gear into the canoe and portaged it across Battery Park.

A homeless guy sat sunbathing on a park bench, his belongings neatly stashed in an A&P shopping basket. He stared at us, wide-eyed. "Say," he said.

"Yeah?" Phil replied.

"Where'd you all come from?"

I was delighted. I had struck out with the waitress the night before, but here, at last, was someone interested in our trip.

But before I could begin what might have been a lengthy discourse on New York City geography—on tides and currents and the beauty of the city as seen from the water—Phil, as if asserting again his idea that we should avoid contact with people on the banks, short-circuited me. "Europe," he said. Then we lashed the canoe atop Phil's station wagon with rubber bungee cords and headed for the Holland Tunnel and home.

6

David Wong Louie was born in 1954 in Rockville Center, New York (his father had come to America from China in the 1940s, and his mother in the 1950s). He graduated from Vassar College, has an M.F.A. in Creative Writing from Iowa, and now teaches at UCLA. His recent novel *The Barbarians are Coming* (2000) chronicles the life of a young Chinese-American man coming to terms with his father and with American culture. This story "Bottles of Beaujolais" is part of his 1991 short story collection *Pangs of Love.* This short story incorporates a love story as part of a complex environmental fable. It begins with a version of human efforts to play god by simulating nature and concludes with its protagonists, including an otter, heading to the real urban nature of Central Park.

Bottles of Beaujolais

David Wong Louie

I will move storms . . .

—*A Midsummer Night's Dream*

It was a little after eight one morning in late November. Fog, fat with brine, snailed uptown. Bits of the wayward cloud beaded between my lashes, crept into the creases of my clothing, and infiltrated my every pore, seeping a dank chill throughout my body. On the radio the man said the fog had set a new record for low visibility. Later, as the taxi pulled in front of the sashimi bar where I worked, the cabbie said that by nightfall the city would be covered with snow.

Unlocking the door to the sashimi bar, I watched Mushimono in the show window standing upright on his hindquarters. He was thick and cylindrical, a furry fireplug. The otter, whose love for fish had inspired my employer to install him as a sales gimmick to lure other fish connoisseurs to the shop, seemed baffled by the fog. From his home—an exact replica of the otter's natural habitat that stretched twelve feet long, reached as high as the ceiling, and jutted six feet into the shop—Mushimono snapped his anvil-like head from side to side, like a blind man lost, following the sounds of traffic he could not see. Mushimono was one of those peculiar creatures evolution had thrown together like a zoological mulligan stew; he had a duck's webbed feet, the whiskered snout and licorice disc eyes of a seal, a cat's quickness, and fishlike maneuverability in water. His fur was a rich burnt-coffee color and it grew thicker with each shrinking day of the year.

Mr. Tanaka, the sashimi master, met me at the door. He had the appearance of a box. The bib of his apron cut across his throat, exaggerating his dearth of neck. An imaginary line that extended up from his thin black necktie and past his purplish lips met his mustache at a perfect perpendicular, reinforcing this illusion of squareness. Above this plane sat two tiny eyes that shimmered like black roe.

Without ceremony Mr. Tanaka told me to make fog. "It not good this way," he said. "Fog outside and no fog inside make Mushimono crazy." He sliced each syllable from his lips with the precision of one of his knives.

The otter stood frozen, as if a mortal enemy were perched nearby. Yet, in spite of this stasis, I saw movement. Perhaps it was the eerie quality of the fog-sifted light or some strange trick of the eye that caused the twin curves of Mushimono's belly and spine to run congruously before tapering together at the S of his thick, sibilant tail. Silken motion where there was none at all. Strong but delicate lines. My thoughts drifted off to a moving figure of another sort: Luna, and the gentle crook of her neck, the soft slope of her shoulders, the slight downward turn of the corners of her mouth.

"Don't forget, only fresh fish for Mushimono," Mr. Tanaka warned.

"I know, I know."

"Sluggishness no substitute for nature," he said, clasping his hands behind his back as he paced the length of the trout-spawning tank. "For Mushimono a fish dead even if it look alive to you. If eyes not clear like—"

"Saki—"

"Their center dark like—"

"Obsidian. Then—"

"They dead," Mr. Tanaka said, completing a favorite adage.

"You mean good as dead."

The sashimi master furrowed his brow, stroked an imaginary beard, and stared at me with those two lightless eyes before he headed for the sashimi bar.

When I was first hired, Mr. Tanaka had promised to teach me the art of sushi and sashimi. In fact, during my interview he had said, "Good mind," a reference to the fact I had graduated cum laude, "make for steady hand." But as the weeks passed, so did my hopes of ever learning how to wield the razor-sharp knives that could turn chunks of tuna into exquisite paper-thin slices. My primary task, as it turned out, was to be Mushimono's keeper. The food fishes and shellfishes were off limits to me. Even when I offered to help scale and shuck, he said, "This operation too delicate a matter for my business, for my sashimi, and for the fish himself for me to permit this ever." I was unhappy at first, but Mr. Tanaka managed to keep me with a more than generous salary. And the job had its share of benefits—all the fish I could eat and Luna's daily stroll past the shop.

I netted three speckled trout from the spawning tank and put them in a pail. All the way to Mushimono's, they nibbled the water's surface and sounded like castanets. As I released the trout into the murky pond in the show window, which extended deep into the basement of the shop, Mushimono regarded me with uncharacteristic calm, undisturbed by my intrusion into his world. I wondered if the odd atmospheric conditions were to blame.

Mushimono's world was an exact reproduction of the lakeshore environment of southern Maine from which he came. Mr. Tanaka had hired experts in the fields of ecology, zoology, and horticulture to duplicate the appropriate balance of vegetation, animals, and micro-organisms found in the wild.

But I made the weather. From an aluminum-plate console attached to the otter chamber, replete with blinking amber lights and grave black knobs, I was the north wind, the cumulonimbus, the offshore breeze, the ozone layer. I was the catalyst of photosynthesis. I was the warm front that collided with my own cold front—I let it rain, I held it up. I greened the grasses, swelled the summer mosses, sweetened the air, and then plucked bare the trees. I was responsible for the death of all summer's children. In time I would freeze the pond. Yes, I had the aid of refrigerators, barometers, thermometers, hydrographs, heaters, humidifiers, sunlamps, and fans. But I threw the switches. I possessed nature's secret formulas. What were all those transistors, tubes, wires, and coils without me? I made the weather. I was night and day. It was no illusion. I turned the seasons. I manipulated metabolism. I made things grow.

Humidifier set high. Saturation point. Dew point. Refrigerated air. Steamy wisps of white rose from the pond—an immense caldron of meteorological soup—and evaporated the further they curled from the water. In no time the show window was filled with fog as dense as surgical gauze. By increments, Mushimono disappeared.

There was a clock inside me. Its alarm—my accelerated pulse, my shortened breaths—went off each day at the same time. I crouched at the foot of the show window beside the weather console, and anticipated Luna's imminent arrival. I fancied there was something organic between us: a chemical bond, a pheromone she emitted that only I could sniff from the air that telegraphed her approach to the shop. Or perhaps it was something mystical, perhaps our souls had been linked in former lifetimes. Or was it some strange configuration of the ions in the atmosphere that drew us together? From the hundreds of feet that shuffled past the sashimi bar each morning, I always knew which belonged to Luna, for hers were like distant fingers snapping. When she walked, there was music on the pavement.

No. It was not some cosmic magnetism that pulled us together, and our molecules were not aligned in any extra-physical way. This was plain, pedestrian infatuation.

Luna's lacquered nails tapped the glass pane. She stopped each day at the same hour to see Mushimono and lavish her attentions on a creature insensitive to her charms. My stomach gurgled in anticipation. I heard a splash of water as the otter dived into his pond. Unable to see Luna through the fog, I pricked up my ears and listened for her. Past the fog and the layers of glass I heard the wet suckling noise, like a child nursing, that she was making with her lips, those succulent, baby shrimp. As always, her kisses were not meant for me.

I longed to see her and I could have satisfied my longing simply by flicking on the sunlamps and burning off the fog. I had the power but not the nerve. Mushimono's welfare was my first priority, my second was to stay employed, and sadly the yearnings of the heart could do no better than a distant third.

Luna tapped once more. Through the fog her red beret was a muted shade of plum. She was no more than a shadow whose substance fluctuated with her proximity to the glass. The fog hid Luna; it caressed her, as Zeus, disguised as a cloud, once caressed Io. And since this cloud was mine, then I was Zeus to Luna's Io.

After several minutes, when Mushimono failed to materialize from the pond, Luna's impatient ghost vanished in the mist.

By the lunch hour the fog outside had worsened. For the very first time, Luna entered the shop. She had a parcel tucked under her arm. Our first meeting without glass. Even sopping wet, she was beautiful. Water droplets sparkled in her hair. Her eyes were as blue as lapis. Her voice was unexpectedly deep. But even more of a surprise was the narrow gap between her two front teeth, a gap so dark and rare and suggestive of the mysteries that draw men to women.

"These are for the weasel," she said as she handed me the parcel. "I hope it likes Nova." She adored Mushimono, Luna explained, and was concerned when he failed to make an appearance that morning. I assured her of his good health. Luna lit a cigarette. Smoke rose and slowly curled up and formed a jagged halo in the damp air around her head. She seemed distracted, gazing at the rear of the shop where Mr. Tanaka's customers lunched at the sushi counter and the Italian-café tables. I leaned my elbow on the weather console and explained—I might have bragged a little, but how could I resist?—that I had made the fog that obscured her view of Mushimono.

"Give me summer," she said, her voice as raspy as July sparklers.

"I'm afraid snow's predicted for tonight."

"Snow, fog, what's the difference?" She drew more smoke into her lungs. "It's a mess any way you slice it. In a month the winter solstice, and your Mistermomo will hibernate for the duration. It's a waste and a shame. I mean it. That weasel makes my day; a little life in all this concrete." She exhaled a long agonized breath. "I'm getting depressed just talking about it." Luna removed her beret and shook off the water. "I think I was a Californian in a former life." She dragged on the cigarette and then added as an afterthought, "Hey, if you're the weather wiz, why don't you do something about this fog?"

I told her that a sudden change in barometric pressure in Mushimono's tank might cause him grave discomfort. This wasn't the total truth but she trusted me at my word. She got ready to leave and said she would stop in on her way home from work if the fog cleared by then. She wanted to make sure Mushimono was in good health. I told her if it was snowing out when she arrived, I would demonstrate how I made snow. She sighed. "All morning long, all I hear is talk of the bottom line; everything with these brokers is the bottom line." Luna crushed her cigarette under the sole of her snakeskin pump. "I come here to get away from all that, to see my Mistermomo, but I don't get weasel. You give me snow. Snow, snow, snow. It's so depressing."

She knotted her belt and turned up the collar of her raincoat. She spun on her heel and started to leave. As she reached for the door, she turned suddenly and apologized for the outburst. "See you later." Here she grinned. "By the way, my name's Peg." Peg! I thought. *Peg?* One hangs coats on pegs. How could my Luna be this monosyllable? This Peg?

By afternoon the fog had lifted, and I burned off the fog from the otter chamber. Mushimono was indifferent to the change in weather, surfacing only for quick breaths before returning to his underwater lair. At three Mr. Tanaka left for the day. I closed shop. In anticipation of Luna's visit, I went shopping and returned with candles and bottles of wine. I lit the candles and waited for Luna. When finally she tapped at the front door, it was already dark and the candles had burned to half their original length.

We had barely said hello, and I was still holding the door open, when she handed me her Burberry and whisked past me, losing me in her perfume. She sped to the little café table I had set up, with its dancing flames and breathing wine. She did not even ask after Mushimono.

Luna took the bottle in her hands, cradling the neck up like the delicate head of a baby. "Beaujolais!" she shrieked. "I can't believe it! How fortuitous. I think I might cry." She sniffed the bottle. "This is the wine of summer, the picnic wine." She lit a cigarette and puffed anxiously. "This is the wine for lovers. Oh, you don't understand, do you? I just had the best summer of my life."

I poured equal amounts of the ruby-red liquid into porcelain saki bowls. The color of her fingertips matched the Beaujolais. We lifted our bowls and, after a moment of deliberation, she offered a toast: "To Mistermomo and Édouard Manet. Or is it Monet? No, Manet." We drank, the bittersweet juice of love. As I sipped, I watched Luna over the rim of my bowl. Her skin glowed as if lit from within.

"Those guys in Manet's, or maybe it is Monet's, 'Déjeuner,'" she said, putting emphasis on the middle syllable, which she pronounced "June," "were crazy for Beaujolais. They drank it by the gallon. Honestly. I read it in an art magazine." Her cheeks were flushed from the wine. I admired her cameo earrings. Luna said the Impressionists were her favorite painters, and they and the wine reminded her of summer.

"Baudelaire—" I began, having recalled his immortal line, *One should always be drunk.*

"No, no, it's pronounced 'Beaujolais,'" Luna said. "See here? Beaujolais." She pointed a finger at the wine label.

"Of course," I said. "My French is terrible." I refilled the bowls.

I never cared for the smell of burning tobacco, but the smoke rings rising from her pursed lips seemed fragrant, almost sweet, as if her body had purified the smoke. Then Luna let out a terrible cough. "Bronchitis," she muttered as she raised the bowl up to her mouth.

"You should take care of yourself," I said. "You ever think what those cigarettes are doing to you? Maybe you can try something athletic, like skating or skiing."

She narrowed her eyes and fixed me with a stare. "What's with you and snow?" And as if that had not already chilled my blood, she said the one thing a lover hates to hear from his beloved: "You sound like my mother."

I apologized. Then she apologized.

"It's me," she said. "The bum lungs, the cigarettes are part of the package. You can say I live life on the edge. I mean van Gogh called it quits before he was forty." She coughed. "This sounds crazy," she said, "but each time I have an attack I feel that much closer to the inner me." Luna drained her bowl and then replenished it with the dregs from the bottle of Beaujolais.

I went behind the sashimi bar to prepare a snack for us. I selected a long shiny knife from Mr. Tanaka's impressive collection. I was surprised by how light it felt in my hand. I removed a block of yellowfin from the refrigerated case and started cutting the fish into crude cubes. The steel seemed to melt through the flesh. At first, I was tentative in my approach to the fish, but soon, caught up in the sensuality of slicing, in the thrill of moving through flesh, I was imitating the sashimi master's speedy hands, approximating his flashy blade act. Where was the mystery of his art? It was mine already. I looked over at Luna and smiled while my busy hands whittled away at the shrinking hunk of fish. I imagined how I might one day audition for Mr. Tanaka, with Luna there for inspiration, and dazzle him with my newfound skills. I glanced down to admire my handiwork. My hand was a bloody mess.

"I fancy myself a burgundy," Luna said.

I clenched my fist, sticky with red pearls of trouble. I felt dizzy but worked hard to hold myself together.

"But, you know," she said, "people like to classify me in the sauterne family."

I wanted to be brave, but every man has his limits, especially when he is watching his blood run from his body.

"I'm bleeding," I said.

"Oh. You say you're a burgundy too?"

"No, I'm bleeding, like a pig!" I flicked my wrist, spattering the pristine countertop with bright red beads.

"Put some mercury on it," she said.

"Some what?"

"Grab ahold of that tuna. It's full of mercury. I read it in—"

"You mean Mercurochrome. That's not the same as—ah, forget it." I tightened my fist, hoping to staunch the flow. I saw my evening with Luna slipping away.

"Call it what you want, it's probably in the tuna anyway."

I ran cold tap water over my hand. My blood turned a rust color in the stainless-steel sink. There were three major cuts—on the thumb, the heel, and the meaty tip of the middle finger—and numerous nicks. Moments later I bandaged my aching hand in a linen napkin.

Luna sipped her Beaujolais and then offered me a taste. I drank. She marked the spot where my lips had come in contact with the bowl and drank the final swallow with her mouth positioned on the very same spot. I retrieved the second bottle of wine, a Chablis, from the refrigerator. I had to ask Luna to uncork it.

"To me, you are a burgundy," I said. Each syllable echoed in my ears long after it had left my lips. My face burned but my extremities felt cold. "There's nothing remotely sauterne about you. You're not even blond." The wines raced through my veins, their friction swelled my wounded hand. I could have sworn my lungs had shrunk—there seemed to be much less air to breathe. "I won't hear another word about you and sauternes. You're definitely burgundy, Luna."

"What did you call me?"

"Burgundy, Luna."

"Peg. I'm Peg."

"You don't have to test me. You're burgundy all the way."

"Yes. Burgundy. Simple and elegant—"

"Rich and full-bodied, Luna."

"Peg!"

"But burgundy—"

"Yes. Earthy, robust, and generous."

"Soft-eyed, soft-lipped, Luna-Peg."

Fires smoldered under my lids. My jaw dropped. My skin drooped from sore bones. And in their core the marrow had hardened.

"Drinking burgundy is an event," she said.

"I adore a fine burgundy."

We drank our wine by the mouthful.

"I don't get it," she said. "Sauternes are such flippant, insignificant wines. Silly vacuous fruit juice—"

"But, Luna, you're not silly or vacant."

"And you, sir, are—let me see—yes, a mature port. I mean it. You have those superior powers of discernment that are the trademark of all good ports." She raised her bowl to my lips. "Drink," she said softly. "You must mend your blood." I gulped her offering, obeying her angelic voice. She refilled her bowl and drank.

I rested my wounded hand on my thigh. The napkin was badly stained. I needed to rest. My heart pounded like the surf, and when the sea receded, I baked under the hot suns beneath my lids until the tide washed over me once more. My head kept time with my pulse, rocking back and forth, from shoulder to shoulder. I unwrapped my hand and dipped the hot digits in the chilled wine. The wounds gaped, the skin around them twitching. The wine rusted. Luna lifted my hand from the bowl and kissed each finger, alternating the kisses with puffs off a cigarette.

"Beaujolais," Luna lamented, staring longingly at the empty bottle. "All gone. The end of summer. No more Monet, Manet—oh, hell. No more of all that crazy light and sun and heat and color; the boys and girls at play. The boys on the beaches and wonderful Beaujolais."

I closed my eyes. They had outgrown their sockets. As I dozed in and out of sleep, I slipped to the borderlines of consciousness where the heres and theres overlap. I sat on my spine with Luna here beside me. But when sleep swept me under, dreams became the intimate here while the things defined by time and space were the distant theres. Luna, repainting her lips as I opened my eyes—here. Then she was there, untouchable, a shadow in my fuzzy dreams. In this place her words turned to music.

"Give me the summer any day of the week," she sang.

I skinned back my lids and was blessed by the sight of her sad cool blues staring at me.

"Luna," I said, smiling. "Burgundy Luna." I took her by the wrist, as big around as a sparrow's breast, and directed her eyes to Mushimono's lakeshore. "Consider it summer again," I said languorously. "Your wish is my command."

"Don't tease," Luna said. "You're two months too late and five months too early."

Her words were lyrics to a love song. What did it matter what they meant? After all, who made the weather? I said, "Who is day and night? Who turns the seasons? Who makes things grow?"

"You sick or what?" She checked my temperature. "You're hot."

I blew out the candles and watched the complex spirals of smoke twist to the ceiling. "Suddenly, it's no more," I said. "Like that, I'll rid us of winter. Summer will be yours again, my dear Luna."

"It's Peg. My name is Peg. You're not well, are you?"

Then the tide inside me ebbed; my body flowed into the chair like a Dali watch. Luna, I thought, is Helen of Troy and Raphael's Madonnas rolled up in one. Luna is Penelope at the loom. Eurydice in Hades. Luna is Mozart at seven. Shirley Temple at eight. Luna is that side of the moon we see, and all we imagine the invisible half to be. Luna is Titania kissing Bottom. Io snatched by Zeus. Marilyn married to DiMaggio. "Luna is Peg," I said out loud, "a lovely mystery, a mysterious loveliness."

"God, if you feel that way, call me Luna. Call me Lunatic. I mean it. Burgundy Luna. I sort of like that."

"I can make summer come and go." My words trickled off my shoulder and down the front of my shirt. "We'll picnic," I said, "picnic."

She sat up excitedly, then slumped back into her seat. "It won't be the same," she said. "How can we have a picnic without the right wine?"

I suggested saki.

"Oh, saki is so—Ceremonial. Let's face facts. Chardonnay goes with fish, cabernet goes with meat, but beaujolais is the stuff of picnics."

I grabbed the empty Beaujolais bottle and funneled some saki into it.

"That's indecent," she said. "That stunt might work on a two-year-old but not on me." She joined me behind the sashimi bar and held the bottle up to the light. "I guess an emergency's an emergency, but the color's all wrong."

Suddenly, she reached for one of Mr. Tanaka's special knives. Silver flashed between us. Luna's eyes were the sky. In them I soared. Back on earth I was trembling. The cold steel parted the earlier, now crusted cuts. Thin red lines appeared across my fingers and palm. She took my hand and smiled mischievously. She squeezed it over the funnel until blood streaked from palm to heel, where droplets hung like lizard tongues. The blood rolled slowly through the funnel and splashed thickly in the saki. In time, we had translated the saki into a bottle of Beaujolais.

"I know we could've pretended," she said as she pressed my hand to her lips. "But why exhaust our imaginations?" The tip of her tongue traced the wounds, splitting, stinging, and soothing them all in the same lick. "You're wonderfully strong port." She squeezed my hand over the funnel once more. The heavy droplets pinged the saki's surface faster and faster until she achieved the coloration she desired. It resembled an orange rosé. Pleased with her work, Luna raised my hand and smeared my blood over her lips. I took the bottle by the neck and intoned, "To Luna."

"To summer," she said, clasping her hand over mine.

Outside the lakeshore, Luna worked the controls of the weather console as I gave her instructions. I was too dizzy and weak to perform the magic myself.

Luna poured Beaujolais into a bowl. "Drink," she beckoned, "wine mends blood." I drank from the bowl she held to my lips. The wine was warm and unpleasantly salty. I felt hot, then cold, then hot again. I closed my eyes. The lids seemed lined with sand. I dreamed of Luna, naked as the otter, standing in the street outside the lakeshore, tapping at the window. Then I woke and saw her at the controls, and this seemed like an equally implausible dream.

The sunlamps burned at noontime intensity. Though the fans were idle, convection stirred a gentle breeze in the lakeshore that rustled the dead leaves along the ground. Soon, because of the contrast between the heat inside and the relative cold outside, dew started to form on the chamber's four glass walls.

"Eighty-two degrees and climbing," Luna sang out. The otter suddenly sprang out of the pond. He scurried up the muddy embankment and darted from one end of the compartment to the other. He pawed the glass, but Luna, fixed on her work at the weather console, did not notice.

"Humidity, let's see, is up to 68 percent," she said. "Barometric pressure reads thirty-point-two-three and rising."

Mushimono stood erect on his haunches and stared devotedly at her, as if he were kneeling, waiting to receive Communion.

We entered the lakeshore. The otter dived into the torpid water. Luna spread her plaid blanket on the ground. I basked under the brilliant suns, whose healing rays sealed my wounds. Beside me Luna arranged a still life of bowls, lox, and the Beaujolais.

"This is great," Luna said as she untied the laces of my shoes. "They won't believe me tomorrow at work."

"Lovely day, if you don't mind me saying so myself." Thick dew clung to the window, blocking any view of the world beyond.

"This is really great. Better than Bermuda. I mean it. Summer in winter, day at night." Luna turned her back to me and rolled her stockings off her ankles. "There's money in this operation. I'll tell the brokers about it. They'll probably flip but they'll know what to do." She stretched out alongside me, undoing the third and fourth buttons of her silky blouse, hiking her skirt past her thighs. She poured a bowl of the new Beaujolais and made me drink. "You remind me of someone. It's your eyes. So big and round and black." She scratched her head for the answer. She picked up the lox. "I see it now," she said, "Mistermomo! You and that sweet weasel."

Luna knelt by the lake and floated the slices of lox, orange-pink rafts, one by one, on the stagnant water. "Oh, Mistermomo," she called, "I have a treat for you." She made her suckling sound, so odd and wet.

"Where's that weasel?"

"He likes fish, not filets."

"Filets," she said, "are fish."

"Mushimono likes his fish with gills and fins."

Luna clenched her teeth, perfect white shells, tightening the skin around her mouth. She glared at me as if I were mad. Tucking the hem of her skirt into the waistband, she waded knee-deep into the lake.

"Jesus, it's freezing!"

With her next step she suddenly plunged into thigh-deep water, stirring a turbulence that sucked the lilylike filets toward her. When the ripples subsided, one filet was clinging to the front of a bare thigh. Rather than removing it, she smoothed the lox against her skin with caresses and pats that produced sounds like those of lovers' stomachs pressed together. The lake, she discovered, was too deep. As she emerged from it, Luna shivered and coughed. She unhitched her algae-blotched skirt and let it fall in a pile at her feet. She seemed frail and small. She gestured for the Beaujolais. I picked up a bowl and was horrified by what I saw. The contents had been retranslated by the suns. The blood had coagulated into a cinnamon crust, sealing in the saki underneath. "I need some wine," she said, "my lovely summery Beaujolais. I'm freezing."

I started to feel the ache in my hand. My head throbbed from the alcohol. "It's gone," I said as I stared at the bowl, the hardened blood, the obscene saki. The sunlamps stung my eyes.

"I'm cold," she said. She reached across me for the bowl, and when she glimpsed the cruel scab bobbing on the dirty saki, she dropped the bowl, and it cracked against a rock. The fire was gone from her eyes and skin. Beads of pond water seemed frozen upon her arms. She trembled. Her pale face was the leaden-gray of cod steak and filled with the indecisiveness of a three-quarters moon. "It's a nightmare," she said.

I wiped a portion of the window clear of dew. No moon in the sky, but snow, lots of snow, just as the cabbie had forecast. Flakes fell in bunches. I shook my sore hand. I heard her pick her raincoat up off the ground, overturning the bowls, the bottle, and all the picnic things that had been resting upon it. I followed the flight of several flakes from the lamplight's nimbus to the white street below. She tiptoed from the show window. A gust of cool air shot in from the shop. Not a soul was on the street. Absolutely quiet, as it must have been at the beginning of time. I could hear my hand throb. In the pond the lox was being semi-poached by the sunlamps, and gave off a rank smell. Not far away I detected the gentle hiss of nylons inching over her legs. Then the rustle of raincoat, the click of her pumps, and the squeak of the front door opening. She crossed the street. Her collar brushed up alongside her ears; each flake seemed to make her flinch and shrink deeper into her coat, like a tortoise into its shell. She struggled, small, shivering, solitary, against the storm.

Peg, I thought. I wiped away some dew. The snowfall was spectacular. "Peg," I whispered. She slipped from sight.

I ran outdoors, following the pair of unbroken footprints leading from the sashimi bar to where she stood on the avenue hailing a cab. "Peg!" I shouted as the cab pulled up to the curb. I began to run. "Peg!" I glided like a cross-country skier in the narrow lane she had cut in the wet snow. "Peg!" There on the sidewalk I saw a salmon filet. "Peg." I was my own echo. Then I became aware of a strange sound coming from behind. Imagine mah-jongg tiles tossed together in a tin can. I took a quick look back, but saw nothing. "Peg." She was climbing into the cab. I ran harder and with my increased speed the mah-jongg tiles grew louder, more urgent. "Peg." My eyes fixed on the amber lamp shining at her shins through the balls of exhaust at the foot of the open car door.

I slid in next to her and slammed the door. Immediately I heard a metallic scratching. I opened the door and there, illuminated by the footlamp, I saw the otter, upright on his hind legs. He was panting, out of breath. "What is it, a dog?" Peg asked. She clutched my arm as she peeked over my shoulder at Mushimono.

"Don't be afraid," I said as the otter flopped into the compartment with us. "He seems very gentle tonight." I closed the door gingerly behind him.

"You've got to take him back," she said, sliding into a corner, away from the otter.

No, I thought, no. Not this night, with my happily aching hand and Peg so near. We were warm and cozy in the cab. She nestled close to me; the otter, stretched to its full length over half of the backseat, seemed to purr; the wheels of our taxi hummed as snow beneath them turned to slush.

I tapped the glass that divided the cab into two compartments. "Central Park," I told the cabbie. "To the lake where you rent those boats in the summer, you know, where the ducks live."

The otter first. Before my hand, before Peg's wet clothes. Before whatever might pass between us next. It was my duty—the otter's care.

The cab swerved uptown. Snow kept falling. It covered the city, softening edges, blurring lines. But I had never seen things any clearer than I did that night. Blizzard-force gusts made our journey difficult. I told the cabbie not to rush. We could not outrace the storm. There would be snow, plenty of snow. I knew by daybreak the snow would turn to rain and by noon it would all be forgotten.

7

Rebecca Johnson was born in Ohio and now lives in Boston; her essay, written as part of a book called *Ecofeminism and the Sacred,* edited by Carol J. Adams, explores the experiences of African-Americans after the great movement from the rural South to the northern cities. Written as she lives and gardens in Jamaica Plain, the essay traces her family's history with the land back to the family home in Tennessee. As she moves back and forth between personal narrative and cultural analysis, Johnson also incorporates many other materials and stylistic approaches, referring to a farmers' almanac, astronomy and astrology, urban history, literary analysis, toxicity, and organic gardening. Also part of her effort to capture the complexity of urban nature are discussions of European imperialism and capitalistic commodification, and the effect that they have had on people of color and on nature.

New Moon over Roxbury

Reflections on Urban Life and the Land

Rebecca Johnson

The wolf moon rises cold
over the concrete ditch called
the Orange Line
where trains blast
through air
through politics
through glass and terrazzo terminals
to the illusion of prosperity
and back again.

The wolf moon (Roberts and Amidon 1991, 405) has been with us all year. The wolf moon is the January moon, the one closest to the earth during the coldest part of the year in the Northern Hemisphere. The 1991 wolf moon brought war. The chill glare of the worst of human intentions acted upon the world. The whole year has felt cold, bone cold, like homelessness in winter, like extinction for misunderstood creatures.

These reflections are about being out in the cold, that is, outside the benevolent concern of ecologist, politician, or big business. These reflections are about gardening in harsh conditions; about being an urban dweller, a feminist, a lesbian, about being black. All those conditions, opportunities, realities which mediate my relationship to all my environments—the urban one I inhabit, the natural one polluted by the city I call home, the psychic one in which memory and poetry and dream dwell and sometimes invite my residence as well. I realized in writing this that I have no answers. In fact, this year I seem to have only questions and doubts, hopes and fears. And poetry. These I hope to share with you.

As I've prepared this piece, I have struggled with the technical language of environmental science and the specific concepts of ecofeminism. In these reflections I am choosing to depend on my own emotional vocabulary to represent concepts important to me. The idea of "The Land" represents the relationship to nature and environmental responsibility with which I grew up. It is a central myth for many black people (Christian 1985, 47–63). Organic gardening is my link with The Land as an idea and a complex corporal system. I garden for sustenance and as spiritual practice. The annual events of germination, waving green life, fruition, and decay are the only things I really believe in anymore. If I worship at all, it is at the compost pile. It receives my most consistent offerings. The experience of black people in the North is my experiential base. The commodification of everything is both metaphor and tool for analysis (Ferguson 1984, 47–57). In the next few pages I will reflect on all of these ideas and concepts.

I am using the occurrence of the full moon in the night sky as organizational reference point. This may seem like an odd structural metaphor for a city dweller.

I have lived in New England for eight years. Before that I lived in Cincinnati, near downtown, in a neighborhood called Over-the-Rhine. My first five years in New England, I lived in near-rural small towns. Those years were my first extended sojourn in a rural setting. They fed my interest in astronomy, which was just developing as I left Cincinnati. When I moved to Boston, I began seriously investigating astrological gardening. I had been exposed to at least the lunar aspects of this approach to planning, planting, and harvesting a garden in Cincinnati. In Boston I learned to join the astrological signs. We (my garden partners and I) only have one year of experience with this technique, but using the astrological signs has given me a sense of integration, joining my relationship with the urban soil with the relatively unspoiled expanses of the cosmos: a kind of chaos redeemed by Chaos. So my reflections are organized around the lunar tradition.

Each full moon has a name and gives a sense of where we are in the year (Roberts and Amidon 1991, 404–27).

January: The Wolf Moon
February: The Snow Moon
March: The Worm Moon
April: The Pink Moon
May: The Full Flower Moon or the Corn Planting Moon
June: The Strawberry Moon or the Rose Moon
July: The Thunder Moon
August: The Red Moon
September: The Harvest Moon
October: The Hunter's Moon
November: The Beaver Moon
December: The Cold Moon

Even those of us living in the big cities of the East Coast can see the moon, if nothing else, in the night sky.

New Moon over Roxbury: Pleiades in Winter

There are places of other suns
new lights burning in the distant sky

we look up call their names
tell stories of their mystery:
seven sisters, singing maidens,

seven stars to show the way
when the moon's face has turned
left our house and closed the door

we wait

we only imagine galaxies
when the moon is new over Roxbury
different lights cluster in our sky
and fall

the staccato flash of automatic weapons fire
sulphurous street lamps
knocked askew
sparks trailing after a fleeing car
the insistent search light of the police helicopter

the lamp in the window night after night waiting
for those of us who have never seen the stars.

Cities have always existed. That is, humans are social beings and have always gathered to create settlements. There may have been a time when these settlements were synchronous with the natural environment, a wholeness built, but not artificial, and reflecting back the wholeness it sought to imitate. That is not the case today. Cities are the cause for and creator of much of the destruction of the natural world. They reflect artifice and decay and an unholy chaos. Yet, in our cities music and art reside and many search for better lives. This search may be unwilling and, as in much of the developing capitalist world, fueled by the wholesale destruction of integrated and functioning ecologies by rampant capitalist speculation and greed. In any event, cities are not about to go away. Experts project that by the year 2000 one-half of the world's population will live in cities (Seager 1989, 40–41, 107).

At one time urban life in the United States was fairly antiseptic. We had been shielded from most of the worst manifestations inherent in dislocation from a familiar and productive rural existence to the squalor and poverty of many urban settlements in the developing capitalist world. Increasingly in the United States, we, too, witness or experience trash picking in dumps, people of all ages and races living on the streets, toxic hot spots rendering large areas unlivable, and the predation that poverty inspires. We prefer the sanitary myth of people coming to this country fleeing war, famine, greed, and natural disaster and finding peace and security. Increasingly, people find here what they would find in many cities of the world: economic stagnation, alienation, and despair. Middle-class urban life permits illusion and ignorance. For those lucky enough to have secure incomes, city life becomes very simple. All can be bought, including the ability to ignore the magnificent complexity of the built and natural environments which make privileged lives possible. Neither do middle-class city dwellers experience the chaos their ignorant consumption inflicts on the land upon which we all depend. Yet poverty is no virtue. It may remove blinders to the inadequacy of urban systems, but it doesn't necessarily bring insight. In choosing urban life, I have neither the resources nor the inclination to claim the class privilege that ignores the consequences of our actions. I stay in urban areas because I still prefer them, even with all the problems I've just listed. It is also the place where much progressive activism originates, where people of color increasingly live, and where fundamental change must be enacted if the natural ecology of the world is to survive.

The Worm Moon

The night after Aunt Bea's funeral, my father and I walked the old family land in Tennessee. He had something important to tell me, his adult daughter who had moved East, grown dreadlocks, and chosen work he didn't quite understand. That night he told me about erosion, how to tell the lay of the land and where erosion might happen. He showed me various remedies. He urged me never to let the land wash away, not like some were, back in his home place.

I come from people who are both urban and rural. As black people they all have an orientation toward the land which went beyond its productivity or the house built on it. It was a resource to be conserved, protected, passed to the next generation with its topsoil, its clean water, its stand of trees intact.

Historically, this attitude was a fundamental orientation of black people in the United States. Our health as a community could be judged by our relationship to the land. Nobody better catches this central myth of black life in this country than Toni Morrison. In her first three novels, *The Bluest Eye, Sula,* and *Song of Solomon,* she explicates the beliefs, conflicts, and crises of a people separated from the land they knew in exchange for the hope of a better political and economic life on land that is new and strange (Christian 1985, 48).

Ms. Morrison's characters are my parents' generation, new to the North, unaccustomed to the demands of industrial life. Their link to the land was their gardens.

One of the hardest resources to locate in a city like Boston is a place to have a garden. Land is scarce. Open spaces which aren't parks or institutionally protected green spaces are generally privately owned and inaccessible or polluted. I live in Jamaica Plain, a part of Boston. The three blocks closest to my home have one tree, but there are several hidden vegetable gardens.

Gardening is hard work, so several of us garden together. My landlady Pauline, and friends Katherine and Diane share responsibility for two, and sometimes three, garden plots. This summer, when we broke ground at our new community garden space, we invited eight friends to clear the plot of volunteer maple trees and (what seemed like) enough rocks to build a fine New England wall.

Soil Analysis Report for Home Gardens[1]
Bag number 87205 for *Rebecca Johnson*
3/11/91
Extractable Aluminum: *9 parts per million (ppm)*
**Lead* (extractable): *29 ppm*
Estimated total lead: *456 ppm*
The lead level in this soil is low.

The soil in our garden is thin as water and dangerous. It is not an exotic threat. For city folks it is as common as street lamps and high-top sneakers. We battle aluminum, lead, and cadmium to grow vegetables.

Over the three years we have gardened in my backyard, we have added soil amendments provided free by Forest Hills Cemetery and the Metropolitan Police Mounted Patrol. We load gardening fork and spade in my car and fill plastic bags with cemetery leaf mold and mounted police horse manure. Through this practice we have reduced the lead content in the soil in my backyard from dangerously high to safely low.

Is there a moon for remembering? Perhaps the Worm Moon in March, the one where you speak hopefully to the dirt in your backyard, can serve that purpose. Just as it is important for the soil to remember its fruitfulness, it is important for us to remember that cities are full of people who want to cooperate with the rhythms of nature, who find community in growing and sharing food, and who quietly struggle to repay the earth for benefits we may have unwittingly and violently wrested from her.

My father was a farmer, escaping his family in Tennessee at eighteen but not escaping the call of the soil and the imperative to grow food. I have a brother and sister. The three of us grew up under my father's insistence that we garden with him. He rented a quarter acre lot to supplement our large Midwestern backyard garden. At ten years old I felt like we had endless rows of green beans to weed and pick. I am the only one of my siblings to continue to garden in adult life, although I am still ambivalent about the cultivation of green beans. My father has been what organic farmers call a "nozzlehead"[2] for most of his life. His use of toxic herbi- and insecticides on the lawn and vegetables was truly terrifying. In the last couple years, he has wanted to know more about organic pest control and fertilizing, and he composts. From my father I learned how much work gardening can be and how to make someone else miserable while doing it.

Ecology

It wasn't for the peaches
but to center our loss on the fringe
Grandma's wake and funeral passing
grandchildren went to touch the tree

The mystery of grief and guilt and terror
engulfed her children our emotion was simpler

Longing for the ecology of her living
the rhubarb thirty years old
and the heat nurturing
apricot and almond

Apple peels and broken beans
caught in the apron folds of her lap
and we rested there for mending

Grandma had a relatively shady yard. She grew some flowers out front. The only food crops I can remember growing at her house were peaches and rhubarb. I think rhubarb is one of the most fascinating plants in the whole world. Its vigorous growth and lively red color are associated in my heart with my grandmother and her absolute joy in gardening.

In Cincinnati I learned housing organizing and organic lunar gardening. I worked with a group of older black women who lived in Over-the-Rhine. They strategized, door-knocked, bake-saled, and picketed their way to a better and more secure housing stock for low-income residents of the neighborhood. They also had a community garden at Spring Grove Cemetery. I shared a plot with two friends. Eddie, Randy, and I would go out in the van with Thelma and Sarah and other members of the Contact Center. We would repair to our plots. Thelma's adjoined our collective plot. On more than one occasion she would lean over the fence between the plots and say, "I wouldn't do that, if I were you." And we wouldn't. We learned which phase of the moon was good for planting leafy plants and root crops, when to water and when to weed, and when to leave well enough alone.

Today we choose organic gardening as the only way to raise food. One of the first realities that escapes us in the privileged industrialized nations is that there can be no waste if a system is to healthily maintain itself and those beings dependent on it. Organic gardening is about cooperation of natural systems—the soil and its microbial life, weather and the human activity of growing food. And for me it is about exploring the interaction of the microcosm of our backyard and community garden plot with the cosmological influences of stars, planets, and the moon.

In the Ohio of the 1960s, most black folks had gardens. All the children in my neighborhood grew up with fresh tomatoes and collard greens. There was a sense of connection to the rural South and the importance of controlling access to as many of the necessities of life as postbellum southern apartheid would allow. As children we never questioned this imperative. There could be no waste.

This culture that taught me to garden was afflicted with a deep ambivalence. Years of apartheid U.S.-style had instilled the longing to be white, and if not white, to pass for something white culture respected. The working-class black families of my youth wanted all that the culture and economy of white people could give. Perhaps they weren't conscious of it, but they hankered after a fundamental disconnection from the earth and the latent traditions of African culture. This connection and those traditions had survived in reasonable if sometimes unconscious forms for most of the centuries of captivity, slavery, and Jim Crow "freedom." Barbara Christian argues that one of the fundamental conflicts for black people new to the urban and industrial North was that between "the natural order" and the illusion of uncomplicated "sweetness and light" presented by the majority white society (Christian 1985, 52). The natural order included "funk and passion," a lack of control. But the folks I grew up with weren't sure they wanted that tradition, with all its pain of poverty, loss, humiliation, and death. "Why couldn't we have store-bought vegetables, straight hair and quiet reverent church services?" was one of the questions my parents' generation was trying to work out for themselves and us. "Who needed that old-timey stuff from the South?" Yet in keeping their gardens, making frequent trips home (that is, south), and worshiping in the fullness of their Afri-Western Christian syncretism, many folks were holding on to an intangible groundedness and truth that would be lost by passing. The city had not taught them how to be rid of Jim Crow or how to find the freedom to keep the best of the culture black people had built in the United States.

Many black people have never known the South. Gardens are our only contact with The Land. We are quickly losing the nourishing link with the natural world which nourished our ancestors. We are becoming, at times, the worst of the culture for which we thought we longed.

The Hunter's Moon

Kimberly Harbor died on Halloween night, 1990. She was a twenty-six-year-old black woman. She was described as a hyperactive child. She became unruly as a teenager, and her parents sent her to boarding school and a foster home. She became pregnant and addicted to cocaine in its many forms. She became a street person and a prostitute.

A gang of black teen men were out Halloween night looking to "rob a prostitute" (Wong 1991, 44). They found Kimberly hanging out around Franklin Field, a park in Dorchester (one of Boston's neighborhoods). Rather than merely robbing her, Kimberly "was raped by several of the defendants, beaten with a tree limb and stabbed with a broken beer bottle and knife . . . sources said the stab wounds—more than 100—were in her stomach, abdomen, back and buttocks"[3] (Ellemont and Murphy 1990, 20).

One father, discussing his son's crime (who has since been convicted of first-degree murder), stated, "It's hard to believe; he's not that kind of kid . . . he's kind of quiet . . . He seemed normal to me. He's always the same. He doesn't show emotion" (Brelis 1990, 20).

Who are these teenagers? They aren't a new kind of predator. One of the legacies of European imperialism is the thoughtless destruction of all life. The young black men who killed Kimberly Harbor, a young black woman, follow in the best tradition of male conquest of this continent. Sadly, they follow in the tradition which conquered their ancestral lands in Africa, Central America, and the Caribbean—a conquest that annihilated whole peoples and enslaved the equivalent of whole countries. All too often, their prey is a woman, more often a woman they know. April 1991 saw a marked increase in the number of women in Massachusetts murdered by their male spouses, partners, and acquaintances. Occasionally, as in Kimberly's case, it was a woman they didn't know. These young men have come to see their lives, and everyone else's life, as expendable. They have absorbed the larger culture's media messages about the worthlessness of certain lives—natural life, colored lives, women's lives—all up for grabs, to be conquered and consumed.

Chinatown

Live chickens
live chickens killed fresh here
is the english translation of the mandarin sign
new mercury street lamps guard the gathering dusk
sentinels over shopper's refuse, wooden crates
the sidewalk cracks bearing a bloody flow
into the street

Fresh girls
fresh girls exposed here no fee
local residents watch their step no translation needed
night-fall shields patrons of the Naked I Cabaret
oblivious to the crimson offering their feet bear
through the entrance way

G-strings and grease paint clad the women dancing for scant
offerings of dollar bills and watery beer
their patrons smoke-stained eyes devouring

No parking
no parking two A.M. street cleaning here
the Naked I weakly blinks as huge amphibious
machines dispense disinfectant
cleaning away the last remnants of the day

One of the legacies of late twentieth-century capitalism is the commodification of every aspect of our lives (Ferguson 1984, 52). Capitalism is fundamentally a predatory system, requiring the consumption of huge amounts of products we don't need and the destruction of natural systems to make that consumption possible.

The first experience of people of color with European imperialism was this nascent commodifying instinct. Black people of African descent and some Native American tribe members were early tools of one of the most effective attempts to commodify human beings. The slavery of North and Central America, the Caribbean, and Brazil was accompanied by destruction of tribes, animal species, and fauna. The early demands of this transplanted European capitalism required that everything on the North American continent be commodifiable. We now live in a world where capitalism appears to be the victor, where all aspects of our lives can be captured, packaged, marketed, and sold.

African-American peoples organized resistance to their degradation. Those first captives knew themselves as a whole people in rhythm with earth's systems. They understood the only survival for future generations of black people was to pass on that sense of synchronicity. Those old Africans probably never anticipated late twentieth-century urban living. They had no way of knowing that there would be a generation of us who would grow up unable to read the sky, earth's creatures and plants, and the spirits that inhabit everything. Certainly those old Africans never anticipated marketing and television. So.

Corn Planting Moon: Soil Conditions/Soul Conditions

The dirt in Boston is nothing like the good Ohio soil back home. I read someplace that it takes at least eight years to help polluted urban dirt become loam, the kind of soil that looks and feels more like chocolate cake than dirt. In the meantime we compost, haul leaf mold, and watch out for chunks of glass and brick as we plant.

Who will devise an eight-year plan for the soul of black people? The steps needed to reclaim a patch of dirt are well known. It is not a process which can be rushed or sold in convenient packages. Similarly, some of the rural black southern tradition applies today, and we can figure out the rest.

Certainly we must maintain whatever link with The Land and growing things we can muster. We need to remember the stories whose only witness is that Land and the water that bore us here. Those stories are not sweet or easy. The loss of hundreds of thousands of lives in the Middle Passage from Africa to North America is a reality we don't acknowledge, yet it is a powerful reminder of the waste capitalism inflicts on all it touches. There can be no waste. Those lives lost to the water must become part of the fertilizer folded back into the souls of black urban people. Perhaps if this story is told, the lure of empty things slickly packaged will be less seductive. Those empty things are made from the legacy of lost lives.

Since so many died coming here and creating America, it is important to see ourselves not as displaced Africans but a people uniting many aspects of (frequently) opposing forces. Our multiculturality is just a starting point. Our ability to survive captivity and build strong, and at times, egalitarian institutions should lead us to help build a different kind of prosperity for ourselves and fellow citizens—one that doesn't tolerate the dumping of environmental hazards in our community (Tyson 1991) or the destruction of the lives of our youngsters. One which balances the need for self-sufficiency with holding government systems responsible for the welfare of all citizens. Black people have lived under and resisted the complex realities of oppression. Today, we can mine that experience to help change the systems that threaten the whole earth. Perhaps then we will be able to read and celebrate the earth's signs again.

Notes

1. Provided by the County Agricultural Extension Service.

2. Heard at the winter conference and annual meeting of New England Organic Farmers Association, January 1991.

3. The number of stab wounds turned out to be 132 and 18 bludgeon wounds (*Boston Globe,* Dec. 19, 1991, 44).

Works Cited

Brelis, Matthew. 1990. "Neighbors, Relatives Express Shock at Arrests of Youthful Suspects." *The Boston Globe* (Nov. 21).

Christian, Barbara. 1985. *Black Feminist Criticism.* New York: Pergamon Press.

Ellemont, John, and Sean P. Murphy. 1990. "Police Defend Low Profile Handling of Franklin Field Murder: Critics Say Community Should Have Been Warned." *The Boston Globe* (Nov. 21).

Ferguson, Kathy E. 1984. *The Feminist Case Against Bureaucracy.* Philadelphia: Temple University Press.

Roberts, Elizabeth, and Elias Amidon, eds. 1991. *Earth Prayers from Around the World.* San Francisco: HarperCollins.

Seager, Joni, ed. 1989. *The State of the Earth Atlas.* New York: Touchstone/Simon and Schuster.

Tyson, Ray. 1991. "We're Not Going to Put Up With It." *USA Today* (Oct. 24).

Wong, Doris Sue. 1991. "Youth Says He Feared Gang." *The Boston Globe* (Dec. 19).

8

Emily Hiestand was born in Chicago in 1947, and she now lives in Cambridge where she serves as editor-at-large for the environmental magazine *Orion.* Her poetry collection *Green the Witch Hazel Wood* (1987) won *The Nation* Discovery prize and a Whiting Writers Award. As a committed environmentalist, Emily Hiestand makes the important point that "*how* we talk about the earth, what kind of language we use, powerfully affects what our species does within the compass of the earth, and what kind of ecosystem ethics we are able to conceive." An earlier version of the following wide-ranging essay on blue jays and the nature of cities appeared in her collection *Angela, the Upside-Down Girl: And Other Domestic Travels* 1999).

Zip-A-Dee-Do-Dah

Emily Hiestand

Each spring for more than a decade, the canopy of the wild black cherry tree outside my living room window has appealed to a pair of blue jays, the showy bird with a smart crest and black necklace. This year's pair has arrived and the birds are commenced on the days-long project of making a nest, the task for which ornithologists have got the lip-pursing, Felix Unger–ish word "nidification." I'm watching the jays from a living room window thirty feet up in the trees, and I am fluctuating between a quiet panic at having a life so marginal that I can spend most of a day watching blue jays nest and the sense that to observe a bit of creation come close to your window is to be at one of life's hubs. (If by hub I can mean one of those many-faceted jewels that are said to fasten the sprawled net of the world.)

The youngest limbs of the black cherry tree have a smooth, lustrous bark flecked with the ruddy gold nicks called sap stripes. Over time, the swelling cambium layer will cause the young sheath to burst, after which the bark will keep growing, thickening finally into the rough, deckle-edged plates in which the older limbs of the cherry and all of its trunk are clad.

I like this tree of two barks. Its leaves are slender boats—in fall a fleet of yellow. Fully leafed, the wild cherry filters the oblique sun of afternoon in such a way that light shimmers, dances on the walls of our rooms, and makes of a solid something more like water. The tree will also appeal to grackles when the hard green cherries of spring have grown as purple-black as the poison berries of *Grimm's Fairy Tales.* In August, flocks of grackles will come flying to gorge on the cherries, so many landing at once that they shake loose the fruits and cause a steady rain. The sidewalk below will gradually become first a deliquescence of pulp and then, as the cherries rot, a pratfall terrain dotted with hard, ochre pits as round and slick as marbles. Anyone might slip on a pit and fall to a hip operation, so in late summer someone from our house will be out sweeping.

In spring, however, the black cherry belongs to nesting jays. To observe them you must slo-mo to the window, for jays, otherwise so tolerant, will not abide fast or sudden movements. As usual, this year the birds are nesting in a junction where three limbs meet and make a shallow pocket. Everything about this wooden pocket must speak to blue jays, must say in their pattern-language "perfect," much the way we may walk through certain rooms and while speaking of something else—a pocket tidetable, the Bodhisattvas—know that we are moving in.

The birds labor over their nest for three days, and they work hard, pausing only to review their construction, to emit their *queedle queedles* and namesake *jeaahs.* A couple building a barbeque over a long weekend, you think, in the decadent nanosecond before you remember your scientific manners. About midway through, when enough material is mounded up, the female jay begins to shape the interior—which she does by plopping herself in the nest, squirming and shifting about in it, pressing and molding everything to the shape of her breast. Whenever the male arrives with more material, she hops out and helps him arrange the new bit. The female also gathers material, but I think she is the only one to fit the nest to her body. I am not sure about that. I am not a student of birds, though I have on occasion traveled with serious birders to blinds and sanctuaries and have watched them (the birders) for many hours and been very moved by their behavior.

But I am going to go out on a limb here, and guess that almost certainly the kind of nest that these blue jays are making has never moved anyone to an encomium to nature's symmetry and perfection. The thing taking shape outside our window is no chambered nautilus shell, with its faultless, secreted spiral of form often invoked when someone wants to take seriously the notion of a great designer—the this-is-all-too-exquisite-to-be-random argument. Nor is the blue jay nest a Greek vase of a nest like that of the cliff swallow, whose small-mouthed, jug-like creations hang in clusters under eaves as well as cliffs. The blue jay nest is not a teacup like the nest of the ruby-throated hummingbird, who binds its concoction with threads from spider webs, finishes the outside with lichens, then slicks down its fancy china with saliva. It is not lined in soft wool like the chough's nest. Is not a fey evening bag of a nest like the nest of the Baltimore oriole. It is not a public works project like the nest of the rufous-breasted castle builder, who erects two chambers and a connecting tunnel, or that of the hammerkop, which smoothes eight thousand twigs into a flying-saucer dome strong enough for a man or woman to stand on. The thing outside our window is not even as organized as the lumpen paper wasp's nest which holds a comb of crisp octagons within its bulbous exterior. None of these possibilities for smoothing out chaos have much impressed the blue jay, and at the end of all their labors the jays' nest most resembles a heap of trash.

It is a temporary, provisional architecture made of material plucked from the yards and gutters within a one-block radius, a landscape that is, thanks to a nearby mom & pop store, teeming with the detritus so attractive to a blue jay eye: glinting lottery tickets, popsicle sticks still sticky with grape or orange goo, newspaper twine, and candy wrappers, especially the Kit-Kat with its shook-foil silver lining. The great man of birds placed the blue jay on the same page of his *Guide to Eastern Birds* with the black-billed magpie, the creature of this and that, of making do with scraps.

What it creates is a motley jumble, but the jay is surely guided, no less than the meticulous nautilus, by some inscribed-in-chains-of-nucleic-acid knowledge. So the bricoleurs of the upper canopy know a good heap when they see one. And they know when that heap is fully realized. When it is, the female takes up her residence, and at some point she lays her eggs. During the next few days, for the rare, fleeting moments when she hops off her nest, anyone sitting close by the window and waiting will see four tiny ovals—smooth, with a faint gloss, some years olive in color, other years the blue of a blue-green sea on a partially cloudy day, shadows stippling, speckling the waves.

And does the blue jays' affection for the motley give them an edge in the urban world, an advantage over fussy, fastidious birds like the lazuli bunting? I must ask a serious birder, a man named Emerson Blake and known as Chip (which is not so unlike the *Cyanocitta cristata* being called Jay). The answer from Chip is yes—an elaborate yes which also tells why birds are particular in the first place, why some are disadvantaged by an urban scene, and why some are having a hard time making any nests at all these days. One hard time is illustrated by the spotted owl, a bird who wants peace and quiet and who wants it over an immense territory, over a great big quiet forest. When it does not get it, the bird's endocrine system simply clams up and its hormones cease to deliver the old imperative.

Other birds, Chip tells me, can be fussy about building materials, may not nest at all without the right twig or grass. It's not whim. Absence of the proper materials would be a sign that larger conditions are not right, that the effort to make young would likely fail. Birds that won't breed unless specific materials or foods are present are specialists. The advantage of being a specialist is to thrive in some uncontested niche, to smoke not only one's competitors, but competition itself. Thus Bachman's warbler prevailed in southern canebrakes. Thus the ivory-billed woodpecker lived in virgin pine forests. Thus snail kites in Florida eat only the apple snail, for which purpose they have grown in a special beak. The risk can be high, of course, for if canebrake, virgin forest, or apple snails disappear, the specialist is, as Chip puts it, "out of business."

That was the fate of the dusky seaside sparrow, perfectly adapted to certain tidal salt marshes along the Florida coast, and not counting on Cape Canaveral or the draining of the marshes for mosquito control. A little planning could have spared the niche of this sparrow (whose name alone is worth sparing), but a bird like the California condor, whose idea of what Southern California should be is profoundly at odds with what Southern California has become, can probably no longer survive without perpetual human assistance.

My birds, the blue jays outside the window, are neither specialists nor maladapted to this century. Blue jays are the most general of generalists. More intelligent than many birds, they are able to withstand competition on several fronts, and if out-maneuvered, they think nothing of taking up life in another site. "The blue jay," Chip muses, "is almost too adaptable." By which he means, he explains, that the success of generalists can mask the demise of specialists, who have the more sensitive bonds to place. Birdwatchers like Chip know what once existed, and they miss it. The way you may feel at a McDonald's if you remember the diner that had red-eye gravy.

Adaptability, however, is what allows blue jays to nest on the margins of an industrial metropolis, and I am glad for that. Naturally I gasp at the colorful gems of rural glades—the rufous breasteds, the golds, the waxwinged, cerulean, and painted. But on this street, where the airborne population is pigeons, grackles, and the occasional blimp, the blue jay passes for beauty. And although I (who require *petit pain* for breakfast, classic-style, *not* sourdough, who will go miles for red-eye gravy) am much in sympathy with the specialists, I do study the blue jay's resiliency: this is the bird of the postmodern, of invention and recycling, of found art.

Above all, this is the bird that comes to our window. It comes like the puppy that toddles across the room from the cardboard birthing box, puts its head in your lap, and chooses you. When life comes to you like that, you refuse it at your own peril. So I am partisan to the jays, and root for their eggs. And however successful in the larger picture, here jay eggs are greatly endangered by the Visigoths of the urban forest—the bushy-tailed gray destroyers who travel the telephone cables and who can turn a nest of eggs into yellow slime in less time than it takes to say "Great Geometer of the Void," less time than it takes to see Samuel Beckett's *Breath.* (The action: curtain rise; cry and one breath; curtain fall.)

It can be just that minimalist, that swift and iconic with these nests. Sometimes a nursery, sometimes a bare choir. In ruin, however, the blue jays do not stand around in stunned silence, they do not reel between the great equanimity where all is balance, and the small, immediate realm where they have been roughed up. They do not mull the more-than-human scheme of justice, variously felt as a benevolence whose eye is on the sparrow, as a magisterial indifference, as a mocking voice in a whirlwind. They just fly away, on those coveted wings.

Eggs, they know every well, are fair game in the gulping world. The eager mouth of the ocean swallows most of its own children, and, it turns out, the blue jay's own favorite food is other bird's eggs. "Trash birds," says another of my bird-world informants, "like the roughnecks of Dickensian London, doing whatever they can to get by, and not thinking much about the ethics of it. Not pretty." (Do Americans deny that class exists so that we can have the fun of projecting it onto flora and fauna?) Well, obviously I do not defend the jays' eating other bird's eggs. They should stop, and should eat more bright-orange and leafy green vegetables, more soy, less fat. And I honestly don't know what trashy things the blue jays do when not by our window being hard-working postmodernists or brooding on their four cloudy-sea eggs, conveying warmth through the ovals, being brave, warm, patient, being all that parents can be, settling over the delicate shells just so. Let's just say that when a creature lays four speckled eggs close by your house, you like for those eggs to hatch.

Because the odds for our local blue jays' eggs are always longish, I root for them with a certain kid of hope. Not the usual sort, which is desire combined with expectation, or even expectation *without* desire—sheer prospect. But the kind of hope that seasoned fans have for the Red Sox and the Cubs, a brand of hope far from pie-eyed optimism, closer to the state of mind that the French call *une douce resignation.* In our new world, the adjective that most often appears before "resignation" is "bitter." But *une douce resignation* is not the defeated mood so repugnant to the American spirit. Although it is of course resigned to the fact that the world is, as Margaret Thatcher put it the week she was (hooray) booted out, "a funny old world," this mood is *douce*—sweet—from kindness and time, says a Belgian poet friend, who also says that if Americans are too doggedly, even eerily optimistic for *une douce resignation* (she doesn't know about baseball), her people, the Flemish, are too taciturn for it. The mood rises most in southern France, in Corsica, also in Italy and Spain, and a Buddhist friend tells me that it is very close to his practice of detachment—a way that fuses passionate caring and letting be, a way of existing within the world's own quite motley assembly of nests, violence, and summer games.

This year's nest is a beauty, an extravagant assembly, a miniature L. A. Watts Tower of a nest, a work that might make Joseph Cornell smile. *Regardez:* A few twigs for a foundation. Then snippets of fine green, and red, and black telephone wire. A yellow plastic garbage-bag tie. Another layer of twigs. A Doublemint gum wrapper. Some shreds of computer paper. Some weeds. Part of a pre-tied drugstore bow. With binoculars, I can see that the birds have incorporated most of the label of a good Beaujolais, George de Boeuf's Brouilly, 1995. The *piece de résistance,* the thing over which the birds have queedled and queedled, is a plastic picnic fork; over the course of two hours, they have gotten it angled into one side of the nest, with the tines pointed outwards, bristling like a pitchfork.

Something to make the destroyer pause? It is a large white fork, a piece of debris that came, I will guess, either from Marcella's on the avenue (which makes the Classico sandwich of prosciutto sliced to translucency) or from the House O' Pizza, where they will, if you ask, make a meatless, cheeseless sub with all the condiments, a delicacy that Sal and I have settled on calling a Nothing With Everything.

9

Chet Raymo was born in Chattanooga, Tennessee, in 1936, and he teaches at Stonehill College in Massachusetts. He received his B.S. in electrical engineering from Notre Dame, an M.S. in physics from UCLA, and a Ph.D. in physics from Notre Dame. He writes a science column for the Boston Globe and has published a number of books, including *365 Nights: An Introduction to Astronomy for Every Night of the Year* (1982) and *Skeptics and True Believers* (1998). Chet Raymo's essays seek to make connections between science and spiritual insight, to reconcile the apparent randomness of life with astronomy and thus the greater natural world. The essay below, from *365 Nights,* aligns a skateboarding accident on Boston's Beacon Street with canoeing a New England stream, and both of these with his astronomer's sense of a larger silence.

The Silence

Chet Raymo

Yesterday on Boston Common I saw a young man on a skateboard collide with a child. The skateboarder was racing down the promenade and smashed into the child with full force. I saw this happen from a considerable distance. It happened without a sound. It happened in dead silence. The cry of the terrified child as she darted to avoid the skateboard and the scream of the child's mother at the moment of impact were absorbed by the gray wool of the November day. The child's body simply lifted up into the air and, in slow motion, as if in a dream, floated above the promenade, bounced twice like a rubber ball, and lay still.

All of this happened in perfect silence. It was as if I were watching the tragedy through a telescope. It was as if the tragedy were happening on another planet. I have seen stars exploding in space, colossal, planet-shattering, distanced by light-years, framed in the cold glass of a telescope, utterly silent. It was like that.

During the time the child was in the air, the spinning Earth carried her half a mile to the east. The motion of the Earth about the sun carried her back again forty miles westward. The drift of the solar system among the stars of the Milky Way bore her silently twenty miles toward the star Vega. The turning pinwheel of the Milky Way Galaxy carried her 300 miles in a great circle about the galactic center. After that huge flight through space she hit the ground and bounced like a rubber ball. She lifted up into the air and flew across the Galaxy and bounced on the pavement.

It is a thin membrane that separates us from chaos. The child sent flying by the skateboarder bounced in slow motion and lay still. There was a long pause. Pigeons froze against the gray sky. Promenaders turned to stone. Traffic stopped on Beacon Street. The child's body lay inert on the asphalt like a piece of crumpled newspaper. The mother's cry was lost in the space between the stars.

How are we to understand the silence of the universe? They say that certain meteorites, upon entering the Earth's atmosphere, disintegrate with noticeable sound, but beyond the Earth's skin of air the sky is silent. There are no voices in the burning bush of the Galaxy. The Milky Way flows across the dark shoals of the summer sky without an audible ripple. Stars blow themselves to smithereens; we hear nothing. Millions of solar systems are sucked into black holes at the centers of the galaxies; they fall like feathers. The universe fattens and swells in a Big Bang, a fireball of Creation exploding from a pinprick of infinite energy, the ultimate firecracker; there is no soundtrack. The membrane is ruptured, a child flies through the air, and the universe is silent.

In Catholic churches between Good Friday and Easter Eve the bells are stilled. Following a twelfth-century European custom, the place of the bells is taken by *instruments des ténèbres* (instruments of darkness), wooden clackers and other noisemakers that remind the faithful of the terrifying sounds that were presumed to have accompanied the death of Christ. It was unthinkable that a god should die and the heavens remain silent. Lightning crashed about the darkened hill of Calvary. The veil of the temple was loudly rent. The Earth quaked and rocks split. Stars boomed in their courses. This din and thunder, according to medieval custom, are evoked by the wooden instruments.

Yesterday on Boston Common a child flew through the air, and there was no protest from the sky. I listened. I turned the volume of my indignation all the way up, and I heard nothing.

There is a scene in Michelangelo Antonioni's film *Red Desert* in which a woman approaches a construction site where men are building a large linear-array radio telescope. "What is it for?" she asks. One of the workmen replies, "It is for listening to the stars." "Oh," she exclaims with innocent enthusiasm. "Can I listen?"

Let us listen. Let us connect the multimillion-dollar telescopes to our kitchen radios and convert the radiant energy of the stars into sound. What would we hear? The random crackle of the elements. The static of electrons fidgeting between energy levels in the atoms of stellar atmospheres. The buzz of hydrogen. The hiss and sputter of matter intent upon obeying the stochastic laws of quantum physics. Random, statistical, indifferent noise. It would be like the hum of a beehive or the clatter of shingle slapped by a wave.

In high school we did an experiment with an electric bell in a glass jar. The bell was suspended inside the jar, and the wires carrying electricity were led in through holes in the rubber stopper that closed the jar's mouth. The bell was set clanging. Then the air was pumped from the jar. Slowly, the sound of the bell was snuffed out. The clapper beat a silent tattoo. We watched the clapper thrashing silently in the vacuum, like a moth flailing its soft wings against the outside of a window pane.

Even by the standard of the vacuum in the bell jar, the space between the stars is empty. The emptiness between the stars is unimaginably vast. If the sun were a golf ball in Boston, the Earth would be a pinpoint twelve feet away, and the nearest star, Alpha Centauri, would be another golf ball (two golf balls, really, two golf balls and a pea; it is a triple star) in Cincinnati. The distances between the stars are huge compared with the sizes of the stars: a golf ball in Boston, two golf balls and a pea in Cincinnati, a marble in Miami, a basketball in San Francisco. The trackless trillions of miles between the stars are a vacuum more perfect than any vacuum that has yet been created on Earth. In our part of the Milky Way Galaxy, interstellar space contains about one atom of matter per cubic centimeter, one atom in every volume of space equal to the size of a sugar cube. The silent vacuum of the bell jar was a million times inferior to the vacuum of space. In the almost perfect vacuum of interstellar space, stars detonate, meteors blast craters on moons, and planets split at their seams with no more sound than the pulsing clapper of the bell in the evacuated jar.

Once I saw the Crab Nebula through a powerful telescope. The nebula is the expanding debris of an exploded star, a wreath of shredded star-stuff eight light-years wide and 5,000 light-years away. What I saw in the telescope was hardly more than a blur of light, more like a smudge of dust on the mirror of the scope than the shards of a dying star. But seeing through a telescope is 50 percent vision and 50 percent imagination. In the blur of light I could easily imagine the outrushing shock wave, the expanding envelope of high-energy radiation, the torn filaments of gas, the crushed and pulsing remnant of the skeletal star. I stood for a quarter of an hour with my eye glued to the eyepiece of the scope. I felt a powerful sensation of energy unleashed, of an old building collapsing onto its foundations in a roar of dust at the precise direction of a demolition expert. As I watched the Crab Nebula, I felt as if I should be wearing earplugs, like an artilleryman or the fellow who operates a jackhammer. But there was no sound.

The Chinese saw the Crab when it blew up. In A.D. 1054 a new star appeared in Taurus. For weeks it burned more brightly than Venus, bright enough to be seen in broad daylight. Then the star gradually faded from sight. The Chinese recorded the "guest star" in their annals. Nine hundred years later the explosion continues. We point our telescopes to the spot in Taurus where the "guest star" appeared in 1054, and we see the bubble of furious gas still rushing outward.

Doris Lessing began her fictional chronicle of space with this dedication: *For my father, who used to sit, hour after hour, night after night, outside our home in Africa, watching the stars. "Well," he would say, "if we blow ourselves up, there's plenty more where we came from."* Yes, there's plenty more, all right, even if one or two blow themselves up now and then. A billion billion stars scattered in the vacuum of space. A star blew up for the Chinese in 1054. A star blew up for Tycho Brahe in 1572, and another for Kepler in 1604. They go in awesome silence.

The physical silence of the universe is matched by its moral silence. A child flies through the air toward injury, and the galaxies continue to whirl on well-oiled axes. But why should I expect anything else? There are no Elysian Fields up there beyond the seventh sphere where gods pause in their revels to glance down aghast at our petty tragedies. What's up there is just one galaxy after another, magnificent in their silent turning, sublime in their huge indifference. The number of galaxies may be infinite. Our indignation is finite. Divide any finite number by infinity and you get zero.

Only a few hundred yards from the busy main street of my New England village, the Queset Brook meanders through a marsh as apparently remote as any I might wish for. To drift down that stream in November is to enter a primeval silence. The stream is dark and sluggish. It pushes past the willow roots and the thick green leaves of the arrowhead like syrup. The wind hangs dead in the air. The birds have fled south. Trail bikes are stacked away for the winter, and snowmobiles are still buried at the backs of garages. For a few weeks in November the marsh near Queset Brook is as silent as the space between the stars.

How fragile is our hold on silence. The creak of a wagon on a distant highway was sometimes noise enough to interrupt Thoreau's reverie. Thoreau was perceptive enough to know that the whistle of the Fitchburg Railroad (whose track lay close by Walden Pond) heralded something more than the arrival of the train, but he could hardly have imagined the efficiency with which technology has intruded upon our world of natural silence. Thoreau rejoiced in owls; their hoot, he said, was a sound well suited to swamps and twilight woods. The interval between the hoots was a deepened silence suggesting, said Thoreau, "a vast and undeveloped nature which men have not recognized." Thoreau rejoiced in that silent interval, as I rejoice in the silence of the November marsh.

As a student, I came across a book by Max Picard called *The World of Silence.* The book offered an insight that seems more valuable to me now than it did then. Silence, said Picard, is the source from which language springs, and to silence language must constantly return to be re-created. Only in relation to silence does sound have significance. It is for this silence, so treasured by Picard, that I turn to the marsh near Queset Brook in November. It is for this silence that I turn to the stars, to the ponderous inaudible turning of galaxies, to the clanging of God's great bell in the vacuum. The silence of the stars is the silence of creation and re-creation. It is the silence of that which cannot be named. It is a silence to be explored alone. Along the shore of Walden Pond the owl hooted a question whose answer lay hidden in the interval. The interval was narrow but infinitely deep, and in that deep hid the soul of the night.

I drift in my canoe down the Queset Brook and I listen, ears alert, like an animal that sniffs a meal or a threat on the wind. I am not sure what it is that I want to hear out of all this silence, out of this palpable absence of sound. A scrawny cry, perhaps, to use a phrase of the poet Wallace Stevens: "A scrawny cry from outside . . . a chorister whose c preceded the choir . . . still far away." Is that too much to hope for? I don't ask for the full ringing of the bell. I don't ask for a clap of thunder that would rend the veil in the temple. A scrawny cry will do, from far off there among the willows and the cattails, from far off there among the galaxies.

The child sent flying by the young man on the skateboard bounced on the pavement and lay still. The pigeons froze against the gray sky. Promenaders turned to stone. How long was it that the child's body lay there like a piece of crumpled newspaper? How long did my heart thrash silently in my chest like the clapper of a bell in a vacuum? Perhaps it was a minute, perhaps only a fraction of a second. Then the world's old rhythms began again. A crowd gathered. Someone lifted the injured child into his arms and rushed with the mother toward help. Gawkers milled about distractedly and dispersed. The clamor of the city engulfed the Common. Traffic moved again on Beacon Street.

10

John Hanson Mitchell was born in 1940 in Gaylewood, New Jersey, and he has his B.A. in comparative literature from Columbia University. He lives outside Boston, where he serves as the editor of *Sanctuary,* the magazine of the Massachusetts Audubon Society, and writes about urban and suburban nature. He is the author of a number of innovative and imaginative books about urban nature that seek out and depict the wildness surviving amidst our proliferating suburbs. In *Ceremonial Time: Fifteen Thousand Years on One Square Mile* (1984), *Living at the End of Time* (1990), and *Walking towards Walden: A Pilgrimage in Search of Place* (1995), he looks at the history of land use in his area and its effect on the natural world. In *Trespassing: An Inquiry into the Private Ownership of Land* (1998), he questions our tradition of private land ownership and its consequences. This brief essay on frogs, which originally appeared as an editor's column in *Sanctuary,* has the whimsical imagination, the concern for wildlife habitat and the history that we humans write upon the land, and the dedication to the richness of nearby nature that characterize his work.

A Paradise of Frogs

John Hanson Mitchell

Years ago I saw a photograph of Mark Twain in his summer whites, standing beside a frog pond with a cane pole fishing rod in his hands. It was his custom, I was told, to tie strips of meat to the end of a line and feed his bullfrogs for entertainment on summer afternoons. The image haunted me for years.

The place where I now live was once a paradise of frogs. There was a fallen barn on the property and an old uncut lawn in back of the house with a few apple trees, backed by deep woods, complete with vernal pools. The yard, such as it was, was characterized mainly by amphibians. Wherever you walked, it seemed that something cold-blooded was hopping out of your way, either a toad, or a wood frog, or sometimes a green frog. I used to keep the pasture grasses down with a scythe, and, nearly every other swing, sleek-bodied pickerel frogs would execute fantastic crisscrossing leaps to escape. I once found a gray treefrog in a hole in one of the old apple trees while I was out scything, and, sometimes, after long rainy spells in spring, we would find frogs inside the very house—wood frogs in the cellar, spring peepers in the kitchen, and, once, a gray treefrog on the dining room window.

Slowly, in the perhaps mistaken course of gentrification of these grounds, I began mowing the lawn and digging in flower beds and cleaning up the fallen barn and the assorted detritus that had collected there ever since the old farmer who once owned this place went to his reward. The constant annual scything of the grasses under the apple trees finally evicted the poison ivy and the multiflora rose and the blackberry. But the pickerel frogs also departed. Toads no longer hopped out of the way on hot summer nights when you crossed a stone terrace in the back of the house, and I rarely saw any frogs on my lawn. What's worse, development began creeping into the former fields and woods around the house, and, sadly, year by year, the spring peeper chorus diminished, and I heard less and less of the beautiful birdlike trilling of the gray treefrogs.

Part of this may have been a sign of a general worldwide decline in frog populations, but I considered that, at least around my property, it was probably all my own handiwork and that my cleaning up projects had forced them out. As a result, some years ago, I started to do something to try to bring them back.

My first act was to dig a frog pond under the apple trees. This was just a shallow, scooped-out area that I lined with concrete. I dug the pond in March, let the concrete set, and then filled it on a rainy day in early April. The next morning, I looked out from the back porch and saw a toad sitting on a rock I had placed in a shallow end. Unfortunately, within a week, through some process like osmosis, the frog pond began to drain itself. I filled it again, and it leaked out once more. I bought sealer and painted the bottom to no avail, and in the end I had to go out and buy one of those little premade fishponds. To disguise its inherent ugliness, I gave this liner a skim coat of cement and then filled it. A week later, no fewer than three green frogs moved in.

Inspired by this, I dug out another small pond farther from the house and put in another premade fishpond someone had given me. Within a few days, more green frogs took up residence, and, at the end of summer, a fine pickerel frog settled there, along with a fat bullfrog.

I had no illusions that a single backyard frog pond, or for that matter ten thousand backyard frog ponds spread out across the suburbs of America, would do anything to halt habitat destruction or the mysterious worldwide decline of frogs. The fact is, I just like frogs. I like to have them around. My pond projects were not that different from maintaining a backyard bird feeder.

To further encourage my frogs, I stopped mowing grass with a lawn mower and resumed scything. With the poison ivy evicted from the grounds under the apple trees, I allowed the grasses to grow all season, save for one or two cuts to keep the woody plants out. I let weeds take over former garden patches and allowed brush to grow along the back walls. I built several little toolsheds that were intended not necessarily for tools but to serve as hiding places for mice and snakes, and eaves for nesting birds, and a sanctuary for toads to hide underneath in the heat of the day. And, finally, although it's not yet complete, I began digging out a larger, deeper frog pond just beyond the apple trees.

My hope is that someday I will attract a permanent bullfrog population. And then in summer, I shall dress in a white suit, tie meat strips to a fishing line, and spend the rest of my days feeding frogs.

II

Edward P. Jones was born in 1950, attended the College of the Holy Cross and the University of Virginia, and now lives in Arlington, Virginia. His short story collection *Lost in the City* was nominated for the 1992 National Book Award. This collection, in which "The Girl Who Raised Pigeons" appeared, depicts the difficult lives of African-Americans in Washington, D.C., with a deliberately matter-of-fact prose style. In the intricate narrative below the fate of homing pigeons—whose fluttering presence and beauty sustain the young protagonist—is paralleled by the destruction of her neighborhood and the displacement of the people there. Urban nature and human community both give way to the destructive "progress" of the railroad, and the result is a pervasive sense of loss.

The Girl Who Raised Pigeons

Edward P. Jones

Her father would say years later that she had dreamed that part of it, that she had never gone out through the kitchen window at two or three in the morning to visit the birds. By that time in his life he would have so many notions about himself set in concrete. And having always believed that he slept lightly, he would not want to think that a girl of nine or ten could walk by him at such an hour in the night without his waking and asking of the dark, Who is it? What's the matter?

But the night visits were not dreams, and they remained forever as vivid to her as the memory of the way the pigeons' iridescent necklaces flirted with light. The visits would begin not with any compulsion in her sleeping mind to visit, but with the simple need to pee or to get a drink of water. In the dark, she went barefoot out of her room, past her father in the front room conversing in his sleep, across the kitchen and through the kitchen window, out over the roof a few steps to the coop. It could be winter, it could be summer, but the most she ever got was something she called pigeon silence. Sometimes she had the urge to unlatch the door and go into the coop, or, at the very least, to try to reach through the wire and the wooden slats to stroke a wing or a breast, to share whatever the silence seemed to conceal. But she always kept her hands to herself, and after a few minutes, as if relieved, she would go back to her bed and visit the birds again in sleep.

What Betsy Ann Morgan and her father Robert did agree on was that the pigeons began with the barber Miles Patterson. Her father had known Miles long before the girl was born, before the thought to marry her mother had even crossed his mind. The barber lived in a gingerbread brown house with his old parents only a few doors down from the barbershop he owned on the corner of 3rd and L streets, Northwest. On some Sundays, after Betsy Ann had come back from church with Miss Jenny, Robert, as he believed his wife would have done, would take his daughter out to visit with relatives and friends in the neighborhoods just beyond Myrtle Street, Northeast, where father and daughter lived.

One Sunday, when Betsy Ann was eight years old, the barber asked her again if she wanted to see his pigeons, "my children." He had first asked her some three years before. The girl had been eager to see them then, imagining she would see the same frightened creatures who waddled and flew away whenever she chased them on sidewalks and in parks. The men and the girl had gone into the backyard, and the pigeons, in a furious greeting, had flown up and about the barber. "Oh, my babies," he said, making kissing sounds. "Daddy's here." In an instant, Mike's head was surrounded by a colorful flutter of pigeon life. The birds settled on his head and his shoulders and along his thick, extended arms, and some of the birds looked down meanly at her. Betsy Ann screamed, sending the birds back into a flutter, which made her scream even louder. And still screaming, she ran back into the house. The men found her in the kitchen, her head buried in the lap of Miles's mother, her arms tight around the waist of the old woman, who had been sitting at the table having Sunday lunch with her husband.

"Buster," Miles's mother said to him, "you shouldn't scare your company like this. This child's bout to have a heart attack."

Three years later Betsy Ann said yes again to seeing the birds. In the backyard, there was again the same fluttering chaos, but this time the sight of the wings and bodies settling about Miles intrigued her and she drew closer until she was a foot or so away, looking up at them and stretching out her arm as she saw Miles doing. "Oh, my babies," the barber said. "Your daddy's here." One of the birds landed on Betsy Ann's shoulder and another in the palm of her hand. The gray one in her hand looked dead at Betsy Ann, blinked, then swiveled his head and gave the girl a different view of a radiant black necklace. "They tickle," she said to her father, who stood back.

For weeks and weeks after that Sunday, Betsy Ann pestered her father about getting pigeons for her. And the more he told her no, that it was impossible, the more she wanted them. He warned her that he would not do anything to help her care for them, he warned her that all the bird-work meant she would not ever again have time to play with her friends, he warned her about all the do-do the pigeons would let loose. But she remained a bulldog about it, and he knew that she was not often a bulldog about anything. In the end he retreated to the fact that they were only renters in Jenny and Walter Creed's house.

"Miss Jenny likes birds," the girl said. "Mr. Creed likes birds, too."

"People may like birds, but nobody in the world likes pigeons."

"Cept Mr. Miles," she said.

"Don't make judgments bout things with what you know bout Miles." Miles Patterson, a bachelor and, some women said, a virgin, was fifty-six years old and for the most part knew no more about the world than what he could experience in newspapers or on the radio and in his own neighborhood, beyond which he rarely ventured. "There's ain't nothing out there in the great beyond for me," Miles would say to people who talked with excitement about visiting such and such a place.

It was not difficult for the girl to convince Miss Jenny, though the old woman made it known that "pigeons carry all them diseases, child." But there were few things Jenny Creed would deny Betsy Ann. The girl was known by all the world to be a good and obedient child. And in Miss Jenny's eyes, a child's good reputation amounted to an assent from God on most things.

For years after he relented, Robert Morgan would rise every morning before his daughter, go out onto the roof, and peer into the coop he had constructed for her, looking for dead pigeons. At such a time in the morning, there would be only fragments of first light, falling in long, hopeful slivers over the birds and their house. Sometimes he would stare absently into the coop for a long time, because being half-asleep, his mind would forget why he was there. The murmuring pigeons, as they did with most of the world, would stare back, with looks more of curiosity than of fear or anticipation or welcome. He thought that by getting there in the morning before his daughter, he could spare her the sight and pain of any dead birds. His plan had always been to put any dead birds he found into a burlap sack, take them down to his taxicab, and dispose of them on his way to work. He never intended to tell her about such birds, and it never occurred to him that she would know every pigeon in the coop and would wonder, perhaps even worry, about a missing bird.

They lived in the apartment Jenny and Walter Creed had made out of the upstairs in their Myrtle Street house. Miss Jenny had known Clara, Robert's wife, practically all of Clara's life. But their relationship had become little more than hellos and good-byes as they passed in the street before Miss Jenny came upon Clara and Robert one rainy Saturday in the library park at Mt. Vernon Square. Miss Jenny had come out of Hahn's shoe store, crossed New York Avenue, and was going up 7th Street. At first, Miss Jenny thought the young man and woman, soaked through to the skin, sitting on the park bench under a blue umbrella, were feebleminded or straight-out crazy. As she came closer, she could hear them laughing, and the young man was swinging the umbrella back and forth over their heads, so that the rain would fall first upon her and then upon himself.

"Ain't you William and Alice Hobson baby girl?" Miss Jenny asked Clara.

"Yes, ma'am." She stood and Robert stood as well, now holding the umbrella fully over Clara's head.

"Is everything all right, child?" Miss Jenny's glasses were spotted with mist, and she took them off and stepped closer, keeping safely to the side where Clara was.

"Yes, ma'am. He—" She pushed Robert and began to laugh. "We came out of Peoples and he wouldn't let me have none a the umbrella. He let me get wet, so I took the umbrella and let him have some of his own medicine."

Robert said nothing. He was standing out of the range of the umbrella and he was getting soaked all over again.

"We gonna get married, Miss Jenny," she said, as if that explained everything, and she stuck out her hand with her ring. "From Castleberg's," she said. Miss Jenny took Clara's hand and held it close to her face.

"Oh oh," she said again and again, pulling Clara's hand still closer.

"This Robert," Clara said. "My"—and she turned to look at him—"fiancé." She uttered the word with a certain crispness: It was clear that before Robert Morgan, *fiancé* was a word she had perhaps never uttered in her life.

Robert and Miss Jenny shook hands. "You gonna give her double pneumonia even before she take your name," she said.

The couple learned the next week that the place above Miss Jenny was vacant and the following Sunday, Clara and Robert, dressed as if they had just come from church, were at her front door, inquiring about the apartment.

That was one of the last days in the park for them. Robert came to believe later that the tumor that would consume his wife's brain had been growing even on that rainy day. And it was there all those times he made love to her, and the thought that it was there, perhaps at first no bigger than a grain of salt, made him feel that he had somehow used her, taken from her even as she was moving toward death. He would not remember until much, much later the times she told him he gave her pleasure, when she whispered into his ear that she was glad she had found him, raised her head in that bed as she lay under him. And when he did remember, he would have to take out her photograph from the small box of valuables he kept in the dresser's top drawer, for he could not remember her face any other way.

Clara spent most of the first months of her pregnancy in bed, propped up, reading movie magazines and listening to the radio, waiting for Robert to come home from work. Her once pretty face slowly began to collapse in on itself like fruit too long in the sun, eaten away by the rot that despoiled from the inside out. The last month or so she spent in the bed on the third floor at Gallinger Hospital. One morning, toward four o'clock, they cut open her stomach and pulled out the child only moments after Clara died, mother and daughter passing each other as if along a corridor, one into death, the other into life.

The weeks after her death Robert and the infant were attended to by family and friends. They catered to him and to the baby to such an extent that sometimes in those weeks when he heard her cry, he would look about at the people in a room, momentarily confused about what was making the sound. But as all the people returned to their lives in other parts of Washington or in other cities, he was left with the ever-increasing vastness of the small apartment and with a being who hadn't the power to ask, yet seemed to demand everything.

"I don't think I can do this," he confessed to Miss Jenny one Friday evening when the baby was about a month old. "I know I can't do this." Robert's father had been the last to leave him, and Robert had just returned from taking the old man to Union Station a few blocks away. "If my daddy had just said the word, I'da been on that train with him." He and Miss Jenny were sitting at his kitchen table, and the child, sleeping, was in her cradle beside

Miss Jenny. Miss Jenny watched him and said not a word. "Woulda followed him all the way back home. . . . I never looked down the line and saw bein by myself like this."

"It's all right," Miss Jenny said finally. "I know how it is. You a young man. You got a whole life in front a you," and the stone on his heart grew lighter. "The city people can help out with this."

"The city?" He looked through the fluttering curtain onto the roof, at the oak tree, at the backs of houses on K Street.

"Yes, yes." She turned around in her chair to face him fully. "My niece works for the city, and she say they can take care of chirren like this who don't have parents. They have homes, good homes, for chirren like her. Bring em up real good. Feed em, clothe em, give em good schoolin. Give em everything they need." She stood, as if the matter were settled. "The city people care. Call my niece tomorra and find out what you need to do. A young man like you shouldn't have to worry yourself like this." She was at the door, and he stood up too, not wanting her to go. "Try to put all the worries out your mind." Before he could say anything, she closed the door quietly behind her.

She did not come back up, as he had hoped, and he spent his first night alone with the child. Each time he managed to get the baby back to sleep after he fed her or changed her diaper, he would place her in the crib in the front room and sit without light at the kitchen table listening to the trains coming and going just beyond his window. He was nineteen years old. There was a song about trains that kept rumbling in his head as the night wore on, a song his mother would sing when he was a boy.

The next morning, Saturday, he shaved and washed up while Betsy Ann was still sleeping, and after she woke and he had fed her again, he clothed her with a yellow outfit and its yellow bonnet that Wilma Ellis, the schoolteacher next door, had given Betsy Ann. He carried the carriage downstairs first, leaving the baby on a pallet of blankets. On the sidewalk he covered her with a light green blanket that Dr. Oscar Jackson and his family up the street had given the baby. The shades were down at Miss Jenny's windows, and he heard no sound, not even the dog's barking, as he came and went. At the child's kicking feet in the carriage he placed enough diapers and powdered formula to last an expedition to Baltimore. Beside her, he placed a blue rattle from the janitor Jake Horton across the street.

He was the only moving object within her sight and she watched him intently, which made him uncomfortable. She seemed the most helpless thing he had ever known. It occurred to him perversely, as he settled her in, that if he decided to walk away forever from her and the carriage and all her stuff, to walk but a few yards and make his way up or down 1st Street for no place in particular, there was not a damn thing in the world she could do about it. The carriage was facing 1st Street Northeast, and with some effort—because one of the wheels refused to turn with the others—he maneuvered it around, pointing toward North Capitol Street.

In those days, before the community was obliterated, a warm Myrtle Street Saturday morning filled both sidewalks and the narrow street itself with playing children oblivious to everything but their own merriment. A grownup's course was generally not an easy one, but that morning, as he made his way with the soundless wheels of the carriage, the children made way for Robert Morgan, for he was the man whose wife had passed away. At her wake, some of them had been held up by grownups so they could look down on Clara laid out in her pink casket in Miss Jenny's parlor. And though death and its rituals did not mean much beyond the wavering understanding that they would never see someone again, they knew from what their parents said and did that a clear path to the corner was perhaps the very least a widow man deserved.

Some of the children called to their parents still in their houses and apartments that Robert was passing with Clara's baby. The few grownups on porches came down to the sidewalk and made a fuss over Betsy Ann. More than midway down the block, Janet Gordon, who had been one of Clara's best friends, came out and picked up the baby. It was too nice a day to have that blanket over her, she told Robert. You expectin to go all the way to Baltimore with all them diapers? she said. It would be Janet who would teach him—practicing on string and a discarded blond-haired doll—how to part and plait a girl's hair.

He did not linger on Myrtle Street; he planned to make the visits there on his way back that evening. Janet's boys, Carlos and Carleton, walked on either side of him up Myrtle to North Capitol, then to the corner of K Street. There they knew to turn back. Carlos, seven years old, told him to take it easy. Carleton, younger by two years, did not want to repeat what his brother had said, so he repeated one of the things his grandfather, who was losing his mind, always told him: "Don't get lost in the city."

Robert nodded as if he understood and the boys turned back. He took off his tie and put it in his pocket and unbuttoned his suit coat and the top two buttons of his shirt. Then he adjusted his hat and placed the rattle nearer the baby, who paid it no mind. And when the light changed, he maneuvered the carriage down off the sidewalk and crossed North Capitol into Northwest.

Miles the barber gave Betsy Ann two pigeons, yearlings, a dull-white female with black spots and a sparkling red male. For several weeks, in the morning, soon after she had dutifully gone in to fill the feed dish and replace the water, and after they had fortified themselves, the pigeons took to the air and returned to Miles. The forlorn sound of their flapping wings echoed in her head as she stood watching them disappear into the colors of the morning, often still holding the old broom she used to sweep out their coop.

So in those first weeks, she went first to Miles's after school to retrieve the pigeons, usually bringing along Ralph Holley, her cousin. Miles would put the birds in the two pigeon baskets Robert would bring over each morning before he took to the street in his taxicab.

"They don't like me," Betsy Ann said to Miles one day in the second week. "They just gonna keep on flyin away. They hate me."

Miles laughed, the same way he laughed when she asked him the first day how he knew one was a girl pigeon and the other was a boy pigeon.

"I don't think that they even got to the place of likin or not likin you," Miles said. She handed her books to Ralph, and Miles gave her the two baskets.

"Well, they keep runnin away."

"Thas all they know to do," which was what he had told her the week before. "Right now, this is all the home they know for sure. It ain't got nothin to do with you, child. They just know to fly back here."

His explanations about everything, when he could manage an explanation, rarely satisfied her. He had been raising pigeons all his life, and whatever knowledge he had accumulated in those years was now such an inseparable part of his being that he could no more explain the birds than he could explain what went into the act of walking. He only knew that they did all that birds did and not something else, as he only knew that he walked and did not fall.

"You might try lockin em in for while," he said. "Maybe two, three days, however long it take em to get use to the new home. Let em know you the boss and you ain't gonna stand for none a this runnin away stuff."

She considered a moment, then shook her head. She watched her cousin peering into Miles's coop, his face hard against the wire. "I guess if I gotta lock em up there ain't no use havin em."

"Why you wanna mess with gotdamn pigeons anyway?" Ralph said as they walked to her home that day.

"Because," she said.

"Because what?" he said.

"Because, thas all," she said. "Just because."

"You oughta get a puppy like I'm gonna get," Ralph said. "A puppy never run away."

"A puppy never fly either. So what?" she said. "You been talking bout gettin a gotdamn puppy for a million years, but I never see you gettin one." Though Ralph was a year older and a head taller than his cousin, she often bullied him.

"You wait. You wait. You'll see," Ralph said.

"I ain't waitin. You the one waitin. When you get it, just let me know and I'll throw you a big party."

At her place, he handed over her books and went home. She considered following her cousin back to his house after she took the pigeons up to the coop, for the idea of being on the roof with birds who wanted to fly away to be with someone else pained her. At Ralph's L Street house, there were cookies almost as big as her face, and Aunt Thelma, Clara's oldest sister, who was, in fact, the very image of Clara. The girl had never had an overwhelming curiosity about her mother, but it fascinated her to see the face of the lady in all the pictures on a woman who moved and laughed and did mother things.

She put the pigeons back in the coop and put fresh water in the bath bowls. Then she stood back, outside the coop, its door open. At such moments they often seemed contented, hopping in and out of cubicles, inspecting the feed and water, all of which riled her. She would have preferred—and understood—agitation, some sign that they were unhappy and ready to fly to Miles again. But they merely pecked about, strutted, heads bobbing happily, oblivious of her. Pretending everything was all right.

"You shitheads!" she hissed, aware that Miss Jenny was downstairs within earshot. "You gotdamn stupid shitheads!"

That was the fall of 1957.

Myrtle Street was only one long block, running east to west. To the east, preventing the street from going any farther, was a high, medieval-like wall of stone across 1st Street, Northeast, and beyond the wall were the railroad tracks. To the west, across North Capitol, preventing Myrtle Street from going any farther in that direction, was the high school Gonzaga, where white boys were taught by white priests. When the colored people and their homes were gone, the wall and the tracks remained, and so did the high school, with the same boys being taught by the same priests.

It was late spring when Betsy Ann first noticed the nest, some two feet up from the coop's floor in one of the twelve cubicles that made up the entire structure. The nest was nothing special, a crude, ill-formed thing of straw and dead leaves and other, uncertain material she later figured only her hapless birds could manage to find. They had not flown back to Miles in a long time, but she had never stopped thinking that it was on their minds each time they took to the air. So the nest was the first solid indication that the pigeons would stay forever, would go but would always return.

About three weeks later, on an afternoon when she was about to begin the weekly job of thoroughly cleaning the entire coop, she saw the two eggs. She thought them a trick of the light at first—two small and perfect wonders alone in that wonderless nest without any hallelujahs from the world. She put off the cleaning and stood looking at the male bird, who had moved off the nest for only a few seconds, rearrange himself on the nest and look at her from time to time in that bored way he had. The female bird was atop the coop, dozing. Betsy Ann got a chair from the kitchen and continued watching the male bird and the nest through the wire. "Tell me bout this," she said to them.

As it happened, Robert discovered the newly hatched squabs when he went to look for dead birds before going to work. About six that morning he peered into the coop and shivered to find two hideous, bug-eyed balls of movement. They were a dirty orange and looked like baby vultures. He looked about as if there might be someone responsible for it all. This was, he knew now, a point of no return for his child. He went back in to have his first cup of coffee of the day.

He drank without enjoyment and listened to the chirping, unsettling, demanding. He would not wake his daughter just to let her know about the hatchlings. Two little monsters had changed the predictable world he was trying to create for his child and he was suddenly afraid for her. He turned on the radio and played it real low, but he soon shut it off, because the man on WOOK was telling him to go in and kill the hatchlings.

It turned out that the first pigeon to die was a stranger, and Robert never knew anything about it. The bird appeared out of nowhere and was dead less than a week later. By then, a year or so after Miles gave her the yearlings, she had eight birds of various ages, resulting from hatches in her coop and from trades with the barber ("for variety's sake," he told her) and with a family in Anacostia. One morning before going to school, she noticed the stranger perched in one of the lower cubicles, a few inches up from the floor, and through he seemed submissive enough, she sensed that he would peck with all he had if she tried to move him out. His entire body, what little there was left of it, was a witness to misery. One ragged cream-colored tail feather stuck straight up, as if with resignation. His bill was pitted as if it had been sprayed with minute pellets, and his left eye was covered with a patch of dried blood and dirt and decaying flesh.

She placed additional straw to either side of him in the cubicle and small bowls of water and feed in front of the cubicle. Then she began to worry that he had brought in some disease that would ultimately devastate her flock.

Days later, home for lunch with Ralph, she found the pigeon dead near the water tray, his wings spread out full as if he had been preparing for flight.

"Whatcha gonna do with him?" Ralph asked, kneeling down beside Betsy Ann and poking the dead bird with a pencil.

"Bury him. What else, stupid?" She snatched the pencil from him. "You don't think any a them gonna do it, do you?" and she pointed to the few stay-at-home pigeons who were not out flying about the city. The birds looked down uninterestedly at them from various places around the coop. She dumped the dead bird in a pillowcase and took it across 1st Street to the grassy spot of ground near the Esso filling station in front of the medieval wall. With a large tablespoon, she dug two feet or so into the earth and dropped the sack in.

"Beaver would say something over his grave," Ralph said.

"What?"

"Beaver. The boy on TV."

She gave him a cut-eye look and stood up. "You do it, preacher man," she said. "I gotta get back to school."

After school she said to Miss Jenny, "Don't tell Daddy bout that dead pigeon. You know how he is: he'll think it's the end of the world or somethin."

The two were in Miss Jenny's kitchen, and Miss Jenny was preparing supper while Betsy Ann did her homework.

"You know what he do in the mornin?" Betsy Ann said. "He go out and look at them pigeons."

"Oh?" Miss Jenny, who knew what Robert had been doing, did not turn around from the stove. "Wants to say good mornin to em, hunh?"

"I don't think so. I ain't figured out what he doin," the girl said. She was sitting at Miss Jenny's kitchen table. The dog, Bosco, was beside her and one of her shoes was off and her foot was rubbing the dog's back. "I was sleepin one time and this cold air hit me and I woke up. I couldn't get back to sleep cause I was cold, so I got up to see what window was open. Daddy wasn't in the bed and he wasn't in the kitchen or the bathroom. I thought he was downstairs warmin up the cab or somethin, but when I went to close the kitchen window, I could see him, peekin in the coop from the side with a flashlight. He scared me cause I didn't know who he was at first."

"You ask him what he was doin?"

"No. He wouldn'a told me anyway, Miss Jenny. I just went back to my room and closed the door. If I'da asked him straight out, he would just make up something or say maybe I was dreamin. So now when I feel that cold air, I just look out to see if he in bed and then I shut my door."

Sometimes, when the weather allowed, the girl would sit on the roof plaiting her hair or reading the funny papers before school, or sit doing her homework in the late afternoon before going down to Miss Jenny's or out to play. She got pleasure just from the mere presence of the pigeons, a pleasure that was akin to what she felt when she followed her Aunt Thelma about her house, or when she jumped double dutch for so long she had to drop to the ground to catch her breath. In the morning, the new sun rising higher, she would place her chair at the roof's edge. She could look down at tail-wagging Bosco looking up at her, down through the thick rope fence around the roof that Robert had put up when she was a year old. She would hum or sing some nonsense song she'd made up, as the birds strutted and pecked and preened and flapped about in the bath water. And in the evening she watched the pigeons return home, first landing in the oak tree, then over to the coop's landing board. A few of them, generally the males, would settle on her book or on her head and shoulders. Stroking the breast of one, she would be rewarded with a cooing that was as pleasurable as music, and when the bird edged nearer so that it was less than an inch away, she smelled what seemed a mixture of dirt and rainy air and heard a heart that seemed to be hurling itself against the wall of the bird's breast.

She turned ten. She turned eleven.

In the early summer of 1960, there began a rumor among the children of Betsy Ann's age that the railroad people were planning to take all the land around

Myrtle Street, perhaps up to L Street and down to H Street. This rumor—unlike the summer rumor among Washington's Negro children that Richard Nixon, if he were elected president, would make all the children go to school on Saturday from nine to twelve and cut their summer vacations in half—this rumor had a long life. And as the boys scraped their knuckles on the ground playing Poison, as the girls jumped rope until their bouncing plaits came loose, as the boys filled the neighborhood with the sounds of amateur hammering as they built skating trucks, as the girls made up talk for dolls with names they would one day bestow on their children, their conversations were flavored with lighthearted speculation about how far the railroad would go. When one child fell out with another, it became standard to try to hurt the other with the "true fact" that the railroad was going to take his or her home. "It's a true fact, they called my daddy at his work and told him we could stay, but yall gotta go. Yall gotta." And then the tormentor would stick out his or her tongue as far as it would go.

There were only two other girls on Myrtle Street who were comfortable around pigeons, and both of them moved away within a month of each other. One, LaDeidre Gordon, was a cousin of the brothers Carlos and Carleton. LaDeidre believed that the pigeons spoke a secret language among themselves, and that if she listened long enough and hard enough she could understand what they were saying and, ultimately, could communicate with them. For this, the world lovingly nicknamed her "Coo-Coo." After LaDeidre and the second girl moved, Betsy Ann would take the long way around to avoid passing where they had lived. And in those weeks she found a comfort of sorts at Thelma and Ralph's, for their house and everything else on the other side of North Capitol Street, the rumor went, would be spared by the railroad people.

Thelma Holley, her husband, and Ralph lived in a small house on L Street, Northwest, two doors from Mt. Airy Baptist Church, just across North Capitol Street. Thelma had suffered six miscarriages before God, as she put it, "took pity on my womb" and she had Ralph. But even then, she felt God had given with one hand and taken with the other, for the boy suffered with asthma. Thelma had waited until the seventh month of her pregnancy before she felt secure enough to begin loving him. And from then on, having given her heart, she thought nothing of giving him the world after he was born.

Ralph was the first colored child anyone knew to have his own television. In his house there had been three bedrooms, but Thelma persuaded her husband that an asthmatic child needed more space. Her husband knocked down the walls between the two back bedrooms and Ralph then had a bedroom that was nearly twice as large as that of his parents. And in that enormous room, she put as much of the world as she and her husband could afford.

Aside from watching Thelma, what Betsy Ann enjoyed most in that house was the electric train set, which dominated the center of Ralph's room. Over an area of more than four square feet, running on three levels, the trains moved through a marvelous and complete world Ralph's father had constructed. In that world, there were no simple plastic figures waving beside the tracks. Rather, it was populated with such people as a hand-carved woman of wood, in a floppy hat and gardener's outfit of real cloth, a woman who had nearly microscopic beads of sweat on her brow as she knelt down with concentration in her flower garden; several inches away, hand-carved schoolchildren romped about in the playground. One group of children was playing tag, and on one boy's face was absolute surprise as he was being tagged by a girl whose cheek was lightly smudged with dirt. A foot or so away, in a small field, two hand-carved farmers of wood were arguing, one with his finger in the other's face and the other with his fist heading toward the chest of the first. The world also included a goat-populated mountain with a tunnel large enough for the trains to go through, and a stream made of light blue glass. The stream covered several tiny fish of many colors which had almost invisible pins holding them suspended from the bottom up to give the impression that the fish were swimming.

What Thelma would not put in her son's enormous room, despite years of pleadings from him, was a dog, for she had learned in childhood that all animals had the power to suck the life out of asthmatics. "What you need with some ole puppy?" she would tease sometimes when he asked. "You'll be my little puppy dog forever and forever." And then she would grab and hug him until he wiggled out of her arms.

By the time he was six, the boy had learned that he could sometimes stay all day in the room and have Thelma minister to him by pretending he could barely breathe. He hoped that over time he could get out of her a promise for a dog. But his pretending to be at death's door only made her worry more, and by the middle of 1961, she had quit her part-time, GS-4 clerk-typist position at the Interior Department, because by then he was home two or three times a week.

Gradually, as more people moved out of Myrtle Street, the room became less attractive for Betsy Ann to visit, for Ralph grew difficult and would be mean and impatient with her and other visiting children. "You stupid, thas all! You just the stupidest person in the whole wide world," he would say to anyone who did not do what he wanted as fast as he wanted. Some children cried when he lit into them, and others wanted to fight him.

In time, the boy Betsy Ann once bullied disappeared altogether, and so when she took him assignments from school, she tried to stay only the amount of time necessary to show politeness. Then, too, the girl sensed that Thelma, with her increasing coldness, felt her son's problem was partly the result of visits from children who weren't altogether clean and from a niece who lived her life in what Thelma called "pigeon air" and "pigeon dust."

When he found out, the details of it did not matter to Robert Morgan: he only knew that his daughter had been somewhere doing bad while he was out doing the best he could. It didn't matter that it was Darlene Greenley who got Betsy Ann to go far away to 7th and Massachusetts and steal candy bars from Peoples Drug, candy she didn't even like, to go away the farthest she had ever been without her father or Miss Jenny or some other adult.

She knew Darlene, fast Darlene, from going to Ralph's ("You watch and see," Darlene would whisper to her, "I'm gonna make him my boyfriend"), but they had never gone off together before the Saturday that Thelma, for the last time, expelled all the children from her house. "Got any money?" Darlene said on the sidewalk after Thelma had thrown them out. She was stretching her bubble gum between her teeth and fingers and twirling the stuff the way she would a jump rope. When Betsy Ann shook her head, Darlene said she knew this Peoples that kinda like y'know gave children candy just for stopping by, and Betsy Ann believed her.

The assistant manager caught the girls before they were out of the candy and toy aisle and right away Darlene started to cry. "That didn't work the last time I told you to stay outa here," the woman said, taking the candy out of their dress pockets, "and it ain't gonna work now." Darlene handed her candy over, and Betsy Ann did the same. Darlene continued to cry. "Oh, just shut up, you little hussy, before I give you somethin to really cry about."

The assistant manager handed the candy to a clerk and was about to drag the girls into a back room when Etta O'Connell came up the aisle. "Yo daddy know you this far from home, Betsy Ann?" Miss Etta said, tapping Betsy Ann in the chest with her walking stick. She was, at ninety-two, the oldest person on Myrtle Street. It surprised Betsy Ann that she even knew her name, because the old woman, as far as Betsy Ann could remember, had never once spoken a word to her.

"You know these criminals?" the assistant manager said.

"Knowed this one since the day she was born," Miss Etta said. The top of her stick had the head of an animal that no one had been able to identify, and the animal, perched a foot or so higher than Miss Etta's head, looked down at Betsy Ann with a better-you-than-me look. The old woman uncurled the fingers of the assistant manager's hand from around Betsy Ann's arm. "Child, whatcha done in this lady's sto?"

In the end, the assistant manager accepted Miss Etta's word that Betsy Ann would never again step foot in the store, that her father would know what she had done the minute he got home. Outside, standing at the corner, Miss Etta raised her stick and pointed to K Street. "You don't go straight home with no stoppin, I'll know," she said to Betsy Ann, and the girl sprinted off, never once looking back. Miss Etta and Darlene continued standing at the corner. "I think that old lady gave me the evil eye," Darlene told Betsy Ann the next time they met. "She done took all my good luck away. Yall got ghosties and shit on yo street." And thereafter, she avoided Betsy Ann.

Robert tanned her hide, as Miss Jenny called it, and then withheld her fifty-cents-a-week allowance for two months. For some three weeks he said very little to her, and when he did, it was almost always the same words: "You should be here, takin care a them damn birds! That's where you should be, not out there robbin somebody's grocery store!" She stopped correcting him about what kind of store it was after the first few times, because each time she did he would say, "Who the grownup here? You startin to sound like you runnin the show."

The candy episode killed something between them, and more and more he began checking up on her. He would show up at the house when she thought he was out working. She would come out of the coop with a bag of feed or the broom in her hand and a bird sitting on her head and she would find him standing at the kitchen window watching her. And several times a day he would call Miss Jenny. "Yo daddy wanna know if you up there," Miss Jenny would holler out her back window. Robert called the school so much that the principal herself wrote a letter telling him to stop.

He had been seeing Janet Gordon for two years, and about three or four times a month, they would take in a movie or a show at the Howard and then spend the night at a tourist home. But after the incident at Peoples, he saw Janet only once or twice a month. Then he began taking his daughter with him in the cab on most Saturdays. He tried to make it seem as if it were a good way to see the city.

Despite his reasons for taking her along, she enjoyed riding with him at first. She asked him for one of his old maps, and, with a blue crayon, she would chart the streets of Washington she had been on. Her father spent most of his time in Southeast and in Anacostia, but sometimes he went as far away as Virginia and Maryland, and she charted streets in those places as well. She also enjoyed watching him at work, seeing a part of him she had never known: The way he made deliberate notations in his log. Patted his thigh in time to music in his head until he noticed her looking at him. Raised his hat any time a woman entered or left the cab.

But the more she realized that being with him was just his way of keeping his eye on her, the more the travels began losing something for her. When she used the bathroom at some filling station during her travels, she found him waiting for her outside the bathroom door, his nail-bitten hands down at his sides, his hat sitting perfectly on his head, and a look on his face that said Nothin. Nothin's wrong. Before the autumn of 1961 had settled in, she only wanted to be left at home, and because the incident at Peoples was far behind them, he allowed it. But he went back to the old ways of checking up on her. "Tell him yes," she would say when Miss Jenny called out her back window. "Tell him a million times yes, I'm home."

Little by little that spring and summer of 1961 Myrtle Street emptied of people, of families who had known no other place in their lives. Robert dreaded coming home each evening and seeing the signs of still another abandoned house free to be picked clean by rogues coming in from other neighborhoods: old curtains flapping out of screenless windows, the street with every kind of litter, windows so naked he could see clean through to the backyard. For the first time since he had been knowing her, Miss Jenny did not plant her garden that year, and that small patch of ground, with alien growth tall as a man, reverted to the wild.

He vowed that until he could find a good place for himself and his child, he would try to make life as normal as possible for her. He had never stopped rising each morning before Betsy Ann and going out to the coop to see what pigeons might have died in the night. And that was what he did that last morning in midautumn. He touched down onto the roof and discovered it had snowed during the night. A light, nuisance powder, not thick enough to cover the world completely and make things beautiful the way he liked. Though there was enough sunlight, he did not at first notice the tiny tracks, with even tinier, intermittent spots of blood, leading from the coop, across his roof and over to the roof of the house next door, the schoolteacher's house that had been empty for more than four months. He did, however, hear the birds squawking before he reached the coop, but this meant nothing to him, because one pigeon sound was more or less like another to him.

The night before there had been sixteen pigeons of various ages, but when he reached the coop, five were already dead and three were in their last moments, dragging themselves crazily about the floor or from side to side in the lower cubicles. Six of them he would kill with his own hands. Though there were bodies with holes so deep he saw white flesh, essence, it was the sight of dozens of detached feathers that caused his body to shake, because the scattered feathers, more than the wrecked bodies, spoke to him of helplessness. He closed his eyes as tight as he could and began to pray, and when he opened them, the morning was even brighter.

He looked back at the window, for something had whispered that Betsy Ann was watching. But he was alone and he went into the coop. He took up one dead bird whose left wing and legs had been chewed off; he shook the bird gently, and gently he blew into its face. He prayed once more. The pigeons that were able had moved to the farthest corner of the coop and they watched him, quivering. He knew now that the squawking was the sound of pain and it drove him out of their house.

When he saw the tracks, he realized immediately that they had been made by rats. He bent down, and some logical piece of his mind was surprised that there was a kind of orderliness to the trail, even with its ragged bits of pigeon life, a fragment of feather here, a spot of blood there.

He did not knock at Walter and Miss Jenny's door and wait to go in, as he had done each morning for some thirteen years. He found them at the breakfast table, and because they had been used to thirteen years of knocking, they looked up at him, amazed. Most of his words were garbled, but they followed him back upstairs. Betsy Ann had heard the noise of her father coming through the kitchen window and bounding down the stairs. She stood barefoot in the doorway leading from the front room to the kitchen, blinking herself awake.

"Go back to bed!" Robert shouted at her.

When she asked what was the matter, the three only told her to go back to bed. From the kitchen closet, Robert took two burlap sacks. Walter followed him out onto the roof and Betsy Ann made her way around Miss Jenny to the window.

Her father shouted at her to go to her room and Miss Jenny tried to grab her, but she managed to get onto the roof, where Walter held her. From inside, she had heard the squawking, a brand-new sound for her. Even with Walter holding her, she got a few feet from the coop. And when Robert told her to go back inside, she gave him the only no of their lives. He looked but once at her and then began to wring the necks of the birds injured beyond all hope. Strangely, when he reached for them, the pigeons did not peck, did not resist. He placed all of the bodies in the sacks, and when he was all done and stood covered in blood and viscera and feathers, he began to cry.

Betsy Ann and her father noticed almost simultaneously that there were two birds completely unharmed, huddled in an upper corner of the coop. After he tied the mouths of the sacks, the two birds, as if of one mind, flew together to the landing board and from there to the oak tree in Miss Jenny's yard. Then they were gone. The girl buried her face in Walter's side, and when the old man saw that she was barefoot, he picked her up.

She missed them more than she ever thought she would. In school, her mind would wander and she would doodle so many pigeons on the backs of her hands and along her arms that teachers called her Nasty, nasty girl. In the bathtub at night, she would cry to have to wash them off. And as she slept, missing them would take shape and lean down over her bed and wake her just enough to get her to understand a whisper that told her all over again how much she missed them. And when she raged in her sleep, Robert would come in and hold her until she returned to peace. He would sit in a chair beside her bed for the rest of the night, for her rages usually came about four in the morning and with the night so near morning, he saw no use in going back to bed.

She roamed the city at will, and Robert said nothing. She came to know the city so well that had she been blindfolded and taken to practically any place in Washington, even as far away as Anacostia or Georgetown, she could have taken off the blindfold and walked home without a moment's trouble. Her favorite place became the library park at Mount Vernon Square, the same park where Miss Jenny had first seen Robert and Clara together, across the street from the Peoples where Betsy Ann had been caught stealing. And there on some warm days Robert would find her, sitting on a bench, or lying on the grass, eyes to the sky.

For many weeks, well into winter, one of the birds that had not been harmed would come to the ledge of a back window of an abandoned house that faced K Street. The bird, a typical gray, would stand on the ledge and appear to look across the backyards in the direction of Betsy Ann's roof, now an empty space because the coop had been dismantled for use as firewood in Miss Jenny's kitchen stove. When the girl first noticed him and realized who he was, she said nothing, but after a few days, she began to call to him, beseech him to come to her. She came to the very edge of the roof, for now the rope fence was gone and nothing held her back. When the bird would not come to her, she cursed him. After as much as an hour it would fly away and return the next morning.

On what turned out to be the last day, a very cold morning in February, she stepped out onto the roof to drink the last of her cocoa. At first she sipped, then she took one final swallow, and in the time it took her to raise the cup to her lips and lower it, the pigeon had taken a step and dropped from the ledge. He caught an upwind that took him nearly as high as the tops of the empty K Street houses. He flew farther into Northeast, into the colors and sounds of the city's morning. She did nothing, aside from following him, with her eyes, with her heart, as far as she could.

12

Betsy Hilbert was born in Brooklyn in 1941, but has lived in Miami since the age of five. She has her B.A. and M.A. from the University of Miami and her Ph.D. from the Union Graduate School. Hilbert has taught in the Independent Studies Department at Miami-Dade Community College since the mid-sixties, and she is known for her scholarly work on women's nature writing as well as her literary essays about the natural world. In the following essay about her efforts on behalf of endangered loggerhead turtles, she conducts a careful examination of the complexities inherent in human efforts to restore the natural world. She concludes that, even in a universe that is "already disturbed" and in a region where the future is already written in concrete, her best choice is to work on behalf of the turtles.

Disturbing the Universe

Betsy Hilbert

Five thirty A.M.; the parking lot of Crandon Park is deserted. An empty plastic drinking cup crunches under the tires as we pull in. Nothing seems worth doing in the world this early. Ute and I climb groggily out of the car. Then the dawn blazes up out over the ocean, rose and gold across the sky. Everything has its compensations.

The beach is still in shadow under the brightening sky, and the dim figures of the morning cleanup crew make a clatter among the trash bins. The two of us are on a cleanup of a different kind this morning, amid the beachwrack and the crumpled potato-chip bags.

"Seen anything?" my partner calls to one of the crew further down the beach, who is slamming a trash can with particular vengeance.

"*No, Señora,*" a voice drifts back, in the soft, mixed-ethnic accents of Miami. "*No tortugas* today."

Actually, we don't want the turtles themselves; it is turtle eggs we're looking for, in their night-laid nests along this populous beach. Our job is to find and rescue the eggs of endangered loggerhead turtles, and to move them to a fenced area nearby maintained by the local Audubon Society, where the hatchlings can be safe from the picnickers and the beach-cleaning machines, and other dangers inherent on a public beach.

We begin our long walk south, where miles ahead the condominiums of Key Biscayne loom in the pale light. Pity the sea turtle who tries to climb their seawalls, or dig her nest in a carefully landscaped patch of St. Augustine grass. A series of grunts and swishes erupts behind us, as an early-morning beach jogger huffs past.

Ute's practiced strides take her up the beach almost faster than I can follow, distracted as I am by the pelican practicing hang-gliding in the morning air and the rippled sand in the tidal shallows. She stops suddenly, taking a soft breath, and I rush up to look. Leading upward from the high-water mark is a long, two-ridged scrape, balanced on either side by the zig-zag series of close, rounded alternating prints. Turtle crawl. Has she nested? Like all good predators, we sniff around a bit before deciding where to dig.

Just below the high dunes, in a circular patch about six feet across, the sand has been conspicuously flailed around. She has tried to discourage nest robbers not by camouflage or hiding, but by leaving too much notice; the disturbed area is so big, and digging in the packed sand so difficult, that the attempt would discourage hunters with less sense of mission than we have. We could poke a sharp stick into the sand until it came up sticky with egg white, as is the traditional technique throughout the Caribbean, but that would damage eggs we are trying to protect. Nothing to do but start digging.

Beneath the turbulence of the dry top sand, the rough, damp subsurface scrapes against the skin of our hands. We run our fingers across the hard sand, hoping to find a soft spot. When no depression becomes apparent—this time it isn't going to be easy—we hand-dig trenches at intervals across the sea. Sometimes it takes an hour or more of digging before the nest is found; sometimes there are no eggs at all.

In my third trench, about four inches down, there is a lump that doesn't feel like rock or shell. A smooth white surface appears, and another next to it and slightly lower. The eggs look exactly like ping-pong balls, little white spheres, but the shell is soft and flexible. With infinite care, I lift the little balls out as Ute counts them, then place them in a plastic container, trying always to keep them in the same position they were laid. Turtle embryos bond to the shells, and turning the eggs as we rebury them might put the infants in the wrong position, with catastrophic results.

One hundred fourteen little worlds come out of their flask-shaped, smooth-sided nest. The eggs are spattered lightly with sand, and my probing fingers hit patches of sticky wetness among them, apparently some kind of lubricating fluid from the mother. The surprising softness of the shells makes sense to me as I dig deeper; hard shells might have cracked as the eggs dropped onto one another.

Carrying the egg container to the reburying place, I am glowing like the sunrise with self-satisfaction. Savior of sea turtles, that's me. Defender of the endangered. Momma turtle would be very pleased that her babies were receiving such good care.

Or would she? I look down at the eggs in their plastic box, and realize that she'd regard me as just another predator, if she regarded me at all. That turtle, if we ever met, would be much more concerned about my species' taste for turtle meat than about my professed interest in her offspring. What would I be to her except another kind of nuisance? Perhaps the Mother of Turtles might respond as the Pigeon in *Alice in Wonderland* does when Alice tries to explain that she's not a snake, but a little girl: "No, no! You're a serpent, and there's no use denying it. I suppose you'll be telling me next that you never tasted an egg!"

What was I to these eggs but just another nest-robber? Did I really know the impact of my actions, the extended chain of events I was setting in motion? With present scientific knowledge, no human alive could chart the course of that one loggerhead as she found her way across the seas. Where she bred and slept, where her food came from, are still mysteries. Not only are there too few scientists searching for the answers, too little money for research, but ultimately there are "answers" we can probably never have. Our ways of knowing are species-locked, our understandings limited by human perceptual processes. I was a shadow on a dusky beach, groping in the dark for more than turtle eggs, digging, shoulder-deep, in holes not of my making.

Suppose we save these eggs, and the turtles that hatch return years later as hoped, to nest on this beach? This land will never be wild any more; the skyscrapers that rise across Biscayne Bay bear monolithic testimony that the future of South Florida is written in concrete. The beach, if preserved, will continue public, and pressured, one of a small number of recreation areas for an ever-growing number of people. So there will never be a time when these animals can live out their lives without the intervention of people like Ute and me. Like so much else of nature now, the turtles of Crandon Park will be forever dependent on human action. Thanks to us, they are surviving; but thanks to us, they are also less than self-sufficient.

And why am I so convinced I'm actually doing good, anyway? Suppose more babies survive than can be supported by their environment, and next year there is a crash in their food supply, or that something we do, entirely unknowing, weakens the hatchlings so that their survival rate is actually lowered? Maybe we should just leave them alone. Maybe they were be better off taking their chances where their mothers first laid them, risking the raccoons and the beach parties.

None of us knows the final outcome of any action, the endless chain of ripples that we start with every movement. We walk in the world blindly, crashing into unidentified objects and tripping over rough edges. We human beings are too big for our spaces, too powerful for our understanding. What I do today will wash up somewhere far beyond my ability to know about it.

And yet, last year, five thousand new turtles were released from the Audubon compound, five thousand members of a threatened species, which would almost certainly not have been hatched otherwise. A friend who urged me to join the turtle project said that on a recent trip to Cape Sable in the Everglades he found at least fifteen nests on a short walk, every one of them dug up and destroyed by raccoons. Whatever chance these hundred fourteen embryos have, nestled inside their shells in the Styrofoam cradle, is what we give them.

In *The Encantadas,* his description of what are now called the Galápagos Islands, Herman Melville depicted the sea tortoises of "dateless, indefinite endurance" which the crew of the whaling ship takes aboard. Melville pointed out that those who see only the bright undersides of the tortoises might swear the animal has no dark side, while those who have never turned the tortoise over would swear it is entirely "one total inky blot." "The tortoise is both black and bright," Melville cautioned. So, too, my morning beach walk has two sides, one purposeful, the other full of doubt.

Whatever my ambivalences may be, the eggs are still in my hands. Ute and I reach the hatchery enclosure and unlock the chain-link fence. We dig another hole as close in size and shape to the original as we can imitate, and then rebury our babies, brushing our doubts back into the hole with the sand. As we mark the location of the new nest with a circle of wire fencing, I am reminded that in the world today there is no way, any more, not to do something. Even if despite our best efforts there will never again be any loggerhead turtles, even if the numbers of the people concerned are few and our knowledge pitifully limited, even if we sometimes do unconscious harm in trying to do good, we no longer have the option of inaction. The universe is already disturbed, disturbed by more than my presence on an early-morning beach, with the sunlight glinting off the blue-tiled hotel swimming pools. While the choice is mine, I choose to walk.

13

Joy Williams was born in Chelmsford, Massachusetts, in 1944, lived in Florida for many years, and now lives in Tucson, Arizona. Her M.A. is from Marietta College in Ohio, and she received her M.F.A. from the University of Iowa; she has taught creative writing at a number of places including the Universities of Houston, California (Irvine), Iowa, and Florida. Her work includes the short story collections *Taking Care* (1982) and *Escapes* (1991) and novels such as *The Changeling* (1978) and *Breaking and Entering* (1989). Over the last decade, however, she has also written essays on the environment. "Florida," first published as part of the collection *The Place Within,* edited by Jodi Daynard, expresses her anger at mankind's assaults on the Florida landscape—especially that of the "most 'interesting' city in Florida"—Key West. Her essay also questions the worth of writing environmental literature and of studying it, asking if literary art still has a viable role in a time of rampant ecological degradation.

Florida

Joy Williams

At any of Florida's state parks you can get a car tag that says: "*Florida State Parks—The Real Florida,*" with the silhouette of a panther on it. It's like saying the Real Iceland, with a picture of the auk, which was exterminated by some guy, some genetic predecessor of the Wise Use movement undoubtedly, who killed the last nesting pair and smashed their single egg in 1844. If the "real" Florida, the natural Florida, hasn't utterly disappeared, it has certainly been pushed to its last redoubt. And still it never ends: the destruction and diminishment. The desecration and degradation. Of Florida.

Poor Florida. Once so pretty and now so battered and worn, she still presents a sunny countenance. Sunny, self-destructive, overcrowded Florida. Where realtors scramble and claw their way to the highest offices in the Audubon Society.

In Europe, Florida is known as Orlando. For many decades, she's been touted as "Vacationland." But the last winter here was cold and wet and many vacationers vowed they would not return, never return, for Florida had become too "unreliable" as a destination. If the sky's not blue and the sun don't shine, what's the point of coming down after all?

And there are those unpleasant incidents—attacks in highway rest areas, murders at tiki bars, bodies being discovered by the maid under the box springs in perfectly nice hotels, jet skis attacking the boats of "wilderness" guides. But Florida hardly needs the vacationer anymore. There is no season: Florida has maxed out with her permanent occupiers. Banks sponsor gala celebrations with fireworks and parades when a city, Jacksonville, hits the one million population mark. Tampa has become Sarasota. Fort Meyers, Naples. Miami sprawls everywhere. But Florida is still a very large state, and as Jax struts and hollers its way into the future as Queen of the Mildew Belt, one thousand miles to the south is the one-of-a-kind, quietly suffocating Everglades.

When I first came to Florida, I was ignorant enough to think that the Everglades National Park *was* the Everglades, when in fact the entire bottom half of the state is; or was, until fifty years ago, when it was diked, drained, channeled and farmed and 'burbed out. The Everglades is a delicate and beautiful ecosystem unequaled on this planet, but it was considered nothing more than a plumbing problem, and treated accordingly. Everyone had pretty much written it off except for some screaming and fussing environmentalists, and it seemed destined to die under the observant eyes and tinkering hands of state bureaucrats, sugar and development interests, and water management boards.

But in February 1996 the Clinton administration did what it had long promised to do and made the shrunken River of Grass the nation's top environmental priority, pledging hundreds of millions of dollars to restore it. Farmland will be bought and turned back to marsh, which sounds wonderful, of course, except to those farmers whose T-shirt of choice says EVERGLADES FARMER—AN ENDANGERED SPECIES. The difficulty is that no one has exactly figured out how farmland is metamorphosized back into viable marsh. When the state recently acquired some long-sought-after farmland that it considered key to its plans for "freshening"—*resuscitating* is more accurate—Florida Bay, the Everglades's immense saltwater nursery, it leased the land back to farmers to farm while it figured out how this restoration idea would proceed. Florida is not a state of mind, but of irony.

Not long ago, on a panel about "place" at a literary seminar in Key West, I remarked that Florida was "toast." This enraged certain members of the audience, who had paid good money to hear how lovely and unique the place was, and to be assured that they had not made a mistake by moving down here. They were sick of people like me, always bad-mouthing everything. Florida wasn't a vanished world, she was still here, wasn't she? There was a lot to still like about Florida, a lot. The weather was still okay. And it's recognizable, the aura. People recognize it as providing the backdrop for lots of nifty crime novels. Writers become "Florida writers" by writing in this genre. They use her as bright and sleazy background. She's reduced to a lurid sunset, a contrivance. She serves, in all her sunny rottenness, as fictive amusement.

Even for the non-genre writer, of course, place matters. Florida has impelled and infused my own writing for twenty-five years. I began on the St. Marks River in northern Florida, then lived for many years on Siesta Key off Sarasota on the west coast. Now I'm as far down as you can go in this exquisitely and peculiarly shaped state: Key West. Florida has served me as backdrop, framework, ambience. I've *used* her. Water and weirdities. Bright irreality. Palmy irresponsibility. Her residents a bit batty. A swell place. Odd but accessible, very accessible. Oh, it was fun. And everything was willing to be shown. The palm would surrender its intense heart for a salad alone. The shark would rise to the bloody bait. Florida was stage and tone. She was my familiar. Surreal and ironic, ironic because her stupendous beauty was so dismissed and debased.

Here in Key West, we have a few salt ponds. A few remnant salt ponds hemmed in by the airport and crisscrossed by filled-in marly trails. People like to come out here, finish off large bottles of vodka, and change the oil in their vehicles of choice. No state-regulated waste disposal fees for them. They're anti-bureaucrat. They prefer to leave the oil where they wish, in this case, in plastic milk jugs at the water's edge. All manner of grotesque debris can be found here, arriving daily. Toilets, gas grills, construction debris. An existential touch (Oh, the environment is a hostile place and man must oppose it by exercising his free will . . .) is the discarded box that once contained *Barbie's Housekeeping Set*—a gift to some lucky little girl—placed on top of a junked sofa, an engine block, some fast-food containers, the entire arrangement nestled in the mangroves. You can see almost anything out at the salt ponds. The place is practically . . . hypnotizing. But it would be rare indeed if you saw any birds. Where *are* the birds? In the Keys there seem to be more birds in the Wildlife Rescue and Rehabilitation Center in Key West and in Islamorada than in the air, and these birds in general are missing something—an eye, a foot, a wing. They're not *entire* birds. Where are the birds? Where's the reef? Where's the view?

For the writer who lives in Florida and was ever nurtured by its natural strangeness and beauty—the beauty and strangeness of the ray and egret, the mangrove and palm—landscape, with its connotations of source and strength, has been replaced by lifeless scenery, something even less than scenery. Florida has been assaulted by mankind for over a hundred years now. She has not withstood that assault. Habitat has been leveled into just another place to live. It all looks pretty much the same now, urban and suburban. Key West is the most "interesting" city in Florida, which of course doesn't mean that it's beautiful, though it has many charms, one of which is that it is not at all representative of the rest of the state. The marvelous poet Elizabeth Bishop, who lived here in the 1940s, wrote: "When somebody says 'beautiful' about Key West you should really take it with a grain of salt until you've seen it for yourself. In general it is really awful and the 'beauty' is just the light or something equally perverse."

The light. Maybe we'll all, in the end, just settle for the light.

Nature writing is enjoying a renaissance. This seems to be in lieu of nature itself, which is not. The humanities in America's colleges have become "green." Environmental Studies is the new hot academic major, with literature professors becoming ecocritics discovering anew how language constitutes reality, and making remarks like "Environmentalism is ultimately a question of design—of ethical design," and "We're seeing a return to realism, to exact and aesthetically pleasing descriptions of nature." All of which is fascinating, given that nature is becoming less aesthetically pleasing all the time, falling as it is to the unethical plow, the bulldozer, the saw, and the ghost net.

Nature is receding in many different ways at once and may in fact, in our time, be utterly subsumed by language, by the writers'—some writers'—increasingly frantic attempts to capture it and preserve its image, somewhat like a pressed fern, between the pages.

Where is literature in all this? Maybe it's too late for literature in this "world of wounds," as Aldo Leopold calls it. Maybe there is just a world of warring words. They are there when I read that businessmen in Crystal River, Florida, although realizing that the manatee is a resource they can capitalize on, nevertheless think that its protection has gone too far when tourists can't swim with it. Or when I read that Miami developers can now get rid of their wetland mitigation obligations (wetland *protection* was an eighties thing) by paying into a wetland bank somewhere else, away from their golf courses and zero-lot line developments. Or when I read the many complaints from people who weren't able to "use" the wilderness areas of the Everglades and Fort Jefferson National Park in the Dry Tortugas during the government shutdown, including the lament of a *Miami Herald* columnist that the fish were lonely, lacking as they did the fishermen. When I read such things, does it drive me to literature? These are assaults on nature at the most careless, unthinking, or cynical level, and it takes more than literature to deal with them.

I think you have only one chance at *place* in this life, your life. A place where your spirit finds a home, a place you cherish and want to protect. All this can take a lifetime. And you can miss your place. Or not recognize it. You can be faithful steward to the wrong place. And when do you leave, abandon it to others? When you see the two-lane bridge to the beach become four? When the four-lane road becomes eight? When you hear motel owners complain bitterly that turtles don't pay taxes, that property owners and tourists do, and that turtle nests just mess up the beach and prohibit proper human use? When a hundred-year-old live oak is slain for a Hooters? When you see an egret trying to fish in the soiled, rain-filled pit of a construction site once too often? When do you leave; what will it take?

Sometimes I despair, which I've heard philosophically speaking is an immature response to reality; joy, in fact, always joy, is the proper, integrated reaction. But sometimes, I must admit—frequently, actually—I despair. Florida has perhaps lost her distinction of place, her vital mystery, and those who love her might be laboring in the wrong vineyard. Knocking at the wrong door. Praying at the wrong church.

But for those who love her this cannot, of course, must not be so.

14

Bob Marshall was born in Macomb, Mississippi, in 1949. His family moved to New Orleans soon afterward, and he graduated from Loyola University there. He writes about nature for national publications as well as for the *New Orleans Times-Picayune* where his series of environmental articles, "Oceans of Trouble," won a Pulitzer Prize in 1997. In the essay below, also first published in the *Times-Picayune,* he describes New Orleans as a city on the edge, one defined by the levees that separate the Bourbon Street tourist areas from the various wildernesses of water around the city. As the essay talks about his trips on the nearby canoe trails, it is clear that Marshall sees his city as being on the edge in another way. It is a place near destruction, one where industry and development threaten the remaining urban wilderness.

Paddling off the Edge of the Big Easy

Bob Marshall

It's midmorning at midweek, and fleets of eighteen-wheelers growl down Interstate 55 heading for Pass Manchac. Exhaust pipes leave plumes of black smoke above the concrete combat zone leading to New Orleans. Truckers jockey with salesmen, students, and shoppers as the wheels of commerce send a steady rumble into a crystal-clear day.

Chris Brown, Melanie Clary, and I don't notice. A wall of cypress and tupelo blocks the interstate from our view, and what noise filters through—past the curtains of Spanish moss, past their canoe, and past my dugout pirogue (a Cajun trapper's boat)—makes no impression. We're already in the grip of sensory overload: The leaves of swamp maple flutter like red flags in the cool autumn breeze; the crowns of cypress glow deep-rust above flowing moss beards; a family of yellow-crowned night herons perches on a snag; willows rain golden leaves on tea-colored water. Three mallards circle overhead, wondering if the open water amid the hyacinths is a safe landing spot—despite the ten-foot-long alligator who suns on a nearby cypress log.

"It's so pleasant back here," says Brown, a local dentist enjoying a swamp outing with his wife and me. "It's so wild, so beautiful, you'd think you were a thousand miles from the city."

But we aren't.

A mere twenty-minute drive from that ten-foot gator, throngs of tourists crowd into the French Quarter. They line up for lunch at Paul Prudhomme's restaurant, attack platters of boiled crayfish and stacks of raw oysters in the seafood houses, and nurse hangovers proudly earned the night before in jazz clubs from Bourbon Street to the Faubourg Marigny. Yet if these same funseekers actually thought about traveling more than a half hour in any one direction, they might slip out of the twentieth century and into a world that would be quite recognizable to the French and Spanish explorers who first traveled this landscape some four hundred years ago.

That's what my friends Chris and Melanie choose to do with me for recreation, any time the mood strikes. For New Orleans residents like ourselves, the neighboring wetlands form an exotic and sprawling backyard. We don't have to travel very far to launch their canoe or my traditional-style pirogue into an ancient, watery world.

One of the easiest options for a nearby paddle is the one I've just described: Shell Bank Bayou near the Bayou LaBranche Wetlands. Shell Bank runs between Lake Maurepas and Lake Pontchartrain and is accessible from Interstate 55, just 20 minutes from the city. To go for a day paddle is effortless and one of the best ways to experience this landscape like a local—or even like the area's first settlers.

The wondrous irony is that the Big Easy—America's unrepentant citadel of hedonism—may be closer to nature than any metropolis on the continent. You'll find more Birkenstocks and Earth Day T-shirts in one square block of Seattle or San Francisco than in the entire French Quarter, but when it comes to trading concrete, steel, and traffic jams for habitat where fur, scales, and feathers rule, you can't make a faster exchange than in the New Orleans area.

That's because the city was started on a small speck of land deep in the delta of North America's greatest river. It was surrounded by a vast wetland wilderness, the largest of its kind on the continent. The big river flowed through lands dominated by expansive cypress swamps, freshwater marshes with acres of waving cane fields, and salt marshes whose knee-high wire grass ran for distances that reminded explorers of the northern prairies.

Travel was strictly by boat—down winding bayous with water as dark as molasses, across lakes and bays, and along the many fingers of a mighty river reaching across the delta.

New Orleans's growth was naturally limited. No matter which direction the developers turned, they soon ran into water. The result: a modern city with a visible edge between civilization and wilderness.

Cities thriving in America's West swoop up and over the mountains that surround them, or gobble expanses of desert at their feet. Midwestern towns eat at the prairie. But New Orleans kept coming up against insurmountable problems: a lake, rivers, bayous, marshes, swamps. When the concrete no longer floated, city builders constructed a levee to keep the storm tides out, then turned in another direction.

Walk atop one of the levees, and you get to see this edge. On one side your eyes will fall on houses, shopping malls, or jazz clubs. On the other you'll see marsh, swamp, bayou, or lake, all arrayed in scenes that might have greeted René-Robert Cavelier Sieur de La Salle in the 1860s when he paddled his birchbark canoe on his first voyage through this area.

Out here, the roar of Mardi Gras fades into the quiet of finger lakes hidden by deep hardwood wetlands. Traces of ancient waterways once paddled by natives are now graced by sentinel oaks and magnolias. There are countless bayous and trenaises (trapper's ditches) winding through tall green marshes hedged by saw grass and bull tongue that's eight feet high. The twenty-three-thousand-acre Bayou Sauvage National Wildlife Refuge, located within city limits, is the winter retreat for about fifty thousand ducks. It's also the permanent home for deer, mink, otters, alligators, egrets, herons, pelicans, and eagles. And only twenty minutes from Bourbon Street is a national park where thousand-year-old cypress preside in cathedral silence over fields of wild iris. The land remains little changed from the days when pirate Jean Lafitte called it home.

None of this is the result of wise urban planning. The wetlands survived because for generations New Orleans's city fathers didn't have the technology to conquer them. By the time they got the know-how, federal laws protected what was left.

But it has suffered. A tour of the surviving wetlands shows just how hard life has been for delta habitats. In its rabid thirst for oil money, the state allowed the dredging of more than twenty thousand miles of canals through priceless coastal marshes and swamps. This opened the door to ruinous saltwater invasions from the Gulf of Mexico. In order to build a city where none should stand, levees were raised that today carry a death sentence for the wetlands outside the mud walls. The result: Louisiana's coast washes away at the rate of thirty-five square miles a year.

It's a catastrophe of historic proportions for North America, one with abysmal consequences for fish, wildlife resources, and people.

Some scientists even think New Orleans should immediately look for a new site for itself, planning ahead for the day when the Gulf eats the last of the wetlands and pounds on the levees of the French Quarter.

Most citizens of the Big Easy wonder what all the hurry and worry is about. They plan to think about the looming catastrophe right after Mardi Gras. Or perhaps after the Jazz Fest, or the Spring Fiesta, or the French Quarter Fest. In the meantime, the city clings to its anthem: *Laissez les bons temps rouler* (let the good times roll)!

For outdoors people, a good time is as simple as a walk out the front door and across a levee. The edge allows a quick escape. Although the increase in oil and gas exploration left a land littered with abandoned wells, pipe fields, storage tanks, and barges, nature lovers can find daisies among the shrapnel.

Lafitte National Historical Park is a favorite of lifelong residents such as myself. On another voyage, on a spring day, I go paddling with a naturalist, and we stop to have lunch. The spontaneous scene belongs on a calendar photo. Our two canoes rest on a yard-wide ribbon of water dotted with white water lilies. On either side, miles of shoulder-high bull tongue reach to the horizon. That sea of green is shattered only by violet islands of iris. Snakes slither. Alligators sun. Cranes, herons, ibis, and ducks call from countless hidden potholes.

We could be marooned in the emerald depths of the Amazon. Yet one look at the northern horizon dispels that fantasy: the New Orleans skyline, equipped with the great white eggshell of the Superdome, looks down upon us. There's no denying it; we are only in the Barataria Unit of Jean Lafitte National Historical Park, in Marrero, a bedroom suburb of New Orleans that's just seven miles from the city's heart.

"People who live five miles from our gate don't even know this park exists," says ranger Bruce Barnes as he peels an orange. Barnes, like the city, has two personalities. When he's not in a ranger's uniform, he's the star of Sun Pie and the Sun Spots, a top Zydeco band, rocking audiences across Europe and the States.

This park protects eleven thousand acres of freshwater wetlands on the north end of the giant Barataria Bay estuary. It also preserves the remnants of a cypress wilderness that was the home of Jean Lafitte, a hero of the battle of New Orleans.

Subdivisions of Marrero push against the park borders, but beyond the levees protecting these homes, the world changes dramatically, peeling back two hundred years of history.

Most park visitors just take one of the elevated walkways through the swamps, near the visitor center on State Highway 45. The walkways can offer a glimpse of a bottomland hardwood swamp, but it's like trying to see the Grand Canyon without leaving the rim.

"Seventy-five percent of the park is accessible only by water," says ranger David Muth. "You've really got to get on the water to experience the landscape. You can spend a few hours or a few days on the canoe trails—and you'll never forget it."

The trail system has three components: bayous, trenaises, and canals. Until the levees were built, natural bayous such as Des Familles and Coquille distributed flow from the Mississippi River. Formerly used by Lafitte to ferry contraband from a base in Barataria Bay, they are now quiet old riverbeds, their banks crowded with ancient cypress, live oak, and magnolia. Curtains of moss hang to the water.

Trenaises meander through floating marshes called floatants. They were originally hand-dug ditches that were wide enough for a pirogue, but trenaises today can be five yards wide. Since shallow water quickly collects vegetation during a long, warm growing season, plastic poles mark trenaise routes to help guide modern-day explorers.

Canals are part of the water traffic system in Jean Lafitte. Some, like Kenta, were dug a century ago, when cypress loggers took trees from this area. Others, such as Tarpaper, were dredged in the last fifty years so oil workers could suck petroleum from under the marshes. Their dredged mud was piled beside the canals, forming levees that soon sprouted hardwoods and shrubs.

Ranger Barnes has planned a route for us that will reveal each type of habitat and watercourse. Yet the choices of where we can go aren't entirely his. "The water levels affect the route," he says. "Everything we do here is controlled by the tides."

Today the water level is below normal, so old bayous will be too shallow to navigate. Barnes's route combines canals and trenaises, and our put-in is at Twin Canals.

Clouds of green duckweed coat the water. Spoil banks host thick hardwoods. An ichthyologist, Barnes never goes anywhere without a fish-sampling net. He pauses every third or fourth stroke to see what's under the surface.

"You won't find water anywhere that has more life in it," he says. "There's so much in these wetlands, it's hard to imagine."

Soon, we are immersed. Small alligators watch our progress from moss beds; others swim several yards ahead. Turtles sun on logs, bream slap at dragonflies, and a great blue heron swoops across the canal and vanishes into a cypress-tupelo swamp behind the spoil levee.

In one mile, we come to a break in the levee that marks the trenaise system's entrance. The bull tongue covers the open marsh for miles, waving in the stiff breeze like broad-leaved wheat.

"A week ago, the bull tongue was a few inches high," Barnes says. "A month ago, it didn't exist—this marsh was just flat and wide open. One month from now, the bull tongue will be six feet tall."

A floatant is built by bull tongue, hyacinths, and other plants. Each winter the greenery dies, leaving brown husks on the water. After many years, a layer of detritus forms and compacts its own weight into a mat several inches or feet thick. The mat becomes a floating marsh as the delta underneath it slowly subsides.

Stepping onto a floatant is like walking on jelly: the surface rolls in small waves under each footfall. Barnes leads us across, carefully probing with a stick for holes—a swamper's equivalent of a crevasse.

"Make the wrong move, and you can sink up to your hips," he says. "If you fall through, you can sink in over your head."

As the trenaise system snakes across a floatant, a paddler gets an alligator's-eye view of this world. Bull tongue, already shoulder high, crowds in on both sides. Stands of wild iris swim above the green tongues. White water lilies grace ponds. Small waterways cut tunnels through groves of wax myrtle dotted with birds' nests. Small fish scurry ahead, gators slither away, snakes watch from the sidelines.

Sometimes the path is blocked by the "living land." Chunks of floatants, moving like green icebergs, break off and drift down the waterway.

"I'm amazed at how fast things change," Barnes says, as he tries to push a piece of floatant out of the trenaise. On the horizon, the New Orleans skyline catches the glow of the evening sun. The ranger looks at the buildings and smiles. "It's a short distance from here to downtown. But it's another world away."

At eight o'clock the next morning, my wife Marie and I decide we'd like to be in that other world. Our heads are still buzzing from the throaty roar of blues mama Marva Wright. And the beers that washed down fiery creations at K-Paul's Louisiana Kitchen didn't help. But I need to do some research to write a paddle-of-the-month article for the newspaper, so we drive west from the French Quarter to make another escape.

Creole cottages give way to suburbia, and then we cross the levee guarding the city's western flank. We're over the edge again. Here the metro area is outflanked by a stretch of freshwater marsh and cypress forest called Bayou LaBranche Wetlands. Wedged between Lake Pontchartrain and U.S. Highway 61, this area is bordered on the west by subdivisions of LaPlace, and on the east by the runways of New Orleans International Airport. Other neighbors include the twin spans of Interstate 10, striding on concrete legs down the lake's south shore, and giant oil refineries and chemical plants whose towers and smokestacks line the horizon, spitting vapor (and worse) into the humid southern air. Beneath, between, and around those eyesores rests a slice of heaven for those who like their world tinted by a rainbow of greens.

Bayou LaBranche once flowed between the southwestern shore of Lake Pontchartrain and the Mississippi River. Before the river levees were built they undoubtedly carried spring overflow into the lake, spreading water into the cypress forests and open freshwater marshes. During dry summers, when the river dropped below its banks, bayou currents probably slowed to a crawl, and the deep quiet of the swamp would have been broken only by the cries of herons, the hoot of owls, and the screech of wood ducks.

Levees ended that relationship with the Mississippi. And some years later, U.S. Highway 61 chopped off the bayou's southern third. It, too, got worked over by loggers and oil miners, and for years developers looked for ways to drain the region. Yet today its future looks wet. Conservation groups and sportsmen's clubs consider it a wetland fragment worth saving.

Our put-in is at a parking area off the shoulder of U.S. Highway 61, about 6.7 miles north of Williams Boulevard in Kenner. The first mile is spent paddling the Cross Bayou Canal, a cypress-lined waterway that struggles to be beautiful: as is typical of south Louisiana canals, its allure is obscured for several hundred yards by litter and garbage tossed from the road and a film of engine oil. But within half a mile, the litter and noise taper off. At the end of the first mile, the canal turns west and empties into Bayou LaBranche, and the world becomes two hundred years younger.

On the east side, a natural levee holds cypress, gum, and maple, a thin line that gives way to the open floating marshes stretching for miles toward the airport. Bird life is abundant. Depending on the season, waterfowl paddle among wading egrets, ibis, and herons.

The west side is another world. It's a cypress swamp with an understory of palmetto. Old timber canals and trenaises, their surfaces coated in duckweed, wind into the swamp like long green snakes. During high water, they offer excellent side trips, twisting through canyonlike walls of cypress and leading to hidden lakes. A quiet paddler is likely to surprise wood ducks, herons, egrets, and perhaps a deer.

After about two miles, a low wooden weir guards the mouth of a small canal on the east bank, and signals another change in character for the bayou. Saw grass and cane begin to line the east bank, and huge cypress have moss-draped branches reaching over the water. Red maples become more abundant, and cattails sway in the breeze.

This is a good place for a break. Hip boots enable Marie and me to step out of our boats and explore higher ground, following our ears toward some curious sounds. Soon we spot the source: a tangle of maples seems alive with white feathers, a writhing mass of noise that grows more animated as we approach. It's a yellow-crowned night heron rookery. Most of the young are just a few days old, sheltered by parents who noisily demand that we leave. These birds have some reason to be nervous. Known locally as "gros becs" (big beaks), the herons are the object of a cultural tug-of-war between Cajuns and federal wildlife agents. The gros becs suffer from a serious problem: they taste good. But since they are a protected species, federal agents are sworn to save them from the ravages of the gumbo pot. That conflict of interest has produced an endless array of folk yarns over the years.

We're not hungry, just curious, and so the birds are left in peace, and we continue down Bayou LaBranche.

After three miles, a westerly wind brings a murmur of faint noise from Interstate 10; a quarter mile later, we can see the elevated bridge spans. But just beyond is the shoreline of huge Lake Pontchartrain, a reminder that for New Orleanians, there is no escape from nature.

The following day, I yearn for more of the outdoors. This time, it's the voice of Dr. John that rattles between my ears, and some crayfish étouffée that provides energy. I'll need it. Today, I'll be taking the ultimate plunge off the edge—exploring the mouth of the Mississippi River with a group of seven other paddlers.

The Mississippi River delta is farther from town than the previous outings, but it's a voyage that encapsulates the south Louisiana paddling experience. Canoeing the great delta takes you through emotional white water—territory where you can be moved from awe to anger in an instant, where each leap of the spirit carries a tug of guilt, like laughter at a funeral. It's a trip everyone should make.

Just seventy miles from the city, remnants of one of the earth's great wildernesses hang on against all odds. Carved to shreds by oil and gas exploration, condemned to death by a system of levees and jetties that rob it of life-giving silt, littered by the ugly garbage of failed oil and gas projects, the place is literally a skeleton of what it was just fifty years ago.

But what a skeleton.

It has more birds on any one day than most places in this country see in a year. Wide and powerful waterways bear two-thirds of the nation's runoff. Delicate, ribbon-thin bayous flow through vast green prairies of elephant ear splashed with islands of yellowtop, violet iris, and startling white spider lilies. Bloody sunsets and dawns are delivered on a dreamlike carpet of fog.

Wreathed about that skeleton are the detritus of the twentieth century and the terrible insults left on this precious land. For those who love wetlands and wildlife, what's left of the delta offers one challenge: to find the beauty within the beast.

Our group of eight accepts the challenge on a two-day trip. it's an eclectic gathering, including a college professor, a massage therapist, a game warden, and a Coast Guard officer. The plan is to paddle south through the federally managed forty-eight-thousand–acre Delta National Wildlife Refuge and into the Pass-a-Loutre Wildlife Refuge, a sixty-six-thousand–acre companion area managed by the state. Both are past the road's end; the only travel within each is by air—or water.

The high waters that come in the spring allow a paddling route off the main river passes and across wide shallow lagoons and natural bayous. We may cover twenty miles in two days—if all goes well. Spring's cooler temperatures provide some relief from mosquitoes and gnats. Bird migrations could be near their peak.

The morning is chilly and windy as the group boards a boat in Venice to reach the put-in, on a canal off Baptiste Collette Pass, about five miles away. This is the last town on State Highway 23, the end of the road. There's no mistaking what rules the morning rush hour. A diesel roar rises as commercial shipping engages in its morning melee: shrimp boats mix with long liners, oil field crew boats, offshore tugs, tiny bass fishing boats, gillnetters, and ocean-going tankers. By the time we reach Baptiste Collette, our ears are ringing and our eyes have had their fill.

Thankfully, silty brown water quickly grabs the canoes, pulling the party south into the heart of the delta—or what's left of it. Signs of humanity's heavy hand are everywhere: straight canals, spoil banks, abandoned oil tanks, rotting barges.

"It gets better," Mike Guidry, a game warden with the U.S. Fish and Wildlife Service, assures us. "It gets really beautiful."

Once, it was one of the most beautiful spots on the continent. The original delta was formed by the huge load of sediment carried by the Mississippi. As the river nears its mouth at the Gulf of Mexico, its flow gradually slows. Eventually, it is not traveling fast enough to carry the silt, and fine-grained particles start dropping out.

In the old days, when the river ran over its banks in floods, those particles fell on the sides of the passes, building the river's delta. Fresh water from the river was critical to the plant life that held the soil together against the ravages of salty storms from the Gulf.

That building of the delta covered an immense area. If the main river is an arm, the delta is its hand and fingers. Major passes branch from the wrist across the land base, and scores of smaller passes and bayous make river fingers, twisting and turning toward the Gulf across hundreds of square miles of green wilderness. Huge marshes once rose from the gifts of the silt and fresh water. Forests of cypress were interspersed with marshes, ponds, and lagoons. That landscape was constantly being reshaped as the river changed courses, surging through high and low cycles.

The first European settlers found a staggering array of wildlife on the delta. It was the winter home of 30 percent of the continent's waterfowl. Mink, otter, and deer were abundant. And the water writhed with fish, shrimp, crabs, and oysters. It was a paradise for wild things. The few humans hardy enough to try to live here were far from the nearest city and exposed to the ravages of the tropical heat, humidity, insects, and storms.

It all stayed relatively unchanged until the 1930s. Then the nation extended its flood protection levees below New Orleans. Communities south of the city no longer had to worry about the flooding Mississippi—but the resources that provided their livelihood had been handed a death sentence. The once-free river was now locked in mud walls. Its load of silt, needed to build and maintain the delta, got shunted right off the continental shelf.

Robbed of its basic building material, the delta is doomed to slowly sink. This process got speeded up dramatically when the canals were dredged for oil, gas, and ship traffic. Thousands of acres of marsh have been destroyed outright. But the canals have had another impact: in low-water years they've provided a direct line for salt water into the interior of the delta. Plants have died, and erosion has increased. Mining for oil and gas has forever affected the wilderness in the delta. Industry is now everywhere.

State and federal wildlife agencies have had some success in slowing the destructive tide. Two wildlife areas preserve a large section of the delta's eastern side. Experiments with silt-trapping fences have helped build new land, but the underlying problem remains: levees continue to squeeze and speed the river. So the delta continues to settle. Huge areas once filled with marsh grass or elephant ear are now open lagoons and bays. Southern edges of the delta, battered by salty waves from the Gulf, collapse at a steady rate.

Everyone on our trip knows this story. That's why they've come.

Within minutes of leaving the put-in, we turn off the main canal into a mile-long lagoon less than six inches deep. Islands of willow grow on the ridges of ancient sloughs, now silted in. Thousands of swallows shuttle overhead, feasting on gnats and other spring insects. Red-winged blackbirds, warblers, and woodpeckers dart between the willow islands. Herons and ibis probe the shallow flats, using long beaks to skewer meals from the muck. Groups of white pelicans float like icebergs across the water's edge.

Soon the roar of diesel engines is forgotten. Eyes are glued to binoculars, and sightings ring out.

"Prothonortary warbler."

"Barn swallow."

"Mottled duck."

"Green heron."

"Blue-winged teal."

The spell is broken as a helicopter lumbers overhead.

"Louisiana wilderness," scoffs Oliver Houck, the college professor. "White pelicans and straight exhaust. What a combination."

Yet soon the chopper is forgotten. Probing the shoreline, we paddle out of the lagoon and find ourselves in a watercourse hardly ten feet wide, lined with patches of cane. A swift current hustles us past ponds alive with birds. Five minutes later, we are deposited in another large, shallow lagoon.

"We're really going with the flow," says Richard Carriere, the masseur. "This is perfect. No rush, just exploring where the water takes us."

That's the way to spend a day crossing between lagoons and trenaises, and bays and bayous. Each choice is an adventure. Although modern aerial photos show most of the watercourses, they don't show depth. One bayou might lead to a lagoon deep enough to paddle; the next, to a dead end on a mudflat.

Each choice can lead to different emotions. One turn could bring wonder: sighting a peregrine falcon, finding a field of iris, watching an osprey fly off with a meal. Another turn brings disappointment: abandoned oil tanks, a wrecked camp, rotting hulks of boats.

Sometimes we fight the flow.

"The highest ground around is the natural levees," says Robert Martin, a state game warden and avid sea kayaker. "The water coming off those passes runs down into lower ground. I guess by staying off the passes, we have more work, but we're also seeing more."

By five o'clock we push through the Delta National Wildlife Refuge, paddle across the Main Pass, and find a campsite on Raphael Pass, just outside the refuge boundary. It's perfect for the total delta experience: A high spoil bank from a dredging operation is flanked by beautiful, willow-lined sloughs. Mudflats are covered with shorebirds and waterfowl, but the scene is marked by camp lights and the sounds of crew boats from nearby Pilottown. In addition, there's a bedtime lullaby of foghorns blaring through the darkness every ten seconds.

The next day our group passes into state-owned Pass-a-Loutre, where the scene shifts delicately. Roseau cane islands are more prevalent and the bays are larger, including Sawdust Bend, which stretches for almost two miles. Like others on the delta, this bay is the spawn of hurricanes.

"Storm tides from hurricanes came through here and just rolled up the floatants like carpets," Guidry says. "Before the hurricane, this was all solid marsh."

By five o'clock we reach Pass-a-Loutre's state research camp and begin pulling out. Our two days and twenty miles of paddling the great delta of the continent's largest river has left some grand impressions.

"It's a surreal mix," Carriere offers. "On one hand, you have this feeling of wildness, these great concentrations of birds and a wonderful stillness of isolation. But you're constantly being yanked back to reality by all the signs and sounds of industry. You're going back and forth. The nice thing is, you can always get away in a hurry."

It has that edge.

15

Rick Bass was born in Fort Worth, Texas, in 1958, grew up in Houston, received his B.S. from Utah State University, and now lives in the Yaak valley of Montana. He has written numerous books of literary nonfiction, including *Winter: Notes from Montana* (1991) and several collections of short fiction, including *The Watch* (1989) and *In the Loyal Mountains* (1995). Although most of his writing focuses on the need for wilderness preservation and protection for the wolves and grizzlies that inhabit large wilderness areas, some of his short stories also look at urban nature. "Swamp Boy," one of the stories included in *The Watch,* takes place in the Houston of his boyhood, at a time when there were undeveloped woods and wetlands between the subdivisions.

Swamp Boy

Rick Bass

There was a kid we used to beat up in elementary school. We called him Swamp Boy. I say we, though I never threw any punches myself. And I never kicked him either, or broke his glasses, but stood around and watched, so it amounted to the same thing. A brown-haired fat boy who wore bright striped shirts. He had no friends.

I was lucky enough to have friends. I was unexceptional. I did not stand out.

We'd spy on Swamp Boy. We'd trail him home from school. Those times we jumped him—or rather, when those other boys jumped him—the first thing they struck was always his horn-rim glasses. I don't know why the thick, foggy-lensed glasses infuriated them so much. Maybe they believed he could see things with them, invisible things that they could not. This possibility, along with some odd chemistry, seemed to drive the boys into a frenzy. We would go after him into the old woods along the bayou that he loved. He went there every day.

We followed him out of school and down the winding clay road. The road led past big pines and oaks, past puddles of red water and Christ-crown brambles of dewberries, their white blossoms floating above thorns. He'd look back, sensing us I think, but we stayed hidden amid the bushes and trees. His eyesight was poor.

Now and then he stopped to search out blackberries and the red berries that had not yet ripened. His face scrunched up like an owl's when he tasted their tart juices. Like a little bear, he moved on then, singing to himself, taking all the time in the world, plucking the berries gingerly to avoid scratching his plump hands and wrists in the awful tangle of daggers and claws in which the berries rested. Sometimes his hand and arm got caught on the curved hooks of the thorns, and he'd be stuck as though in a trap. He'd wince as he pulled his hand free of the daggers, and as he pulled, other thorns would catch him more firmly; he'd pull harder. Once free, he sucked the blood from his pinprick wounds.

And when he'd had his fill of berries and was nearing the end of the road, he began to pick blossoms, stuffing them like coins into the pockets of his shirt and the baggy shorts he always wore—camper-style shorts with zip-up compartments and all sorts of rings and hooks for hanging compasses and flashlights.

Then he walked down to the big pond we called Hidden Lake, deep in the woods, and sprinkled the white blossoms onto the surface of the muddy water. Frogs would cry out in alarm, leaping from shore's edge with frightened chirps. A breeze would catch the floating petals and carry them across the lake like tiny boats. Swamp Boy would walk up and down the shore, trying to catch those leaping frogs.

Leopard frogs: *Rana utricularia.*

We followed him like jackals, like soul scavengers. We made the charge about once a week: we'd shout and whoop and chase him down like lions on a gazelle, pull that sweet boy down and truss him up with rope and hoist him into a tree. I never touched him. I always held back, only pretending to be in on it. I thought that if I touched him, he would burn my fingers. We knew he was alien, and it terrified us.

With our hearts full of hate, a terrible, frantic, weak, rotting-through-the-planks hate, we—they, the other boys—would leave him hanging there, red-faced and congested, thick-tongued with his upside-down blood, until the sheer wet weight of the sack of blood that was his body allowed him to slip free of the ropes and fall to the ground like a dead animal, like something dripped from a wet limb. But before his weight let him fall free, the remaining flowers he'd gathered fluttered from his pockets like snow.

Some of the boys would pick up a rock or a branch and throw it at him as we retreated, and I was sickened by both the sound of the thuds as the rocks struck his thick body and by the hoots of pleasure, the howls of the boys whenever one of their throws found its target. Once they split his skull open, which instantly drenched his hair, and we ran like fiends, believing we had killed him. But he lived, fumbling free of the ropes to make his way home, bloody-faced and red-crusted. Two days after he got stitched up at the hospital, he was back in the woods again, picking berries and blossoms, and even the dumbest of us could see that something within him was getting strong, and that something in us was being torn down.

Berry blossoms lined the road along which we walked each afternoon—clumps and piles of flowers, each mound of them indicating where we'd strung him up earlier. I started to feel bad about what I was doing, even though I was never an attacker. I merely ran with the other boys for the spectacle, to observe the dreamy phenomenon of Swamp Boy.

One night in bed I woke up with a pain in my ribs, as if the rocks had been striking me rather than him, and my mouth tasted of berries, and I was frightened. There was a salty, stinging feeling of thorn scratches across the backs of my hands and forearms. I have neglected to say that we all wore masks as we stalked and chased him, so he was probably never quite sure who we were—he with those thick glasses.

I lay in the darkness and imagined that in my fright my heart would begin beating faster, wildly, but instead it slowed down. I waited what seemed like a full minute for the next beat. It was stronger than my heart had ever beaten before. Not faster, just stronger. It kicked once, as if turning over on itself. The one beat—I could feel this distinctly—sent the pulse of blood all through my body, to the ends of my hands and feet. Then, after what seemed again like a full minute, another beat, one more round of blood, just as strong or stronger. It was as if I had stopped living and breathing, and it was the beat of the earth's heart in my hurt chest. I lay very still, as if pinned to the bed by a magnet.

The next day we only spied on him, and I was glad for that. But even so, I awakened during the night with that pain in my chest again. This time, though, I was able to roll free of the bed. I went to the kitchen for a glass of water, which burned all the way down as I drank it.

I got dressed and went out into the night. Stars shone through the trees as I walked toward the woods that lay between our subdivision and the school, the woods through which Swamp Boy passed each day. Rabbits sat hunched on people's front lawns like concrete ornaments, motionless in the starlight, their eyes glistening. The rabbits seemed convinced that I presented no danger to them, that I was neither owl nor cat. The lawns were wet with dew. Crickets called with a kind of madness, or a kind of peace.

I headed for the woods where we had been so cruel, along the lazy curves of the bayou. The names of the streets in our subdivision were Pine Forest, Cedar Creek, Bayou Glen, and Shady River, and for once, with regard to that kind of thing, the names were accurate. I work in advertising now, at the top of a steel-and-glass skyscraper from which I stare out at the flat gulf coast, listening to the rain, when it comes, slash and beat against the office windows. When the rain gives way to sun, I'm so high up that I can see to the curve of the earth and beyond. When the sun burns the steam off the skin of the earth, it looks as if the whole city is smoldering.

Those woods are long gone now, buried by so many tons of houses and roads and other sheer masses of concrete that what happened there when I was a child might as well have occurred four or five centuries ago, might just as well have been played out by Vikings in horn helmets or red natives in loincloths.

There was a broad band of tallgrass prairie—waist high, bending gently—that I would have to cross to get to the woods. I had seen deer leap from their beds there and sprint away. I could smell the faraway, slightly sweet odor of a skunk that had perhaps been caught by an owl at the edge of the meadow, for there were so many skunks in the meadow, and so many owls back in the woods. I moved across the silver field of grass in starlight and moonlight, like a ship moving across the sea, a small ship with no others out, only night.

Between prairie and woods was a circle of giant ancient oaks. You could feel magic in this spot, could feel it rise from centuries below and brush against your face like the cool air from the bottom of a deep well. This "buffalo ring" was the only evidence that a herd of buffalo had once been held at bay by wolves, as the wolves tried, with snarling feints and lunges, to cut one of the members out of the herd. The buffalo had gathered in a tight circle to make their stand, heads all facing outward; the weaker ones had taken refuge in the center. Over and over, the sun set and the moon rose and set, again and again, as the wolves kept them in this standoff. Heads bowed, horns gleaming, the buffalo trampled the prairie with their hooves, troughed it up with nose-stinging nitrogen piss and shit in their anger and agitation.

Whether the wolves gave up and left, or whether they darted in, grabbed a leg, and pulled out one of the buffalo—no matter, for all that was important to the prairie, there at the edge of the woods along the slow bayou, was what had been left behind. Over the years, squirrels and other animals had carried acorns to this place, burying them in the rich circular heap of shit-compost. The trees, before they were cut down, told this story.

Swamp Boy could feel these things as he moved across the prairie and through the woods, there at the edge of that throbbing, expanding city, Houston. And I could too, as I held my ribs with both arms because of the strange soreness. I began going into the woods every night, as if summoned.

I would walk the road he walked. I would pass beneath the same trees from which we had hung him, the limbs thick and branching over the road: the hanging trees. I would walk past those piles of flower petals and berry blossoms, and shuffle my feet through the dry brown oak leaves. Copperheads slept beneath the leaves, cold and sluggish in the night, and five-lined skinks rattled through brush piles, a sound like pattering rain. Raccoons loped down the road ahead of me, looking back over their shoulders, their black masks smudged across their delicate faces.

I would walk past his lake. The shouting frogs fled at my approach. The water swirled and wriggled with hundreds of thousands of tadpoles—half-formed things that were neither fish nor frog, not yet of this world. As they swirled and wriggled in the moonlight, it looked as if the water were boiling.

I would go past the lake, would follow the thin clay road through the starlit forest to its end, to a bluff high above the bayou, the round side of one of the meandering S-cuts that the bayou had carved. I know some things about the woods, even though I live in the city, have never left this city. I know some things that I learned as a child just by watching and listening—and I could use those things in my advertising, but I don't. They are my secrets. I don't give them away.

I would stand and watch and listen to the bayou as it rolled past, its gentle, lazy current always murmuring, always twenty years behind. Stories from twenty years ago, stories that had happened upstream, were only just now reaching this spot.

Sometimes I feel as if I've become so entombed that I have *become* the giant building in which I work—that it is my shell, my exoskeleton, like the seashell in which a fiddler crab lives, hauling the stiff burden of it around for the rest of his days. The chitin of things not said, things not done.

I would stand there and hold my hurt ribs, feel the breezes, and look down at the chocolate waters, the star glitter reflecting on the bayou's ripples, and I would feel myself fill slowly and surely with a strength, a giddiness that urged me to *jump, jump, jump.* But I would hold back, and instead would watch the bayou go drifting past, carrying its story twenty more years down the line, and then thirty, heading for the gulf, for the shining waters.

Then I'd walk back home, undress, and crawl back into bed and sleep hard until the thunder rattle of the alarm clock woke me and my parents and my brothers began to move about the house. I'd get up and begin my new day, the real day, and my ribs would be fine.

I had a secret. My heart was wild and did not belong among people.

I did what I could to accommodate this discrepancy.

We continued to follow him, through the woods and beyond. Sometimes we would spy on him at his house early in the evenings. We watched him and his family at the dinner table, watched them say grace, say amen, then eat and talk. It wasn't as if we were homeless or anything—this was back when we all still had both our parents, when almost everyone did—but still, his house was different. The whole house itself seemed to come alive when the family was inside it, seemed to throb with a kind of strength. Were they taking it from us as we watched them? Where did it come from? You could feel it, like the sun's force.

After dinner they gathered around the blue light of the television. Our spying had revealed to us that *Daniel Boone* was Swamp Boy's favorite show. He wore a coonskin cap while he watched it, and his favorite part was the beginning, when Dan'l would throw the tomahawk and split the tree trunk as the credits rolled. This excited him so much each time that he gave a small shout and jumped in the air.

After *Daniel Boone,* it would be time for Swamp Boy's mother and father to repair his glasses, if we'd broken them that day. They'd set the glasses down on a big long desk and glue them, or put screws in them, using all sorts of tape and epoxy sealers, adjusting and readjusting them. Evidently his parents had ordered extra pairs, because we had broken them so often. Swamp Boy stood by patiently while his parents bent and wiggled the earpieces to fit him.

How his parents must have dreaded the approach of three in the afternoon, wondering, as it drew near the time for him to get out of school and begin his woods walk home, whether today would be the day that the cruel boys would attack their son. What joy they felt when he arrived home unscathed, back in the safety of his family.

We grew lean through the spring as we chased him toward the freedom of summer. I was convinced that he was absorbing all of our strength with his goodness, his sweetness. I could barely stand to watch the petals spill from his pockets as we twirled him from the higher and higher limbs, could barely make my legs move as we thundered along behind him, chasing him through the woods.

I avoided getting too close, would not become his friend, for then the other boys would treat me as they treated him.

But I wanted to watch.

In May, when Hidden Lake began to warm up, Swamp Boy would sometimes stop off there to catch things. The water was shallow, only neck deep at the center, full of gars, snakes, fish, turtles, and rich bayou mud at its bottom. It's gone now. The trees finally edged in and spread their roots into that fertile swamp bottom, taking it quickly, and no sooner had the trees claimed the lake than they were in turn leveled to make way for what came next—roads, a subdivision, making ghosts of the forest and the lake.

Swamp Boy kept a vegetable strainer and an empty jar in his lunch box. He set his tape-mended glasses down on a rotting log before opening his lunch box, flipping the clasps on it expertly, like a businessman opening his briefcase. He removed his shoes and socks and wiggled his feet in the mud. When his glasses were off like that, we could creep to within twenty or thirty feet of him.

A ripple blew across the water—a slight mystery in the wind or a subtle swamp movement just beneath the surface. I could feel some essence, a truth, down in the soil beneath my feet—but I'd catch myself before saying to the other boys, "Let's go." Instead of jumping into the water or giving myself up to the search for whatever that living essence was beneath me, I watched.

He crouched down, concentrating, looking out over the lake and those places where the breeze had made a little ring or ripple. Then came the part we were there to see, the part that stunned us: Swamp Boy's great race into the water. Building up a good head of steam, running fast and flat-footed in his bare feet, he charged in and slammed his vegetable strainer down into the reeds and rushes. Just as quickly he was back out, splashing, stumbling, having scooped up a big red wad of mud. He emptied the contents onto the ground. The mud wriggled with life, all the creatures writhing and gasping, terrible creatures with bony spines or webbed feet or pincers and whiskers.

After carefully sorting through the tadpoles—in various stages of development; half frog and half fish, looking human almost, like little round-headed human babies—angry catfish, gasping snapping turtles, leaping newts, and hellbenders, he put the catfish, the tadpoles, and a few other grotesqueries in his jar filled with swamp water, and then picked up all the other wriggling things and threw them back into the lake.

Then he wiped his muddy feet off as best as he could, put his shoes and socks and strainer in his lunch box, and walked the rest of the way home barefoot. From time to time he held the jar up to the sun, to look at his prizes swimming around in that dirty water. The mud around his ankles dried to an elephant-gray cake. We followed him to his house at a distance, as if escorting him.

That incredible force field, a wall of strength, when he disappeared into his house, into the utility room to wash up—the whole house glowed with it, something emanated from it. And once again I could feel things, lives and stories, meaningful things, stirring in the soil beneath my feet.

I continued to walk out to the woods each night, awakening with a pain so severe in my chest and ribs, a pain and a hunger both, that I could barely breathe.

Could I run out and catch a frog or a tadpole, launch myself wild-assed into the muddy water? Could I bring a shovel out to the prairie one night and dig down, deep down, in search of an old buffalo skull that would still smell rank and earthy but gleam white in the moonlight when I pulled it up? If I had intended to do any of those things, if I had dared to—if I had had the strength and the courage—I should have done so then.

In the evenings, after spying on him as he watched TV, we'd go home to our own suppers, then return and look in on him again. We wouldn't devil him, just watch him. We'd line up, a couple of us at each window, and peer in from the darkness like raccoons.

In his room Swamp Boy had six aquariums set beneath neon lights. He kept the other lights turned off, so that all you could see were his catfish and the hellish tadpoles. There were filters and air pumps bubbling away in those aquariums, humming softly. The water was so clear that it must have seemed like heaven to those poor rescued creatures that had been living in a Houston mud hole.

The catfish were pretty, as were even the feather-gilled tadpoles—morpho-frogs whose hind legs trailed uselessly behind them. He went from tank to tank, bending over to examine the creatures with his patched-up glasses that made him look like a little surgeon. He pressed his nose against the glass and stared in wonder, open-mouthed, touching the sides of the aquarium with his fingers while the sleek, wild-whiskered catfish and bulge-bellied tadpoles circled and swarmed in lazy schools, rising and falling as if with purpose. He tried to count his charges. We'd see him point at them with his index finger, saying the words out loud or to himself, softly, "One, two, three, four . . ."

There was a bottle of aspirin on his desk and a heater in each of the tanks, for cold winter nights. Whenever he suspected that a catfish or a tadpole was feeling ill, he'd drop an aspirin in the water. It would make a cloudy trail as it fell.

Sometimes he'd lie in bed with his hands behind his head and watch the fish and tadpoles go around and around in their new home. When the moon was up and the lights were off it looked as though his room were under water—as if *he* were under water among the catfish.

God, we were devils. It occurred to a couple of the older boys to see how far he could run. Usually we caught him and strung him up fairly quickly, after only a short chase, but one day we tried to run him to exhaustion, to try and pop his fat, strong heart.

After school we put on wolf masks and made spiked collars by driving nails through leather dog collars, which we fastened around our necks. We spoke to one another in snarling laughs, our voices muffled through the wolf masks.

We started out after him the minute he hit the woods, bending our heads low to the ground and pretending to sniff his scent, howling, trotting along behind him, loping and barking. We chased him through the woods and down along the bayou on the other side of a forested ridge. In his fear he started making sounds like a lost calf. There was cane along the bayou, flood-killed, dry-standing ghost bamboo, and Swamp Boy plowed through that as if going through a dead corn field, snapping the bamboo in all directions, running as if the forces of hell had opened up.

All we were going to do was throw mud on him, once he got too tired to go any farther. Roll him around in the mud a little, maybe. And break his glasses, of course.

But this time he was really afraid.

It was exciting, chasing him through the tiger-slash stripes of light, following the swath of his flight through all that knocked-over dead bamboo. It was about the most exciting thing we had ever done.

We chased him to the small bluff overlooking the bayou, and Swamp Boy paused for only the briefest of seconds before making a Tarzan dive into the milky brown water. He swam immediately for the slick clay bank on the other side, toward north Houston where the rich people lived, where I imagined he would skulk up to some rich person's back yard, shivering, shoeless, smelling like some vile swamp thing, waiting until dark, so large was his shame. He'd hide in their bushes, perhaps, before creeping up to the back porch—still dripping wet and muddy, and bloody from where the canes had stabbed him—and then, crying, ask if he could use the telephone.

If this were not all a lie, a re-creation or manipulation of the facts, and if I were the boy who had chased the other boy through the cane, rather than the boy who had leapt into the muddy bayou, then what I would have done, what I should have done, was something heroic: I would have held out my hands like an Indian chief, stopping the other boys from jumping in and swimming after him, or even from gloating. I would have said something noble, like, "He got away. Let him go."

I might even have gone home and called Swamp Boy's parents, so that he wouldn't have to lurk in the shadows in some rich person's yard—afraid to walk home through the woods because of the masked gang, but also afraid to go ask to use the phone.

That's what I'd have done if I were the boy who chased him, rather than the boy who got chased, and who made that swim. Who kept, and worshiped, those baroque creatures in his aquarium.

I was that boy, and I was the other one too. I was at the edge of fear, the edge of hesitancy, and had not yet—not then—turned back from it.

There's a heavy rain falling today. The swamps are writhing with life.

16

Wendell Mayo was born in Corpus Christi, Texas, in 1953. He received his B.S. degree in chemical engineering from Ohio State University and his B.A. in journalism from the University of Toledo. He also has an M.F.A. in creative writing from Vermont College and a Ph.D. in twentieth-century literature and creative writing from Ohio University. He has published numerous short stories as well as three collections of short fiction: *Centaur of the North* (1996), *In Lithuanian Wood* (1999), and *B. Horror and Other Stories* (1999). He won the 1996 Premio Aztlán Award for *Centaur of the North,* a collection that included his short story "Conquistador." In this story the narrator revises his earlier attitudes as he revisits where he lived as a young man. The narrative explores the complex interweaving of family heritage and financial circumstances, gender roles, and attitudes toward nature.

Conquistador

Wendell Mayo

The heroes of the world have been feared and admired.

—Martin Decoud, *Nostromo*

Summer nights, ghost crabs come into Corpus Christi, clamber up the rocks, and swagger across the sands from the east bay, north to the tiny islands of the archipelago, Mustang Island, and still further south to San Padre Island, where they come onto the laps of shallow coves in droves, and in the moonlight, a soft, strange violet light, their bodies reach the near point of translucence. Their presence here is a silent contradiction: the mind conceives of the hard armor carapaces over their backs and broad, jutting chests, yet their images in the night light are soft and strange, like spirits wandering onto shore to meet other spirits, to whisper among themselves of their other lives in tidal pools, or to speak of their cousins, the blue crabs, who live many months in the deeper, darker parts of the Gulf, in another watery terrain, perhaps the sunken, shifting hull of a Spanish galleon, or in the skull of a drowned sea captain, or among the itinerant bones of my grandfather's ancestor, Francisco Durante, that ancient captain of the Spanish Main whose name my grandfather reportedly took from him, as my grandmother Eva tells it.

I have also seen droves of fiddlers near the salt marshes as they tack across the compacted sandy mud among blades of sea grass, each carrying its absurdly proportioned chela high like a diminutive soldier wielding a lance, but I have always walked alone with the ghosts and fiddlers, always without Eva or Francisco, and without my parents who were lost to me in consecutive years: my father in 1962 when his rig loaded with pipe string headed for the Anadarko Gas Fields went off the road outside Tivoli; my mother in 1963 to cancer. So I belonged to Eva on my father's side when I was nine years of age, and from that time on I became a conquistador, a product of old ways, so Eva told me: her dead husband, she explained, was the descendant of Francisco Durante . . . *el conquistador. . . . Someday,* she said, *you will be anything you want.*

We lived on Old Brownsville Road in a small white house like many of the houses dotting the outlying areas of Corpus, in and around the groves of pecan trees and fields of cotton. The house was a square single story, with a tar-paper roof, bubbled and peeling siding, and a dark, forbidding crawl space under the back porch. The kitchen was located directly to the right of the back door at the porch. A single window permitted light to fall in a square over the sink, a low black gas range, a small table, and a plank shelf fixed halfway up the opposite wall, upon which the entire assortment of Eva's cookery rested: several wooden spoons, a deep cast iron skillet, a flat stone platter, a wooden rolling pin, and a stone pot Eva called her *olla* and in which she cooked *olla podrida.* Several knives my grandfather had peened, tempered, and sharpened also lay scattered between the pots and pans. In another corner of the tiny kitchen Eva kept empty coffee tins for flour, beans, rice, corn—and one for her old chicken bones she used for crabbing at the breakwater in Corpus Christi Bay.

Eva and I took our meals at a small square table in the center of the kitchen, not in the larger dining room where Francisco had eaten his meals. Eva explained to me that this was tradition, and that tradition was important to a conquistador. But I believed that Eva set our table in the kitchen out of habit, or because she was somehow more comfortable there.

One day, soon after I came to live with Eva, she said, "Someday you will head a great table of your own. . . . You will have a loving wife and many *niños y niñas.*"

From that day on, knowing that Francisco and she had dined in two rooms in the same house, I began to feel separate from Eva. But even with my sense of separateness, I followed Eva everywhere in my first days with her. We were each with our own recent losses—she, her Francisco, me with my father and mother. I trailed her into the back yard, and to the small coop she kept at the side of Francisco's tool shed. I watched her reach in and pull a chicken out by its legs. She carried the struggling bird to the back porch as if she were walking onto a stage. She took the chicken by the neck, swung it over her head in a wide circle—and snapped her wrist and its neck at the same time. I was amazed that her small, brown, wrinkled hands could so suddenly take the life of anything. Yet my astonishment soon vanished in the shadow of Francisco Durante. Evenings, she would kneel by Francisco's chest, take out his First World War clothes, helmet, medals, and rusty bayonet, and spread them all on the bed:

"He was a brave man, your grandfather Francisco."

Of course, I mulled over this business of being a conquistador, as children ponder things of such importance. Eva's assertion that I was a conquistador was incongruous with my surroundings. How could such an important man as Francisco Durante have left his wife in such modest circumstances? A tiny tar-papered house on a broken asphalt strip one dared not to call "road," just "Old Brownsville"? Still, I was interested in her remarks about conquistadors and bravery, so I sat and thought about it while feeding her chickens, and later drawing stick figures in the dust across Old Brownsville. One afternoon I announced my conclusions to Eva as she stood in the kitchen stirring pintos in her old stone pot: if I was indeed a conquistador, then it was my wish to be a great treasure hunter, and to find the sunken galleon my great ancestor had captained.

"Oh," Eva said, "you will find many riches in the Gulf, and you will become a famous treasure hunter."

But though I wanted to believe her, her appearance made me suspicious. Eva was such a tiny woman, with a flat rump, a small waist, short dark hair, and a flat smooth nose. Her skin was olive-green, and her hair coal-black, not like mine. I never bothered her about her ancestors because it was obvious, even to so young a boy in Corpus Christi, that she was Mexican . . . more precisely Mexican Indian. It was this that kept me from believing her about my more important ancestors, those of Francisco Durante, but she pulled the wooden spoon out of her *olla* and set it aside.

"Look," she said, and she reached for something on the window ledge over her sink. She handed me a small coin, deeply worn and tarnished gray. "A diver found this many years ago," she said. "The diver said he found it at the wreck of *El Aliento.*"

El Aliento was the elder Francisco's fabled galleon, part of, Eva said, a Spanish treasure fleet of twenty ships beset by a hurricane and lost off Padre Island in 1553. I turned the coin over and over in my hand. I made out the letters CINCO PESOS on one side of the coin, and the vague image of a dragonlike animal on the other side.

"Is it gold?" I asked her.

"*Sí, sí,*" she laughed, "*el oro.*"

I did not know at the time if she kidded me or not, but it didn't matter. Eva bought a pair of diving goggles, and we took her dead Francisco's old pale-green Ford Falcon to the breakwater, with two fishing poles and a bucket of old chicken bones Eva saved from several meals.

I am never sure if it was more my imagination, but Corpus Christi Bay that day—my christening as a great treasure hunter—was blue and deep as the sky. The bay, as I knew it, had many moods—gray, green, or brown-green in the winter when the jellyfish came in and left themselves in the low tide like gelatin buttons over stretches of beach. But this day the surface of the bay under the glow of the sun in the cloudless sky was passionately blue. The breakwater ran through the bay like the white, scaly back of a great serpent, bending away from the sea wall in a lazy *S* north toward Aransas Pass and the Gulf. And I believed I possessed unfathomable strength, like that of a magnificent serpent. I believed I could put my arms the whole way around one of the large palms leaning over the beach and climb to the top of it in an instant, and there see as no man has ever before—as no one would ever again—all the lands and seas of my domain.

I left Eva a short distance out on the breakwater with her bucket of bones and fishing poles, and raced around it to the beach, to a spot just north of the pilings at the pier nearby.

I slipped on my new goggles, put my chest out, and skipped into the surf until I felt the sea full and deep around me. I knifed through the swells beyond the breaking flat sheets of froth, and bore into the next swell and the next. . . . I was the great treasure hunter, and I tore open the water with my skull and stuck my eyes in their goggles to the task of looking into the sea, yet I saw only bits of debris and the most murky sorts of shapes coming and going in my field of vision. I came up for air, saw Eva wave to me from the breakwater beyond the pier, then felt, as I was at the very height of my disappointment, dozens of impressions on my body—as if many fingers touched me all over, all at once—and around me I saw a myriad of tiny splashes, like a thousand pebbles suddenly dashed into the water. I tore for the shore with both arms sailing around me like the vanes of a windmill, and raced through the surf back to the beach. There I removed my goggles and threw them onto the sand.

I sat for a time watching Eva bait her poles, then I slowly walked back to her on the breakwater.

"Well," she said, tugging at the line of one pole with her index finger, "have you found Francisco's treasure?"

I sat and took the other pole in my lap.

"Not yet," I said.

"Someday, you will," she said, and pulled up a blue crab with her pole, its claw clamped around the smaller broken half of a wishbone. She dropped the crab into her bucket, cut the line, then smiled and pointed at the spot in the water from which I had just fled. The surface of the water suddenly broke and thousands of tiny rifts appeared then vanished. "So many little fish."

I ignored Eva's enthusiasm for the bounty of the sea, and instead pointed to the crab, which was pressing its hard greenish claws, its legs and paddles, all simultaneously against the sides of the bucket. The crab turned itself round and round.

"He is so stupid," I said to Eva. "All he wants is that stupid wishbone, and he never lets it go—even when you pull him in, all the way out of the sea." When I said this, Eva looked surprised, but she set about tying another chicken bone on her line, and I added, "He deserves to die."

I am never sure if Eva felt this was a horrible thing for me to say. She never mentioned it. We caught six more crabs that afternoon, boiled and ate them that night, and Eva said to me, "Some day you will be very smart—a doctor or a painter. I will be so proud of you."

She put her hand on my shoulder and I ran from her into my room. I am not certain if I fled because I was ashamed of my cowardice in the face of the vicious little fishes, or if, somehow, Eva's premonitions about my future—my being a conquistador—set me forever above her. After all, compared to the boy my father's blood and his father's blood had brought forth, what was she? A tiny Indian woman who caught crabs with old dried chicken bones and stood in the tiny square of light made by the narrow window in her kitchen and boiled pintos and *podrida* in her old stone *olla* all day for my meals. But I was the grandson of Francisco Durante, who was the descendant and namesake of a daring captain of the Spanish Main—who might have become, had not the fortunes of adventure sunk him in the Gulf, a famous soldier, doctor, or artisan in his time.

Eva did not immediately come to find me in my room. I suspect she sensed the difference between my blood and her blood and stayed away. Still, I reasoned, she was part of me, the small boyish part, and though I was sure I would soon shed this part of myself—of her—it made me think a long while about my mother and father in the only way I could bear their loss: they were in Heaven together, happier than I ever knew them to be, happier than I would ever be here in Corpus, here in this humid, slow old patch of seaside dust and rock. I had to, somehow, strike out from here, even if it meant joining them in their afterlives . . . yet Eva's words kept coming to me, *someday, someday,* and others, *wait, not yet . . .*

Later that evening, I stood in Francisco's dining room and watched Eva in her kitchen plucking the chicken for tomorrow's dinner; she was whispering to the chicken in Spanish . . . *lo siento* . . . and pulling its feathers with her tiny worn hands with great care and tenderness, which seemed to me a foolish thing to do since the bird was stone-cold dead.

Eva did not mention how rough this whole business of being a conquistador could be. She had plans for me, and now that I began to accept my destiny as a great conqueror, she set her plans in motion—she must have, that is, because her preparations seemed so queer—and her plans seemed to me far above even my expectations of a conquistador, certainly far above those parents had of other boys I knew at school. Naturally, Spanish was not taught at school, so Eva taught me the Spanish of the Royal Academy of Spain, which never failed to get me in trouble with my friends who, rather than thinking me regal or refined, simply did not understand me, or laughed at my clumsy use of *vosotros* instead of *ustedes.* Eva bought a paint set, an easel, and glittering paints of lapis lazuli, gold and silver, and rich blacks and purples. I painted Spanish galleons, though I had never seen one: barklike crafts with crooked, angular sails and ridiculous stick men on their decks. Later, she gave me a book of illustrations and I copied the ships as best I could. Still, from my early failures to my poor duplications of ships of the Spanish Armada, she would stand by the easel, cross her arms over her chest, and sigh, "Oh, these are lovely—you see, you see!"

I am never sure what she saw or expected me to see, but all of my training seemed innocuous enough, with the possible exception of my use of the King's Spanish with the boys at school, which I remedied by simply speaking differently with them.

But other matters of my training were more painful. I was confirmed and made First Communion late since my father and mother had never gotten to it, but Eva could not see the least bit embarrassment in it. I stood a head higher than all the other children at First Communion Mass, and the whole matter of kneeling was foreign to me; I did so shakily, and only after all the other children kneeled obediently. Perhaps if I had been younger I would not have felt such resistance. . . . I was sure the priest paused and smiled before he laid the wafer on my tongue. I had forgotten to hold my hands at my sides, and I *reached* for it . . .

Eva was deeply moved: "You are with God now. He is with you now, forever."

I was too young to feel the deep mysteries of faith and, unlike the other children of six and seven, too old to believe the whole matter just plain fun. But it was good to know God was with me, especially that next week at school when I punched out George Ramírez for calling me an orphan. Eva came to school and sat by my side in the principal's office. She looked sadly at the principal, Mr. Lynch, with her big brown eyes.

"He's a good boy. . . . He just lost his father and his mother. . . . He's a good boy."

Whatever Eva did, whatever special quality of voice or manner she possessed, she got me out of many scrapes at school. The other children tortured me for not having parents; but I believed older people were easy, and with time I could slug any kid for saying anything; I would suffer only a royal scolding from Mr. Lynch, then Eva would come to rescue me. God was with me, and I suppose with His help I won a kind of victory: eventually none of the children would say anything to me—only the most obligatory and polite salutations.

A year passed, and I had no more a notion of what it was to be the son of a son of a son . . . of a son of a conquistador than the Man in the Moon. I was old enough then to study the great explorers: Balboa, Cortez, Pizarro, Ponce de León, as well as Alonso Alvarez de Piñeda, who reportedly first sighted and named the city on the day of Corpus Christi in 1519. Yet even this historical fact baffled me. Had Piñeda the honor of first sight? No one can say he *saw* Corpus Christi, and what if he had been looking at something else all together? Later that year in school we learned that the French explorer René Robert Cavelier, sieur de La Salle, perhaps sailed by Corpus Christi in 1685—had *he* been keeping his eyes peeled? Or had Alonso de León seen the bay on two trips while chasing after the Frenchman La Salle?—or was it the English?—Ingram, Bourne, and Twide, the survivors of a sea battle with the Spanish in 1568? I imagined a great compression of time, and in that compression, the Spanish chasing the English chasing the Spanish chasing the French, like some mad animal chasing its tail: León after La Salle—the Spanish Fleet after Ingram, et al.—and Piñeda, blithely sailing by and mumbling *Corpus Christi*—all the while the indigenous Karankawa Indians, later to be called "Water-Walkers" because of their ability to cross unseen shallow reefs and shifting sand bars on foot, stood by and watched the carnival at a distance.

Although I was only a boy, as near as I could tell, Piñeda had named the thing I came to know: *Corpus.* And I cursed Piñeda for discovering this old Corpus. And while I felt no urgent need to quest for other legendary lands in the New Spanish World—such as the Fountain of Youth—it seemed entirely reasonable to me that I should be questing or conquering or discovering—something. Were not these men—these explorers—the standard-bearers for generations to come? And should not I somehow follow in their footsteps? Should not I be on one knee, somewhere, claiming something in the name of someone? But how, with so many explorers before me, could I hope to be sure I would be the first to discover whatever it was I discovered? Of course, it occurred to me that my ancestor Francisco Durante was not a conquistador at all, which in itself was only part of my greatest dread: was it possible that my intellectual training and Eva's late attention to my manners would amount to nothing? She read the Chivalric Code to me nights before bed, parts of which impressed me little: all the trouble over women and being smitten by them. We began *Don Quijote,* very slow, but I did my best to stay with it, especially since Eva spoke of the old book with such reverence . . . *El Quijote,* she called it, the *One and Only.* She also made me recite verse in Latin from grandfather Francisco's primer of the same. All this I felt would be wasted if the legend of my ancestor were not true: a whole year of conquistador training down the drain.

One morning, I sat in the kitchen and watched Eva chop tomatoes, corn, chicken, and beans and drop them with her tiny hands into her pot for her *olla podrida.* I asked her:

"What kind of conquistador am I? I'm bored. What should I *do?*"

She wiped the backs of her hands on her apron. "You will be what you will be—it's your destiny."

And so we pressed on with my training. I completed my introduction to Latin by reciting, to Eva's adoring satisfaction, the epigraph to Wordsworth's "Ode to Duty," one of grandfather Francisco's favorites:

Jam non consilio bonus, sed more eo
perductus, ut non tantum recte
facere possim, sed nisi recte
facere non possim . . .

Now at last I am not consciously good
but so trained by habit that I not only
can act rightly but cannot act
otherwise than rightly . . .

I thought the epigraph was perfect, and since I had memorized it so carefully, I felt I knew its profound and yet simple meaning. During that year I came to believe I could not do anything wrong—that the habits of a trained conquistador could not be anything but feared and admired by the worlds of less fortunate people. I could not, I believed, act unless it was right—so I decided to run away—rather, to *quest* for what I began to believe was my *destiny*—a strange word, and vague idea. I thought, I would be who I would be. Well, then, I would be a runaway, thereby seeking and finding at the same time, as I understood the concept, my *destiny.*

While Eva was feeding her chickens I went to her room and broke into Francisco's chest, knowing I would find his First World War clothes. I put them on, found his dull, rusty bayonet, and tried on his wide-brimmed iron helmet, but it kept slipping front to back over my eyes and off my head, down my back and onto the floor. So I left it.

I rolled up the sleeves and pant legs of Francisco's gray musty-smelling war clothes and struck out for Corpus Christi Bay and the Gulf of Mexico. The sun was low on the horizon, changing from white to yellow over the ocean; an orange corona hugged it at last, and mobs of clouds clumped around it like purple grapes. As I approached the beach, the sky was dark, and the wind strong against my face. I sat for a long while near the beach with Francisco's bayonet across my knees. I could hear the long ragged fronds of a palm tree rattling together above me. Then I walked out to the beach, this time south of the breakwater. There, I decided to strike south, to walk the coast to South America.

The tide was in, and at the line of surf that pushed thin sheets of water to my feet were clumps of sea moss, and yellow, black, and red ropy strands of weed, among which lay several Portuguese men-of-war with their long, dark, tapered stingers tangled in the weed, and their gelatinous, pale-blue sails poking up. Further ahead of me, ghost crabs zigzagged among humps of weed and men-of-war, always just beyond the full range of human sight—beyond absolute, positive identification. That I felt I knew they were ghosts came only with experience, and with a kind of faith in the existence of creatures who live just out of light's reach. I was not far south of the breakwater, when I came to a small tidal pool with a few blades of grass standing out of it. . . . Suddenly, dozens of fiddler crabs were at my feet, holding their absurd little lances high, tacking sideways with me as I walked, their eyes like tiny black beads dead on me. I was enraged at the stupid little creatures, and I struck at them with Francisco's bayonet. I tipped them over one by one and, when I could slow one enough with the blade, jabbed the bayonet into its underside.

I felt an odd, frightening, yet uncontrollable need to kill, and kill, and keep killing, followed by the voice I'd heard inside me before: *perhaps,* I thought, then, *not yet, not yet,* then, *perhaps I am,* but I grew more and more distracted by the need to kill the fiddlers and by their legs, quivering and moving in circles as they struggled to right themselves.

The helpless gearlike workings of their legs amazed me more and more, and I slaughtered dozens of them—before I spotted the headlights of Francisco's Falcon parked near the breakwater behind me, then Eva, stooping and falling to her knees, then rising and crawling down the rocks toward me. I threw the bayonet down and ran; I twisted my ankle; I crawled and stumbled as fast as I could, yet Eva managed to tackle me, haul me up, and—miraculously—lift me in her arms.

"Don't touch me!" I screamed with my face in my hands. "Don't look at me! I am a conquistador!"

I said this to her over and over—I am never sure if Eva responded in any way to my commands. I do know I was amazed all the while at the old woman's strength as she crawled up the rocks of the breakwater with me in her arms to Francisco's Falcon.

She let me go when we reached the car. I stood by the bumper on one leg and rubbed my ankle.

"You are a conquistador," Eva said, panting. "You are also a bad little boy."

"But my destiny!" I reproached, and she smiled a moment which calmed me—I was sure my esteemed ancestry had gotten me out of another bind.

Then she said, "It is your destiny, little boy, to be spanked and to spend tomorrow in your room."

I have carried the humiliation of Eva's hand to my bare backside all these years—yet I never whimpered once—stroke after stroke of her hand—sting after sting until the pain fairly glowed in my lower body. But I never whimpered, and I have never asked to this day how Eva might have felt about the humiliation she so passionately put upon her conquistador, the grandson of Francisco Durante—and I shall never know. I do know that from that day on I was utterly alone in whatever quest destiny might throw my way . . .

By the grace of God, and I know it must have been by His grace alone, I graduated high school, happy to have the uneasy days living with Eva after my humiliation behind me. But that seemed to be the extent of His guiding hand. I joined the Navy in 1971 and was assigned duty on a destroyer. But I soon spent six months in the brig for slugging an Army sergeant who said sailors sail, soldiers fight. I expect I showed him the difference. When I got out of the brig, I saw many places and the people in them: the stony outlines of people at Pompeii, the pyramids and their regal sarcophagi in the tombs of the Pharaohs, the temples of Montezuma, the stone steps leading to sacrificial altars; yet never in my travels did I ever quest for one thing; never did my destiny speak to me to say *this way* or *that way;* still, like the wilder days of my youth, other voices, such as those a wanderer is wont to hear, rose in me aboard ship as I lay awake nights with the diesels humming: *not yet, not yet, not yet* . . . followed by silence and my utter dread of my heritage, the dark idea of it all, that my true self lay buried and shifting in the watery catacombs of the Gulf.

Eva died in her little tar-papered house in Corpus while I was on duty at sea, aboard my destroyer, and I'll never know precisely where I was or what my thoughts were when she passed away. I returned to Corpus Christi—a short leave granted only for that purpose—to settle her affairs. As I remember, after the funeral, I came upon the tiny white house suddenly, and as I turned the steering wheel quickly left to enter the crushed seashell drive, my only thought was to find Francisco's chest, and to save his possessions from the last rites of surveyor, bank, and land agent. I entered through the front of the house and came to the room—Francisco's, and Eva's room for the years after his passing—where I knew his chest rested, but I heard again the propellers of my destroyer moaning in my ears, *not yet.* So I turned from Francisco's room, and went straight down the hall, past the kitchen, and into the back yard, where three chickens still paced Eva's coop. I tossed them some corn from the coffee can nailed near the gate, then stood there awhile watching them take up the corn, and hearing, I imagined, the fiddlers around me scratching over the sand, and the same voice again I had heard all the years since I left Eva, and the memory of Francisco Durante, and my humiliation . . . *not now . . . not now . . . not here . . .*

I turned and went back to the house, through the wooden screen door and into Eva's kitchen. There, all in a single square of light thrown from the narrow window over the sink, where the worried surfaces of a stone pot and platter, where three wooden spoons and the cans of pintos and chicken bones for crabbing at the breakwater rested—there, I named her—*mi abuela,* my Eva—there, and not on the silent slopes of Darien overlooking the Pacific, not in the prison of night where the naked palms shake against the sky, or in the dark, shifting bottom of the Gulf that so stubbornly kept the bones of my ancestors—there, where by the small table in the center of the kitchen I lowered myself to one knee.

17

Stephen Harrigan was born in Oklahoma City in 1948, grew up in Corpus Christi, received his B.A. from the University of Texas, and now lives in Austin. "The Soul of Treaty Oak" first appeared in *Texas Monthly* magazine where Harrigan worked as a senior editor, and it is part of his collection *Comanche Midnight* (1995). He also has published another essay collection, *A Natural State* (1988), a book of non-fiction, *Water and Light: A Diver's Journey to a Coral Reef* (1992), and three novels: *Aransas* (1980), *Jacob's Well* (1984), and *The Gates of the Alamo* (2000). In this essay, Harrigan records citizen response to the deliberate poisoning of a very old, well-loved Austin tree, juxtaposing the ongoing destruction of Austin's environment with the outpouring of love for this particular tree.

The Soul of Treaty Oak

Stephen Harrigan

According to Stephen Redding, a mystical arborist who lived on a farm in Pennsylvania called Happy Tree, the Treaty Oak expired at 5:30 in the afternoon on Tuesday, July 25, 1989. Redding felt the tree's soul leave its body. He heard its last words—"Where are my beloved children?"

Redding had read about the bizarre plight of the Treaty Oak in the *Philadelphia Inquirer,* and he had come to Austin to help ease the tree's suffering, to be with it in its terrible hour. The Treaty Oak by that time was an international celebrity. People in London, Tokyo, and Sydney had heard the story of how Austin's massive, centuries-old live oak—once showcased in the American Forestry Association's Tree Hall of Fame—had been *poisoned;* how a feedstore employee named Paul Cullen allegedly had poured a deadly herbicide called Velpar around the base of the tree in patterns that suggested some sort of occult mischief. It was an act of vandalism that the world immediately perceived as a sinister and profound crime. As the Treaty Oak stood there, helplessly drawing Velpar through its trunk and limbs, it became an unforgettable emblem of our ruined and innocent earth.

Stephen Redding—a big man with dark swept-back hair and a fleshy, solemn face—was only one of many people who felt the tree calling out to them in anguish. Over the years Redding had been in and out of jail for various acts of civil disobedience on behalf of threatened trees, and he hinted darkly that the car wreck that had left him dependent on a walker may not have been an accident ("It was very mysterious—a dark night, a lonely intersection"). In preparation for his visit to the Treaty Oak, Redding fasted for six days, allowing himself only a teaspoon of maple syrup a day ("My means of partaking a little bit of the lifeblood of the tree kingdom"). On his second night in Austin, he put his hand on the tree's root flare and felt its slow pulse. He tied a yellow ribbon around its trunk and planted impatiens at its base. For almost a week he camped out under the tree, criticizing the rescue procedures that had been prescribed by a task force of foresters, plant pathologists, chemists, and arborists from all over the country. Finally Redding grew so pesty that the city decided to escort him away from the tree. That was when he felt it die.

"It was so intense," he told me in his hotel room a few days later. "I just kind of fell back on my cot without the energy even to sit. I felt like someone had dropped a sledge on my chest."

"I heard that you saw a blue flickering flame leave the tree," I said.

"I'd prefer not to speak about that. If you want to enter the rumor, that's okay. I don't want to confirm it. You could suggest that rumor has it that it looked like a coffee cup steaming. And if the rumor also said there was a hand on the loop of the coffee cup you could say that too."

I was surprised to realize, after an hour or so of hearing Redding expound upon the feelings of trees and the secret harmony of all living things, that I was listening not just with my usual journalist's detachment but with a kind of hunger. Anyone who went by to pay respects to the Treaty Oak in the last few months would recognize that hunger: a need to understand how the fate of this stricken tree could move and outrage us so deeply, how it could seem to call to each of us so personally.

When I read about the poisoning, I took my children by to see Treaty Oak, something I had never thought to do when it was in good health. The tree stands in its own little park just west of downtown Austin. Although in its present condition it is droopy and anemic, with its once-full leaf canopy now pale and sparse, it is still immense. It has the classic haunted shape of a live oak—the contorted trunk, the heavy limbs bending balefully down to the earth, the spreading crown overhead projecting a pointillistic design of light and leaf shadow.

The historical marker in front of the tree perpetuates the myth that Stephen F. Austin signed a treaty with a tribe of Indians—Tonkawas or Comanches—beneath its branches. The marker also states that the tree is six hundred years old, an educated guess that may exaggerate the truth by two hundred years or so. But the tree is certainly older than almost any other living thing in Texas, and far older than the idea of Texas itself. Stephen F. Austin may not have signed his treaty beneath the Treaty Oak, but even in his time it was already a commanding landmark. According to another legend, the tree served as a border marking the edge of early Austin. Children were told by their mothers they could wander only as far as Treaty Oak. Beyond the tree was Indian country.

It was a cool evening in early June when we went by Treaty Oak that first time. I looked down at the kids as they looked up at the tree and thought that this moment had the potential to become for them one of those childhood epiphanies that leave behind, in place of hard memory, a mood or a shadowy image that would pester them all their lives. The several dozen people who had gathered around the tree that evening were subdued, if not downright heartsick. This thing had hit Austin hard. In its soul Austin is a druid capital, a city filled with sacred trees and pools and stones, all of them crying out for protection. When my neighborhood supermarket was built, for instance, it had to be redesigned to accommodate a venerable old pecan tree, which now resides next to the cereal section in a foggy glass box. Never mind that Austin had been rapaciously destroying its environment for years. The *idea* of trees was still enshrined in the civic bosom. In Austin an assault on a tree was not just a peculiar crime; it was an unspeakable crime, a blasphemy.

"Oh, poor thing," a woman said as she stood in front of the ailing oak. Like everyone else there, she seemed to regard the tree as if it were a sick puppy rather than an implacable monument of nature. But you could not help personifying it that way. The tree's inanimate being—its very *lack* of feeling—only made it seem more helpless. Someone had left flowers at its base, and there were a few cards and brave efforts at poems lying about, but there was nowhere near the volume of weird get-well tokens that would come later. On the message board that had been set up, my children added their sentiments. "Get well Treaty Oak," my seven-year-old daughter wrote. "From a big fan of you."

Would it live? The answer depended on the experts you asked, and on their mood at the time. "The Treaty Oak was an old tree before this happened," John Giedraitis, Austin's urban forester, told me as we stood at the base of the tree a few days after Stephen Redding had declared it dead. "It's like an old lady in a nursing home who falls down and breaks her hip. She may survive, but she'll never be the same afterward."

Giedraitis was sipping from a Styrofoam cup half filled with coffee. "If this were a cup of Velpar," he said, holding it up, "about half of the liquid that's in here would have been enough to kill the tree. We think this guy used a whole gallon."

The Treaty Oak poisoning had thrust Giedraitis from his workaday position in an unsung city bureaucracy into a circus of crisis management. His passionate way of speaking had served him well in countless television interviews, and now when he walked down the street in Austin, people turned to him familiarly to inquire about the welfare of the tree. He replied usually in guarded language, in a tone of voice that betrayed his own emotional attachment to the patient. Two years earlier, Giedraitis had proposed to his wife beneath Treaty Oak's branches.

"There was never any question in my mind that Treaty Oak was where I would propose," he said. "That's the power spot. That's the peace spot."

"This is a magnificent creature," he said, standing back to survey the ravaged tree with its startling network of life-support equipment. A series of screens fifty-five feet high guarded the tree from the sun and made the site look from a distance like a baseball stadium. A system of plastic pipes, carrying Utopia Spring Water donated by the company, snaked up its trunk, and every half hour the spring water would rain down upon the leaves.

"You know," Giedraitis went on, "it's hard to sit here over the last six weeks like I have and think it doesn't have some sort of spirit. You saw those roots. This thing is pressed to the earth. This thing is *alive!*"

Giedraitis said he thought the tree might have been poisoned as long as five months before the crime was discovered. He first noticed something wrong on March 2, when he took a group of visiting urban foresters to see Treaty Oak and happened to spot a few strips of dead grass near the tree. The dead grass was surprising but not particularly alarming—it was probably the result of a city employee's careless spraying of a relatively mild chemical edger at the base of the tree.

Treaty Oak seemed fine until the end of May, when a period of heavy rains caused the water-activated Velpar that was already soaking the roots of the tree to rise from its chemical slumber. On the Friday before Memorial Day weekend, Connie Todd, who worked across the street from the tree, noted with concern that its leaves were turning brown. She thought at first it must be oak wilt, which had been decimating the trees in her South Austin neighborhood. But when she looked closer at the leaves, she saw they were dying not from the vein out—the classic symptom of oak wilt—but from the edge inward. Todd called Giedraitis, who looked at the leaves and knew that the tree had been poisoned.

But by what, and by whom, and why? Whoever had applied the poison had poured it not only around the base of the tree but also in a peculiar half-moon pattern to the east. Giedraitis called in tree experts from Texas A&M University and the Texas Forest Service. Samples were taken from the soil to see what kind of poison had been used. Eight inches of topsoil were removed. Amazonian microbes and activated charcoal were injected into the ground.

When the lab reports came back on the poison, Giedraitis was stunned. Velpar! Velpar is the sort of scorched-earth herbicide that is used to eliminate plants and competing trees from pine plantations and Christmas-tree farms. Velpar does not harm most conifers, but it kills just about everything else. The chemical is taken up into a tree by its roots and travels eventually to the leaves, where it enters the chloroplasts and short-circuits the chemical processes by which photosynthesis is conducted. The tree's reaction to these nonfunctioning leaves is to cast them off and bring on a new set. But in a Velpar-infested tree, the new leaves will be poisoned too. The tree dies by starvation. It uses its precious reserves of energy to keep producing new leaves that are unable to fulfill their function of turning sunlight into food.

When Giedraitis and his colleagues discovered that Velpar was the poison, they immediately realized that Treaty Oak was in a desperate condition. As its tainted leaves fell to the ground and a deadly new crop emerged to replace them, outraged citizens called for the lynching of the unknown perpetrator from the very branches of the tree. They suggested that he be forced to drink Velpar. Du Pont, the maker of Velpar, offered a ten-thousand-dollar reward for information leading to the conviction of the person who had so callously misused its product. The Texas Forestry Association chipped in another thousand dollars. Meanwhile a twenty-six-person task force bankrolled by H. Ross Perot convened in Austin and considered courses of treatment. The sun screens were erected, and the tree's upper branches were wrapped in burlap to prevent them from becoming overheated because of the loss of the leaf canopy overhead. Samples showed that the soil was contaminated to a depth of at least thirty-four inches, and so the dirt around the base of the tree was dug out, exposing the ancient roots that had bound the earth beneath the oak for hundreds of years. When the root system became too dense to dig through, the poisoned soil was broken with high-pressure hoses and sluiced away.

A Dallas psychic named Sharon Capehart, in Austin at the invitation of a local radio station, told Giedraitis that the workers had not dug far enough. The tree had spoken to her and told her what their samples confirmed—that there were still six inches of poisoned soil.

Capehart took off her shoes and crawled down into the hole and did a transfer of energy to the tree.

"It was a tremendous transfer," she told me. "But she needed it so much. It was like she was drawing it out of me."

Capehart had determined that Treaty Oak was a female. In another lifetime—when the tree was in human form—it had been Capehart's mother in ancient Egypt. The tree had a name, which it passed on to Capehart, stipulating that she could release it only to the person her spirit guides had revealed to her.

Meanwhile the vigil in front of the Treaty Oak continued. Sharon Capehart wasn't the only one beaming positive energy to the tree. To the protective chain that now cordoned off the Treaty Oak, visitors attached all sorts of get-well exotica: holy cards, photographs, feathers, poems ("Hundreds of you / Fall everyday / The lungs of the World, / by our hands taken down. / Forgive us ancient one"), even a movie pass to the Varsity Theatre, made out in the name of Treaty Oak. People had set coins into the brass letters of the historical marker, and on the ground before it were flowers, cans of chicken soup, crystals, keys, toys, crosses, everything from a plastic unicorn to a bottle of diarrhea medicine.

All of this was so typical of Austin. Looking at this array of talismans, I was convinced anew that Austin would always be the never-never land of Texas. What other city would take the plight of an assaulted tree so grievously to heart or come to its rescue with such whimsical resolve?

There was a suspect. Sharon Capehart had an intimation of a "sandy-haired gentleman with glasses, around the age of thirty-eight," and that was about what the police turned up, though the man was forty-five. His name, Paul Stedman Cullen, had been put forward to the police by several different informants. Paul Cullen worked in a feed store in the nearby suburb of Elroy and lived alone in a truck trailer, where he read science fiction and books on occult magic with solitary fervor. According to the police, his arrest record—for drunken driving, for drug possession, for burglary—dated back more than twenty years. He had lived in California in the sixties, during the salad days of the drug culture, and now he drove a truck with a sign in the rear window that read "Apollyon at the Wheel" and was a self-confessed member of the Aryan Brotherhood.

Paul Cullen had poisoned the tree, the informants told the police, because he wanted to entrap its spiritual energy to win the love of a woman or to ward off a rival. They described the poisonous circle he had drawn at the base of Treaty Oak and mentioned the books—including one called *The Black Arts*—that he might have used as ritualistic manuals.

"Any pagan knows better than to kill a tree," an outraged Austin pagan known as Bel told me. "And *The Black Arts* is nothing but metaphysical masturbation. The reaction of the pagan community to this act is one of disgust."

Before Cullen could be charged with a crime, the tree had to be coolly appraised, using a complicated formula devised by the Council of Tree and Landscape Appraisers. The formula takes into account a tree's species, location, condition, historical value, and trunk size. (According to the guidelines, the current value of a "perfect specimen shade tree" is $27 per square inch of trunk cross section: "The cross section area is determined by the formula 0.7854D, where D equals the diameter measured.") When all the figures were applied, the mighty entity of Treaty Oak was judged to be worth $29,392.69. Because the tree's value was more than $20,000, Cullen was charged with second-degree felony mischief.

"It's tree worship!" Cullen's attorney, Richard C. Jenkins, shouted at me over the phone as he proclaimed his client's innocence. "In my opinion, Paul is a political prisoner. He's being sacrificed in a new kind of witchcraft rite. He could go to jail for *life!* People have really jumped off the deep end on this one. Usually this kind of treatment is reserved for murder victims. Rape victims! Child-molestation victims! But a tree? Come on! I mean, it's a *tree!*"

Though the poisoned soil had been removed from the base of Treaty Oak, the tree was still full of Velpar, and the chemical crept slowly up its trunk and branches, killing off the leaves flush by flush. As a last desperate measure, the tree scientists drilled holes in the trunk of the tree and injected thirty-five gallons of a weak potassium-chloride solution, hoping that this salty flood would help the tree purge itself of the poison.

Sharon Capehart, in Abilene for a radio talk show, felt the tree weeping and calling out to her for another energy transfer. As soon as she was able, she got in her car and headed toward Austin. "Around Georgetown I could really feel her weeping and wanting me to hurry hurry. I told her, 'Just wait. I'm putting the pedal to the metal. I'm getting there.'"

Capehart arrived at Treaty Oak wearing high heels, a tight black skirt, and a red jacket. Her blond hair was teased in a manner that made it look as if it were flaring in the wind. There were four or five other women with her, students and assistants, and they made a circle around the tree, holding out their hands and drawing the negative energy—the Velpar itself—into their bodies and then releasing it into the atmosphere. I was told I would be able to smell the poison leaving the tree, and I did detect an ugly gassy smell that may have been Velpar or may have been fumes from the Chevrolet body shop next door.

Capehart and her team did one transfer and then took a break, smoking cigarettes and waiting for their bodies to recharge their stores of positive energy.

During the second transfer the women each held a limb of the tree, and then they all converged on the trunk, laying their hands flat against the bark. Capehart's head jerked back and forth, and she swayed woozily as a couple of squirrels skittered around the trunk of the tree just above her head.

"Are we doing it, or what?" she called from the tree in triumph. "Two squirrels!"

Capehart's spirit guides had told her that I was the person to whom she should reveal the name of the tree. "Your name was given to me before you ever called," she told me in her hotel room after the transfer. "They let me know you'd try to understand."

She dabbed at her lipstick with a paper napkin and tapped the ash off her cigarette.

"Her name is Alexandria," she said. "Apparently Alexander the Great had started the city of Alexandria in the Egyptian days, and she was named after that. She was of royalty. She had jet-black hair, coal-black, very shiny. She was feminine but powerful. She had slate-blue eyes and a complexion like ivory."

Alexandria had been through many lifetimes, Capehart said, and had ended up as a tree, an unusual development.

"None of the guides or spirits I've communicated with have ever come up in a plant form before," Capehart said. "This is my first as far as plant life goes."

The energy transfer, she said, had gone well. Alexandria had told Capehart that when she began to feel better, she would drop her leaves upon the psychic's crown chakra. Sure enough, as Capehart stood at the base of the tree, she felt two leaves fall onto her head.

"There ain't no way that tree is dead. That spirit has not left that tree. She is a high-level being. They never leave without letting everybody notice."

Entrusted with the name of the tree, I felt compelled to visit it once again. She—I could not help but think of it as a female now—did not look to me as if she could ever recover. There was a fifth flush of poisoned leaves now, and the tree's branches seemed saggy and desiccated. There was not much cause for optimism. At the very best, if Treaty Oak survived, it would not be nearly the tree it had once been.

But even in its ravaged state it remained a forceful presence, a hurt and beckoning thing that left its visitors mute with reverence. And the visitors still came, leaving cards and crystals and messages. All of the attention paid to the tree had created, here and there, a discordant backlash. An anti-abortion crusader had left a prophecy, saying that, because of all the babies "slaughtered without mercy" by the city of Austin, "the tree that she loved will wither and die. Tho' she care for it night and day forever, that tree will not survive." Others complained, in letters to the editor, in press conferences, in editorials, that the money and resources that had been bestowed on the tree should have been used for the poor, the mentally ill, the Indians. They saw the circus surrounding the tree as a sign of cruel indifference, as if this spontaneous display of concern subtracted from, rather than added to, the world's store of human sympathy.

I talked for a while to a man named Ed Bustin, who had lived across the street from Treaty Oak for years and who used to climb it as a boy, working his way up its steady branches to its spreading summit. Another neighbor, Gordon Israel, had gathered up some of Treaty Oak's acorns with his children a year before and now had some eight seedlings that in another five or six hundred years might grow to rival the parent tree. A local foundry operator had put forth the idea to cast the tree in bronze, so that in years to come a full-size statue would mark the spot where Treaty Oak lived and died. And there were other memorial acts planned: The Men's Garden Club of Austin would take cuttings from the dying tree, and corporate sponsors were being sought out to pay for an expensive tissue culture that would ensure genetically identical Treaty Oak clones.

"I hope you live so I can bring my children to see you," read a note left at the tree by J. J. Albright, of La Grange, Texas, age nine. There were innumerable others like it—from other children, from grownups, from bankers, from pagans and Baptists, all of them talking to the tree, all of them wanting in some way to lay their hands upon its dying tissue and heal it. Perhaps this was all nonsense and I had just been living in Austin too long to realize it or admit it to myself. But I was enough of a pagan to believe that all the weirdness was warranted, that Treaty Oak had some message to deliver, and that no one could predict through which channel it would ultimately be received.

My own sad premonition was that the tree would die, though not in the way Sharon Capehart had predicted, in an ascending glory of light. I felt that at some point in the months to come its animate essence would quietly slip away. But for now it was still an unyielding entity, mysteriously alive and demanding, still rooted defiantly to the earth.

Standing there, feeling attuned to the tree's power and to the specter of its death, I recalled with a shudder a ghastly incident I had not thought of in years. When I was in college, a young woman I knew slightly had burned herself to death at the foot of Treaty Oak. I remembered her as bright and funny, carelessly good-looking. But one day she had walked to the tree, poured gasoline all over her body, and struck a match.

The newspaper report said that a neighbor had heard her moan and rushed to her rescue with a half-gallon wine bottle filled with water. By the time he got there she was no longer on fire, but her hair and clothes were burned away and she was in shock, stunned beyond pain. Waiting for the ambulance, they carried on a conversation. She asked the man to kill her. He of course refused, and when he asked her why she had done this to herself, she would not respond. But why here? he wanted to know. Why do it here at the Treaty Oak? For that she had an answer.

"Because," she said, "it's a nice place to be."

18

Sandra Cisneros was born in Chicago in 1954 and now lives in San Antonio. Her undergraduate degree is from Loyola University, and she received her M.F.A. from the University of Iowa. Cisneros has published two books of poetry, but she is best known for her two works of fiction, *The House on Mango Street* (1983) and *Woman Hollering Creek and Other Stories* (1991). "The Monkey Garden" is one of the many evocative stories and vignettes that feature the character of Esperanza, the autobiographical protagonist of *The House on Mango Street.* This story frames her first sexual awareness with her exploration of urban nature in Chicago. It moves from a catalogue of the extravagant vitality and beauty of the urban nature in a nearby open lot to consideration of the interrelated questions of gender and power, ownership and displacement.

The Monkey Garden

Sandra Cisneros

The monkey doesn't live there anymore. The monkey moved—to Kentucky—and took his people with him. And I was glad because I couldn't listen anymore to his wild screaming at night, the twangy yakkety-yak of the people that owned him. The green metal cage, the porcelain table top, the family that spoke like guitars. Monkey, family, table. All gone.

And it was then we took over the garden we had been afraid to go into when the monkey screamed and showed its yellow teeth.

There were sunflowers big as flowers on Mars and thick cockscombs bleeding the deep red fringe of theater curtains. There were dizzy bees and bow-tied fruit flies turning somersaults and humming in the air. Sweet sweet peach trees. Thorn roses and thistle and pears. Weeds like so many squinty-eyed stars and brush that made your ankles itch and itch until you washed with soap and water. There were big green apples hard as knees. And everywhere the sleepy smell of rotting wood, damp earth, and dusty hollyhocks thick and perfumy like the blue-blond hair of the dead.

Yellow spiders ran when we turned rocks over and pale worms blind and afraid of light rolled over in their sleep. Poke a stick in the sandy soil and a few blue-skinned beetles would appear, an avenue of ants, so many crusty ladybugs. This was a garden, a wonderful thing to look at in the spring. But bit by bit, after the monkey left, the garden began to take over itself. Flowers stopped obeying the little bricks that kept them from growing beyond their paths. Weeds mixed in. Dead cars appeared overnight like mushrooms. First one and then another and then a pale blue pickup with the front windshield missing. Before you knew it, the monkey garden became filled with sleepy cars.

Things had a way of disappearing in the garden, as if the garden itself ate them or as if with its old-man memory it put them away and forgot them. Nenny found a dollar and a dead mouse between two rocks in the stone wall where the morning glories climbed, and once when we were playing hide and seek, Eddie Vargas laid his head beneath a hibiscus tree and fell asleep there like a Rip Van Winkle until somebody remembered he was in the game and went back to look for him.

This, I suppose, was the reason why we went there. Far away from where our mothers could find us. We and a few old dogs who lived inside the empty cars. We made a clubhouse once on the back of that old blue pickup. And besides, we liked to jump from the roof of one car to another and pretend they were giant mushrooms.

Somebody started the lie that the monkey garden had been there before anything. We liked to think the garden could hide things for a thousand years. There beneath the roots of soggy flowers were the bones of murdered pirates and dinosaurs, the eye of a unicorn turned to coal.

This is where I wanted to die and where I tried one day but not even the monkey garden would have me. It was the last day I would go there.

Who was it that said I was getting too old to play the games? Who was it I didn't listen to? I only remember that when the others ran, I wanted to run too, up and down and through the monkey garden, fast as the boys, not like Sally who screamed if she got her stockings muddy.

I said Sally come on, but she wouldn't. She stayed by the curb talking to

Tito and his friends. Play with the kids if you want, she said, I'm staying here. She could be stuck-up like that if she wanted to, so I just left.

It was her own fault too. When I got back Sally was pretending to be mad . . . something about the boys having stolen her keys. Please give them back to me she said punching the nearest one with a soft fist. They were laughing. She was too. It was a joke I didn't get.

I wanted to go back with the other kids who were still jumping on cars, still chasing each other through the garden, but Sally had her own game.

One of the boys invented the rules. One of Tito's friends said you can't get the keys back unless you kiss us and Sally pretended to be mad at first but she said yes. It was that simple.

I don't know why, but something inside me wanted to throw a stick. Something wanted to say no when I watched Sally going into the garden with Tito's buddies all grinning. It was just a kiss, that's all. A kiss for each one. So what, she said.

Only how come I felt angry inside. Like something wasn't right. Sally went behind that old blue pickup to kiss the boys and get her keys back, and I ran up three flights of stairs to where Tito lived. His mother was ironing shirts. She was sprinkling water on them from an empty pop bottle and smoking a cigarette.

Your son and his friends stole Sally's keys and now they won't give them back unless she kisses them and right now they're making her kiss them, I said all out of breath from the three flights of stairs.

Those kids, she said, not looking up from her ironing.

That's all?

What do you want me to do, she said, call the cops? And kept on ironing.

I looked at her a long time, but couldn't think of anything to say, and ran back down the three flights to the garden where Sally needed to be saved. I took three big sticks and a brick and figured this was enough.

But when I got there Sally said go home. Those boys said, leave us alone. I felt stupid with my brick. They all looked at me as if *I* was the one that was crazy and made me feel ashamed.

And then I don't know why but I had to run away. I had to hide myself at the other end of the garden, in the jungle part, under a tree that wouldn't mind if I lay down and cried a long time. I closed my eyes like tight stars so that I wouldn't, but I did. My face felt hot. Everything inside hiccupped.

I read somewhere in India there are priests who can will their heart to stop beating. I wanted to will my blood to stop, my heart to quit its pumping. I wanted to be dead, to turn into the rain, my eyes melt into the ground like two black snails. I wished and wished. I closed my eyes and willed it, but when I got up my dress was green and I had a headache.

I looked at my feet in their white socks and ugly round shoes. They seemed far away. They didn't seem to be my feet anymore. And the garden that had been such a good place to play didn't seem mine either.

19

Susan Power, a member of the Standing Rock Sioux tribe, was born in Chicago in 1961. She attended Radcliffe College, received her J.D. from Harvard Law School and M.F.A. from the University of Iowa Writers Workshop. Her writing, including a novel *Grass Dancer* (1995), explores Native American experience, often focusing on a search for connections with the past and with nature. "Chicago Waters" first appeared in *The Place Within,* edited by Jodi Daynard. It examines how we know nature in an urban setting by comparing her mother's nature experiences on the reservation in Fort Gates, North Dakota, with her own adventures on Lake Michigan. As the essay relates her own stories and the tales she has heard from the community, it also explores the role of gender issues in shaping the individual's relationship with nature.

Chicago Waters

Susan Power

My mother used to say that by the time I was an old woman, Lake Michigan would be the size of a silver dollar. She pinched her index finger with her thumb to show me the pitiful dimensions.

"People will gather around the tiny lake, what's left of it, and cluck over a spoonful of water," she told me.

I learned to squint at the 1967 shoreline until I had carved away the structures and roads built on landfill and could imagine the lake and its city as my mother found them in 1942 when she arrived in Chicago. I say "the lake and its city" rather than "the city and its lake" because my mother taught me another secret: the city of Chicago belongs to Lake Michigan.

But which of my mother's pronouncements to believe? That Chicago would swallow the midwestern sea, smother it in concrete, or that the lake wielded enough strength to outpolitic even Mayor Richard J. Daley?

Mayor Daley, Sr., is gone now, but the lake remains, alternately tranquil and riled, changing colors like a mood ring. I guess we know who won.

When my mother watches the water from her lakeside apartment building, she still sucks in her breath. "You have to respect the power of that lake," she tells me. And I do now. I do.

I was fifteen years old when I learned that the lake did not love me or hate me, but could claim me, nevertheless. I was showing off for a boy, my best friend, Tommy, who lived in the same building. He usually accompanied me when I went for a swim, but on this particular day he decided the water was too choppy. I always preferred the lake when it was agitated because its temperature warmed, transforming it into a kind of Jacuzzi.

Tommy is right, I thought, once I saw the looming swells which had looked so unimpressive from the twelfth floor. Waves crashed against the breakwater wall and the metal ladder that led into and out of the lake, like the entrance to the deep end of a swimming pool.

I shouldn't do this, I told myself, but I noticed Tommy watching me from his first-floor window. "I'm not afraid," I said to him under my breath. "I bet you think that I'll chicken out just because I'm a girl."

It had been a hot summer of dares, some foolish, some benign. Sense was clearly wanting. I took a deep breath and leapt off the wall into the turmoil since the ladder was under attack. How did I think I would get out of the water? I hadn't thought that far. I bobbed to the surface and was instantly slapped in the face. I was beaten by water, smashed under again and again, until I began choking because I couldn't catch my breath.

I'm going to die now, I realized, and my heart filled with sorrow for my mother, who had already lost a husband and would now lose a daughter. I fought the waves, struggled to reach the air and the light, the sound of breakers swelling in my ears, unnaturally loud, like the noise of Judgment Day. *Here we go,* I thought. Then I surprised myself, becoming unusually calm. I managed a quick gasp of breath and plunged to the bottom of the lake, where the water was a little quieter. I swam to the beach next door, remaining on the lake floor until I reached shallow waters. I burst to the surface then, my lungs burning, and it took me nearly five minutes to walk fifteen feet, knocked off balance as I was by waves that sucked at my legs. This beach now belongs to my mother and the other shareholders in her building, property recently purchased and attached to their existing lot. But in 1977 it was owned by someone else, and a barbed-wire fence separated the properties. I ended my misadventure by managing to climb over the sharp wire.

I remained downstairs until I stopped shaking. Tommy no longer watched me from his window, bored by my private games, unaware of the danger. I didn't tell my mother what had happened until hours later. I was angry at myself for being so foolish, so careless with my life, but I was never for a moment angry at the lake. I didn't come to fear it either, though it is a mighty force that drops 923 feet in its deepest heart. I understand that it struck indifferently; I was neither target nor friend. My life was my own affair, to lose or to save. Once I stopped struggling with the great lake, I flowed through it, and was expelled from its hectic mouth.

My mother still calls Fort Yates, North Dakota, home, despite the fact that she has lived in Chicago for nearly fifty-five years. She has taken me to visit the Standing Rock Sioux Reservation where she was raised, and although a good portion of it was flooded during the construction of the Oahe Dam, she can point to hills and buttes and creeks of significance. The landscape there endures, outlives its inhabitants. But I am a child of the city, where landmarks are man-made, impermanent. My attachments to place are attachments to people, my love for a particular area only as strong as my local relationships. I have lived in several cities and will live in several more. I visit the country with curiosity and trepidation, a clear foreigner, out of my league, and envy the connection my mother has to a dusty town, the peace she finds on a prairie. It is a kind of religion, her devotion to Proposal Hill and the Missouri River, a sacred bond that I can only half-understand. If I try to see the world through my mother's eyes, find the point where my own flesh falls to earth, I realize my home is Lake Michigan, the source of so many lessons.

As a teenager I loved to swim in the dark, to dive beneath the surface where the water was as black as the sky. The lake seemed limitless and so was I, an arm, a leg, a wrist, a face, indistinguishable from the wooden boards of a sunken dock, from the sand I squeezed between my toes. I always left reluctantly, loath to become a body again and feel more acutely the oppressive pull of gravity.

It was my father who taught me to swim, with his usual patience and clear instructions. First he helped me float, his hands beneath my back and legs, his torso shading me from the sun. Next he taught me to flutter-kick, and I tried to make as much noise as possible. I dog-paddled in circles as a little girl, but my father swam in a straight line perpendicular to shore, as if he were trying to leave this land forever. Just as he had left New York State after a lifetime spent within its borders, easily, without regret. His swim was always the longest, the farthest. Mom and I would watch him as we lounged on our beach towels, nervous that a boat might clip him. It was a great relief to see him turn around and coast in our direction.

"Here he comes," Mom would breathe. "He's coming back now."

My father also showed me how to skip a stone across the water. He was skillful, and could make a flat rock bounce like a tiny, leaping frog, sometimes five or six hops before it sank to the bottom. It was the only time I could imagine this distinguished, silver-haired gentleman as a boy, and I laughed at him affectionately because the difference in our years collapsed.

My mother collects stones in her backyard—a rough, rocky beach in South Shore. She looks for pebbles drilled with holes, not pits or mere scratches, but tiny punctures worn clear through the stone.

"I can't leave until I find at least one," she tells me.

"Why?" I ask. I've asked her more than once because I am forgetful.

"There are powerful spirits in these stones, trying to tunnel their way out."

Ah, that explains the holes. What I do not ask is why she selects them, these obviously unquiet souls, why she places them in a candy dish or a basket worn soft as flannel. What good can it do them? What good can it do her to unleash such restless forces on the quiet of her rooms?

I finger my mother's collection when I'm home for a visit. I have even pressed a smooth specimen against my cheek. The touch is cool, I believe it could draw a fever, and the object is mute and passive in my hand. At first I think there is a failing on my part, I cannot hear what my mother hears, and then I decide that the spirits caught in these stones have already escaped. I imagine them returning to the lake, to the waves that pushed them onto the beach and washed their pebble flesh, because it is such a comfort to return to water.

And then I remember my own weightless immersion, how my body becomes a fluid spirit when I pull myself underwater, where breath stops. And I remember gliding along the lake's sandy bottom as a child, awed by the orderly pattern of its dunes. Lake Michigan is cold, reliably cold, but occasionally I passed through warm pockets, abrupt cells of tepid water that always came as a surprise. I am reminded of cold spots reputedly found in haunted houses, and wonder: Are these warm areas evidence of my lost souls?

A young man drowned in these waters behind my mother's building some years ago. Mom was seated in a lawn chair, visiting with another tenant on the terrace. They sat together facing the lake so they could watch its activity, though it was calm that day, uninteresting. A young man stroked into view, swimming parallel to the shore and headed north. He was close enough for them to read his features; he was fifteen feet away from shallow depths where he could have stood with his head above water. He called to them, a reasonable question in a calm voice. He wanted to know how far south he was. The 7300 block, they told him. He moved on. A marathon swimmer, the women decided. But eventually my mother and her friend noticed his absence, scanned the horizon unable to see his bobbing head and strong arms. They alerted the doorman, who called the police. The young man was found near the spot where he'd made his cordial inquiry.

"Why didn't he cry for help? Why didn't he signal his distress?" my mother asked the response unit.

"This happens all the time with men," she was told. "They aren't taught to cry for help."

So he is there too, the swimmer, a warm presence in cold water or a spirit in a stone.

I have gone swimming in other places—a chlorinated pool in Hollywood, the warm waters of the Caribbean, the Heart River in North Dakota—only to be disappointed and emerge unrefreshed. I am too used to Lake Michigan and its eccentricities. I must have cold, fresh water. I must have the stinking corpses of silver alewives floating on the surface as an occasional nasty surprise, discovered dead and never alive. I must have sailboats on the horizon and steel mills on the southern shore, golf balls I can find clustered around submerged pilings (shot from the local course), and breakwater boulders heavy as tombs lining the beach. I must have sullen lifeguards who whistle to anyone bold enough to stand in three feet of water, and periodic arguments between wind and water which produce tearing waves and lake-spattered windows.

When I was little, maybe seven or eight, my parents and I went swimming in a storm. The weather was mild when we first set out, but the squall arrived quickly, without warning, as often happens in the Midwest. I remember we swam anyway, keeping an eye on the lightning not yet arrived from the north. There was no one to stop us since we were dipping into deep water between beaches, in an area that was unpatrolled. The water was warmer than usual, the same temperature as the air, and when the rain wet the sky, I leapt up and down in the growing waves, unable to feel the difference between air and water, lake and rain. The three of us played together that time; even my father remained near shore rather than striking east to swim past the white buoys. We were joined in this favorite element, splashing, ducking. I waved my arms over my head. My father pretended to be a great whale, heavy in the surf, now and then spouting streams of water from his mouth. He chased me. My mother laughed.

Dad died in 1973 when I was eleven years old, before my mother and I moved to the apartment on the lake. We always thought it such a shame he didn't get to make that move with us. He would so have enjoyed finding Lake Michigan in his backyard.

We buried him in Albany, New York, because that is where he was raised. My mother was born in North Dakota, and I was born between them, in Chicago. There is a good chance we shall not all rest together, our stories playing out in different lands. But I imagine that if a rendezvous is possible—and my mother insists it is—we will find one another in this great lake, this small sea that rocks like a cradle.

We are strong swimmers in our separate ways, my mother like a turtle, my father like a seal. And me? I am a small anonymous fish, unspectacular but content.

20

Leonard Dubkin was a self-described "sidewalk naturalist" who delighted in the nature of Chicago. He was born there in 1904, began studying urban natural history at age nine, and started writing a newspaper column on urban nature (on typewriters from Jane Addams's Hull House) at fifteen. He later wrote a syndicated nature column for the *Chicago Tribune* and essays for *The Atlantic Monthly* and *Coronet.* His books include *Enchanted Streets: The Unlikely Adventures of an Urban Naturalist* (1947), *The White Lady* (1952), *Wolf Point* (1953), *The Natural History of a Yard* (1955), and *My Secret Places: One Man's Love Affair with the City* (1972). He died in Chicago in 1972. As his essay demonstrates, Dubkin's eye for the engaging comic situation often intertwined with his love for urban nature.

Some Experiences with Insects

Leonard Dubkin

A wealth of life exists just above the surface of the earth, between the blades of grass, under fallen leaves and twigs and stones, on and under the bark of trees, and on the leaves and stem and flowers of every plant. There, creatures that vary in size from a tiny fraction of an inch to three and four inches live out their lives, unseen by human eyes, never exciting the wonder or the curiosity of the two-legged animals with whom they share this planet, unaware of the vast changes that man has wrought on the face of this earth. Little beings as weird in appearance as though they had been dreamed in a nightmare, as fantastically made as though their organs had been thrown together haphazardly, with habits as varied and as strange as though they had been conceived by a madman; and yet each one singularly fitted for a particular role in life, for a particular duty on earth, for an honored place in the scheme of existence.

Just to study the ants alone, to observe the habits of the different kinds of ants and try to solve the enigmas of their actions and behavior, would take many lifetimes. There are ants that spend their entire lives capturing slaves to do their work for them; others keep herds of plant lice, or aphids, which they milk. One variety of ant does nothing but plant and cultivate huge underground gardens of the mushrooms on which they feed; others march through the grass in long lines with bits of leaves they are bringing home held over their heads like umbrellas. There are individual ants of one species which attach themselves to the ceiling of the burrow and hang there for months, fed by the others until they are round little barrels that act as food reservoirs. There are ants that have a highly developed sense of social consciousness, others that are predaceous. Some live in trees, others in the ground. Some species are carnivorous, others eat only a particular kind of fungus.

And yet ants are only one kind of insect in the vast multitude that inhabit the earth. There are also the beetles; those that roll carrion into huge balls, those that drag dead birds or mice underground, embalm them, and raise their young on the flesh, those that fly and others that are earthbound. There are also many different kinds of bees, and wasps, and flies, and butterflies and moths, and dragonflies and mosquitoes and midges, and spiders, and grasshoppers and leafhoppers and crickets and ticks—and a thousand others. And then there are a host of insects so insignificant to man, of so little interest to the ordinary human being, that they do not even have common names, but, if they are ever referred to at all, are called simply "bugs"—except by entomologists, who have long Latin names for them.

To me the most amazing thing about these tiny creatures is that they abound everywhere; every field in the country is filled with them, as well as every yard and alley and empty lot in the city, and even the cracks in the city pavement. It is true that some tropical insects are found only in the jungles of Africa and South America; but on the other hand hundreds of common northern insects do not breed in the tropics, so that as many different species can probably be found on a front lawn in the city on a summer day as anywhere in Africa. Yet no one in the city would think of sitting on his front lawn for an hour to watch the strange, incredible, fantastic little beings going about the business of living out their lives. Many people will read books about them: they will read Maeterlinck on the bees, Fabre on ants, and magazine articles about the engineering abilities of spiders; but after they have read and marveled their curiosity is satisfied, they have no desire to watch these things themselves. It is too bad that this should be so, for there is as much difference between, for example, a magazine description of a spider spinning her web and the actual observance of a spider running back and forth from twig to leaf to grass stem, tightening the threads of her web, as there is between a newspaper description of a sunset and the observance of the changing colors of the western sky at evening.

During the period of my unemployment the world of insects was for me a refuge from the human world in which I felt myself an outcast. Whenever I felt depressed and melancholy, when, after answering help-wanted ads in the newspapers and going from building to building "seeing" my friends, it seemed to me that there was no place for me in the society of my kind, that I was a useless individual in a busy world, I would walk to one of the little parks near the Loop, or to a grassy place beside the river, and spend an hour or two watching the insects. And unlike the feeling of superiority I got from looking down on the city from a great height, watching the insects on the ground had the effect of completely obliterating the world of human beings from my mind, it was like a drug that deadened my memory, and left no aftereffect, no hangover.

At first when I sat down in the grass, with the noises of the city all about me, the rattle and clang of streetcars, the blowing of auto horns, the chugging of a locomotive somewhere in the distance, and the shrill blowing of a policeman's whistle, there would be no sign of activity on the ground, nothing moving in the grass. I had chosen a barren spot, I would think, there were no insects here at all. But as I continued to stare at the ground and my eyes became focused to the small, I would become aware of a movement in the grass, perhaps an ant, or a hairy brown caterpillar, or a little fly with golden body. Once the first thing I saw was a spotted ladybug moving sedately up a blade of grass. When she came to the top she went over and continued down the other side, then on to the next blade of grass. I got down on one elbow and watched her go from stem to stem, up one side and down the other, until she came to a spot of black on a grass stem, where she stopped. I moved my head directly behind her for a closer look and saw that the black spot was made up of tiny aphids or plant lice, each with its threadlike beak stuck into the stem sucking the juice. The ladybug was methodically gobbling up the aphids, one to a mouthful, until there were none left. Then she continued up and down the grass stems until she came to another colony of aphids, where she duplicated the voracious procedure.

Another time, on a leaf of a small bush, I saw a queerly shaped green bug that looked like a tiny triangle with two bulging eyes on top. I had often seen these bugs when I was a boy, and had marveled at their strange appearance.

Why were they shaped like triangles, I wondered, and what were they for, what purpose did they serve in the insect world? In those days I believed that every living thing had a purpose in life, that every species of animal was like a gear wheel that meshed with the other species to form the vast machine of nature. There were plants to manufacture the foodstuffs essential to life from a synthesis of sunlight, water, and the bacteria in the ground, and insects to spread the pollen and keep destructive plants down, and birds and animals to scatter the seeds and consume the foodstuffs; and when the birds and animals died they were eaten by the bacteria in the ground to complete the cycle. If there was some form of life that did not seem to fit into this scheme, it was only because I had not yet discovered its purpose. Maybe when I was grown-up and had become a naturalist, I would think, I would know what it was.

So I used to watch these bugs closely every time I saw one, and the only thing I ever saw them do was walk about on leaves, then lift their heavy wing covers, like a little old lady lifting her skirts to cross a street, and fly off. I had heard them called stinkbugs, because when they were disturbed they shot off a little vapor of evil-smelling stuff; but the descriptions of them in the books on entomology I had read did not mention a common name, and the scientific name was so long and meaningless that I never could remember it.

Another thing that puzzled me about this bug was the location of its thorax. I could not afford a cyanide jar in which to kill the insects I wanted for my collection, but I had read somewhere that a practical and inexpensive method of killing insects was to pinch the thorax firmly. This method served me very well, and the slight disfigurement of my insect specimens was hardly noticeable when they were mounted. But where was the thorax of this triangular bug? It was shaped somewhat like an armored tank, and its thorax was hidden somewhere within the armor. Each time I tried to kill one I would invariably pinch the wrong part of its anatomy, and the body fluids would come oozing out, leaving a shapeless mass unfit for mounting. So I never had a stinkbug in my collection.

But to return to the present—I once saw one of these bugs on a leaf of a small bush that grew in an empty lot east of Michigan Boulevard, where I had gone to recuperate from a day of looking for work. I put my head down close to the leaf and stared at it, marveling at its odd shape. I was not interested in the location of its thorax now, for there would be no purpose in killing it—I no longer had a collection. The little bug walked to the edge of the leaf, then turned and went under it. I turned the leaf about by the stem so I could watch it, and saw, peacefully grazing on the underside of the leaf which was uppermost now, a green caterpillar with two rows of yellow dots along its back. The triangular bug approached the caterpillar, and as it came close there issued from its head, under the armor, a long, jointed, pipelike affair with a point at the end, like a plumber's pipe that had not been joined together evenly. Then the bug rushed fiercely at the caterpillar, and I thought of an armored knight with a crooked lance attacking a huge dragon.

The end of the stinkbug's pipe penetrated the side of the caterpillar, and the bug quickly raised his pipe high in the air and held the squirming caterpillar impaled there. For a long time he stood motionless, holding that wriggling dragon that must have weighed five times as much as himself. What was he doing with it? I wondered. Was he some insect sadist watching the death throes of an impaled caterpillar? Or was he merely waiting for it to die so he could eat it?

After a time the caterpillar stopped squirming, it hung limp and lifeless from the bug's pipe. Then the bug lowered its pipe, brushed the caterpillar off on the edge of the leaf, and walked away. I picked the caterpillar up from the ground where it had fallen and held it between my fingers. It was thin and hollow inside; the stinkbug had drained it of its juices. What a horrible way to die, I thought, to have one's insides slowly drained out while hanging in the air. And yet it seemed horrible only to me, to the human observer. Delicacy of feeling did not exist in nature, and no creature but man had ever felt either pity or remorse. The stinkbug had been provided with only one method of getting its food, and this was it. To the caterpillar it was a natural death, neither better nor worse than any other. There was no question of cruelty involved here, for cruelty was a concept that had been evolved in the brain of man, and it had no existence for these little creatures, nor anywhere in nature.

Late one afternoon I was walking on the east side of Michigan Boulevard, near the Art Institute, when I decided to sit down on the grass for a while and rest. There were others sitting there, a few ragged old men who looked like vagrants, and a young girl sitting cross-legged with a book open in her lap. It was a hot day, and the passers-by were mopping their faces with damp handkerchiefs, the men with their coats off, collars open and sleeves rolled up. I sat for a time watching the cars rushing by, then stopping in a row when the traffic light was red. What a silly, senseless life people led in a big city, I thought. Here were these men and women driving cars, they rushed madly down the Boulevard as fast as the law would allow them to go, zipping around cars that were moving too slowly, honking their horns wildly when it seemed as though they might have to slow down to let some pedestrian cross the street. Then they came to a traffic light that was red, and they calmly sat in their motionless cars staring out of the windshield, waiting for the light to change so they could go tearing ahead again.

As I sat there I heard, through the noise of the traffic and the talking of the passers-by, the thin, high, intermittent shrilling of a cricket somewhere under the grass. Now the singing of a cricket has always been a sort of challenge to me; it sets off in my mind, each time I hear it, some compulsion to track the little insect down and watch it producing its rasping sound. Hundreds of times, both as a boy and as a man, I have crept cautiously up to the spot from which the shrilling came, and dozens of times I have been close enough to see the cricket, but each time the insect has become aware of my presence and stopped singing, so that all I ever succeeded in seeing was a little black insect scurrying away under the grass. I have read, of course, that they produce the sound by rubbing their wing-covers together, but that is not the same as seeing the sound being produced, it is as though all one knew about human speech was the fact that it is produced by a vibration of the vocal chords.

I got up, looked about to be sure no one was watching me, then cautiously approached the place from which the sound was coming. Twice the cricket became frightened and stopped singing, and each time I stopped where I was and stood motionless until the singing started again. When I was directly above the sound I lowered myself carefully to the ground, looked about again, then lay down on my stomach with my head a few inches above the grass. As slowly and as gently as I could I brought my head down to the level of the grass and peered between the blades.

At first I could not see anything, there was only a dim blackness between the grass and the earth. The cool, dank, heavy smell of earth and growing grass filled my nostrils, and the piercing clamor of the cricket's song so close to my ears obliterated the city sounds all around me; I might have been lying on my stomach in some country field miles from any house or town. As my eyes became accustomed to the darkness under the grass I began to make out little objects, a twig and a few stones, an old curled-up brown leaf, and the grass stems going into the ground. A black ant came into view, rushed about busily first one way and then another, and finally disappeared under the curled-up leaf. But I could not see the cricket, though the scraping of his wing-covers filled my ears.

Then at last I saw him. He was standing on the end of a little twig that came out of the ground at an angle, his legs gripping the twig, his long, angular hind legs projecting out behind him like two braces. I could see him start his song, by raising his wing-covers and vibrating them against each other for a few seconds, then slow the vibrations until the shrill rasping trailed off into little clicks of sound. After each burst of song he changed his position on the twig, loosening his grip and revolving a little to the right or left, like an opera singer shifting his stance for another aria.

Soon I became aware of another cricket, smaller than the first, crawling up the twig toward the singer. It was, I decided, a female, for she crawled slowly up the twig with a sort of feminine meekness, as though she were attracted by the song but was not sure what sort of reception she would get from the singer. While he was singing she did not move, but crouched low on the twig as though overcome with worshipful adoration, as though she did not dare interrupt his singing; it was only during the short silent intervals that she dared to move toward him.

When she stood before him he stopped his scraping, lowered his head toward her, and felt her with his antennae. Then he raised his head and went on with his singing, while she stood meekly before him. Well, I thought, this is a fine situation. His beautiful singing has won him a mate, but he doesn't want her, she doesn't appeal to him. Perhaps he's an aesthetic cricket, rubbing his wing-covers together just for the joy of hearing his own song. He probably believes in art for art's sake, and is repulsed by the thought of using his song for material ends, like attracting a female.

But the lady knew her rights; when she saw that he was paying no attention to her she rushed at him fiercely, butting him so hard that he broke off his singing and rolled over on the twig, hanging under it by his legs. Then he turned so he was standing atop the twig again, and for a few seconds the two insects looked into each other's eyes. What thoughts were going on behind those eyes, in those rudimentary little brains? The situation seemed similar to one in which two human beings might find themselves: it was a case of a girl who had thrown herself at the feet of a man she worshiped, and had been repulsed. And yet how could I know that these insects were thinking what a man and a woman would think in like circumstances? I could only guess at their reactions, I could only be certain that some sort of drama was being enacted here, on a tiny twig underneath the grass. It might be a drama like a million others that were taking place in and on the earth, beneath stones, under the bark of trees, on waving grass-stems, on leaves high in the air, and in the homes of people. But these little creatures standing on their twig looking into each other's eyes could not know that; to them it was a singular affair, so personal to themselves that it could not possibly occur to anyone else.

When the two crickets had looked their fill the smaller one turned about and crouched down on the twig, the end of her glossy black body glistening in the other's face. They must have reached some agreement, I thought, for now the male rose to the occasion, he scrambled quickly between her legs. It was then that I became aware of voices about me, and I realized with a start where I was.

"Why doesn't somebody call an ambulance?" a woman's voice was saying.

Then a man's voice said, "He's probably just drunk. Come on, help me turn him over."

I turned over and sat up in one swift motion, and, blinking my eyes in the sudden strong light, saw a crowd of people grouped around me in a circle. For a second no one moved, they all stared down at me as though I were a corpse that had suddenly come to life. Finally one man leaned down toward me and asked, "You all right?"

"Yeah," I said, "I'm all right." Then I got up hurriedly, pushed my way through the gaping crowd, and walked as quickly as I could down Michigan Boulevard, acutely conscious of the eyes that were following me, my face burning with embarrassment.

21

Ronald L. Fair was born in Chicago in 1932. He has taught at Wesleyan University, Northwestern University, and Columbia College of Chicago; and he won an Arts and Letters Award from the National Institute of Arts and Letters. His fiction about African-American life includes *Many Thousand Gone: An American Fable* (1965), *We Can't Breathe* (1972), and *Hog Butcher* (1975). The short story "Thank God It Snowed" first appeared in the *American Scholar* where it was erroneously described as an essay. It was then expanded to become the first chapter of his autobiographical novel *We Can't Breathe.* This short story, like the rest of Fair's Chicago fiction, describes the harsh realities of ghetto life in a prose style that fuses naturalistic description and symbolic commentary. It conveys how poverty and ethnicity shape the protagonist's view of nature.

Thank God It Snowed

Ronald L. Fair

But there were cool times, too. There were the rains that came in the spring and the fall. The rain.

Sometimes it rained so hard that the sewers plugged up within three minutes. We would be outside, playing in a vacant lot, and before we could reach cover we were soaked, and the lot, weeds worn down and away by our persistent feet, was turned to mud. The rain fell like heavy hands on a drum, and the mud thinned, and colored the rain.

We ran. We ran to shelter. Not so much because we were afraid of getting wet, but because none of us wanted to go through that painful experience of having our parents look at us and accuse us of not having enough sense to come in out of it. We ran. And no matter how fast we ran, we could never keep time with the rapid cadence of the thousands, of the millions of raindrops. The rain came on us like a great mysterious, cleansing thing that cleared the air of all dust and brightened and recolored things with a kind of gentle rendering that lasted for days; that sometimes lasted long enough for us to forget how dirty things had been before it came with the sweet breezes from the lake.

The sewers were totally ineffective, and we were delighted, because it meant that we had pools of water for sailing our popsicle-stick boats, the tarred streets and curbs refusing to let the water escape. Those of us who were truly adventurous wandered into the vacant lots and sailed our tiny cruisers on much more lavish waters.

Strange, now that I look back on the rain of my childhood, that I never think of it as being an unpleasant experience to be wet with rain. Oh, we sang songs about chasing the rain away, and we had little sayings that were passed on from generation to generation; some of them had probably come to us from as far back as the superstitious people hundreds of years before. When there was a flash of lightning that streaked across the sky, a child would say, "The devil's beatin' his wife." And when the deafening explosion of thunder followed, another child would reply, "Yeah, man, but she's fightin' back." And strange, too, that I think of it as being always a blessing that cooled the city. But I cannot forget the icy rain that fell in the fall and winter, chilling us through our heavy wool jackets and two sweaters, and a shirt, and even through our long underwear. We laughed at each other, mocking the one who shivered the most and then ultimately praising him. "Man, this cat keeps himself warm by shivering. Must be the warmest cat outside today."

Those fall rains were a prelude to the heavy gray cloud that would be with us for months to come. There would be snow after them, but the snow would be transformed almost immediately as it worked its way through the perpetual grit-cloud that hovered over our city, so that the grayness of the outside would blend with the grayness of our worlds inside where we spent the winter months keeping our roaches and rats fat so that they could go on producing their newborns along with us come the spring.

I remember that spring I became aware of the necessity of rain. I remember that spring I realized that had the rain not come, had it not washed down the buildings, had it not methodically worn away the industrial waste from the trees and shrubbery, had it not washed away the millions of tiny particles in swirling whirlpools that only little children can appreciate, had it not brightened, as it fell through the almost invisible powder that formed a poisonous gas working on our lungs, had it not given us pure air to breathe, we would have been asphyxiated by our misery. The spring rains would go on for about two months, and during that time we were distracted from the unpleasantness inside by the brightness and beauty the rain created outside. (Even weeds growing six feet high in a vacant lot can be beautiful when there is nothing else growing.) The rains would continue and we would try to soak them into our souls because soon the heat of summer would be with us, and with it would come the extreme depression of that gray grit-cloud that tried to remind us of our place in society.

But of all the seasons, winter was the most impressive. It was always beautiful in the winter. Everything was clean and smelled even better than it did after a spring rain. The temperature was often zero or below, and, with holes in our shoes and no rubbers, our feet were always wet and cold. But it was a good time of year. Most of us carried pieces of newspaper in our pockets and when the paper in our shoes became too wet we would step inside someone's doorway and change the expendable linings. There was snow everywhere and the half-dozen or so sleds on the block were enough to accommodate the thirty or forty children.

Snowplows never came through our neighborhood. It was good they didn't because the snow was a wedge against a reality we were glad not to face. I thank God it snowed as much as it did when we were young. I thank God we were freed from everything that was familiar.

Sometimes it seemed to snow for days; as if the elements had contrived to free us by transforming ugliness into beauty. There were other parts of the city that hated to see the snow come, and their snowplows worked almost daily trying to set the calendar back. But we prayed for it in our neighborhood. There were no landscaped gardens for us. There had been no year of fun on the golf course. There was no grass to be covered up, only broken glass and pages of old newspapers dancing in the wind with the leaves from the big cottonwoods that were always shedding something. There were no rose bushes that had to be protected against the subzero temperature, only weeds that were more than strong enough to fend for themselves. There was really not much beauty at all, only a gray, dirty, sad world we had lived in for nine months, and we were delighted to see it changed.

In the alleys the snow packed down hard on the mounds of garbage and provided us with hills for sliding. It leveled the uneven sidewalks. It even painted the buildings and filled the holes in the streets and in yards, and laid lawns, for once, over all the neighborhood. It was clean. It was pure. It was good.

With the coming of the snow, life became gentler as sounds became muffled. The snow was so special that all the children in the neighborhood respected its holiness and played more quietly.

Sampson would still come through three days a week, but he didn't sell much ice now. Who needed ice when every windowsill was a refrigerator? The other four days of the week he would deliver coal. But there was one very cold winter when he figured out a way to sell both at the same time. He built wooden platforms on both sides of his truck and he lined them with ice and then covered the ice with canvas so it didn't get coal dust on it. And then, inside the truck, he dumped two or three tons of coal. He still didn't sell much ice, but at least he was able to travel the alleys in good conscience that year.

When we were very young we ate the snow. As we grew a little older, we washed girls' faces in it. And as we became of age, we rolled it up in little balls and threw them at shiny new cars driven by white people passing through our neighborhood on their way to work.

It was indeed beautiful in the winter. I remember one year the snow was so high that, as we ran down the wavy path that led in front of the buildings, we had to jump up to see over the top. And it was always clean! An empty wine bottle was swallowed up by it, and tucked away so we wouldn't have to see it for a while. Old Jesse, who was always vomiting his insides up early in the morning so that we'd see it on the way to school, was temporarily forgotten because the snow covered over his chili-mack and sweetened the air again. Inside the doorways of the buildings the urine smell was still there, but not outside in the gangways like it was the rest of the year. Outside it smelled like it did everywhere else in the city; like it smelled where people had jobs and money. Outside it was like a dream and it was a pleasure to get soaked with it; chilled and shivering until we could stand it no longer. And even then we didn't want to go in, for inside was a reality that no climatic conditions could change. Even on Christmas Day with snow everywhere and a few toys under the trees and the radio playing Christmas music, and people saying "God bless you" everywhere in the world, even on *Christmas Day* when it grew late and we stepped inside our dungeons we realized that those God-bless-yous were not meant for us.

22

Jan Zita Grover is a former AIDS worker who moved from San Francisco to Minnesota after she became exhausted by her intense relationships with friends who were dying. In her essay collection, *North Enough and Other Clear-Cuts* (1997), Grover explores the similarities between the bodies of her dying friends and the north country woods devastated by logging. *Northern Waters* (1999) describes what happens when she submits herself to "the tutelage of waters" by learning to flyfish. She now lives in Duluth, Minnesota, but the "Minnehaha Creek" essay from that book describes her unique Zen fishing experiences in Minneapolis. The essay engages the reader through an instructive paradox: how fishing these fishless city waters enabled her to acquire a deeper understanding of place and urban nature.

Minnehaha Creek

Jan Zita Grover

My home stream for four years was a Zen fishing paradise: a mazy, meandering tailwater that ran twenty-eight miles from dam to mouth, most of it beneath a pleached archway of elms, ashes, cottonwoods, and poplars. Kingfishers, green-backed herons, great blue herons, white-breasted nuthatches, tree and barn swallows, swifts, hooded mergansers, goldeneyes, and Canada geese rode its waters and dived from its streamside trees. A few warm days in winter opened up channels broad enough for casting, and in summer the water was usually high enough to provide two to three feet midstream, and often more along the grass-lined outer bank.

But a *Zen* stream? Well, yes. This creek offered fishing, but no fish—a daily ritual of casting, feeling the water eddy 'round my legs, noting the changes in water level and temperature, the progress of seasons marked by vegetation, insects, and birds. But as for fish, those were few and far between—according to the DNR's metro manager, a few sunfish, bluegills, the vagrant bass or pike who washed over the dam far upstream.

In any case, the creek's few finned beings were wholly safe from me. I not only didn't seek them, I didn't even cast a fly. But I was nonetheless gratified when I ran into fish—or rather, when one of them ran into me. One late spring morning, for example, I was standing midstream, casting against the current, when something with the resilience of an inflated inner tube bumped hard into my left calf and briefly wrapped itself around my leg. A dark shape glimpsed, then gone beneath the hard-running water. My first and only thought was a pike—several years ago, a child angler had caught a respectable eighteen-inch snake, as small pike are sometimes called locally, in a pool just upstream of where I now stood. But before I could further puzzle out the fish's identity, rain began dimpling the water, and the crowns of the creekside trees fanned open beneath a heavy northwest wind. A late May storm was coming on, thunder predicted, so I reluctantly reeled in and left the water for the morning. Five minutes later, when the storm broke, I was already at home in southwest Minneapolis.

My homewater was Minnehaha Creek, which is fed by Lake Minnetonka and regulated at Gray's Bay Dam by the Minnehaha Creek Watershed District (MCWD). The creek may have been fishless for all intents and purposes by the time it reached Fifty-second Street and Xerxes, where I faithfully haunted its waters each day, but it was in every other way an interesting stream.

Before it was dammed for lumber, furniture, and grist mills in the 1850s to 1870s, Minnehaha Creek swam with pike, bass, sunfish, and suckers. In 1852, Colonel John Owens, publisher of the weekly *Minnesotan* (St. Paul), wrote about an expedition he and his party had made to Lake Minnetonka, during which they "caught fish enough to feed all twelve hungry men" from Minnehaha Creek. "Fishing for about twenty minutes more, they brought in more than a total of about forty pounds." Even the first generation of dams on the creek apparently didn't destroy its fish populations; Coates P. Bull, whose family farmed alongside one of the creek's tributaries around 1900, recalled pickerel, bass, sunfish, and other fish in great numbers: "Suckers and Redhorse each spring swam from Lake Harriet through the outlet into Minnehaha. . . . They 'paid toll' aplenty; for settlers, even from Eden Prairie and miles to the west, brought their spears to harvest bushels of these fish to eat and to feed pigs."[1]

But as the wetlands adjoining Lake Minnetonka and the creek were drained for farms, roads, and homes, the creek's water level began to drop and to fluctuate dramatically. There were years when the creek almost dried up. By 1928, when Otto Schussler published his *Riverside Reveries,* Minnehaha Creek had "almost ceased, for a great part of each year at any rate, to be a stream." Finally, in 1963, the MCWD was formed to regulate water levels and water quality in the creek's 169-square-mile watershed. At the Gray's Bay Dam on Lake Minnetonka, waters above a set minimum level are released into the creek. Creek levels are also increased during peak canoeing/tubing season (July to August) unless there's a drought. In 1979, the Creekside chapter of the Izaak Walton League cleaned up the creek from Gray's Bay down to Minneapolis; the garbage they collected filled two dump trucks.

Living about twenty-one miles downstream from Gray's Bay Dam, I witnessed the creek's almost daily and seemingly fickle fluctuations. In early May, despite snowmelt and ice going out on Lake Minnetonka, the creek was usually starved for water throughout its Minneapolis course. Even the old mill pond below East Minnehaha Parkway at Thirty-fourth Avenue receded from its usually brimming banks. Farther upstream, every storm drain leading into the creek hung suspended three or four feet above the usual water level. Ducks waiting for open water crowded into discontinuous puddles like so many commuters pressing onto rush-hour trains.

And then, just as inexplicably, sometime during the night near the end of the month, the water would begin spilling over the dam again. The next morning, the creek was a good three feet higher, its muddy flats vanished. Buffleheads and mallards floated contentedly on winter-cold pools beneath the naked trees.

Most of the Minneapolis miles of Minnehaha Creek provided great opportunities for everything that makes fly fishing gratifying *except* the likelihood of hooking fish. The creek's width varied roughly between ten and twenty-five feet when the water was running 150 cubic feet per second or faster. Its structure was classic: runs, riffles, pocket waters, pools filled with many of the same aquatic invertebrates I had learned to expect to find in trout waters: stonefly, mayfly, and caddis-fly nymphs colonized the rocks that dotted its sand bottom; black-fly larvae clung there, too, swaying by silk threads in the current. Winter and summer, fine blooms of midges lifted suddenly into the air at twilight, followed in summer by great cartwheeling hoards of swallows and swifts, who picked them off as quickly as they arose from the water. In late June and July, iridescent blue damselflies courted and mated in midair, on the surface of the water, on the yellow flag and cattails at the water's edge.

By foregoing the opportunity to cast for fish, I was able to sample other pleasures in a focused, relaxed way. No two and a half-hour drive, no burning of hydrocarbons to get my conservation-minded self farther and farther out of town; no night driving. In exchange for an absence of fish, I got everything else that made small-stream fishing worthwhile. Need I add that the creek was uncrowded? The only time I found anyone else casting there, it was because I had told Sam and Kim about it. But I did not see them on the creek again.

Plenty of people stopped their cars alongside my stretch to ask if there were really fish in Minnehaha Creek or to comment on my casting. After I told them that the creek was practically fishless and pulled my line from the water to show them the yarn at the end of my tippet, most of them just stared at me, bemused or disgusted, shook their heads, and climbed back into their cars. I, in turn, was bemused by sidewalk anglers whose view of fishing was so instrumental that they were flummoxed by my admission that I wasn't even rigged to catch anything. But I savored the company of others who stopped to reminisce about their favorite streams, try a few casts with my rod, or comment that midcity, midstream casting looked like a great way to unwind after a day's work.

The last year I haunted Minnehaha Creek, I was occasionally tempted to tie on a fly, *just in case.* Like the boy in Dr. Seuss's *McElligott's Pool,* how did I *know* what I might find swimming in those clear rushing waters below the roadway? But I didn't really want to connect with any of the creek's few fish via a hook. Life in that creek of wildly fluctuating temperature and depth was hard enough for them; why add to their stresses? I had come to value the creek for itself and for the complex community of creatures who populated its banks and streambed.

Occasionally, as if stringing me along, the creek presented me with fishy surprises. I found the little pike floating head down in the shallow water of the creek one late July evening, his V-shaped lower jaw pointed toward the sand, his tubular body stiff with muscle—or was it with death? I filled a plastic bucket from the car with the water he had died in and took him home.

Over the sink, I took the pike out and turned him over and over. Sheathed in a transparent film like human snot, he slid through my fingers speedily, as if even dead he still wanted to get away. His scales were so embedded that he seemed scaleless, suited instead in a shiny green lamé cape that paled where it descended his sides to an opal white belly. Pale yellow-green jottings fretted his back as if he had been stippled with a Magic Marker. His eyes were still clear, a large luminous yellow, and flat. He would have seen well to the sides but perhaps not immediately ahead.

I admired his head: long-billed, like a fishing duck's. His gill covers were bright green, and behind them bristled rows of short, thick gill rakers, waxy-white prison bars of bone. I pried open his mouth and ran my fingers lightly over the dog teeth in his lower jaw, the volmer teeth crowding the roof of his mouth like stalactites, and those that heaved upward from his tongue, the teeth of a predator who clamps down on his prey and shakes or crunches it to death. (It is not uncommon for anglers to catch pike with the tails of their most recent prey still protruding from their bills.) On his belly I found the tiny anal opening—an inny like a child's umbilicus—and dorsal and anal fins riding his body far to the rear, faintly red, just like in pictures. I held him up to my nose and sniffed: *Fresh.* He smelled of fertile water and the creatures living in it.

Next I laid the pike on his back on my cutting board and sliced him open from throat to peduncle. This was not an easy task; his skin was a sturdy tegument, for all its slithy suppleness. In the end, I used my kitchen shears below the first inch of incision, cutting rather than slicing my way toward his tail. It was like cutting through particularly thick felt or leather. His skin and muscle lifted away from the bones beneath and parted like an open shirt beneath my blades. The bones were transparent and delicate, almost weightless: they had none of the gravity and opacity of mammal bones, having no need to support the animal's weight in his weightless medium of water. Instead, they merely wrapped and secured his organs, provided anchors for the muscles that attached his fins.

Within him the scent of creek was stronger and more distinct than without. I smelled water, dust, decay, mold, green bottom grasses, elodea, and algae, as if the incision I made had torn open the creek itself. They were pleasing, pungent smells, ones I knew I could not easily erase. They bloomed into my kitchen, which became odorous and charged with the smell of water and dying. The dogs gathered at my ankles and cocked their heads, beating their tails softly against the linoleum, questioning, hoping.

The pike's liver was long and pale. Over it hung his swim bladder, a deflated balloon. Behind and below the liver I found his heart and kidney, dark glowing stones, and farther down, his testicles, creamy and elongated. I took these out and returned them to the bucket of water.

His stomach and intestine were what I was after. Like his predator cousin, the human, the pike has a sizable stomach capable of expanding or contracting dramatically with the fortunes of feeding, and a simple intestine—a straight-shot tube for absorbing flesh. I removed the stomach and intestine and opened them. They were pale, glassy organs, almost vitreous in appearance, shining and clean. Both were empty, untenanted. They hardly seemed to be doing the job of absorptive organs: they had no apparent work.

Had the small pike starved, then, or had he simply died after absorbing his final meal? He was about sixteen inches long from the tip of his snout to mid-peduncle, and in girth no more than five inches. He would have found few creatures other than bottom-dwelling nymphs of mayfly, stonefly, damselfly and caddis fly in the creek's low waters, and few of them at this time of year. I had found him twenty-one miles downstream from the dam where he would have entered the creek. Only the first four miles below the dam are rich with crustaceans in the muddy bottoms; only those first four miles and the mill pond farther below are deep enough to provide a coolwater fish with the temperature range his kind prefers.

He had appeared, already dead or dying, in less than three inches of warm downstream water, the dam at Gray's Bay having been mysteriously closed for over a week, sending others, I am sure, to a similar fate.

But had he starved to death? Pike feed at the top of the food chain they are links of. They are versatile predators who eat insects, crustaceans, other fish, birds, and small mammals, including, if popular lore is to be credited, pet toy poodles. Larry Finnell's 1982 to 1986 study of fish in Elevenmile Reservoir, Colorado, found that the stomach contents of pike consisted of about 7 percent kokanee salmon; 9 percent other fish (suckers, bullhead, dace, etc.); 18 percent crayfish; 25 percent rainbow trout; 36 percent miscellaneous invertebrates (scuds, damselfly and mayfly nymphs). Thirty-seven percent had empty stomachs. No one knows what to make of the high incidence of pike with empty stomachs. They are opportunistic feeders, more sluggish in warm weather than in cool, so perhaps they simply weren't feeding heavily when caught. In a reservoir whose level was less manipulated by humans than Minnehaha Creek, the pike would either have been eaten or have found adequate prey of his own, not this death in what amounted to a watery desert after the floodgates had closed.

Warm, shallow water: little of the dissolved oxygen a fast-moving, ambushing predator relies on. Even to my 37° C human toes, the water had felt ripe with rot, and sun-warm. Perhaps, then, he had suffocated? Suffocated, or starved?

The underside of his jaw was waxy white, the skin over his submaxilla pierced by ten sensory pores, five to a side. The gill covers flared. His throat skin was crêpey and fine as pongée silk. I sunk my index and middle fingers beneath the archway of his lower jaw, using what is known as the Leech Lake lip lock, a method for handling living pike without being bitten by them. I hefted him for weight: perhaps two pounds. Then I cut off his head and opened his gills, whose rakers promptly sliced open the palm of my hand.

You cannot look at a fish's bones and think of them as you do a dog's or human's. In fact, as I discovered when I foolishly set the pike's head in simmering water to remove the fat and skin, the skull I so coveted melted away as promptly as its casings. I have boiled frogs' and small mammals' bones for hours in brine and they only grew harder, more marmoreal; this pike instead dissolved back into the medium that had grown him.

I took him back to the stream the next morning to release his jellified bones and skin into the water so he could feed the other creatures who lived there. I stood and watched as his graying remains floated down the current, then almost imperceptibly sank beneath it, like rotten ice. In a day or so, I reflected, whatever of him hadn't been eaten might reach the Mississippi below Minnehaha Falls. The current might take that pike all the way downstream to gar country and beyond that to the Gulf of Mexico. These were fine thoughts with which to pick up my rod and cast in the direction of the Mississippi, as if I could lash the water into compliance: *Take him, take him,* the line seemed to urge.

The summer I found the small pike, after two years of faithful attendance on the mostly fishless waters of Minnehaha Creek, I woke one day and decided I wanted to fish not so much *for* fish as *in the presence of* them. I wanted to stand in waters that the DNR had designated as trout waters. This had less to do with my growing appetite for blood or hookups than with my curiosity about how fishy waters differed from what I knew about Minnehaha Creek. My curiosity had grown, as had my confidence: I thought I knew now what to look for when exploring new waters for fish. So I began driving to the nearest certified trout streams: Eagle Creek, Hay Creek, the Kinnickinnic and Rush rivers, the

Brule. And I found that what I had learned on Minnehaha Creek served me well: sometimes I found fish where I expected to, and occasionally I even caught them.

But those streams, beautiful and "productive" (as fisheries biologists call them) though they were, lacked the heart-tugging familiarity of Minnehaha Creek. I missed knowing what occurred on those distant streams during the many days when I couldn't visit them; I missed the dailiness of time spent on a nearby stream. What those fine waters offered in terms of fish per mile couldn't compensate me for what they couldn't give: the knowledge earned through daily intimacy. Was the creek up or down today? How close to hatching were the caddis flies in the riffle downstream of the big cottonwood? Had the chubs and shiners built their nests yet?

Today I am lucky enough to live close to not only two neighborhood streams but to ones with resident trout and lake-run fish. Like Minnehaha Creek, stretches of them are cool, leafy, seemingly untouched. In spring I can lie on warm streamside boulders and stare down into their transparent miniature pools at shiners and nervous little brook trout, just as I used to watch chubs on Minnehaha. These are streams I not only savor, but work to protect; I have come to see the need to fight for such precious urban waters. I doubt that I shall ever be more fond of them, though, than I was—still am—of Minnehaha Creek.

It is the place I first fell under the spell of moving waters and came to see them as animate, storied, and plastic enough to accommodate and challenge me, no matter how little or much I knew. It is the place where I first kept faith with a part of myself I hadn't known before: the creature capable of a great, unexpected patience, a faith that I could crack the code of waters, the skills of casting and fishing. It is the place that taught me that faithful attendance on a single place—in this case, a stretch of stream no more than five hundred yards long—could yield unimagined complexity, a microcosm so rich that I am still its beginner, its postulant.

Minnehaha Creek taught me a way of seeing that enriches my life and my writing. Just now, on a visit to Minneapolis, as I sat alongside the creek's edge once again, admiring it from my truck on a mid-June morning, a great blue heron drifted weightlessly across the opaque white sky. A leaf green inchworm bobbed from his silk line beneath a drooping elm branch, and I saw both of them. Because my eyes had been opened in and by this place, I knew how succulent a surface-feeding fish would find the inchworm, and how such fish would gather eagerly beneath the branch, waiting for him to drop.

The rains had finally come after an exceptionally hot, dry spring, and now the creek flowed wide and shallow. Watergrasses that wouldn't have been there most years until mid-July streamed in the current, and the heavy thickets of grasses anchoring the north bank crowded out over the water, their pale heads already seeding up.

This was a place that humans nearly destroyed and then helped to rebuild. That handsome curve on the inside of the creek just below me covered with mosses and grasses wasn't even there three years ago when I moved north to Duluth. It was a human-made structure concocted of sandbags, mesh, and soil designed to narrow the creek where it was throwing up sand and cutting back into the bank.

I felt enormous satisfaction in these evidences that people could partially heal what we have damaged, that a place like Minnehaha Creek has restorative powers of its own. I learned these lessons on an urban stream, and I believe they made me a different and a better person. The prospect of revisiting the creek whenever I travel to Minneapolis remains exquisitely exciting. Each time, I strain forward over the steering wheel, peering eagerly through the windshield, waiting for my first sight of it.

"Jeez, *Mom,*" my daughter protests. "It's not like you ever caught anything there."

But I did. Fishing in that nearly fishless place taught me what I most wanted to learn: the patience, attentiveness, and submission needed to love a place well.

Notes

1. The pickerel whom Bull refers to would have been snake or hammerhandle pike; pickerel are not native to the Upper Mississippi drainage. Redhorse are a variety of sucker.

Bull's, Owen's, and Schussler's reminiscences were collected by Jane King Hallberg and published in her *Minnehaha Creek, Laughing Waters* (Minneapolis: Cityscape Publishing Co., 1995).

23

Gerald Vizenor was born in Minneapolis in 1934; his father was an Ojibwa from the Minnesota White Earth Reservation and his mother was Euro-American. Vizenor attended New York University, received his B.A. from the University of Minnesota, and did graduate work at Minnesota and Harvard. He has taught at a number of schools including the University of Minnesota, the University of Oklahoma, and Berkeley. Although he began writing as a poet, Vizenor's many books include numerous novels, essays, and memoirs such as *The Heirs of Columbus* (1992) and *Dead Voices: Natural Agonies in the New World* (1992). This short story from his collection called *Landfill Meditation* (1991) is like much of his work in its mix of autobiographical elements with strikingly imaginative material and in its use of the trickster figure. The "feral lasers" in this story function as a "tribal pen"—a way to rewrite demeaning colonial histories and to imagine an alternative wilderness, one that can exist above the interstates and cities.

Feral Lasers

Gerald Vizenor

Almost Browne was born twice, the sublime measure of a crossblood trickster. His parents, a tribal father and a white mother, had been in the cities and ran out of gas on the way back to deliver their first son on the White Earth Reservation in Minnesota.

Almost earned his nickname in the back seat of a seventeen-year-old hatchback. The leaves had turned, the wind was cold. Two crows bounced on the road, an auspicious chorus near the tribal border.

Father Browne pushed the car to a small town; there, closer to the reservation, he borrowed two gallons of gas from a station manager and hurried to the hospital at White Earth.

Wolfie Wight, the reservation doctor, an enormous woman, opened the hatchback; her wide head, hard grin, and cold hands menaced the child. "Almost brown," the doctor shouted. Later, she printed that name on the reservation birth certificate, with a flourish.

Almost was concerned with creations; his untraditional birth and perinatal name would explain, to some, his brute dedication to trickster simulations. No one, not even his parents, could remember much about his childhood. He was alone, but not lonesome, a dreamer who traveled in trickster stories. He learned to read in back seats and matured in seven abandoned cars, his sanctuaries and private mansions on the reservation. Station wagons were his beds, closets, hospitals, libraries; and in other cars he conversed with mongrels, counted his contradictions, and overturned what he heard from the elders. He lived in the ruins of civilization and shouted at trees, screamed into panic holes; he was, in his own words, "a natural polyvinyl chloride partisan."

Almost started a new tribal world with the creation of a winter woman, an icewoman as enormous as the reservation doctor; she saluted and laughed at men. Hundreds of people drove from the cities and other reservations to hear the icewoman laugh, to watch her move her arms. The sound of her cold voice shivered into summer, into rash rumors that ran down the trickster. He was secure in the blood, a bold protester, an eminent romancer, but censure was a cold tribal hand.

Almost was never a failure in the tribal sense; he resisted institutions and honored chance but never conclusions or termination. His imagination overcame last words in education; he never missed a turn at machines, even those dead in the weeds.

Once, when he applied for work, he told the reservation president that he had earned a "chance doctorate" at the Manifest Destiny Graduate School in California. The president was impressed and hired the trickster as a tribal computer consultant. "Chance," he boasted later, was a "back seat degree." He wired the reservation with enough computer power to launch it into outer space.

Theories never interested the trickster, but he was a genius at new schemes and practices, and the mechanical transanimation of instincts. He saw memories and dreams as three dimensional, colors and motion, and used that to understand race and laser holograms. "Theories," he said, "come from institutions, from the scared and lonesome, from people who fear the realities of their parents." "Theories," he said, were "rush hours."

Almost never said much; he worked on computers and held hands with a teacher at the government school. Em Wheeler lived in the woods with two gray mongrels; she was lonesome, thin at the shoulders, and she listened to tricksters. He told her that "creations were obvious, a rope burn, a boil on the nose, warm water, and much better than theories." He mussed theories and harnessed instincts, natural responses. For instance, the icewoman was animated by a caged mongrel wired to a solenoid, the source of electromotivation. When the mongrel moved, when his heartbeat leaped, the icewoman saluted. The wires, gears, and pulleys, hidden beneath chicken mesh and wire, were powered by solar batteries. "There you have it, sun, snow, and a cold sleight of hand," he mocked, "considerate winter moves." The mongrels barked, and the icewoman laughed and laughed at the visitors.

The trickster was an instinctive mechanician; communal sentiments and machines were his best teachers. He was a bear, a crow in a birch, a mongrel, and he reached in imagination to a postbiological world. Cold robotics and his communion with bears caused the same suspicious solicitude on the reservation. He practiced seven bear poses under a whole moon. Much later, when he was on trial in tribal court, he said he was a shaman, a bear shaman selenographer. "Tricksters have the bear power to enchant women with the moon." He persuaded seven women, three tribal and four white, to bare their bottoms to the moon each month.

The icewoman, snow machines that saluted, bears, and moon studies, however, were not cited as the main reasons for his banishment late that summer. He was responsible for those postshamanic laser holotropes that hovered over the reservation; lucent presidents from old peace medals and other figures danced, transformed the lakes and meadows, and terrified tribal families.

Almost was tried and removed to the cities because he studied electromagnetism, luminescence, and spectral memories; more than that, he deconstructed biological time and paraded western explorers in laser holograms. The pale figures loomed over the mission pond and blemished the clear summer nights on the reservation.

The Quidnunc Council, dominated by several mixed femagogues, gathered to consider the grimmest gossip about the trickster and his laser holotropes: the ghosts of white men returned to steal tribal land, harvest wild rice, and net fish. Sixgun, a detached stump puller, said he saw a white monster sprout six heads and suck up the lake six times. "Sucker Lake is down six feet from last year."

The best stories on the reservation would contain some technologies, the electromagnetic visuals of the trickster mechanism. The femagogues, in the end, told the tribal court to settle for the terror he had caused on the reservation with his laser holograms. The court convened in the preschool classroom; the trickster, the judge, other court officials, and witnesses were perched on little chairs.

"Almost, some say you are a wicked shaman, not with us the whole time," said the tribal judge. He leaned back on the little chair. His stomach rolled over his belt. His feet were wide. His thumbs were stained and churned when he listened. "Your dad and me go back a long time, we hunted together, so what is this business about six white heads sucking off a lake?"

"Lasers, nothing more," said Almost.

"Who are they?"

"Nobody," he said. "Laser light shows."

"Whose lights?"

"Laser holotropes."

"Indian?" asked the judge. "Where's he from then?"

"Nowhere, laser is a light."

"Laser, what's his last name again?"

"Holotropes, but that's not a real name."

"Does he shine on our reservation?"

"Laser is an image."

"Not when he shines our deer," said the judge.

"Listen," said the trickster. "Let me show you." Almost drew some pictures on a chalkboard and talked about reflections, northern lights, and natural luminescence, but not enough to understand laser holotropes. His mother told him that a real healer, a trickster with a vision, "must hold back some secrets." The tribal court, wise elders but not healers, would not believe a chalk and talk show in a preschool classroom. The tribal judge ordered the crossblood to demonstrate his laser holotropes that night over the mission pond at White Earth.

The court order reached tribal communities more than a hundred miles from the reservation. The loons wailed at the tribunal on the pond; mosquitoes whined in the moist weeds; fireflies traced the wide shore; bats wheeled and turned over the black water.

Christopher Columbus arose from the white pine, he saluted with a flourish, turned his head, circled the pond once, twice, three times, and then posed on the water tower. The school windows shimmered, blue and green light swarmed the building. Then, bright scuds carried the explorer to the center of the pond; there, his parts—an arm, hands, his loose head—protruded from the lucent scuds. Tribal families, the casual juries that night, gathered on the shore and cheered the dismemberment; later, when the explorer was put back together again and walked on water, most families retreated to the woods. One femagogue shouted that she could smell white diseases, the crotch of Christopher Columbus.

Almost Browne never revealed how he created the postshamanic laser holograms over the mission pond, but he told the tribal court that white men and diseases were not the same as electroluminations. "Columbus was here on a laser and withered with a wave of my hand," he said. "Laser holograms created the white man, but we set the memories and the skin colors."

"Not your life," said a crossblood.

"Darker on the inside," the trickster countered.

"Never," she shouted.

"The laser is the new trickster."

"Not on this reservation, not a chance," said the tribal judge. Almost was held accountable for accidents, diseases, and death on the reservation that summer. He was shamed as a shaman and ordered to remove his machines and laser demons from the reservation; he was the first tribal member to be removed to the cities, a wild reversal of colonial histories. The trickster moved no one but the preschool teacher who held his hand and nurtured his imagination.

Em Wheeler had lived on the reservation for nineteen years, nine months, seventeen nights. She counted lonesome nights, and she held a calendar of contradictions and denials. The trial was held in her classroom; she listened, turned morose, and threatened to leave the reservation if the crossblood was removed.

Em and Almost lived in a camper van with two mongrels and a songbird in a bamboo cage. She smiled behind the wheel, liberated by a light show; he laughed, ate corn chips, and read newspaper stories out loud about their trickster laser shows. He was a natural at interviews. "Name the cities and we'll be there before winter," he told a television reporter. "We're on laser relocation." The reporter nodded and told him to repeat what he had said for a sound check. "Back on the reservation we presented holograms, white men over ponds and meadows," the trickster continued, "but in the cities we launched wild animals, tribal warriors, and presidents over the interstates."

"Will lasers replace traditions?"

"We need three lasers to create our light bears out there," he told the reporter, "so we bought two junkers with sun roofs and parked them in strategic places."

"How does it work?"

"Which one?"

"The bear over the interstate."

"Can't tell you," said the trickster.

"How about the presidents?"

"Peace medals."

"Show me your best president," she said to the camera.

"The nudes?"

"The police said your presidents are obscene."

"Light is no erection."

"Show me," the reporter teased.

"Lasers undress the peace presidents."

"Show me," she insisted.

"Lasers substantiate memories, dreams, with no obverse, no other, no shadows," he said. The trickster turned to the camera and pounced at the words; then he moved his mouth, saying in silence, "Lasers are the real world."

Hologramic warriors and wild animals over urban ponds were natural amusements, but when the trickster chased a bear and three moose over a rise on the interstate, no one on the road was pleased. Late traffic was slowed down for several miles; the bear was too close to the dividers and scared hundreds of drivers. Later, several people were interviewed on television and complained about the wild animals.

"That's why we spent billions for interstates," said a retired fireman, "to keep wild animals where they belong, in the woods, and out of harm's way in traffic."

"But the animals are light shows," said an interviewer.

"Right, but this guy ought to keep his lights to himself, his creation is not for me on the road," said the fireman. "Indians should know that much by now."

Almost and Em stopped traffic in several cities between Minneapolis and Detroit. The laser tricksters were cursed on the interstates, but he was celebrated on television talk shows and late night radio. Instant referenda revealed that native tribal people had natural rights to create animals over the cities; these rights, one woman insisted, were part of the treaties.

"These people have suffered enough," said a librarian, a caller on late night radio. "We took their land and resources; the least we can do now is be amused with their little light shows and metamorphoses."

"We watched in bed through our skylight," said another night talker. "Wild men, wild neighborhoods in the sky, me on my back, the tribes above, the whole thing is turned around somehow."

"We drove into the wilderness," a man whispered.

"Next thing you know we'll need a hunting license to drive home from work at night," said a woman on a television talk show. She was a trucker who drove cattle to market.

The trickster and the schoolteacher were precious minutes from arrest in most cities. At last, the two were located by the military, a special surveillance plane used to track drug smugglers, and cornered on a dead end road at a construction site in downtown Milwaukee.

The police impounded their lasers and ordered them to appear in court later that week. They were charged with causing a public disturbance, endangerment on an interstate, and amusements without a license.

Editorial columnists and media interviewers defended their tribal rights to the air, where there were no legal differences between light and sound. "Indians show, we sound; our rights are the same," a constitutional lawyer said on public radio.

The prosecutor, however, argued in court that the "two laser shiners" should be tried "because a light show is neither speech nor art, and is not protected by current copyright laws."

"The prosecutor is a racist," said a student.

"The creator in this case is a digital code, not a tribal artist," said the prominent prosecutor. "Furthermore, bright lights like loud music are a public nuisance and put basic transportation at risk."

Almost and Em represented themselves at the hearing. "Your honor, my chest is white but my heart is tribal," she said. The judge, on loan from a northern rural district, smiled, and others laughed in the crowded courtroom. "Remember when you were a child, silhouettes on the bedroom wall at night?"

"Make your point," said the judge.

"Well, lasers heal in three dimensions, a real silhouette, and besides, an animal of the light has a natural tribal right to the night, more so than a trucker with higher beams," said Em.

"You have a point there."

"Your honor, our presentation is procedural," pleaded the prosecutor. "This is not the proper forum for a lecture on candlepower." He pinched his chin, a measure of his pleasure over his last phrase. "We are prepared for trial."

"Christopher Columbus," shouted the trickster.

"Your witness?"

"Would you hold the right to his image over the road?" Almost pounded his chest several times, a filmic gesture, and then posed at the prow of the polished bench. "Columbus is our precedence."

"New World indeed, but the issue here is an interstate, not a novel port for the Niña, Pinta, Santa Maria," the prosecutor lectured. "Real bears and laser simulations have no legal voice in our courts, your honor. Their beams are not protected, not even in tribal courts."

"Then cut the lights."

"What?"

"Plead in the dark," said the trickster.

"Your honor, please. . . ."

"Then we have a right to be tried with our light."

"Your honor, please, the accused was removed from the reservation for the same cause, the perilous light that comes before this court," said the prosecutor. "Their new cause is not sacred but postbiological as we read Hans Moravec in *Mind Children,* and this world 'will host a great range of individuals constituted from libraries of accumulated knowledge.' "

"Can the lard," said the judge.

"Christopher Columbus is all over the place," the trickster continued, "in lights, kites, trailers on planes, but his image is no more important than a warrior, a bear over the road at night."

"What is the cause here?"

"Light, light," lauded the trickster, "is a tribal right."

"First Amendment lights?"

"First and Sixth," shouted Em, "lights and rights."

"Due process?"

"Feral lasers," said the trickster, and then the lights were turned out. Lucent animals, superconductors on the dark, appeared as defendants. Then the spectators chanted two words, feral laser, feral laser, faster and faster. The trickster lasers created a wild Mount Rushmore National Memorial. George Washington, Jefferson, Lincoln, and Theodore Roosevelt beamed over the bench; however, tribal warriors eclipsed the presidents in a new tribunal.

Meanwhile, in old and troubled cities across the nation, people by the thousands bought lasers to revise histories, to hold their memories, and to create a new wilderness over the interstates. The cities came alive with laser holograms, a communal light show, a right to come together in the night. Lights danced over the cities; lonesome figures returned to their lost houses.

"The laser is a tribal pen, a light brush in the wild air," the judge pronounced, overcome with light amusement, "and these warriors are new creations, an interior landscape, memories to be sure, an instance of communal rights and free expression." The judge ruled in favor of light rights and dismissed the case; he appeared that night with the animals over seven cities.

Antoine de la Mothe Cadillac, tribal mummers in the new fur trade, peace medal presidents, bears, and crows appeared with Almost Browne and Em Wheeler in a comic opera, trickster lasers on a summer night over the Renaissance Center in Detroit.

24

Jesús Salvador Treviño was born in El Paso, Texas, in 1946, and he has lived in East Los Angeles since he was three years old. He graduated from Occidental College with a B.A. in philosophy. Mr. Treviño, a noted film director as well as a writer, wrote and produced the landmark documentary "Yo Soy Chicano" (1972) as well as the powerful "Seguin" (1982) for "PBS Playhouse." He has also directed segments of such television shows as "Chicago Hope," "The Practice," "NYPD Blue," and "Star Trek: Voyager." *Eye Witness,* a memoir of his activities as a civil rights activist / filmmaker, will be published soon. The short story "The Amazing Sinkhole" is from his collection *The Amazing Sinkhole and Other Stories* (1995). The story is set in Arroyo Grande, a fictional small Texas city patterned after Treviño's grandmother's neighborhood in Juarez, Mexico. The magical eruption of water in a small border city, its connections to the lives of the many different individuals who view it, and its power to generate wonder, a sense of community, and a new appreciation for life—all engage the reader in envisioning new possibilities for the mystery and power of city wilds.

The Fabulous Sinkhole

Jesús Salvador Treviño

The hole in Mrs. Romero's front yard erupted with the thunderous whoosh of a pent-up volcano, sending a jet of water dancing eight feet into the air. It stood there for a moment, shimmering in the sun like a crystal skyscraper, before it fell back on itself and settled into a steady trickle of water emanating from the earth.

The gurgling water made a soft, sonorous sound, not unlike music, as it quickly spread, inundating the low lawn surrounding the sculpted hole, painting a swirling mosaic of leaves, twigs, and dandelion puffs.

Pages of the weekly *Arroyo Bulletin News* were swept up by the fast moving water, creating a film of literary discourse that floated on the surface of the water before becoming soaked and eventually sinking into the whirlpool created by the unusual hole.

Within moments of the unexpected appearance of the geyser, the serenity of Mrs. Romero's ordinary, predictable world was disrupted. On that Saturday morning Mrs. Romero's life, and that of the other residents of Arroyo Grande, a border town along the Rio Grande river, was forever transformed by an event as mysterious as the immaculate conception and as unexpected as summer snow.

The routine of Mrs. Romero's Saturday mornings—the leisurely watering of her philodendrons, Creeping Charlies, and spider plants, the radio recipe hour, and the morning *telenovelas*—evaporated the moment that she stepped out the back door to feed Junior, her three-year-old poodle-Afghan mix.

No sooner had she opened the door to the back yard than the dog, whom she let sleep in the house with her, caught a whiff of something and ran around to the front of the house. He bounded back in a moment and began to jump, yelp, whine, bark, and engage in other canine theatrics to draw Mrs. Romero's attention to something unusual that was happening in her front yard.

"¿Qué trae ese perro?" Mrs. Romero asked herself as she circled her house and walked out to the front of her modest stucco home. She then saw that Junior was barking at a hole in her front yard.

The hole was about three feet in diameter. It was located ten feet from the white picket fence that framed her front yard and a few yards from the cement walkway leading from her porch to the sidewalk.

As she walked down the porch steps, she noticed the most pleasant vanilla odor in the air. "*Qué bonito huele,*" she thought to herself.

She started to waddle across the lawn, but saw that it was flooded and opted to use the cement walkway instead. When she got to the point on the walkway that was closest to the hole, she stooped over to examine the depression and noticed that there was water bubbling up from the earth.

Mrs. Romero's first thought was that some of the neighborhood kids had dug the hole during the night. "*Chavalos traviesos,*" she surmised. But when she saw that there was water coming up from the ground, she had second thoughts about this being the mischievous work of local juveniles.

Where was the water coming from? Perhaps it was a broken water main. Just then, a clump of grass fell into the hole as it expanded further. The hole seemed to be growing.

"*Qué raro,*" she said as she stood up.

Mrs. Romero was not someone easily buffaloed by much of anything in her long and eventful life. She had weathered the deportations of the Thirties (eventually returning to Arroyo Grande by foot, thank you), the Second World War, six children (all living), sixteen grandchildren, three husbands (deceased), four wisdom-tooth extractions, an appendectomy, the Blizzard of '52, an Internal Revenue audit, and weekly assaults on her privacy by Jehovah's Witnesses.

She was not about to be bamboozled by a mere hole in the ground.

She walked into her house and returned with a broom, which she proceeded to stick into the hole, handle first, to see if she could determine how far down the hole went.

When the broom handle had gone in to the point where she was holding the broom by the straw whiskers, she gave up and pulled the broom out. "What a big hole," she said out loud.

About this time, thirteen-year-old Reymundo Salazar, who lived in the adjacent block and was well known for the notorious spitball he pitched for the Arroyo Grande Sluggers, happened to be walking by Mrs. Romero's house on his way to Saturday morning baseball practice. Seeing Mrs. Romero taking the stick out of the hole in the lawn, he stopped and asked what was up.

"*Mira, m'ijo,*" she said. "Come look at this hole that just now appeared *aquí en mi patio.*"

Reymundo opened the gate and entered the yard, scratching Junior under his left ear. The dog by now had forgotten the mystery of the hole and was trying to get up a game of ball with the boy.

"Did you dig this hole, *Señora?*" Reymundo asked.

"No, *m'ijo,* that's the way I found it," Mrs. Romero said, somewhat defensively. She wiped her wet hands on the apron that circled her ample midriff and shook her head in wonder. "Look, it's getting bigger."

Sure enough, as Reymundo and Mrs. Romero watched, another large clump of earth fell into the hole as more and more water bubbled up from the earth below.

"You'd better get a plumber, *Señora,*" advised Reymundo as he started back to the sidewalk, "It's probably a broken water pipe."

"*Ay Dios mío,*" said Mrs. Romero, shaking her head once again. "If it's not one thing it's another."

As he walked away, Reymundo, who had been raised by his mother to be polite to older people, thought he'd compliment Mrs. Romero for the wonderful smell which permeated the air. He assumed it came from something she had dowsed herself with. "Nice perfume you're wearing, Mrs. Romero," he called out to her. "Smells real nice!"

Within an hour, news of the hole in Mrs. Romero's front yard had spread throughout Arroyo Grande as neighbors from as far away as Mercado and Seventh Street came to see the sight. Mrs. Romero's next-door neighbors, Juan and Eugenia Alaniz, were the first over.

Mrs. Romero explained the appearance of the strange hole to the couple, and Juan said he'd see what he could find out. He want back to his garage and returned with a long metallic pole with which he began to plumb the depths of the sinkhole. Like young Reymundo, he was certain it was a broken water pipe and thought he might locate it with the metal pole.

But after much probing, and getting his worn Kinney casuals soaked, Juan reported back to Mrs. Romero that he could find no pipes under her yard. "Beats me," he said.

By now the hole had enlarged to about six feet across. More and more water kept bubbling up, undermining the earth around the edges of the hole until eventually another bit of the lawn went into the hole. It appeared to sink to a bottom. Juan Alaniz extended his twenty-foot measuring tape to its full length and stuck it into the hole and still it did not hit bottom.

"It's deep," he said authoritatively to Mrs. Romero and his wife Eugenia, showing them the twenty-foot mark on the measuring tape. "Real deep."

"*Qué bonito huele,*" said Eugenia. "Smells like orange blossoms."

"No," said Juan, "smells like bread pudding. You know, *capirotada.*"

"Yes," said Mrs. Romero. "I noticed the smell, too. But it smells like vanilla to me. No?"

"Cherry-flavored tobacco," said grumpy Old Man Baldemar, who had crossed the street to see what the commotion was about. "It definitely smells of cherry-flavored tobacco."

Old Man Baldemar was known on the block for his foul mouth and his dislike of the neighborhood kids. He seldom spoke to anyone, kept to himself, and most people just stayed clear of him. That he would go out of his way to be social was just another indication of the deep feelings the hole stirred in those who saw it.

While Mrs. Romero and her neighbors discussed the powerful aroma that came from the hole, Reymundo Salazar returned from the baseball field along with the members of the Arroyo Grande Sluggers. They descended on Mrs. Romero's on their skateboards, looking like a swarm of fighter planes coming down *Calle Cuatro.* Reymundo had told his friends about the doings at Mrs. Romero's, and all were eager to see the mysterious water hole.

"Maybe it goes all the way to China!" Reymundo joked as he came to a stop in front of the white picket fence that surrounded Mrs. Romero's yard.

"Nah, a hole can't go all the way through the earth," said twelve-year-old Yoli Mendoza, taking it all very seriously as she finished off a perfect street-to-sidewalk ollie and came to a stop next to him. Yoli was advanced for her age, a real brain at school, and the tomboy of the group. She never missed a chance to show the boys in the neighborhood that she knew more about most things than they did, or that she could outskate them.

"In the center of the earth there's thick molten rock," she said professorially. "The *magma* and nothing can get through it—not even this hole."

At this point, chubby Bobby Hernández, also twelve years old but nowhere near Yoli's intellect, started arguing with Yoli, hoping to browbeat her into admitting that it *was* possible for a hole to extend from Mrs. Romero's yard all the way to China.

"Itcanitcanitcanitcanitcan," he said, as if repeating it enough times would make it so.

"You are an ignoramus and a lout," Yoli said emphatically, adjusting the ribbon at the end of her ponytail, "and not worth the time it takes to argue with you."

"Maybe we'd better call the Department of Water and Power," said Juan Alaniz as he examined the hole. "I'll do that and see if they can't get somebody out here. After all, it's water—they should know what to do."

While Juan went off to his house to place the call, Eugenia and Old Man Baldemar stayed to talk to Mrs. Romero. Meanwhile, other neighbors on *Calle Cuatro* were beginning to gather to see what all the commotion was about.

Mrs. Domínguez, the neighborhood gossip, who had spied the crowd coming down the street and presumed there had been a car accident, immediately called Sally Mendez and Doña Cuca Tanguma and told them to meet her at Mrs. Romero's. When the three arrived and found there was no accident but only an ever-widening water hole, Mrs. Domínguez was only momentarily embarrassed.

"Why, this is much better than an accident," she said to her friends as she regained her composure, "because no one's been hurt."

Miguelito Pérez, driving to work at the Copa de Oro restaurant bar, pulled his '73 Chevy over when he saw the crowd on *Calle Cuatro,* and got out to investigate. Within moments he, too, was integrated into the crowd.

"Hey, *Señora* Romero," he said, pointing to the picket fence that separated the expanding hole from the cement sidewalk. "If this hole continues to grow, it's going to wreck your fence."

Don Sabastiano Diamante, an expatriate Spaniard who laced his conversation with Biblical quotations and aphorisms, heard the commotion as far away as *Calle Diez.* He found the long walk to Mrs. Romero's rewarded by an ideal opportunity to dazzle a few more souls with his knowledge of the Good Book. He was always quick to point out how the scriptures neatly underscored the socialist ideals that had led him in and out of the Spanish Civil War and eventually brought him to Arroyo Grande.

"*And God said, Let the waters under the heaven be gathered together unto one place,*" Don Sabastiano quoted as he walked his Dachshund Peanuts slowly around the body of water, "*and the gathering together of waters he called the Seas.* Genesis One, Ten."

Choo Choo Torres, who would later give an account of the day's events to his sixth-grade class during the afternoon "Tell-a-Story" hour, arrived early on with the other Sluggers and made a list of the people who visited Mrs. Romero's front yard that day.

Among the five pages of names that Choo Choo Torres painstakingly compiled were: Old Man Baldemar, Don Carlos Valdez, Ed Carillo, Eddie Martinez, Cha Cha Mendiola, Juan and Eugenia Alaniz, Raúl and Simón Maldonado, Braulio Armendáriz, Pablo Figueroa, Raoul Cervantes, Sam Bedford (from the City Bureau of Public Works), the Méndez family (six in all), the Márquez family (father and three kids), the Baca family (four in all), the Armenta family (eight in all), the Arroyo Grande Sluggers (eleven kids in all, including Reymundo Salazar, Bobby Hernández, Tudí Domínguez, Choo Choo Torres, Beto Méndez, Robert and Johnnie Rodríguez, Junior Valdez, Smiley Rojas, Jeannie De La Cruz, and, of course, Yoli Mendoza), Howard Meltzer (the milkman), Chato Pastoral, Kiki Sánchez, Richard and Diane Mumm (visiting from Iowa), Mrs. Ybarra, Mrs. Domínguez, Sally Méndez, Doña Cuca Tanguma, Dr. Claude S. Fischer (who was conducting a sociological survey of barrio residents), Rolando Hinojosa, Miguelito Pérez, Rosalinda Rodríguez, Mr. and Mrs. Alejandro Morales, Charles Allen (who connected Arroyo Grande homes with cable TV), Lefty Ramírez, the Cisneros family (nine in all), Don Sabastiano Diamante and his dog Peanuts, Julia Miranda, One-Eyed Juan Lara, Sylvia Morales, Rusty Gomez (from the Department of Water and Power), David Sandoval, Max Martínez, 'Lil Louie Ruiz, Rudy "Bugs" Vargas, Pete Navarro, Bobby Lee and Yolanda Verdugo, the

Torres family (four not counting Choo Choo), Elvis Presley, Ritchie Valens, César Chávez, Frida Kahlo, John F. Kennedy, Che Guevara, Michael Jackson, and Pee Wee Herman.

The last several names, of course, were scoffed at by Choo Choo's classmates. Yoli Mendoza, who sat two seats behind Choo Choo, lost no time in openly accusing him of being a big fat liar, to which other classmates joined in with a chorus of "yeahs" and "*orales.*"

Truth to tell, Choo Choo *had* gotten a bit carried away with his list-making, but didn't see any need to admit his minor human idiosyncrasies to riff-raff the likes of his classmates.

With brazen, dead-pan bravado that—years later—would serve him in good stead at the poker table, Choo Choo insisted that each and every one of the people on his list had been at Mrs. Romero's house that day, and that he had personally seen them with his own two eyes.

Had it been a weekday with everyone off to work, the crowd that gathered in front of Mrs. Romero's might not have been very big. But it was a Saturday morning, and quite a warm, sunny day at that. An ideal day for neighbors to come together and get caught up on each other's lives. And that they did.

By eleven o'clock that morning the crowd in front of Mrs. Romero's yard was easily over fifty people and growing bigger and bigger by the hour.

For Mrs. Romero it was quite a delight. She had not had so many visitors in years, not since her husband Maclovio had passed away. Her husband's death had taken the spark out of Mrs. Romero's life—they had been married for thirty-six years—and no matter what her daughters, son, and grandchildren tried to do to cheer her up, her laughter always seemed forced and her smile polite. There were some who said she was merely biding time waiting to join her husband. Her children, caught up in their own lives, came to visit less and less frequently. On the day of the sinkhole, it had been a long month since she had been visited by anyone.

But now, hearing the lively chatter from her neighbors, she wondered why she hadn't made more of an effort to get out and meet people *herself.*

She felt warmed by the company of her neighbors and the cheerful sound of their laughter. Then and there she resolved that from now on she'd make it a point to visit her neighbors on a regular basis and would demand that her children and grandchildren visit more often. *"Va!"* she thought to herself, "I'm not in the grave yet."

Tony Valdez, who ran the corner store, heard about the crowd gathering at Mrs. Romero's, and his money-making mind immediately sprang into action.

He sent his son Junior, who made the mistake of returning from baseball practice to tell his dad about the doings at Mrs. Romero's, to the location with a grocery cart full of cold Cokes.

Before long a *tamalero,* a *paletero,* and a fruit vendor had joined the boy, and all were doing brisk business in front of Mrs. Romero's house.

By noon there was quite a festive air to the day as neighbors sipped Cokes, munched *tamales,* chomped on popsicles, and carried on the kind of conversation they normally reserved for weddings and funerals. Old friendships were renewed, new friends made, and, in general, more gossip and telephone numbers exchanged that day than had been exchanged in months.

One-Eyed Juan Lara stopped to examine the crowd at the ever-widening hole and speculated that if the hole got any bigger, Mrs. Romero could charge admission for the neighborhood kids to swim in it.

"You'll have your own swimming pool, *Señora,*" he said, "just like the *ricos.*"

Frank Del Roble, who had grown up on *Calle Cuatro* and now worked as a reporter for the *real* town newspaper, the *Arroyo Daily Times,* overheard Don Luis and countered that this probably wasn't such a good idea. "If this water is coming from a broken sewer line," he said, "the water might be contaminated, might get people sick."

"But look how clear it is," Juan Lara replied, pointing to the bubbling aperture.

Frank had to admit that the water flooding Mrs. Romero's front lawn was quite clear and not at all looking like a sewage spill.

Frank had been driving to the office when he had seen the crowd gathered outside Mrs. Romero's and had gotten out to investigate. Now, he pulled out his trusty spiral notepad and began taking notes.

Bobby Hernández, meanwhile, was still contending that the hole went all the way to China, and Yoli was still arguing that he was crazy, an ignoramus, and going against accepted scientific fact.

Bobby wasn't sure what an ignoramus was, but was damned if he was going to ask Yoli about it.

About this time a large "plop" sound announced the arrival of the first of many items that would bubble up in Mrs. Romero's front yard that day.

"Look!" Bobby said smugly, pointing to the hole. "I told you so!"

All heads turned to the hole and a hush fell over the group of spectators as they stared in wonder at the item floating on top of the water.

To Yoli's astonishment and Bobby's delight it was a large, straw hat, pointed in the center, not unlike those worn by millions of Chinese people halfway around the world.

"No, it's not a broken pipe," said Rusty Gómez, who worked for the Department of Water and Power and had been sent over to investigate the commotion on *Calle Cuatro.* He had measured and prodded the watery hole for half an hour before announcing to the sizable group gathered at Mrs. Romero's his conclusion.

"What you have here," he said, "is a sinkhole!"

A murmur coursed through the crowd as they played the new word on their lips.

"What's a sinkhole?" Mrs. Romero asked. She was determined to know all about this thing that had disrupted her day and was creating such ever-widening chaos in her yard.

"It's a kind of depression in the ground; it caves in when undermined by water from an underground river or stream. You don't know it's there until the ground gives way and the water surfaces."

"Yeah?" said Juan Alaniz cautiously. "So where's the river?"

"Years ago," continued Rusty, "there used to be an *arroyo* going through this neighborhood, right along *Calle Cuatro.* When it rained, a good-sized stream used to run through here, right down to the Rio Grande. There's probably an underground stream someplace and that's where this water is coming from."

"That," Rusty mused, "or an underground cavern connecting to the Rio Grande itself. Hell, it's only a half mile away. Yeah, I'd say this water's coming from the Rio Grande."

"Well, what can I do about it?" Mrs. Romero asked.

"Don't know, *Señora.* If I were you, I'd call the City Bureau of Public Works. They've got an engineering department. This is more their field of work. Say what is that, a bird cage?" Rusty Gómez pointed to the sinkhole where a shiny aluminum bird cage had suddenly popped up from the ground.

Old Man Baldemar, who lived alone in a single-room converted garage, and whose only companions were two parakeets which he had named *el gordo y el flaco,* fished the bird cage out of the water.

"*Señora* Romero," he said. "If you don't mind, I'd like to keep this here bird cage. The one I have for my *pajaritos* just this morning rusted through in the bottom. Those birds will get a real kick out of this."

"*Cómo no, Señor Baldemar,*" Mrs. Romero replied. "If you can use it, *pos* take it!" And that is how one of the first of the articles that popped into Mrs. Romero's front yard was taken away by one of the residents of Arroyo Grande.

Within an hour, more and more items began to float to the surface of the sinkhole, now about fifteen feet across. Choo Choo, Reymundo, Yoli, Bobby, and the rest of the neighborhood kids kept themselves busy by pulling objects out of the sinkhole and laying them on the sidewalk to dry.

Frank del Roble, who had already gotten a couple of quotes from Mrs. Romero for the piece he was now sure he'd write on the event at *Calle Cuatro,* stooped over the sidewalk and started making a list of the artifacts.

Throughout the day, Frank kept a careful record of the items that came bubbling up through Mrs. Romero's sinkhole, and this is what the list looked like:

a brown fedora, size 7½,
fourteen football player cards, three of Joe Montana,
one baseball player card of Babe Ruth,
a Gideon Bible,
a pair of plastic 3-D glasses,
a paperback edition of Webster's dictionary,
three paperback science-fiction novels,
four Teenage Mutant Turtle comic books,
a baseball bat,
three baseball gloves, one of them for a left-hander,
one basketball,
fourteen golf balls,
four unopened cans of semi-gloss paint primer,
an aluminum bird cage,
a 1975 world globe,
a tuba,
a yellow plastic flyswatter,
one yard of blue ribbon,
a toy magnifying glass,
a 1965 Smith Corona typewriter,
an April 1994 issue of *Art News* magazine,
a July 16, 1965, issue of *Life* magazine,
an August 1988 issue of *Life* magazine,
a July 4, 1969, issue of *Time* magazine,
the *Los Angeles Times* for October 9, 1932,
an issue of *TV Guide* for the week of April 18–23, 1988,
an unused package of condoms,

a blank certificate of merit,
fourteen Mexican coins of various denominations,
a three peso Cuban note,
$3.17 in U.S. currency including a silver dollar,
a 500 yen note,
a size 14.5 steel-bolted Goodyear radial tire,
the frame of a black, 1949 Chevy Fleetline,
a New York Mets baseball cap,
a deck of Hoyle playing cards with the ten of clubs and the three of diamonds missing,
a finely crafted silver pin,
a brochure for travel to *Macchu Picchu,*
a claw-toothed hammer,
three screwdrivers,
a pair of compasses,
a ruler,
a leatherbound copy of *David Copperfield,*
three pairs of jeans,
sixteen shirts of different kinds, sizes, and colors,
a white terry-cloth robe with the initials RR on it,
eight sets of men and women's shoes,
a broken Mickey Mouse watch,
a 14K gold wedding band,
a bronze belt buckle,
a fake pearl brooch,
a tambourine,
three empty wine bottles made of green glass,
an orange pet food dish,
a wooden walking cane with a dragon carved on the handle,
two umbrellas, one bright red and one yellow with brown stripes,
a twenty-foot extension cord,
thirty-two empty soft-drink bottles of assorted brands,
a pair of Zeitz binoculars,
a mint set of U.S. postage stamps commemorating rock and roll/rhythm and blues,
a Max Factor makeup kit,
five brand-new #2 pencils,
a Parker fountain pen,
four ball-point pens,
a set of ceramic wind chimes,

six pairs of sunglasses, one with a lens missing,
the figures of Mary, the baby Jesus, Joseph, and a camel from a porcelain nativity scene,
a framed autographed photo of Carmen Miranda,
a bag of clothespins,
a three-speed Schwinn bicycle with one wheel missing,
six size C Duracell batteries,
six record albums: *La Jaula de Oro* by Los Tigres del Norte, a collection of "Top Hits from 1957," a Sesame Street Singalong album, an album by The Jackson Five, "Learn to Mambo with Pérez Prado," and The Beatles' white album,
A black and red Inter-Galactic lasergun with accompanying black plastic communicator and extraterrestrial voice-decoder,
a sturdy, wooden push broom with a large bristle head,
an 8 × 10 wooden frame,
a red brick,
a map of Belkin County, Texas,
a book of Mexican proverbs,
a desk stapler,
two large black and white fuzzy dice,
a plastic swizzle stick with a conga dancer at one end, a rounded ball at the other end, and "Havana Club" printed along its side,
a subway token,
a red and white packet of love lotion labeled "*Medicina de Amor,*"
a 5 × 7 artist sketch pad,
five auto hubcaps, four of them matching,
a St. Christopher's medal,
a four-inch metal replica of the Eiffel Tower,
a New York auto license,
a large ring of assorted keys,
a plastic hula hoop, and lastly,
a Chinese sun hat.

As curious as Frank's exhaustive list was, the fact is that by the end of the day every single article had found a home in the hands of one or another of the people who stopped by Mrs. Romero's.

In quite a number of cases, the article seemed ideally suited for the person who picked it up. Like Old Man Baldemar walking away with a new bird cage for the one that had broken that morning, or Miguelito Pérez finding a hubcap to replace the one he had lost the week previous. Alejandro Morales found a red brick with the company name "Simmons" embossed on it, and was inspired to use it as the centerpiece for the new brick front porch he was adding to his house.

In other cases, the link between what a person took away from the sinkhole and a particular need in their life was not apparent at all.

Tudí Domínguez, for example, walked away from Mrs. Romero's having collected all thirty-two soft drink bottles and intending to return them to a recycling center for the rebate.

But on the way home he ran into Marcy Stone, a blond-haired, blue-eyed *gringita* on whom he had a devastating crush, and, rather than be seen carrying the bag of empty bottles, dumped them in a nearby trashcan. The bottles never surfaced again.

Marcy continued to ignore Tudí throughout the sixth and seventh grade until her family moved out of town, and Tudí grew up to be a used-car salesman. Never once did he ever think of the coke bottles he abandoned that day, nor were any of the four wives he married in the course of his otherwise uneventful life either blond or blue-eyed.

For most people at Mrs. Romero's, it wouldn't be until weeks, months, or even years later that they would associate an item they had carried off from the sinkhole on that peculiar Saturday afternoon with a specific influence in their lives.

By one o'clock, the sinkhole had undermined the earth on which Mrs. Romero's white picket fence was built and, just as Miguelito Pérez has predicted, the fence, pickets and all, plopped into the water.

Juan Alaniz helped Miguelito pull the picket fence out as a favor to *la señora,* and they neatly stacked the broken sections of the fence on her front porch.

Sam Bedford, from the City Bureau of Public Works, finally showed up at two o'clock that afternoon.

The balding city employee was grumpy because his afternoon game of golf had been disrupted by an emergency call to see about potholes on Fourth Street.

"Well that's definitely more than a pothole," Sam said, whistling in astonishment at the sinkhole which now measured twenty feet across.

By now the neighborhood kids had collected several dozen items and had them neatly drying on the sidewalk in front of Mrs. Romero's house.

The crowd now numbered about a hundred people as neighbors continued to call friends and relatives to see the unusual event.

Sam strutted about the hole for about an hour, comparing the yard and the street with several city maps and sewage charts he carried under his arm. Now and then he'd say "uh-huh" or "yeah," as if carrying on a deep conversation with himself.

Finally he returned to Mrs. Romero's porch where the elderly woman sat sipping lemonade with Mrs. Domínguez, Sally Méndez, and Doña Cuca Tanguma.

"Don't know what to tell you, lady," Sam said, putting his maps away. "It sure looks like a sinkhole, though I've never seen one so large. We won't be able to do anything about it till Monday. I'll put in a request for a maintenance crew to come out here first thing."

"But what about in the meantime?" Mrs. Romero asked.

Sam just shook his head. "Sorry, I can't help you. Just keep people away so no one falls in." As he walked away he noticed something amid the pile of junk that was accumulating on the sidewalk. "Oh, by the way," he continued, "do you mind if I take some of those golf balls lying over there?"

If there were two incidents that would be remembered by everyone on the day of Mrs. Romero's sinkhole, it was the argument between Father Ronquillo and his parishioner, *Señora* Florencia Ybarra, and the appearance of the largest item to pop out of the sinkhole, something that occupied the concentrated energy of five well-built young men and a tow truck for over an hour.

The Father Ronquillo incident began innocently enough when Mrs. Ybarra, whose devotion to the Blessed Mother was renowned, saw a Gideon Bible pop out of the sinkhole. She fished it out of the water and found, to her amazement, that although the leatherette cover of the book was wet, when she opened it up, the inside pages were on the whole pretty dry.

She examined the Bible carefully and came to a conclusion she immediately shared with her neighbors.

"It's a miracle!" she said, waving the Bible in the air. "Look, *la Santa Biblia* is dry! This water hole is a sign from the Lord and this Bible proves it!"

Mrs. Domínguez and several other women gathered about Mrs. Ybarra to examine the Bible. They all agreed that the Bible, though damp, should have been soaked and that some divine intervention was not out of the question.

What capped the argument was the sudden appearance of a porcelain figure of Mary from a nativity scene, followed in swift succession by a porcelain baby Jesus and a porcelain Joseph.

"*¡Milagro!*" The murmur spread through the crowd.

Father Ronquillo, dressed in his work-out sweats and out on his morning jog, happened by Mrs. Romero's at precisely this moment. The crowd spent little time ushering him to the sinkhole to witness for himself the Holy Bible and figurines of the Blessed Mother, Joseph, and the baby Jesus that had miraculously appeared in the water.

"Oh, thank God you are here, Father." Mrs. Ybarra said. "Look, it's a miracle!"

The parish priest was silent for a moment as he examined the figures and the still widening sinkhole. He listened to Rusty Gómez's explanation of the sinkhole, then talked with Sam Bedford, then listened once again to Mrs. Ybarra, and then examined the figurines.

He hadn't counted on facing a theological debate on his morning jog, but he was only too eager to responsibly shoulder his life work when the challenge presented itself.

"Well, there's certainly nothing miraculous about this," he said, pointing to the underside of the figures. "Look, it says JCPenney." He passed the figurines around for everyone to examine and, sure enough, the store name was printed on price labels stuck to the underside of each figurine.

"Of course it's no miracle," Frank Del Roble said emphatically as he compiled his list of the objects assembled on the sidewalk. Frank's university education had trained him to loathe superstitious people. "It's what keeps the *barrio* down," he was often heard to say. "Superstition and religion and no respect for science."

He surveyed the sizable collection laid out on the sidewalk. "I think Rusty's right. This stuff's probably been dragged here by some underground current of the Rio Grande. There's a scientific explanation for everything."

"It's from South America, that's what!" said Bobby Hernández. "The Rio Grande is connected to the Amazon. I betcha all these things come from down South!"

"The Rio Grande definitely does *not* connect to the Amazon," Yoli countered, only too eager to show off her knowledge of geography. "The Rio Grande starts in Colorado and empties into the Atlantic Ocean in the Gulf of Mexico."

"It *is* connected to the Amazon," Bobby replied, secretly convinced that Yoli made up the facts that she announced with such authority. "Itisitisitisitisitis!"

"*Es un cuerno de abundancia,*" said Don Sabastiano. "It's a cornucopia bringing something for everyone here."

"Definitely the Rio Grande," Juan Alaniz said, ignoring Don Sabastiano and nodding to Father Ronquillo. "That would explain where all this stuff is coming from." He picked up a silver dollar from the collection of artifacts laid out on the sidewalk and flipped it in the air. "All this stuff is probably from some junk yard up river."

Father Ronquillo, however, was not eager to allow the faith of his parishioners to be dispelled so easily. After all, if their faith was allowed to be undermined on these little matters, where would it end?

"There is a scientific explanation for everything," he agreed, examining a twenty-foot extension cord that had been drying on the sidewalk. He remembered that the parish needed one.

"But remember that our Lord invented science." He turned to the crowd around him and assumed his best clerical demeanor, at least the best he could dressed in jogging sweats.

"All of this may come from some junk yard," he said, putting the extension cord under the elastic of his jogging pants, "but that doesn't mean that some higher power did not arrange for all of this to happen."

"Then it *is* a miracle," said Mrs. Ybarra feeling vindicated.

"For those who believe, there will always be miracles," he said with reassuring eloquence. "And those unfortunate souls so tainted by the cynicism of the world that they cannot believe," he eyed Frank Del Roble pointedly, "are only the lesser for it."

"I still think that all this stuff is coming from South America," said Bobby, not giving up.

"I must prepare for the afternoon Mass," Father Ronquillo said, moving through the crowd and back on his running route. "Mrs. Romero," he said as he passed her, "you should call the city to see about filling in this hole before it does much more damage."

Indeed by now the hole had expanded to the edge of the walkway and sidewalk. There, the cement had put a halt to its growth. But on the far side of the yard, where there was no cement, the hole had gone on a gluttonous rampage, devouring so much of Mrs. Romero's front yard that when Don Sabastiano paced off the hole it measured fully forty feet across. It was enormous by any standard. It now appeared it might endanger Mrs. Romero's house.

Father Ronquillo's none too subtle barb at Frank Del Roble had left the reporter muttering under his breath. "Superstitious fools, that's what," he reiterated to himself.

Frank's dream was to someday work for the *Los Angeles Times,* a newspaper of record with an enormous readership that Frank considered worthier of his considerable journalistic talents than the few thousand readers of the *Arroyo Daily News.* Frank believed that his strict adherence to scientific truth was his ticket to the big time.

As if to prove to himself and those around him that he was not in the least bit superstitious, he challenged in a voice loud enough for everyone in the crowd around him to hear, "If this is a miracle, may the earth open up and swallow me!"

No sooner had the words left his mouth than a deep reverberation began in the ground immediately underneath Frank. The journalist's face blanched white as the whole area around Mrs. Romero's front yard began to tremble and rock, knocking several people off their feet and forcing everyone to struggle for balance.

Don Sabastiano, who in his many travels had experienced more than his share of life's wonders, immediately called out a warning to his neighbors. "Hold on to something, it's an earthquake!"

But an earthquake it was not. For just as quickly as it had started, the shaking subsided and was replaced by a loud rumbling sound rolling from under the sinkhole. While Frank caught his breath, reassured that the ground on which he stood was firm, the attention of the crowd was focused on the sinkhole as water began spouting up into the air.

The rolling rumble grew to a crescendo. When the noise had risen to a level that caused people to hold their hands over their ears, the sinkhole emitted a deafening whoosh.

With a power that sent water spraying a hundred yards in all directions, the sinkhole suddenly belched up the full frame of a 1949 black Chevy Fleetline.

"Get the hook around the front bumper," seventeen-year-old Pete Navarro called out as he stuck his head out of the cab of his Uncle Mickey's tow truck. It was four o'clock in the afternoon, an hour after the appearance of the 1949 Chevy Fleetline.

Rudy Vargas, Pete Navarro, David Sandoval, 'Lil Louie Ruiz, and Arroyo Grande, teenagers whose reputations were murky but who had never actually been caught doing anything illegal, had agreed to haul the car out of Mrs. Romero's yard as a favor to *la señora* and for whatever parts they might strip from the vehicle.

As they prepared to haul the car, which looked like a giant bloated cockroach, out of the sinkhole, they discovered to their surprise that it was in remarkably good shape for having been completely submerged in water for who knows how long.

"Look," said Rudy, sitting atop the roof of the car still floating in the middle of the sinkhole, "it's a little rusty, but this chrome can be polished up." The steady bubbling of water from under the sinkhole seemed to keep the car afloat.

"We give it a new paint job," he continued, "replace the engine, some new upholstery, and this could be quite a nice ride."

"Doesn't look like it was in the water very long at all," 'Lil Louie agreed, sipping a coke as he sat on Mrs. Romero's porch. Somehow when Rudy, Pete, David, and Louie undertook enterprises, it was always Rudy, Pete, and David who wound up doing the work, and Louie who managed to oversee the operation. "My managerial talents at work," he would explain.

The neighbors of Arroyo Grande gawked in wonder at the durable automobile defying the laws of nature by floating on the surface of the sinkhole. The water line went up to the car wheels.

"All set?" Pete cried out.

"¡Dale!" Rudy replied.

With a lurch, Pete began to edge the tow truck away from the sinkhole, slowly turning the car on its axis in the water and bringing it up to the shore of what could now be properly called the pond in Mrs. Romero's front yard.

The crowd watched with anticipation as the cable on the tow truck lifted the front end of the Fleetline out of the water. "Let me get off," yelled Rudy as he jumped off the hood of the car.

Pete waited until Rudy was clear and then continued to lift the car out of the water and over the sidewalk. But then the lifting stopped.

The tow truck alone could not get the Chevy's back wheels onto the sidewalk where Mrs. Romero's white picket fence had been. The car's upper end was in the air and its bottom end in the sinkhole.

"Come on guys," said Rudy to the men in the crowd, "*pasa mano.*"

Miguelito Pérez, Rudy Vargas, David Sandoval, Frank Del Roble, and 'Lil Louie gathered themselves under the car and began to push extra hard from below as Pete tried the lift again. Slowly the Chevy's rear end rose out of the water. The men shoved some more, each one straining to the limit of his strength.

Finally, the car's rear wheels touched the sidewalk.

It was a dramatic moment and the crowd could not help but give out a collective "Ah" as the back wheels of the vehicle caught hold of the ground. Within seconds Pete was driving the tow truck down the street, dragging the dripping Chevy behind it.

"*¡Gracias a Dios!*" Mrs. Romero said. "I don't know how I would have gotten that thing out of there. You boys, *son tan buenos muchachos.*"

As the commotion of the Chevy Fleetline's departure quieted down, Choo Choo Torres noticed something along the edge of the sinkhole's water line.

He called Frank Del Roble over and the two conferred in whispers for a moment. Frank took a stick and held it against the side of the hole for a moment and then nodded to Choo Choo that he was right. Choo Choo turned to the crowd and announced loudly, "Mrs. Romero. Look! The water's going away."

Mrs. Romero and her neighbors gathered at the edge of the pond and saw that, sure enough, like the water in a sink when the plug is pulled, the water in her sinkhole seemed to be receding slowly into the depths of the earth.

The Chevy Fleetline had been the last item to come out of the sinkhole, and now it seemed as if some master magician had decided that the show was over and it was time to go home.

Indeed, with the sun now low in the sky, people began to remember those things they had set out to do on that Saturday before the commotion at Mrs. Romero's had distracted them—the shopping, the wash, the mowing of the lawn, the repairs around the house. One by one, Mrs. Romero's neighbors began to drift away.

"*Adiós, Señora Romero,*" said Mrs. Domínguez as she and her friends Sally and Doña Cuca left the sinkhole. They each carried something from the sinkhole: Mrs. Domínguez, a fake pearl brooch and a bright red umbrella; Sally, a yellow and brown umbrella and a pair of harlequin style sunglasses; and Doña Cuca, a set of ceramic wind chimes and a book of *adivinanzas.* They were joined by Bobby Lee Verdugo, who had picked up a shiny brass tuba, and his wife Yolanda who had picked up an old issue of *Life* magazine and a tambourine. A noisy and colorful spectacle they all made walking up *Calle Cuatro* together, Bobby blowing notes on the tuba, Doña Cuca tapping the wind chimes, and Yolanda banging the tambourine in time to the music.

"*Sí, hasta luego,*" said Juan Alaniz, flipping the silver dollar he had picked up earlier. Eugenia, his wife, carried off a pile of shirts and a bag of shoes. "For the homeless," she had explained earlier. "I'll drop them by the Goodwill on Monday."

Fearful that she would have to call a trash man to haul away what remained of the collection of artifacts, Mrs. Romero urged her neighbors to take what they wanted home. *"¡Llévenselo todo!"* she said, "take anything you want!"

Don Sabastiano complied by carting off a sturdy wooden push broom with a wide bristle head.

Ed Carillo took a couple of old magazines that caught his eye. Thirty-five-year-old spinster Rosalinda Rodríguez took a white terry-cloth robe with her initials on it. The robe fit her perfectly, which was surprising since the poor woman was constantly ridiculed for being the most overweight person in Arroyo Grande.

Don Carlos Vasquez, who owned the Copa de Oro bar as well as several empty lots in Arroyo Grande, took a deck of Hoyle playing cards and a ring of assorted keys.

Twenty-two-year-old Julia Miranda, a dark-haired beauty who had been voted most likely to succeed by her high-school graduating class, and whose ambition was to someday star in a Hollywood movie, took an autographed photo of Carmen Miranda, a pair of sunglasses, and a New York subway token.

No one really took note of who took what from the sinkhole—except perhaps when seven-year-old Moisés Armenta walked up to his mother with an unopened package of condoms.

With the adults in the crowd chuckling, Mrs. Armenta quickly took the condoms from the child and put them in her purse where they remained for several weeks until discovered by her husband Arnulfo when he was rifling through her purse looking for cigarette money.

By six that evening, when the street lamps began to go on up and down *Calle Cuatro,* all the items but an orange dog food dish, a yellow flyswatter, and the Pérez Prado album had been taken away.

It was then that Mrs. Romero remembered that the whole day had started with her going into the back yard to feed Junior, and that in the course of the day's confusion she had forgotten to do that.

She looked out at her watery front yard, lit up by the street lights, and considered herself lucky.

The accidental appearance of the sinkhole had disrupted the mundane pattern of her daily activities and had given her a new appreciation for life. She wasn't sure what, if anything, it had done for her neighbors—but what a nice day it had turned out to be for her! Mrs. Romero was not an overly philosophical person, but as she stood on her porch watching the evening wrap itself around the modest houses of *Calle Cuatro,* she did have to wonder about the day's events.

Perhaps it was the mysterious workings of God, as Father Ronquillo had suggested. Or perhaps it was some other playful, magical force that had nudged her life and that of her neighbors. Or perhaps it was simply the overflow of the Rio Grande through a junk yard, all of it quite explainable by science.

Whatever the case, she was tired of thinking about it and eager to get on with the Pedro Infante movie, *Nosotros los pobres,* scheduled for TV that night. "Come on, Junior," she said, picking up the food dish, the flyswatter, and the album. "*Pobrecito,* it's time we got you some breakfast."

25

Sergio Troncoso was born in El Paso in 1961 (after his parents moved there from Chihuahua, Mexico), and he grew up in Ysleta, a community on El Paso's East Side. He graduated from Harvard University with a focus on Mexican and Latin American studies, took a Fulbright Scholarship in Mexico City, and studied philosophy and international relations at Yale. Although some of his fiction is set in New York's Upper West Side where he now lives, most of Troncoso's short story collection—*The Last Tortilla and Other Stories* (1999)—takes place where he grew up. "The Snake" is an autobiographical story depicting a young protagonist's exploration of urban nature. Troncoso's story carefully complicates that exploration by situating it within the complexities of family life and of cultural life on the border.

The Snake

Sergio Troncoso

The chubby boy slammed the wrought-iron screen door and ran behind the trunk of the weeping willow in one corner of the yard. It was very quiet here. Whenever it rained hard, particularly after these thunderstorms that swept up the dust and drenched the desert in El Paso during April and May, Tuyi could find small frogs slithering through the mud and jumping in his mother's flower beds. At night he could hear the groans of the bullfrogs in the canal behind his house. It had not rained for days now. The ground was clumped into thick white patches that crumbled into sand if he dug them out and crushed them. But he was not looking for anything now. He just wanted to be alone. A large German shepherd, with a luminous black coat and a shield of gray fur on its muscular chest, shuffled slowly toward him across the patio pavement and sat down, puffing and apparently smiling at the boy. He grabbed the dog's head and kissed it just above the nose.

"Ay, Princey hermoso. They hate me. I think I was adopted. I'm not going into that house ever again! I hate being here, I hate it." Tuyi put his face into the dog's thick neck. It smelled stale and dusty. The German shepherd twisted its head and licked the back of the boy's neck. Tuyi was crying. The teardrops that fell to the ground, not on the dog's fur nor on Tuyi's Boston Celtics T-shirt, splashed into the dust and rolled up into little balls as if recoiling from their new and unforgiving environment.

"They give everything to my stupid sister and my stupid brothers and I get nothing. They're so stupid! I always work hard, I'm the one who got straight A's again, and when I want a bicycle for the summer, they say I have to work for it, midiendo. I don't want to, I already have twenty-two dollars saved up, Oscar got a bicycle last year, a ten-speed, and he didn't even have anything saved up. He didn't have to go midiendo. Diana is going to Canada with the stupid drum corps this summer, they're probably spending hundreds of dollars for that, and they won't give me a bicycle! I don't want to sit there in the car waiting all day while Papá talks to these stupid people who want a new bathroom. I don't want to waste my summer in the hot sun midiendo, measuring these stupid empty lots, measuring this and that, climbing over rose bushes to put the tape right against the corner. I hate it. Why don't they make Oscar or Ariel go! Just because Oscar is in high school doesn't mean he can't go midiendo. Or Ariel could go too, he's not so small, he's not a baby anymore. And why don't they put Diana to work! Just because she's a girl. I wish I was a girl so I could get everything I wanted to for free. They hate me in this house."

"Tuyi! Tuyi!" his mother yelled from behind the screen door. "¿En dónde estás, muchacho? Get over here at once! You're not going outside until you throw out the trash in the kitchen and in every room in this house. Then I want you to wash the trashcans with the hose and sweep around the trash bins outside. I don't want cucarachas crawling into this house from the canal. When I was your age, young man," she said as he silently lifted the plastic trash bag out of the tall kitchen can and yanked it tightly closed with the yellow tie, "I was working twelve hours a day on a ranch in Chihuahua. We didn't have any *summer* vacation." As he lugged it to the backyard, to the corner where the rock wall had two chest-high wooden doors leading to the street and a brick enclosure over which he would attempt to dump the trash bag into metal bins, a horrible, putrid smell of fish—he hated fish, they had

had fish last night—wafted up to Tuyi's nose and seemed to hover around his head like a cloud.

"¡Oye, gordito! Do you want to play? We need a fielder," said a muscular boy, about fifteen years old, holding a bat while six or seven other boys ran around the dead end on San Simon Street, which had just finally been paved by the city. When the Martínez family had moved into one of the corner lots on San Simon and San Lorenzo, Tuyi remembered, there had been nothing but dirt roads and scores of empty lots where they would play baseball after school. His older brother, Oscar, was a very good player. He could smack the softball all the way to Carranza Street and easily jog around the bases before somebody finally found it stuck underneath a parked car and threw it back. When it rained, however, the dirt streets got muddy and filthy. Tuyi's mother hated that. The mud wrecked her floors and carpets. No matter how much she yelled at the boys to leave their sneakers outside they would forget and track it all in. But now there was black pavement, and they could play all the time, especially in the morning during the summer. You couldn't slide home, though. You would tear up your knee.

"Déjalo. He's no good, he's too fat," a short boy with unkempt red hair said, Johnny Gutiérrez from across the street.

"Yeah. He's afraid of flies. He drops them all the time in school and el coach yells at him in P.E.," Chuy sneered.

"Shut up, pendejos. We need a fielder," the older boy interrupted again, looking at Tuyi. "Do you want to play, Tuyi?"

"No, I don't want to. But Oscar will be back from washing the car, and I think he wants to play," Tuyi said, pointing to their driveway as he began to walk away, down San Lorenzo Street. He knew Oscar would play if they only asked him.

"Ándale pues. Chuy, you and Mundis and Pelón will be on my team, and Maiyello, you have the rest of them. Okay? When Oscar comes we'll make new teams and play over there," he said, pointing to a row of empty lots down the street. "There's more room and we can slide. I'll be the fielder, you pitch, Pelón. And don't throw it so slow!"

Tuyi looked back at them as he walked down the new sidewalk, with its edges still sharp and rough where the two-by-fours had kept the cement squared. Here someone had scrawled "J + L 4/ever" and surrounded it with a slightly askew heart when the cement had been wet. Tuyi (no one called him

Rodolfo, not even his parents) was happy to have won a reprieve from midiendo and from cutting the grass. He was not about to waste it playing baseball with those cabrones. He just wanted to be alone. His father had called home and had told his mother to meet him after work today. They were going to Juárez, first to a movie with Cantinflas and then maybe for some tortas on 16 de Septiembre Street, near the plaza where they had met some twenty years before. Tuyi had heard this story so many times he knew it by heart. His father, José Martínez, an agronomy and engineering student at the Hermanos Escobar School, had walked with some of his university buddies to the plaza. There, young people in the 1950s, at least those in Chihuahua, would stroll around the center. The boys, in stiff shirts with small collars and baggy, cuffed slacks, looking at the girls. The girls, in dresses tight at the waist and ruffled out in vertical waves toward the hem, glancing at the boys. If a boy stopped to talk to a girl, her friends would keep walking. Sometimes whole groups would just stop to talk to each other. In any case, this was where Papá had first seen Mamá, in a white cotton dress and black patent leather shoes. Mamá had been a department store model, Tuyi remembered his father had said, and she was the most beautiful woman Papá had ever seen. It took him, Papá told Tuyi, five years of going steady just to hold her hand. They were novios for a total of eight years before they even got married! Today they were going to the movies just as they had done so many times before. His father had told his mother that he and Tuyi could instead go midiendo tomorrow, for a project in Eastwood, on the east side of El Paso, just north of the freeway from where they lived. Mr. Martínez was a construction engineer at Cooper and Blunt in downtown El Paso. On the side he would take up design projects for home additions, bathrooms, porches, new bedrooms, and the like. The elder Martínez had already added a new carport to his house and was planning to add another bathroom. He would do the construction work himself, on the weekends, and his sons would help. But today he wanted to go to the movies with his wife. They were such a sappy couple.

"Buenos días, Rodolfito. Where are you going, my child?" a woman asked, clipping off the heads of dried roses and wearing thick black gloves. The house behind her was freshly painted white, with a burnt orange trim. A large Doberman pinscher slept on the threshold of the front door, breathing heavily, its paw stretched out toward nothing in particular.

"Buenos días, Señora Jiménez. I'm just off for a walk," Tuyi answered politely, not knowing whether to keep walking or to stop, so he stopped. His mother had told him not to be rude to the neighbors and to say hello whenever he saw them on his walks.

"Is your mother at home? I want to invite her to my niece's quinceañera this Saturday at the Blue Goose. There's going to be mariachis and lots of food. I think Glenda is going too. You and Glenda will be in 8-1 next year, in Mr. Smith's class, isn't that right?"

"Yes, señora, I'll be in 8-1. My mother is at home now, I can tell her about the party."

"You know, you're welcome to come too. It will be lots of fun. Glenda told me how the whole class was so proud of you when you won those medals in math for South Loop School. I'm glad you showed those snotty Eastwood types that a Mexicano can beat them with his mind."

"I'll tell my mother about the party. Hasta luego, señora," Tuyi muttered as he walked away quickly, embarrassed, his face flushed and nervously smiling. As he rounded the corner onto Southside Street, his stomach churned and gurgled. He thought he was going to throw up, yet he only felt a surge of gases build somewhere inside his body. He farted only when he was sure no one else was nearby. He had never figured out how he had won three first places in the citywide Number Sense competition. He had never even wanted to be in the stupid competition, but Mr. Smith and some other teachers had asked him to join the math club at school, pressured him in fact. Tuyi finally stopped avoiding them with his stoic politeness and relented when he found out Laura Downing was in Number Sense already. He had a crush on her; she was so beautiful. Anyway, they would get to leave school early on Fridays when a meet was in town. Tuyi hated the competition, however. His stomach always got upset. Time would be running out and he hadn't finished every single problem, or he hadn't checked to see if his answers were absolutely right. His bladder would be exploding, and he had to tighten his legs together to keep from bursting. Or Laura would be there, and he would be embarrassed. He couldn't talk to her; he was too fat and ugly. Or he wanted to fart again, five minutes to go in the math test. After he won his first gold medal, all hell broke loose at South Loop. The school had never won before. The principal, Mr. Jácquez, announced it over the intercom after the pledge of allegiance and the club and pep rally announcements. Rodolfo Martínez won? The kids in Tuyi's class, in 7-1, stared at Tuyi, the fat boy everybody ignored, the one who was always last running laps in P.E. Then, led by Mrs. Sherman, they began to applaud. He wanted to vomit. After he won the third gold medal in the last competition of the year at Parkland High School, he didn't want to go to school the next day. He begged his parents to let him stay at home. He pleaded with them, but they said no. The day before the principal had called to tell them about what Tuyi had done. He should be proud of himself, his mother and father said, it was good that he had worked so hard and won for Ysleta. The neighborhood was proud of him. His parents didn't tell him this, but Mr. Jácquez had told them that there would be a special presentation for Tuyi at the last pep rally of the year. He *had* to go to school that day. When Mr. Jácquez called him up to the stage in the school's auditorium, in front of the entire school, Tuyi wanted to die. A rush of adrenaline seemed to blind him into a stupor. He didn't want to move. He wasn't going to move. But two boys sitting behind him nearly lifted him up. Others yelled at him to go up to the stage. As he walked down the aisle toward the stage, he didn't notice the wild clapping or the cheering by hundreds of kids. He didn't see Laura Downing staring dreamily at him in the third row as she clutched her spiral notebook. Everything seemed supernaturally still. He couldn't breathe. Tuyi didn't remember what the principal had said on the stage. Tuyi just stared blankly at the space in front of him and wished and prayed that he could sit down again. He felt a trickle of water down his left leg which he forced to stop as his face exploded with hotness. Thank God he was wearing his new jeans! They were dark blue; nobody could notice anything. Afterward, instead of going back to his seat, he left the stage through the side exit and cleaned himself in the boy's bathroom in front of the counselor's office. The next day, on the last day of school, when the final bell rang at 3:30, as he walked home on San Lorenzo Street with everything from his locker clutched in his arms, he was the happiest person alive in Ysleta. He was free.

Tuyi walked toward the old, twisted tree just before Americas Avenue, where diesel trucks full of propane gas rumbled toward the Zaragoza International Bridge. He did not notice the Franklin Mountains to the west. The huge and jagged wall in the horizon would explode with brilliant orange streaks at dusk, but now, at mid-morning, was just gray rock against the pale blue of the big sky. His shoulders were slumped forward. He stared at the powdery dirt atop the bank of the canal, stopping every once in a while to pick up a rock and hurl it into the rows of cotton around him. He threw a rock against the 30 mph sign on the road. A horribly unpeaceful clang shattered the quiet and startled him. A huge dog—he was terrified of every dog but his own—lunged at him from behind the chainlink fence of the last house on the block. The black mutt bared its teeth at him and scratched its paws into the dust like a bull wanting so much to charge and annihilate its target. At the end of the cotton field and in front of Americas Avenue, Tuyi waited until a red Corvette zoomed by going north, and then ran across the black pavement and down the hill onto a perpendicular dirt road that hugged the canal on the other side of Americas. There would be no one here now. But maybe during the early evening some cars would pull up alongside the trees that lined this old road. Trees that grew so huge toward the heavens only because they could suck up the moisture of the irrigation canal. The cars would stop under the giant shade, and groups of men, and occasionally a few women, would sit and laugh, drink some beers, throw and smash the bottles onto rocks, just wasting time until dark, when the mosquitoes would swarm and it was just better to be inside. Walking by these trees, Tuyi had often seen used condoms lying like flattened centipedes that had dried under the sun. He knew what they were. Some stupid kids had brought condoms to school for show and whipped them around their heads at lunch time, or hurled them at each other like giant rubber-band bombs. Tuyi had also found a ring once, made of shiny silver and with the initials "SAT" inside. He didn't know anyone with these initials. And even if he had, he probably wouldn't have returned the ring anyway: he had found it, it was his. Tuyi imagined names that might fit such initials: Sarah Archuleta Treviño, Sócrates Arturo Téllez, Sigifredo Antonio Torres, Sulema Anita Terrazas, or maybe Sam Alex Thompson, Steve Andrew Tillman, Sue Aretha Troy. After he brought the ring back home and hid it behind the books on the shelves his father had built for him, he decided that "SAT" didn't stand for a name at all but for "Such Amazing Toinkers," where toinkers originally referred to Laura Downing's breasts, then later to any amazing breasts, and then finally to anything that was breathtaking and memorable. The sun sinking behind the Franklin Mountains and leaving behind a spray of lights and shadows was a "toinker sun." The cold reddish middle of a watermelon "toinked" in his mouth whenever he first bit into its wonderful juices.

About a half mile up the dirt road, Tuyi stopped. He was at his favorite spot. He shuffled around the trunk of the oak tree and found a broken branch, which he then trimmed by snapping off its smaller branches. In the canal, he pushed his stick into mud—the water was only a couple of inches deep—and flung out globs of mud. He was looking for tadpoles. The last time he had found one, he had brought it up to a rock near the tree. Its tail was slimy and slick. He found a Styrofoam cup, which he filled up with water. Under the tree, he watched it slither around the cup, with tiny black dots on its tail and a dark army green on its bulletlike body. After a few minutes, he flicked open his Swiss army knife and slit the tadpole open from head to tail. The creature's body quivered for a second or two and then just lay flat like green jelly smeared on a sandwich. Tuyi noticed a little tube running from the top of the tadpole's head to the bottom, and a series of smaller veins branching off into the clear green gelatinous inside. He found what he took to be one of the eyes and sliced it off with the blade. It was just a black mass of more gushy stuff, which was easily mashed with the slightest pressure. He cut the entire body of the tadpole in thin slices from head to tail and tried to see what he could see, what might explain how this thing ate, whether it had any recognizable organs, if its color inside was different from the color of its skin.

But today he didn't find anything in the mud except an old Pepsi bottlecap and more black mud. He walked toward the edge of the cotton field abutting the canal. Here he found something fascinating indeed. An army of large black ants scurried in and out of a massive anthole, those going inside carrying something on their backs, leaves or twigs or white bits that looked like pieces of bread, and those marching out of the hole following, in the opposite direction, the paths of the incoming. The ants would constantly bump into each other, go around, and then follow the trail back toward whatever it was that kept them busy. How could ants follow such a trail and be so organized? Did they see their way there? But then they wouldn't be bumping into each other all the time. Or did they smell their way up the trail and back home? Maybe they smelled each other to say hello, such as one might whose world was the nothingness of darkness. Tuyi wondered if these black ants were somehow communicating with each other as they scurried up and down blades of grass and sand and rocks, never wavering very far from their trails. Was this talking audible to them? Was there an ant language? There had to be some sort of communication going on among these ants. They were too organized in their little marching rows for this to be random. Maybe they recognized each other by smell. He thought this might be the answer because he remembered what a stink a small red ant had left on his finger after he had crushed it between his fingertips. This might be its way of saying, "Don't crush any more red ants or you'll be smeared with this sickly sweet smell," although this admonition could be of no help to one already pulverized. This warning might have been to help the red ants of the future. Maybe, ultimately, red ants didn't care if any one of them died as long as red ants in general survived and thrived without being crushed by giant fingers. Anyway, this would make red ants quite different from humans, who were individualistic and often didn't really care about anyone else except themselves. For the most part, humans were a stupid, egotistical mob. Tuyi decided to find out if black ants could somehow talk to each other.

Finding one ant astray from the rest, Tuyi pinned it down with his stick. This ant, wriggling underneath the wooden tip, was a good two feet from one of the trails near the anthole. Its legs flailed wildly against the stick, tried to grab on to it and push it off, while its head bobbed up and down against the ground. After a few seconds of this maniacal desperation—maybe this ant was screaming for help, Tuyi thought—six or seven black ants broke off from a nearby trail and rushed around the pinned ant, coming right to its head and body and onto the stick. They climbed up the stick, and just before they reached Tuyi's fingers, he let it drop to the ground. It worked. They had freed their friend from the giant stick. Tuyi looked up, satisfied that he had an answer to whether ants communicated with each other. Just about halfway up from his crouch he froze: about three feet away, a rattlesnake slithered over the chunks of earth churned up by the rows of cotton and onto the caked desert floor. He still couldn't hear the rattle, although the snake's tail shook violently a few inches from the ground. Tuyi was a little hard of hearing, probably just too much wax in his head. The snake stopped. It had been crawling toward him, and now it just stopped. Its long, thick body twisted tightly behind it while its raised tail still shook in the hot air. He didn't move; he was terrified. Should he run, or would it spring toward him and bite him? He stared at its head, which swayed slowly from left to right. It was going to bite him. He had to get out of there. But if he moved, it would certainly bite him, and he couldn't move fast enough to get out of its way when it lunged. He was about to jump back and run when he heard a loud crack to his right. The snake's head exploded. Orange fluid was splattered over the ground. The headless body wiggled in convulsions over the sand.

"God-damn! Git outta' there boy! Whatcha doin' playin' w'th a rattler? Ain't ye got no *sense?* Git over here!" yelled a burly, red-headed Anglo man with a pistol in his hand. There was a great, dissipating cloud of dust behind him; his truck's door was flung open. It was an INS truck, pale green with a red siren and search lights on top of the cabin.

"Is that damn thing dead? It coulda' killed you, son. ¿Hablas español?

Damn it," he muttered as he looked at his gun and pushed it back into the holster strapped to his waist, "I'm gonna haf'ta make a report on firin' this weapon."

"I wasn't playing with it. I was looking at ants. I didn't see the snake."

"Well, whatcha doin' lookin' at ants? Seems you should be playin' somewhere else anyways. Do you live 'round here, boy? What's yer name?"

"Rodolfo Martínez. I live over there," Tuyi said, pointing at the cluster of houses beyond the cotton fields. "You work for the Immigration, right? Can you shoot mojados with your gun, or do you just hit them with something? How do you stop them if they're running away?"

"I don't. I corner the bastards and they usually giv' up pretty easy. I'm takin' you home, boy. Git in the truck."

"Mister, can I take the snake with me? I've never seen a snake up close before and I'd like to look at it."

"Whatha hell you want w'th a dead snake? It's gonna stink up your momma's house and I know she won't be happy 'bout that. Shit, if you wanna take it, take it. But don't git the thang all over my truck. Are you some kinda' scientist, or what?"

"I just want to see what's inside. Maybe I could take the skin off and save it. Don't they make boots out of snake skin?"

"They sure as hell do! Nice ones too. They also make 'em outta elephant and shark, but ye don't see *mae* cutting up those an'mals in my backyard. Here, put the damn thang in here." The border patrolman handed him a plastic Safeway bag. Tuyi shoved the headless carcass of the snake into the bag with his stick. The snake was much heavier than he thought, and stiff like a thick tube of solid rubber. He looked around for the head and finally found it, what was left of it, underneath the first row of cotton in the vast cotton field behind him. As the INS truck stopped in front of the Martínez home on San Lorenzo Street, and Tuyi and the border patrolman walked up the driveway, the baseball game on San Simon stopped. A couple of kids ran up to look inside the truck and see what they could see.

"They finally got him. I told ya' he was weird! He's probably a mojado, from Canada. They arrested him, el pinchi gordito."

"Shut up, you idiot. Let's finish the game. We're leading 12 to 8. Maybe la migra just gave him a ride. Why the hell would they bring 'em back home if he was arrested?"

"Maybe they don't arrest kids. He's in trouble, wait till his father gets home. He's gonna be pissed off. They're gonna smack him up, I know it."

"Come on! Let's finish the game or I'm going home. *Look* it, there's blood on the seat, or something."

"I told ya, he's in trouble. Maybe he threw a rock at the guy and he came to tell his parents. Maybe he hit 'em on the head with a rock. I tell ya, that Tuyi is always doin' something weird by himself. I saw him in the canal last week, digging up dirt and throwing rocks. He's loco."

"Let's go, I'm going back. Who cares about the stupid migra anyway?"

"Ay, este niño, I can't believe what he does sometimes. And what did the migra guy tell you, was he friendly?" asked Mr. Martínez, glancing back at the metal clanging in the back of the pickup as he and his wife pulled up into the driveway. The moon was bright tonight. Stars twinkled in the clear desert sky like millions of jewels in a giant cavern of space.

"Oh, Mr. Jenkins was muy gente. I wish I could've given him lunch or something, but he said he had to go. He told me Tuyi wanted to keep the snake. Can you believe that? I can't even stand the thought of those things. I told Tuyi to keep it in the backyard, in the shed. The bag was dripping all over the kitchen and it smelled horrible. I hope the dog doesn't get it and eat it."

"It looks like everyone's asleep. All the lights are out. Let me get this thing out of the truck while you open the door. Do you have your keys? Here, take mine."

"I'm gonna put it in the living room, está bien? That way we can surprise him tomorrow. Pobrecito. He must've been scared. Can you imagine being attacked by a snake? This was a good idea. I know he'll be happy. He did so well in school too."

"Well, if it keeps him out of trouble, I'll be happy. I hope he doesn't get run over by a car, though," said Mrs. Martínez while pouring milk into a pan on the stove. Only the small light over the stove was on, and that was nearly covered up as she stood waiting for the milk to bubble. "¿Quieres leche? I'm going to drink a cup and watch the news. I'm tired, but I'm not really sleepy yet."

The house was quiet except for the German shepherd in the backyard who scratched at the shed door, smelling something powerful and new just beyond it. Princey looked around, sniffed the floor around the door, licked it, and after trotting over to the metal gate to the backyard lay down with a thump against the gate, panting quietly into the dry night air. Inside the house, every room was dark except for the one in the back corner from which glimmered the bluish light of a television set, splashing against the white walls in sharp, spasmodic bursts. In the living room, a new ten-speed bicycle, blue with white stripes and black tape over the handlebars, reclined against its metal stop. Some tags were still dangling from its gears. The tires needed to be pressurized correctly because it had just been the demonstration model at the Wal-Mart on McCrae Boulevard. It was the last ten-speed they had.

26

Chicana fiction writer and playwright Denise Chávez was born in 1948 in Las Cruces, New Mexico, where she now lives. She has a B.A. degree from New Mexico State University, an M.A. from the University of New Mexico, and an M.F.A. from Trinity University, San Antonio; she has taught at several places including the University of Houston and New Mexico State. Her short story collection *The Last of the Menu Girls* (1986) won the Puerto del Sol fiction award, and her novel *The Face of an Angel* (1995) won the Premio Aztlan Award. This short story, from *The Last of the Menu Girls,* traces a child's geography of flowers, irrigation ditches, and a triangle of trees that shaped and graced her childhood.

Willow Game

Denise Chávez

I was a child before there was a South. That was before the magic of the East, the beckoning North, or the West's betrayal. For me there was simply Up the street toward the spies' house, next to Old Man W's or there was Down, past the Marking-Off Tree in the vacant lot that was the shortcut between worlds. Down was the passageway to family, the definition of small self as one of the whole, part of a past. Up was in the direction of town, flowers.

Mercy and I would scavenge the neighborhood for flowers that we would lay at Our Lady's feet during those long May Day processions of faith that we so loved. A white satin cloth would be spread in front of the altar. We children would come up one by one and place our flowers on that bridal sheet, our breathless childish fervor heightened by the mystifying scent of flowers, the vision of flowers, the flowers of our offerings. It was this beatific sense of wonder that sent us roaming the street in search of new victims, as our garden had long since been razed, emptied of all future hope.

On our block there were two flower places: Old Man W's and the Strongs. Old Man W was a Greek who worked for the city for many years and who lived with his daughter who was my older sister's friend. Mr. W always seemed eager to give us flowers; they were not as lovely or as abundant as the Strongs' flowers, yet the asking lay calmly with us at Old Man W's.

The Strongs, a misnamed brother-and-sister team who lived together in the largest, most sumptuous house on the block, were secretly referred to by my sister and me as "the spies." A chill of dread would overtake both of us as we'd approach their mansion. We would ring the doorbell and usually the sister would answer. She was a pale woman with a braided halo of wispy white hair who always planted herself possessively in the doorway, her little girl's legs in black laced shoes holding back, sectioning off, craning her inquiry to our shaken selves with a lispy, merciless, "Yes?"

I always did the asking. In later years when the street became smaller, less foreign, and the spies had become, at the least, accepted . . . it was I who still asked questions, pleaded for flowers to Our Lady, heard the high piping voices of ecstatic children singing, "Bring flowers of the fairest, bring flowers of the rarest, from garden and woodland and hillside and dale. . . ." My refrain floated past the high white walls of the church, across the Main Street irrigation ditch, and up our small street. "Our pure hearts are swelling, our glad voices telling, the praise of the loveliest Rose of the Dale. . . ."

One always came down . . .

Down consisted of all the houses past my midway vantage point, including the house across the street, occupied by a couple and their three children, who later became my charges, my baby-sitting responsibilities, children whose names I have forgotten. This was the house where one day a used sanitary napkin was ritually burned—a warning to those future furtive random and unconcerned depositors of filth, or so this is what one read in Mr. Carter's eyes as he raked the offensive item to a pile of leaves and dramatically set fire to some nameless, faceless woman's woes. I peered from the trinity of windows cut in our wooden front door and wondered what all the commotion was about and why everyone seemed so stoically removed, embarrassed or offended. Later I would mournfully peep from the cyclopian window at the Carters' and wonder why I was there and not across the street. In my mind I floated Down, past the Marking-Off Tree with its pitted green fruit, past five or six houses, houses of strangers, "los desconocidos," as my Grandmother would say, "¿Y pues, quién los parío?" I would end up at my aunt's house, return, find myself looking at our house as it was, the porch light shining, the lilies' pale patterns a diadem crowning our house, there, at night.

The walk from the beginning to the end of the street took no longer than five to ten minutes, depending on the pace and purpose of the walker. The walk was short if I was a messenger to my aunt's, or if I was meeting my father, who had recently divorced us and now called sporadically to allow us to attend to him. The pace may have been the slow, leisurely summer saunter with ice cream or the swirling dust-filled scamper of spring. Our house was situated in the middle of the block and faced a triangle of trees that became both backdrop and pivot points of this child's tale. The farthest tree, the Up Tree, was an Apricot Tree that was the property of all the neighborhood children.

The Apricot Tree lay in an empty lot near my cousin's house, the cousin who always got soap in her nose. Florence was always one of the most popular girls in school and, while I worshipped her, I was glad to have my nose and not hers. Our mothers would alternate driving us and the Sánchez boys, one of whom my father nicknamed "Priscilla" because he was always with the girls, to a small Catholic school that was our genesis. On entering Florence's house on those days when it was *her* mother's turn, I would inevitably find her bent over the bathroom basin, sneezing. She would yell out, half snottily, half snortingly, "I have soap in my nose!"

Whether the Apricot Tree really belonged to Florence wasn't clear—the tree was the neighborhood's and as such, was as familiar as our own faces, or the faces of our relatives. Her fruit, often abundant, sometimes meager, was public domain. The tree's limbs draped luxuriously across an irrigation ditch whose calm, muddy water flowed all the way from the Río Grande to our small street where it was diverted into channelways that led into the neighborhood's backyards. The fertile water deposited the future seeds of asparagus, weeds, and wild flowers, then settled into tufted layers crossed by sticks and stones—hieroglyphic reminders of murky beginnings.

Along with the tree, we children drew power from the penetrating grateful wetness. In return, the tree was resplendent with offerings—there were apricots and more, there were the sturdy compartments, the chambers and tunnelways of dream, the stages of our dramas. "I'm drowning! I'm drowning!" we mocked drowning and were saved at the last moment by a friendly hand, or, "This is the ship and I am the captain!" we exulted having previously transcended death. Much time was spent at the tree, alone or with others. All of us, Priscilla, Soap-in-her-Nose, the two dark boys Up the street, my little sister and I, all of us loved the tree. We would oftentimes find ourselves slipping off from one of those choreless, shoreless days, and with a high surprised "Oh!" we would greet each other's aloneness, there at the tree that embraced us all selflessly.

On returning home we may have wandered alongside the ditch, behind the Westers' house, and near the other vacant lot which housed the second point of the triangle, the Marking-Off Tree, the likes of which may have stood at the edge of the Garden of Eden. It was dried, sad-looking. All the years of my growing up it struggled to create a life of its own. The tree passed fruit every few years or so—as old men and women struggle to empty their ravaged bowels. The grey-green balls that it brought forth we used as one uses an empty can, to kick and thrash. The tree was a reference point, offering no shade, but always meditation. It delineated the Up world from the Down. It marked off the nearest point home, without being home; it was a landmark, and as such, occupied our thoughts, not in the way the Apricot Tree did, but in a subtler, more profound way. Seeing the tree was like seeing the same viejito downtown for so long, with his bottle and his wife, and looking into his crusty white-rimmed eyes and thinking: "How much longer?" Tape appears on his neck, the voice box gargles a barking sound, and the bruises seem deeper.

There, at that place of recognition and acceptance, you will see the Marking-Off Tree at the edge of my world. I sit on the front porch at twilight. The power is all about me. The great unrest twitters and swells like the erratic chords of small and large birds scaling their way home.

To our left is the Willow Tree, completing this trinity of trees. How to introduce her? I would take the light of unseen eyes and present the sister who lives in France, or her husband who died when he was but thirty. I would show you the best of friends and tell you how clear, how dear. I would recall moments of their eternal charm, their look or stance, the intrinsic quality of their bloom. You would see inside an album a black and white photograph of a man with a wide, ruddy face, in shirtsleeves, holding a plump, squinting child in front of a small tree, a tree too frail for the wild lashes, surely. On the next page an older girl passing a hand through windblown hair would look at you, you would feel her gentle beauty, love her form. Next to her a young girl stands, small eyes toward godfather, who stares at the photographer, shaded by a growing-stronger tree. Or then you would be at a birthday party, one of the guests, rimmed in zinnias, cousins surrounding, Soap-in-her-Nose, the two dark boys (younger than in story time) and the others, miniaturized versions of their future selves. Two sisters, with their arms around each other's child-delicate necks, stand out—as the warps and the twinings of the willow background confuse the boys with their whips and the girls with their fans.

In this last photograph one sees two new faces, one shy boy huddled among the girls, the other removed from all contact, sunblinded, lost in leaves.

Next to us lived the Althertons: Rob, Sandy, Ricky, and Randy. The history of the house next door was wrought with struggle. Before the Althertons moved in, the Cardozas lived there, with their smiling young boys, senseless boys, demon boys. It was Emmanuel (Mannie) who punched the hole in our plastic swimming pool and Jr. who made us cry. Toward the end of the Cardoza boys' reign, Mrs. C, a small breathless bug-eyed little woman, gave birth to a girl. Mr. C's tile business failed and the family moved to Chiva Town, vacating the house to the Althertons, an alternately histrionically dry and loquacious couple with two boys. Ricky, the oldest, was a tall, tense boy who stalked the Altherton spaces with the natural grace of a wild animal, ready to spring, ears full of sound, eyes taut with anticipation. Young Randy was a plump boy-child with deep, watery eyes that clung to Mrs. Altherton's lumpish self while lean and lanky Papa A ranged the spacious lawn year round in swimming trunks in search of crab grass, weeds, any vestiges of irregularity. Lifting a handful of repugnant weed, he'd wave it in the direction of Sandy, his wife, a pigeon of a woman who cooed, "You don't say . . ."

Jack Spratt shall eat no fat, his wife shall eat no lean, and between them both, you see, they licked the platter clean.

The Altherton yard was very large, centered by a metal pole to which was attached the neighborhood's first tetherball. From our porch where my sister and I sat dressing dolls, we could hear the punch and whirr of balls, the crying and calling out. Ricky would always win, sending Randy racing inside to Mrs. A's side, at which time, having dispatched his odious brother, Ricky would beat and thrash the golden ball around in some sort of crazed and victorious adolescent dance. Randy and Mrs. A would emerge from the house and they would confer with Ricky for a time. Voices were never raised, were always hushed and calm. The two plump ones would then go off, hand in hand, leaving the lean to himself. Ricky would usually stomp away down the neighborhood, flicking off a guiltless willow limb, deleafing it in front of our watchful eyes, leaving behind his confused steps a trail of green, unblinking eyes, the leaves of our tree.

Every once in a while Randy would walk over to us as we sat dressing dolls or patting mud pies, and hesitantly, with that babyish smile of his, ask us to come play ball. We two sisters would cross the barriers of Altherton and joyfully bang the tetherball around with Randy. He played low, was predictable, unlike Ricky, who threw the ball vehemently high, confounding, always confounding. Ricky's games were over quickly, his blows firm, surprising, relentless. Ricky never played with my sister and me. He was godlike and removed, as our older sister, already sealed in some inexplicable anguish of which we children had no understanding. It was Randy who brought us in, called out to us, permitted us to play. And when he was not there to beckon us, it was his lingering generosity and gentleness that pushed us forward into the mysterious Altherton yard, allowing us to risk fear, either of Mr. Altherton and his perennial tan, or Ricky with his senseless animal temper. Often we would find the yard free and would enjoy the tetherball without interruption, other times we would see Ricky stalk by, or hear the rustling approach of clippers, signifying Mr. Altherton's return. If we would sense the vaguest shadow of either spectre, we would run, wildly, madly, safely home, to the world of our Willow where we would huddle and hide in the shelter of green, labyrinthine rooms, abstracting ourselves from the world of Ricky's torment or Mr. Altherton's anxious wanderings.

I have spoken least of all of the Willow Tree, but in speaking of someone dead or gone, what words can reach far enough into the past to secure a vision of someone's smiling face or curious look, who can tame the restless past and show, as I have tried, black and white photographs of small children in front of a tree?

The changes of the Willow were imperceptible at first. Mr. W, the Greek, through an oversight in pronunciation, had always been Mr. V. The spies became individualized when Mr. Strong later became my substitute history teacher and caused a young student to faint. She who was afraid of blood looked up into the professor's nose and saw unmistakable flecks of red. The two dark boys grew up, became wealthy, and my cousin moved away. The irrigation ditch was eventually closed. Only the Willow remained—consoling, substantial. The days became shorter and divided the brothers while the sisters grew closer.

Ricky, now a rampaging, consumed adolescent, continued his thoughtless forays, which included absently ripping off willow limbs and discarding them on our sidewalk. "He's six years older than Randy," said my mother, that dark mother who hid in trees, "he hates his brother, he just never got over Randy's birth. You love your sister, don't you?" "Yes, mother," I would say.

It was not long after Ricky's emerging manhood that the Willow began to ail, even as I watched it. I knew it was hurting. The tree began to look bare.

The limbs were lifeless, in anguish, and there was no discernible reason. The solid, green rooms of our child's play collapsed, the passageways became cavernous hallways, the rivers of grass dried and there was no shade. The tree was dying. My mother became concerned. I don't know what my little sister thought; she was a year younger than I. She probably thought as I did, for at that time she held me close as model and heroine, and enveloped me with her love, something Randy was never able to do for his older brother, that bewildered boy.

It wasn't until years later (although the knowledge was there, admitted, seen) that my mother told me that one day she went outside to see Ricky standing on a ladder under our Willow. He had a pair of scissors in his hands and was cutting whole branches off the tree and throwing them to one side. Mother said, "What are you doing, Ricky?" He replied, "I'm cutting the tree." "Do you realize that you're killing it?" she responded calmly. It is here that the interpretation breaks down, where the photographs fade into grey wash, and I momentarily forget what Ricky's reply was, that day, so many years ago, as the limbs of our Willow fell about him, cascading tears, willow reminders past the face of my mother, who stood solemnly and without horror.

Later, when there was no recourse but to cut down the tree, Regino Suárez, the neighborhood handyman, and his son were called in.

Regino and his son had difficulty with the tree; she refused to come out of the earth. When her roots were ripped up, there lay a cavity of dirt, an enormous aching hole, like a tooth gone, the sides impressed with myriad twistings and turnings. The trunk was moved to the side of the house, where it remained until several years ago, when it was cut up for firewood, and even then, part of the stump was left. Throughout the rest of grade school, high school, and college—until I went away, returned, went away—the Willow stump remained underneath the window of my old room. Often I would look out and see it there, or on thoughtful walks, I would go outside near the Althertons' old house, now sealed by a tall concrete wall, and I would feel the aging hardness of the Willow's flesh.

That painful, furrowed space was left in the front yard, where once the Willow had been. It filled my eyes, my sister's eyes, my mother's eyes. The wall of trees, backdrop of the traveling me, that triangle of trees—the Apricot Tree, the Marking-Off Tree, the Willow Tree—was no longer.

One day Ricky disappeared and we were told that he'd been sent to a home for sick boys.

As children one felt dull, leaden aches that were voiceless cries and were incommunicable. The place they sprung from seemed so desolate and uninhabited and did not touch on anything tangible or transferable. To carry pain around as a child does, in that particular place, that worldless, grey corridor, and to be unable to find the syllables with which to vent one's sorrow, one's horror . . . surely this is insufferable anguish, the most insufferable. Being unable to see, yet able, willing, yet unwilling . . . to comprehend. A child's sorrow is a place that cannot be visited by others. Always the going back is solitary, and the little sisters, however much they love you, were never really very near, and the mothers, well, they stand as I said before, solemnly, without horror, removed from children by their understanding.

I am left with recollections of pain, of loss, with holes to be filled. Time, like trees, withstands the winters, bursts forth new leaves from the dried old sorrows—who knows when and why—and shelters us with the shade of later compassions, loves, although at the time the heart is seared so badly that the hope of all future flowerings is gone.

Much later, after the death of the Willow, I was walking to school when a young boy came up to me and punched me in the stomach. I doubled over, crawled back to Sister Elaine's room, unable to tell her of my recent attack, unprovoked, thoughtless, insane. What could I say to her? To my mother and father? What can I say to you? All has been told. The shreds of magic living, like the silken, green ropes of the Willow's branches, dissolved about me, and I was beyond myself, a child no longer. I was filled with immense sadness, the burning of snow in a desert land of consistent warmth.

I walked outside and the same experience repeated itself; oh, not the same form, but yes, the attack. I was the same child, you see, mouthing pacifications, incantations . . . "Bring flowers of the fairest, bring flowers of the rarest. It's okay, from garden and woodland and hillside and dale. Our pure hearts are swelling. It's all right, our glad voices are telling, please, the praise of the loveliest rose of the dale."

Jack Spratt could eat no fat, his wife could eat no lean, and between them both, you see, they licked the platter clean . . .

My mother planted a willow several years ago, so that if you sit on the porch and face left you will see it, thriving. It's not in the same spot as its predecessor, too far right, but of course, the leveling was never done, and how was Regino to know? The Apricot Tree died, the Marking-Off Tree is fruitless now, relieved from its round of senseless birthings. This willow tree is new, with its particular joys. It stands in the center of the block . . . between.

27

Poet and essayist Alison Hawthorne Deming (the great-great-granddaughter of the writer Nathaniel Hawthorne) was born in Hartford, Connecticut, in 1946, and received her M.F.A. from Vermont College. She now directs the University of Arizona Poetry Center in Tucson. Her poetry collection *Science and Other Poems* (1993) won the Academy of American Poets Walt Whitman Award; a second book of poetry about butterflies, *The Monarchs,* was published in 1998. She also has published two collections of nonfiction including *Temporary Homelands* (1994) and *The Edges of the Civilized World* (1998). This essay, from her first collection, chronicles her efforts at coming to terms with Tucson's Sonoran desert climate by working in her yard, that "curious border zone between the wild and the domestic in which we invite nature to come close but not too close."

Claiming the Yard

Alison Hawthorne Deming

Autumn, time to cut back the overgrowth again. The pyracantha hedge has gone shapeless as uncombed hair. The paloverde has pressed a limb against the stucco chimney running up the east wall of my house. And the bougainvillea has sprawled beyond its capacity to hold its boughs upright. Even the aloes and agaves have sent satellite growths out from their roots, the outlyers offending my idea of symmetry in the semicircular garden by the front door. The profusion always surprises me, though I have had three years to get used to desert living. When I'm not cutting back and pulling up, I'm struggling to keep alive plants that don't belong here—peppermint, petunias, tomatoes, and marigolds. Since the temperature in Tucson has been over one hundred degrees for most of the past four months, my attempts at gardening look pretty crisp these days. I have mastered only clove-scented basil. "My basil trees," I call them. The cluster of glistening sweetness has thrived for six months in the backyard shade, growing three feet tall, sporting woody stalks an inch thick and leaves big as serving spoons. Though it is already October, I don't have the heart to whack them down to make pesto.

My friends who know my dreamy penchant for oceans and woods find it strange that I live in the sun-beaten starkland of the Sonoran Desert. To be honest, so do I. At times I feel green deprived, and I would not be surprised to learn that there exists a psychic malady that can be cured only by the visual ingestion of green wildness—a syndrome similar to the one that afflicts the light-deprived residents of the Pacific Northwest. But I love not only nature's beauty; I love also her weirdness and pig-headed persistence against hostile conditions. And the desert is nothing if not weird and pig-headed. Consider the spadefoot toad that uses its namesake appendages to dig a home underground, lies there without breathing for months—even years in severe drought—absorbing oxygen through its skin, then emerges to feed and breed at the first music of raindrops hitting the soil. Consider the range of desert dwellers requiring venom in order to survive—Gila monster, ten species of rattlesnake, coral snake, scorpion, centipede, tarantula, black widow, brown recluse, and the venomous Colorado river toad known to kill the dog that laps it. Consider the placid saguaro, a cool phallic water cask that takes its sweet time growing—fifty years before it bothers making arms. Living here has been humbling, teaching me that I don't know much about nature after all, that I am no master even of the small domain of my yard.

A yard, anywhere, is an expression of one's relationship with nature, a curious border zone between the wild and the domestic in which we invite nature to come close, but not too close. Nature does not belong in the house. We buy chemical products to keep our space clear of fungi, molds, bacilli, mites, and fleas. Plants can come inside, if they are content to live in pots. We seal basement windows and crawl spaces to keep out feral cats. And, when a crusty cockroach or lacy newt crawls out of the drain into our kitchen sink, we are shocked at its lack of respect for the border we've drawn. The shaping and ordering of the yard is a warning to nature: here dwells human will.

In the desert the conscientious homeowner gives up on lawn, replacing it with gravel and a few pleasingly arrayed arid-land shrubs and trees—Sonoran bird of paradise, oleander, prickly pear, Joshua tree, Chilean mesquite. After the January rains, the gravel sprouts with mustard, wild onion grass, tumbleweed, penstemon, and globe mallow. Most of my neighbors use Rapid-Kill or

Round-Up to keep the gravel bare, so that it provides a more attractive background for their shrubs. Gallon jugs of the stuff are sold at grocery and drug stores. Or one can use the preemergents, which one neighbor assured me don't kill anything; they just stop the seeds from germinating. For the first two years I resorted to arduous biannual weed pulling. This fall I decided to let the front yard go wild and see what comes up.

I was inspired to do so by my earlier experiment with Arizona lupines. I had been accustomed to lupines from the Northeast. They grow in manic meadows along the coast of Maine and New Brunswick—startling spires of peppery deep blue, fuchsia, white, and pink quilting the roadsides. The deep blues predominate in most years, though once I saw the fuchsias and pinks take over. Lupines in the Northeast are bigger and more sturdy than most wildflowers; in fact, they are a runaway garden variety, or, as the field guide calls them, "escapes." Shortly after moving to Arizona, I made a road trip north from Tucson to Globe. It was April and I had no idea what to expect from spring in the desert. The route made a gradual ascent from creosote bush and saguaro terrain to one of varied grasses. The shoulder lit up with the burgundy tassels of bromegrass, and then deep blue began to line both sides of the road—a linear bouquet that extended for fifty miles. Pulling off to identify the blooms, I was surprised to discover that they were lupines, smaller in stature and in leaf and flower size, their color more subdued, but morphologically identical to the eastern runaways. A few miles farther on, lupines blanketed entire hillsides and arroyos, the ground tinted as if a cloud shedding a blue shadow had drifted over.

The bloom passed nearly as quickly as a cloud. I returned two weeks later to gather seed and the task was a challenge. Not only had the flowers passed, the plants had become entirely desiccated, blown flat and empty by hot, dry winds. I collected what pods I could find and brought them home to scatter in the yard. The following spring my captives bloomed out of the gravel by my mailbox. When that small wild blue meadow flared up and passed into dross, I began to feel at home.

Though my eagerness to control nature in the borderland of my yard is less developed than that of many of my neighbors, this past summer I was forced by termites to enter the chemical marketplace. There is not much wood on the outside of my adobe house, but it sits on wooden beams all too accessible to the ground-dwelling insects. The queen of a termite colony can lay thirty thousand eggs in a day, so once the drills and sawdust trails are found in the cellar, one tends to leap for corrective measures. In the rush of a busy work week there were miscommunications with the pest people. Before I'd had time to fully understand the treatment plan, what biocide they would use, what risks there might be, what options I had, I came home to find a crew of gloved, goggled, and masked workers pumping something called Dragnet into every seam and crevice that might provide access for the bugs. Things went from bad to worse. The workers drilled through a cement slab and burst a water pipe, which soaked the carpet in my bedroom. By the time I had finished arguing with the company's owner about who was responsible for fixing the mess, the rug had begun to stink of fungus and mold. The carpet man came, made a diagnosis from the stench, sprayed on an antifungal. What is it? I asked him. MBI, he said. What's that? I asked. We just call it a microbiological inhibitor, he said. Does anyone sleep in here? I do, I replied. Well, I wouldn't, he warned. He installed a huge fan under the carpet, clipping down the edges so that the surface waved like Jell-O, and the stink wafted throughout the house. We'd better let that dry for a few days, he said, and left me in the chemical haze.

I admit that I'm among the first to claim our species would be better off if we had a closer relationship with nature—one of understanding rather than exploitation. But this domestic debacle got me thinking that there are limits to the claim. We may need to be close to the song of the mockingbird and the Swainson's thrush because their music wakes up a benevolent part of our minds that is usually sleeping. We may need to be close to the sustaining power of the land because it feeds us body and soul; to trees because they manufacture oxygen and teach us by the example of their long and rooted lives to slow down. We may need the lessons in endurance, in the heroic capacity for healing and regeneration that nature provides. But we need also to distance ourselves from nature—from the random forces that would wreck our health and homes; from the microbial upstarts that would colonize our blood; and from certain tendencies of mind, which are only natural, such as the lust for killing.

The geneticists say that evolution favors complex brains such as ours because our intelligence, at least in theory, enables us to change faster than does the slow dance of genetic selection and drift. But we seem to be too slow for our own ambitions in this regard. Take killing. For thousands of years (a blink in evolutionary time) human beings have lived with a collective moral decision that killing others is wrong. We have decided to kill our killing, to quell that aspect of our animality. Yet a resume for our species would have to report that we have not come close to accomplishing that goal. Indeed it seems that the three things most troubling to us—violence, sex, and death—all speak of our struggle with our animal nature. Our relationship with nature, both inside our bodies and outside in our yards, is as complicated as our intimate tangles with one another. I guess that's why we like to tame nature by thinking of it as something *out there* that we can visit on the weekend to improve our frame of mind.

Time to cut back the overgrowth again, to stake my claim for order and beauty against the chaos of nature's profusion. While I'm out there whacking and hoeing, puling up and pruning, cutting down one plant so another will thrive, I'll remember how good that work feels. I get a little crazy when my hands are out of dirt for too long, like my house cats, who climb the windows and walls if I don't let them out to do some killing.

28

Susan J. Tweit was born into a family of naturalists in Evanston, Illinois, in 1956. She has her B.S. in botany and photography from Southern Illinois University, and she has written seven books about the American West. These books include *Pieces of Light: A Year on Colorado's Front Range* (1990), *Seasons in the Desert: A Naturalist's Notebook* (1998), *Barren, Wild, and Worthless: Living in the Chihauhan Desert* (1995), *City Foxes* (with Wendy Shattil; 1997), and *Seasons on the Pacific Coast: A Naturalist's Notebook* (1999). She now lives in Salida, Colorado, where she is engaged in restoring a creek that runs through the center of the downtown area. She also writes for *Audubon* magazine and teaches writing seminars around the country. As these selections from *Pieces of Light* demonstrate, she built her book about urban nature in Boulder, Colorado, in the traditional form of the nature journal, recording her observations and reflections over the course of her year in the city.

From *Pieces of Light*

Susan J. Tweit

Wednesday, 23 September

Today is the first day of fall—last night was the autumnal equinox. The nights and days are now about equal length, but soon the days will be shorter. The year is winding towards the long cold nights of winter. Autumn is a season of transition, between summer, the season of abundant and exuberant life, and winter, the quiet season when much of life is dormant, waiting for the earth to move closer to the sun again and the days to lengthen. Hormones direct the rituals of change: leaves on maples, cottonwoods, oaks, and other deciduous trees turn brilliant, gradually lose their color, and finally drop; birds from hawks to hummingbirds, some animals, and even fragile monarch butterflies migrate to wintering areas; raccoons, skunks, mice, and other animals and insects prepare to hole up for the winter; the pace of human lives slows too, we succumb to melancholia more frequently, we sleep longer hours. . . . Even fall weather is in transition: gusty, strong winds; days running the gamut from summer's heat to winter's snapping cold; precipitation from rain to sleet to snow. Rarely is the weather forecast the same for two successive fall days.

The equinoxes and the solstices are the turning points for the seasons, markers in the sun's yearly cycle. Historically, human cultures revolved around the changing seasons. The solstices and equinoxes signaled the times to plant or harvest, or the end of deepening winter. Rituals, feasts, and celebrations marked these crucial celestial events. Our modern culture, though, largely ignores the changing seasons. We pass our lives in climate-controlled buildings, detached from the rhythms of life outside our homes, offices, schools, and cars.

The study of astronomy began with the need to chart the cycles of the sun and moon in order to predict the times of the equinoxes and solstices. It has only been in the rational era of modern science, with its emphasis on logic instead of emotion, that we have lost interest in celebrating the solar rhythm. Perhaps that will change. If the earth really is a giant self-regulating organism as some theories now suggest, then the solar cycle regulates the beat of its life. Today, after the autumnal equinox, the beat is beginning to slow in preparation for winter.

Tonight, Richard walked with me to my class on the university campus. On the way he showed me another walk that he discovered. He is really the explorer of the two of us. I explore only until I find a path or walking route that suits me and then I walk that route every day, learning its details—colors, textures, patterns, smells, and sounds—until it becomes familiar. Richard is always pushing at the boundaries of his territory, scouting a new route, a different alley, walking several blocks out of his way to check out a park or a place with a view. We walked over the hill and through downtown to the greenbelt along Boulder Creek, and followed the path downstream.

The greenbelt is a linear park, only several hundred yards wide, but nearly five miles long, a verdant ribbon winding along Boulder Creek from the mouth of Boulder Canyon east right through downtown and out onto the plains. A hard-surfaced path follows the creek for the whole length of the park. Along the way are benches and picnic tables in eight pocket parks—wide places in the greenbelt—and in two larger parks. It is a wonderful place. Despite being bridged by numerous busy city streets, hemmed in by houses, yards, commercial districts, and even a football field, and losing part of its flow to diversion dams, the creek and its green ribbon of vegetation host trout and raccoons, dippers and other wild lives. The strip of rushing mountain stream, shadowed by enormous cottonwoods and peach-leaved willows, stitches the foothills to the plains.

It is a popular park, and last night was no exception—we were passed by joggers and cyclists, roller skaters, people in wheelchairs, and a skateboarder. Warm days year-round bring hordes of people out of downtown offices and shops to sit in the shade of the big trees along the creek, or run and cycle the path. On weekends, the path is choked with people young and old, large and small, of every variety and description, walking, running, skateboarding, bicycling, or just sitting. People float the creek's cool waters with inner tubes. Late spring and early summer high water lures kayakers to dance the creek's obstacle course of low bridges and diversion dams. Fly-fishing season brings out numerous anglers to try their skill on trout. In winter, skiers use the path when sufficient snow falls on Boulder. The cool shade and wild tangle of vegetation also attracts a small population of homeless people, both residents and passers-through, who find the greenbelt attractive warm-weather camping and panhandling space.

I'd walked parts of the path before, upstream from downtown to Richard's office near the mouth of the canyon; downstream past the Arapahoe Avenue bridge, but never wandered downstream as far as we walked tonight. The creek muttered and gurgled as it flowed along its rocky bed, a cool downstream breeze rustled the jungle of leaves all around us, golden evening sunlight pierced the shady canopy in dust-flecked rays. The rumble of traffic and other city noises receded, washed away by soft sounds. The air was filled with the pungent sweetness of peeling cottonwood bark. A belted kingfisher gave its rattling cry as it flew downstream. We stopped to watch for trout in the clear water but didn't see any. It didn't matter. We forgot about the surrounding city, strolling in another time, free of the march of seconds, minutes, hours.

Overhead was a nearly continuous, dancing green canopy: the waxy deltoid leaves of big cottonwood trees; shiny, long, lance-shaped leaves dangling from multi-trunked peach-leaved willows; bleached green, three-parted box elder leaves already fading to the pale yellow of fall. At eye level was a mosaic of shrubs and small trees: cottonwoods and willows, chokecherry and wild rose, box elder and green ash trees, wild plums, all stitched to the overstory by the strong ropes of wild grape and clematis vines.

It is hard to imagine Boulder without the greenbelt and creek path. It seems such a logical part of the city. But the idea of preserving Boulder Creek as a strip of natural park running through urban Boulder has been a long time germinating. Eighty years ago, in 1910, Frederick Law Olmstead, Jr., son of the designer of New York's Central Park, created a master plan that recommended protecting Boulder Creek as a free-flowing, wild creek. The idea, and the creek's riparian vegetation and trout population, languished for decades. In the meantime, gravel was dredged from the creek bed and parts of the creek were channelized for flood control. Construction encroached on the downtown section of the creek bed, and overgrazing broke the banks on the east end. Cottonwoods were removed or died as water was drawn down for irrigation and lawn watering. Where the cottonwood overstory was breached, the balance failed and the remaining riparian vegetation wasted away, no longer able either to filter runoff or to shade the creek bottom from the summer's hot sun. Populations of trout and other riparian and aquatic creatures dwindled. Finally, in 1983, the city brought alive Olmsted's grand vision with the Boulder Creek Project, including protection of the greenbelt, construction of the Boulder Creek Path, and extensive stream rehabilitation to make Boulder Creek not only pleasant for people, but liveable for wildlife also. That meant reconstruction of the actual creek channel to provide good habitat for trout and other aquatic life—adding boulders and other structures so the stream would regain pools and riffles; revegetation of denuded bank sections to provide shelter, food, and cover; and negotiations between the city and major water users to ensure a sufficient year-round streamflow to keep trout populations alive. It worked: the trout are back in the upper sections, belted kingfishers patrol the creek, at least one pair of great horned owls nests in the cottonwoods, great blue herons fish the pools, dragonflies hawk sunny spots above the water—and we humans crowd the path in hordes.

The greenbelt is a good example of the problems of competing land uses along the Front Range, and in any arid area. Riparian areas like this—because of the available water, dense and verdant vegetation, cover and shade, and resultant diversity—are critical to the survival of more mammal, bird, fish, reptile, amphibian, and insect populations than any other habitats. Even the species that do not actually live in riparian habitats depend on them as travel corridors, feeding areas, migration rest stops—the list goes on and on. Yet riparian ecosystems are the tropical rain forests of North American arid areas: the most likely ecosystems to be thoughtlessly abused for short-term gains. We dam the streams to store water, creating widely fluctuating reservoirs that eventually silt up; we cut down the cottonwoods and replace them with "more desirable" trees; we divert the flows, de-watering the streams to maintain our green lawns; we straighten out the kinks and line their banks with concrete for flood control. And so the riparian jungles disappear. When we do preserve a relatively free-flowing stream and its green ribbon of cottonwood forest, we put a path along it, displacing the wildlife with joggers, walkers, cyclists—a monoculture of humans.

I love walking this path, but is my pleasure worth the cost of displacing the myriad species of wildlife from one of the precious few remaining riparian areas? Given the choice between developing a path through Boulder along this creek or putting the path somewhere else and keeping the creek wild to accommodate the white-tailed deer, great horned owls, northern orioles, dippers, ducks, leopard frogs, salamanders, and other wildlife, what should we choose? The trade-offs are not clear. Some of the wildlife live here anyway, deer certainly continue to travel the creek corridor at night, and raccoons and other urban wildlife use the creek, but without the enormous numbers of humans using the slender riparian zone, there would be more space for other lives. On the other hand, the creek path does much good in terms of education, by exposing people to the beauty and wonder of the natural world. The question involves rights: do we humans have the right to preempt other beings' habitat? I don't think so. We are acting like greedy children, grabbing the whole plate of cookies, asserting that they belong to us, and refusing to share. Still, there is no simple solution, along Boulder Creek, or anywhere.

We crossed the creek on a creaky suspended footbridge and climbed a switchbacking path onto the university campus. Below, the steep hillside was shaded by the box elders and cottonwoods of the riparian forest, the ground festooned with thick brown stems of wild grape vines. At the top of the hill, above the green canopy, we turned and stood under the spreading branches of a ponderosa pine, looking north along the cresting wave of the foothills where the plains suddenly bend upwards into mountains. Below us wandered the green line of the creek, cutting through the regular pattern of the city streets; past town, the wide sweep of ochre plains stretched to the horizon. The sun slanted low, coloring the world with dusty golden light.

After my class I walked back across the university campus to meet Richard in the student center. It is a big campus, cluttered with buildings and twisted walkways. I became absorbed in watching the stars in the obsidian-black sky and forgot to pay attention to where I was. I missed the student center and had to backtrack between a group of old buildings, through enchanting archways leading to dark courtyards full of trees and in one case, a pond. All mysterious and obscure, inviting exploration.

Friday, 9 October

Last night, three raccoons ran up the stairs outside our living room window, their nails clacking loudly on the wooden stair treads. The large grey mother led, the two smaller young of the year followed hard behind. It was quite startling to look out the window and see raccoons there. I suspect that they come for cat food; one of the apartments upstairs is home to a large ginger cat whose owner keeps a dish of cat food outside the door. This must be a regular dining stop for the raccoons because they seemed to know where they were going—after they passed the window the steady rhythm of their nails told me that they headed purposefully along the balcony with no pausing to sniff and cast about.

Boulder's urban wild mammal population is large and surprisingly diverse, partly because of the lush habitat created by thousands of planted trees and acres of landscaping. Raccoons are one of the three most commonly sighted wild animals in Boulder, along with deer and skunks. Other members of our urban fauna include bats, shrews, mice, weasels, ground squirrels, cottontail rabbits, and muskrats. All are opportunistic species, able to adapt to human activity and common in town wherever pockets of usable habitat exist. Therein lies a problem: what seems like usable habitat to a raccoon may be hotly contested by the humans who live there. At this time of year, the problem is exacerbated by the approach of denning season. Wildlife from bats to raccoons are on the prowl for winter homes and will take up residence in whatever suitable space they find, including attics, chimneys, crawl spaces, porches, garages, woodpiles.

Our relationship with wild animals is a bit schizophrenic: how we behave depends partly on whether we think of the animal as a "good" animal or not; basically, whether they compete with us in any way. If a numerous and opportunistic species prefers the habitat we humans prefer, we see the species as "bad" animals, and we generally resolve the conflict by transplanting or killing them. It doesn't take much soul-searching to decide to transplant a group of skunks that have invaded your crawl space for the winter—you can be pretty sure that they will find another shelter and survive. But what about other species, for instance, grizzly bears, whose habitat is now scarce and also, because much of it is "pristine" and beautiful wilderness, increasingly pressured by human use? When conflicts arise with the big bears, it is not nearly as easy to transplant them since so little usable habitat remains for grizzlies. How do we resolve conflicts with species, like the grizzlies, with which we don't seem to be able to coexist? Would we ever think of closing a wilderness area to human use in order to allow grizzlies to have an undisturbed home?

Later last night I heard the raccoons hissing and squealing right outside our bedroom window under the apple trees. They come in the evening to eat the apples and often get into fights with the feral cats that consider that tangle of trees and shrubs their turf. My sympathies are entirely with the raccoons; although I might prefer a backyard with shortgrass prairie, burrowing owls, prairie dogs, and rattlesnakes, at least the raccoons are wild. But even those sympathies carry a value judgment. Are raccoons really "wilder" than feral cats? I fell asleep to the unearthly symphony of squealing and hissing, still wondering.

29

Robert Michael Pyle is a well-known nature writer who was born in Denver in 1946 and now lives in Grays River, Washington. He received his B.S. and M.S. degrees from the University of Washington, and his M.Phil. and Ph.D. from Yale. He is a respected lepidopterist who wrote *The Audubon Society Guide to the Butterflies of North America* (1981). Pyle has also written a number of books about nature including *Wintergreen: Listening to the Land's Heart* (1987), which won the John Burroughs Medal for nature writing, and *Chasing Monarchs: Migrating with the Butterflies of Passage* (1999). The essay below is from *The Thunder Tree: Lessons from an Urban Wildland* (1993) where he tells how a "secondhand land"—the High Line Canal near the Denver suburb of Aurora—shaped his love of nature. What he discovered there about how children come to love nature becomes the basis for the compelling observations in "The Extinction of Experience."

The Extinction of Experience

Robert Michael Pyle

We need not marvel at extinction; if we must marvel, let it be at our own presumption in imagining for a moment that we understand the many complex contingencies on which the existence of each species depends.

—Charles Darwin, *The Origin of Species*

I became a nonbeliever and a conservationist in one fell swoop. All it took was the Lutherans paving their parking lot.

One central, unavoidable fact of my childhood was the public school system of Aurora, Colorado. My path to school for ten out of twelve years followed the same route: down Revere Street, left at the fire hall, along Hoffman Park to Del Mar Circle, then around the Circle to Peoria Street, and on to whichever school was currently claiming my time. Detours occurred frequently.

The intersection of Hoffman Boulevard and Peoria Street was two corners sacred, two profane. On the southeast squatted the white brick Baptist church. Across Del Mar lay a vacant lot full of pigweed, where Tom and I cached brown bananas and other castoffs foraged from behind Busley's Supermarket in case we needed provisions on some future expedition. Then came the Phillips 66 gas station and the Kwik Shake, a nineteen-cent hamburger stand whose jukebox played "Peggy Sue" if you so much as tossed a nickel in its direction. On the northeast corner lay Saint Mark's, the red brick lair of the Lutherans, marginally modern, with a stained glass cross in the wall. I spent quite a lot of time dawdling in the vacant lot among the pigweed and haunting the Kwik Shake after school, but I seldom loitered in the precincts of the churchgoers.

Lukewarm Methodists at best, my parents flipped a coin and took us to Saint Mark's for the Easter service. The next Christmas I was roped into being a wise man, and I felt both silly and cold in my terry cloth robe. Later, when my great-grandmother came to live with us, she hauled me off Sundays to the Southern Baptists. Gimma desperately wanted me to go down the aisle and be saved. A shy boy, I wasn't about to prostrate myself in public before a bunch of people with big smiles and bad grammar. Besides, I couldn't see the sense in confessing to sins I didn't feel I had properly enjoyed as yet. Had I been compelled to choose among them, I'd have taken the cool, impersonal approach of the Lutherans over the Baptists' warm-hearted but embarrassing bear hug of a welcome. But Gimma passed on, and my parents pushed in neither direction, so I opted for the corporeal pleasures of "Peggy Sue" and pigweed and put the soul on hold.

Behind the Lutheran Church lay another, smaller vacant lot, where the congregation parked in the mud. The new community of Hoffman Heights had been built partly on a filled-in lake. The water poked up here and there, making marshy spots full of plants that grew nowhere else around, like cattails and curly dock. The far corner of the Lutherans' lot held one of the last of these.

One September day, coming home from school, I cut across the boggy corner, almost dried out with late summer and tall with weeds. Pink knotweed daubed the broken mud and scented the afternoon air. Then I noticed, fully spread on the knotweed bloom, a butterfly. It was more than an inch across, richly brown like last year's pennies, with a purple sheen when the sun caught it just right. I knelt and watched it for a long time. There were others flitting around, some of them orange, some brown, but this one stayed put, basking. Then a car drove by, disturbing it. The last thing I noticed before it flew was a broad, bright zigzag of fiery orange across its hind wings.

A couple of years later, when I became an ardent collector, I remembered the butterfly in the Del Mar marshlet clearly. My Peterson field guide showed me that it was, without question, a bronze copper. The orangey ones had been females. Professor Alexander Klots wrote in his *Peterson Field Guide* that it is "the largest of our coppery Coppers" and "not uncommon, but quite local. Seek a colony," he wrote, "in open, wet meadows." Dr. F. Martin Brown, in my bible, *Colorado Butterflies,* explained that the species extended no farther west than the plains of eastern Colorado, and called it *very* local (which I translated as "rare"). He went on to say that "the best places to seek [*Lycaena*] *thoe* in Colorado are the weedy borders of well-established reservoirs on the plains," which the Hoffman Heights lake had certainly been. I eagerly prepared to return to the spot at the right time and obtain *Lycaena thoe* for my collection.

Then, in early summer, the Lutherans paved their parking lot. They dumped loads of broken concrete and earthfill into the little marsh, then covered it with thick black asphalt. Gone were the curly docks, the knotweeds, the coppers. Searching all around Aurora over the next few years I failed to find another colony, or even a single bronze copper. Concluding that a good and loving god would never permit his faithful servants to do such a thing, I gave up on the Lutherans and their like for the long run.

Biologists agree that the rate of species extinction has risen sharply since the introduction of agriculture and industry to the human landscape. Soon the decline might mirror ancient mass extinction episodes that were caused by atmospheric or astronomic events. In response, we compile lists and red books of endangered species and seek to manage conditions in their favor. This is good, if only occasionally successful.

Our concern for the absolute extinction of species is highly appropriate. As our partners in earth's enterprise drop out, we find ourselves lonelier, less sure of our ability to hold together the tattered business of life. Every effort to prevent further losses is worthwhile, no matter how disruptive, for diversity is its own reward. But outright extinction is not the only problem. By concentrating on the truly rare and endangered plants and animals, conservationists often neglect another form of loss that can have striking consequences: the local extinction.

Protection almost always focuses on rarity as the criterion for attention. Conservation ecologists employ a whole lexicon of categories to define scarceness. In ascending order of jeopardy, the hierarchy usually includes the terms "of concern" (= "monitor"), "sensitive," "threatened" (= "vulnerable"), and "endangered." All types so listed might fairly be called "rare." But people tend to employ that term when some other word might be more precise.

Most species listed as endangered are genuinely rare in the absolute sense: their range is highly restricted and their total number is never high. Biologists recognize a fuzzy threshold below which the populations of these organisms should not drop, lest their extinction likely follow. That level is a kind of critical mass, the minimum number necessary to maintain mating and other essential functions. A creature is profoundly rare when its members are so few as to approach this perilous line.

Perceived rarity is often a matter of the distribution of a species over time and space. The monarch butterfly, for example, is virtually absent from the Maritime Northwest owing to the lack of milkweed, while across most of North America it is considered a commonplace creature. Patchy and fluctuating from year to year when dispersed in the summertime, monarchs become incredibly abundant in their Mexican and Californian winter roosts. Yet the migration of the North American monarch is listed as a threatened phenomenon because of the extreme vulnerability of the winter clusters.

Another orange and black butterfly, the painted lady, appears in northern latitudes by the millions from time to time. In certain springs, such as those of 1991 and 1992, these butterflies block entire highways with their very numbers. In drier years, when their southern winter habitat produces little nectar, nary a lady might be seen in the temperate regions come summertime. Nevertheless, this thistle-loving immigrant is so widespread globally that its alternate name is the cosmopolite. Are these insects common or rare? Evidently they can be either. Painted ladies and monarchs stretch our sense of rarity.

The concept becomes a little less slippery when we speak of sedentary or specialized animals and plants such as the bronze copper. But are such creatures actually rare, or merely "local," as Professor Klots described the copper in 1951? The fact is that as the countryside condenses under human influence, that which was only local has a way of becoming genuinely scarce.

Somewhere along the continuum from abundance to extinction, a passenger pigeon becomes a pileated woodpecker, then a northern spotted owl, then nothing at all.

In light of the relativity of rarity, it is not surprising that scarce wildlife preservation resources go almost entirely to the more truly rare species. But, as with Ronald Reagan's decision to restrict federal aid to those he considered "truly needy," this practice leaves many vulnerable populations subject to extinction at the local level.

Local extinctions matter for at least three major reasons. First, evolutionary biologists believe that natural selection operates intensely on "edge" populations. This means that the cutting edge of evolution can be the extremities of a species' range rather than the center, where it is more numerous. The protection of marginal populations therefore becomes important. Local extinctions commonly occur on the edges, depriving species of this important opportunity for adaptive change.

Second, little losses add up to big losses. A colony goes extinct here, a population drops out there, and before you know it, you have an endangered species. Attrition, once under way, is progressive. "Between German chickens and Irish hogs," wrote San Francisco entomologist H. H. Behr to his Chicago friend Herman Strecker in 1875, "no insect can exist besides louse and flea." Behr was lamenting the diminution of native insects on the San Francisco Peninsula. Already at that early date, butterflies such as the Xerces blue were becoming difficult to find as colony after colony disappeared before the expanding city. In the early 1940s the Xerces blue became absolutely extinct. Thus local losses accumulate, undermining the overall flora and fauna.

The third consequence amounts to a different kind of depletion. I call it the *extinction of experience.* Simply stated, the loss of neighborhood species endangers our experience of nature. If a species becomes extinct within our own radius of reach (smaller for the very old, very young, disabled, and poor), it might as well be gone altogether, in one important sense. To those whose access suffers by it, local extinction has much the same result as global eradication.

Of course, we are all diminished by the extirpation of animals and plants wherever they occur. Many people take deep satisfaction in wilderness and wildlife they will never see. But direct, personal contact with other living things affects us in vital ways that vicarious experience can never replace.

I believe that one of the greatest causes of the ecological crisis is the state of personal alienation from nature in which many people live. We lack a widespread sense of intimacy with the living world. Natural history has never been more popular in some ways, yet few people organize their lives around nature, or even allow it to affect them profoundly. Our depth of contact is too often wanting. Two distinctive birds, by the ways in which they fish, furnish a model for what I mean.

Brown pelicans fish by slamming directly into the sea, great bills agape, making sure of solid contact with the resource they seek. Black skimmers, graceful ternlike birds with longer lower mandibles than upper, fly over the surface with just the lower halves of their bills in the water. They catch fish too, but avoid bodily immersion by merely skimming the surface.

In my view, most people who consider themselves nature lovers behave more like skimmers than pelicans. They buy the right outfits at L. L. Bean and Eddie Bauer, carry field guides, and take walks on nature trails, reading all the interpretive signs. They watch the nature programs on television, shop at the Nature Company, and pay their dues to the National Wildlife Federation or the National Audubon Society. These activities are admirable, but they do not ensure truly intimate contact with nature. Many such "naturalists" merely skim, reaping a shallow reward. Yet the great majority of the people associate with nature even less.

When the natural world becomes chiefly an entertainment or an obligation, it loses its ability to arouse our deeper instincts. Professor E. O. Wilson of Harvard University, who has won two Pulitzer prizes for his penetrating looks at both humans and insects, believes we all possess what he calls "biophilia." To Wilson, this means that humans have an innate desire to connect with other life forms, and that to do so is highly salutary. Nature is therapeutic. As short-story writer Valerie Martin tells us in "The Consolation of Nature," only nature can restore a sense of safety in the end. But clearly, too few people ever realize their potential love of nature. So where does the courtship fail? How can we engage our biophilia?

Everyone has at least a chance of realizing a pleasurable and collegial wholeness with nature. But to get there, intimate association is necessary. A face-to-face encounter with a banana slug means much more than a Komodo dragon seen on television. With rhinos mating in the living room, who will care about the creatures next door? At least the skimmers are aware of nature. As for the others, whose lives hold little place for nature, how can they even care?

The extinction of experience is not just about losing the personal benefits of the natural high. It also implies a cycle of disaffection that can have disastrous consequences. As cities and metastasizing suburbs forsake their natural diversity, and their citizens grow more removed from personal contact with nature, awareness and appreciation retreat. This breeds apathy toward environmental concerns and, inevitably, further degradation of the common habitat.

So it goes, on and on, the extinction of experience sucking the life from the land, the intimacy from our connections. This is how the passing of otherwise common species from our immediate vicinities can be as significant as the total loss of rarities. People who care conserve; people who don't know don't care. What is the extinction of the condor to a child who has never known a wren?

In teaching about butterflies, I frequently place a living butterfly on a child's nose. Noses seem to make perfectly good perches or basking spots, and the insect often remains for some time. Almost everyone is delighted by this, the light tickle, the close-up colors, the thread of a tongue probing for droplets of perspiration. But somewhere beyond delight lies enlightenment. I have been astonished at the small epiphanies I see in the eyes of a child in truly close contact with nature, perhaps for the first time. This can happen to grown-ups too, reminding them of something they never knew they had forgotten.

We are finally discovering the link between our biophilia and our future. With new eyes, planners are leaving nature in the suburbs and inviting it back into the cities as never before. For many species the effort comes too late, since once gone, they can be desperately difficult to reestablish. But at least the adaptable types can be fostered with care and forethought.

The initiatives of urban ecologists are making themselves felt in many cities. In Portland, Oregon, Urban Naturalist Mike Houck worked to have the great blue heron designated the official city bird, to have a local microbrewery fashion an ale to commemorate it, and to fill in the green leaks in a forty-mile-loop greenway envisioned decades ago. Now known as the 140-Mile Loop, it ties in with a massive urban greenspaces program on both sides of the Columbia River. An international conference entitled "Country in the City" takes place annually in Portland, pushing urban diversity. These kinds of efforts arise from a recognition of the extinction of experience and a fervid desire to avoid its consequences.

Houck has launched an effort to involve the arts community in refreshing the cities and devoted himself to urban stream restoration. When streams are rescued from the storm drains, they are said (delightfully) to be "daylighted." And when each city has someone like Mike Houck working to daylight its streams, save its woods, and educate its planners, the sources of our experience will be safer.

But nature reserves and formal greenways are not enough to ensure connection. Such places, important as they are, invite a measured, restricted kind of contact. When children come along with an embryonic interest in natural history, they need free places for pottering, netting, catching, and watching. Insects, crawdads, and tadpoles can stand to be nabbed a good deal. Bug collecting has always been the standard route to a serious interest in biology. To expect a strictly appreciative first response from a child is quixotic. Young naturalists need the "trophy," hands-on stage before leapfrogging to mere looking. There need to be places that are not kid-proofed, where children can do damage and come back the following year to see the results.

Likewise, we all need spots near home where we can wander off a trail, lift a stone, poke about, and merely wonder: places where no interpretive signs intrude their message to rob our spontaneous response. Along with the nature centers, parks, and preserves, we would do well to maintain a modicum of open space with no rule but common courtesy, no sign besides animal tracks.

For these purposes, nothing serves better than the hand-me-down habitats that lie somewhere between formal protection and development. Throwaway landscapes like this used to occur on the edges of settlement everywhere. Richard Mabey, a British writer and naturalist, describes them as the "unofficial countryside." He uses the term for those ignominious, degraded, forgotten places that we have discarded, which serve nonetheless as habitats for a broad array of adaptable plants and animals: derelict railway land, ditchbanks, abandoned farms or bankrupt building sites, old gravel pits and factory yards, embankments, margins of landfills. These are the secondhand lands as opposed to the parks, forests, preserves, and dedicated rural farmland that constitute the "official countryside."

Organisms inhabiting such Cinderella sites are surprisingly varied, interesting, and numerous. They are the survivors, the colonizers, the generalists—the so-called weedy species. Or, in secreted corners and remnants of older habitat types—like the Lutherans' parking lot—specialists and rarities might survive as holdouts, waiting to be discovered by the watchful. Developers, realtors, and the common parlance refer to such weedy enclaves as "vacant lots" and "waste ground." But these are two of my favorite oxymorons: What, to a curious kid, is less vacant than a vacant lot? Less wasted than waste ground?

I grew up in a landscape lavishly scattered with unofficial countryside—vacant lots aplenty, a neglected so-called park where weeds had their way, yesterday's farms, and the endless open ground of the High Line Canal looping off east and west. These were the leftovers of the early suburban leap. They were rich with possibility. I could catch a bug, grab a crawdad, run screaming from a giant garden spider; intimacy abounded.

But Aurora slathered itself across the High Plains, its so-called city limits becoming broader than those of Denver itself. In reality it knew no limits, neither the limit of available water nor that of livability. Of course the lots filled in, losing the legacy of their vacancy. The park actually became one, and almost all of its fascination fled before the spade and the blade of the landscaper's art. By the time the canal became an official pathway, part of the National Trail System, most of the little nodes of habitat embraced within its curves and loops were long gone. As butterflies fled before bulldozers, the experience I'd known was buried in the 'burbs.

In a decade I recorded about seventy kinds of butterflies—a tenth of all the North American species—along the canal. In doing so, I learned perhaps the most important thing the High Line had to teach, which was also the saddest. It had to do with the very basis of ecology, that organisms ask their own specific needs of the landscape, and when these cease to be met, they vanish unless adaptation happens fast enough to accommodate change and allow species to survive.

The admiral butterflies flitting along the High Line Canal were survivors. Butterflies related to both red and white admirals lived in central Colorado approximately thirty-five million years ago, as shown by Oligocene fossils from the shale beds of Ancient Lake Florissant. Sharing many characteristics with today's relatives, they kept up with changing landscapes and climates and prospered. They will change further, just as wood nymphs change their spots over time, refining their protection. But because few butterflies can adapt fast enough to outpace a Caterpillar tractor, they must depart or die out when development comes. Altered habitats along the High Line have provided all too many examples.

At first, faunal changes on the canal were largely additive. Itself a product of human intrusion, the old irrigation ditch came to provide habitats for many opportunistic animals and plants. When I began studying its butterflies in the late fifties, the High Line was probably at the peak of its diversity. Habitats had matured and gained complexity for the better part of a century. New species were still coming in, riding the long pipeline of life downstream from the Rockies or up from the prairie.

One season, my mother and I found a large colony of painted crescentspots in a field beside Toll Gate Creek. This southern butterfly had never been recorded in Colorado outside the Arkansas River drainage. Here it was, deep within the basin of the Platte. How it crossed the Divide, the piney plateau that serves as a biogeographical barrier between the watersheds, we hadn't a clue. But once beyond, it began spreading rapidly. The Platte River flood of 1965 took out most of the original colony, but it came back from remnants. Then the painted crescent, more adaptable to disturbance of canalside habitats, began to replace the formerly common pearl and field crescentspots. The painted and gorgone crescentspots, feeding on bindweed and sunflower, respectively, became the common species on much of the eastern High Line, while the pearl and field crescents, dependent on asters, retreated to a few less disturbed sites. With change, something was lost and something else gained.

As change intensified with the growing population of Aurora, losses began to outnumber additions. Many of the habitats I'd known were erased by rampant development of housing tracts and malls. Places where black swallowtails, purplish coppers, and silvery blues once flew became other kinds of places, where they didn't. The only colony of Olympia marblewings was sacrificed, along with their crucifer hosts, mourned by no one but my butterflying buddy, Jack Jeffers, and me. A bluegrass playing field for a new school appeared in their place—the very field where I would throw the discus all through ninth grade. Even as the platter flew high above the new green turf, I thought of the mustards and marbles that would not be back.

None of these butterflies became extinct in the strict sense, for they survived elsewhere, in places still wild and rural. Still, through these local losses, I learned about extinction. Like spelling or multiplication tables, it was a lesson learned by rote, for it was repeated again and again. My work with the butterflies of the High Line Canal has gone on for thirty years. For half that long, a group of friends has gathered each July to hold a butterfly count centered at the site of the Thunder Tree. These ongoing censuses have revealed that since 1960, some 40 percent of the butterfly species on my High Line Canal study sites have become extinct or endangered. This is a greater rate of loss than Los Angeles, San Francisco, or Staten Island has experienced. The decline corresponded with the growth of Aurora's population from about forty thousand to more than a quarter of a million human beings.

On a recent visit, I saw many more kids walking along the canal than in my day, and in many more colors, but none of them were catching bugs, trapping crawdads, or running from spiders. Merely putting people and nature together does not ensure intimacy; to these kids, the canal path might have meant little more than a loopy sidewalk, a shortcut home from school. But I wondered how much was left to find, if anyone wanted to look.

The next day I followed the High Line Canal out onto the plains. A few dozen tall cottonwoods marked off an unspoiled mile strung between a freeway and a new town. Where the ditch dove into a culvert beneath a road, an old marshy margin survived. Monarchs sailed from milkweed to goldenrod.

Then I spotted a smaller brilliancy among the fall flowers. Netting it, I found it was a bronze copper—the first I'd seen in more than thirty years, since the Lutherans paved the parking lot. It was a male, and a female flew nearby. Maybe, I thought, releasing the copper near her, some kid with a Peterson field guide will happen across this little colony before the end of it.

Had it not been for the High Line Canal, the vacant lots I knew, the scruffy park, I'm not at all certain I would have been a biologist. I might have become a lawyer, or even a Lutheran. The total immersion in nature that I found in my special spots baptized me in a faith that never wavered, but it was a matter of happenstance too. It was the place that made me.

How many people grow up with such windows on the world? Fewer and fewer, I fear, as metropolitan habitats disappear and rural ones blend into the urban fringe. The number of people living with little hint of nature in their lives is very large and growing. This isn't good for us. If the penalty of an ecological education is to live in a world of wounds, as Aldo Leopold said, then green spaces like these are the bandages and the balm. And if the penalty of ecological ignorance is still more wounds, then the unschooled need them even more. To gain the solace of nature, we all must connect deeply. Few ever do.

In the long run, this mass estrangement from things natural bodes ill for the care of the earth. If we are to forge new links to the land, we must resist the extinction of experience. We must save not only the wilderness but the vacant lots, the ditches as well as the canyonlands, and the woodlots along with the old growth. We must become believers in the world.

30

David Wicinas was born in 1953 in Pittsburgh. He has his B.A. from the University of Pennsylvania and his M.F.A. from the University of Southern California, and he now lives near San Francisco where he writes about the environment. His essay "The Dark Constable" is part of his book about urban nature entitled *Sagebrush and Cappuccino: Confessions of an L.A. Naturalist* (1995). As Wicinas attempts to come to terms with that most cataclysmic feature of Los Angeles nature—the earthquake, his efforts take shape around a very traditional way of knowing nature, the nature walk. The site that he selects for this particular hike, however, takes him along the San Andreas fault in the wake of the Northridge quake of 1994.

The Dark Constable

David Wicinas

When the first pulse of the earthquake hit at 4:31 in the morning, the building started chattering. Windows throbbed in their casings. Two-by-fours in the walls creaked as they rocked against nails that have held them upright for forty-five years. Pamela and I jerked awake, threw off the blankets, and leapt for the doorway.

Then the second pulse hit. The chattering cranked up into thundering booms, the sound of the building—and the city—bouncing on its foundation. Compounding the horrendous din was the noise of glass and ceramics shattering, furniture toppling, people screaming. Although my life didn't quite flash before my eyes, it seemed like it was cued up and ready to roll.

After the earth stopped moving, we pried our hands from the door frame and surveyed the situation. The building had stood. All that we had lost were material possessions—and a lot of plaster. At the time none of that seemed to matter. Material losses could be replaced. Vastly more important was the fact that we had survived, unharmed.

Soon afterward the words from a song came into my head—lines from a classic Mexican mariachi ballad, "Caminos de Guanajuato."

No vale nada la vida. La vida no vale nada. Nothing is worth life. Life is worth nothing.

We humans are flyspecks. All our edifices, possessions, plans, dreams—they are grains of sand cast to the wind when the Earth chooses to shrug its shoulders. Yet insignificant as we may be, nothing is worth relinquishing our flyspeck of a life spent here on Earth.

Within minutes KFWB News Radio was broadcasting earthquake information. Cal Tech, the seismic soothsayer of Southern California, calculated the epicenter to be located thirteen miles away, in the San Fernando Valley—an area called Northridge. Early reports gauged the strength of the temblor as 6.6 on the Richter scale.

When I heard these pronouncements I snarled, "You mean we lived through that and it wasn't even *the Big One?*"

The specter of an apocalyptic earthquake looms over the future of all Californians. Popularly known as "the Big One," this presumed catastrophe could hit a hundred years from now—or it could strike today. Seismologists say the Big One will result from the collision between two tectonic plates—pieces of the Earth's crust thousands of miles wide that move, often in opposing directions. Pressure builds up in the crust where plates collide. Occasionally the stress is relieved when the plates slip, releasing energy in the form of an earthquake.

The San Andreas fault, one of the biggest tectonic collision zones in the world, runs most of the length of California. Like myself, thirty million Californians have chosen to spend their brief days here on Earth within miles of the San Andreas fault—a force that could make those days substantially briefer.

I have always viewed earthquakes with healthy respect, but after January 17, 1994, they moved way up in my personal cosmology. Previously I had established my own system of classifying temblors. They came in two types: little and scary. The little ones prompted me to remark, "Hmm, it's an earthquake." The bigger ones sent me running for a doorway where I would pray to any divine entities that were tuned in, "Please stop please stop please stop."[1]

Up until January 17 the shaking had always stopped. But that morning, as the floor rolled beneath me like the deck of a sailboat, as I watched pictures leap from the walls—pictures I had installed to withstand an earthquake—I offered no commentary except an awestruck "my God."

One friend of mine, a dedicated Buddhist, told me after the earthquake, "I'm very proud of myself. My years of training paid off. When I realized what was happening, I calmly prepared myself for the death experience."

Regrettably I can't claim that kind of mental discipline. I evidently wasn't ready to relinquish the life experience.

In the days after January 17 I grew edgy and irritable. Though I hated being alone, when I was with other people I rarely laughed and often as not lapsed into silence. Incessantly my mind replayed those predawn moments, especially the sound—the pounding that comes from everywhere. Sleep became nearly impossible. When I did doze off, I bolted awake at the slightest creak. During those long nights I frequently recalled a favorite line from Hemingway. As the war-scarred Jake Barnes observes in *The Sun Also Rises,* "It is awfully easy to be hard-boiled about everything in the daytime, but at night it is another thing."

Had I consulted a psychologist, I would mostly likely have been diagnosed as suffering from post-traumatic stress syndrome—normally the affliction of combat veterans and victims of violence. During the weeks after the quake, the appointment books of L.A.'s mental health professionals were doubtless full, even without my business, because post-traumatic stress syndrome had instantly become a profound concern for hundreds of thousands of Angelenos. Well, it wasn't exactly instant. The pathology took thirty seconds to develop.

The passage of time helped a little, but hundreds of aftershocks only made matters worse. To hasten my psychological adjustment to a seismically active bedroom, I decided to confront my newfound fear of earthquakes. I would peer straight into the eyes of the Big One.

And that is what led me to be standing on the shore of a mountain lake, breathing the clean aroma of pine. A mile high in the San Gabriel Mountains, Jackson Lake is a small finger-shaped tarn that lies at the base of a long valley. As I watch the sun sparkle on the lake's rippling surface, I stand with one leg on the North American tectonic plate moving southeast, the other on the Pacific plate bound for the northwest. My legs are spreading apart at an average rate of one mile every sixty thousand years.

When I was in college my geology professor assured me and my classmates that no matter what your religious training may suggest, the ground does not open up during earthquakes and swallow people—be they sinners or saints.

Standing here astride the fault, I certainly hoped he was correct. He seemed knowledgeable, but I can't help questioning his guarantee when my flesh and bones would make a tasty tidbit to a tectonic plate awakening from a long nap.

The valley in which I stand is part of a region called the San Andreas rift zone, a series of valleys paralleling the southwestern boundary of the Mojave Desert and the northern edge of the Tehachapi, San Gabriel, and San Bernardino mountain ranges. For two centuries these mountains have blocked the northwestern advance of the city of Los Angeles. In the last twenty years, however, several hundred thousand pioneers willing to tolerate two-hour commutes broke through these topographic barriers. (They were led, of course, by those intrepid scouts, the real estate developers.) The region where many of these hyper-commuters settled, near the high-desert town of Palmdale, constitutes the seismic front lines—Tectonic Ground Zero. This was the region I hoped to explore. By spending some time there, I thought I might better understand the time bomb ticking beneath the California soil.

To reach the San Andreas rift zone from my house, I must traverse a freeway interchange where several bridges collapsed at 4:31 A.M., January 17. In thirty seconds those two-hour commutes for thousands of high-desert dwellers turned into five-hour epic journeys. Each way.

Consequently, I plan to rise at 5:30 to get an early start on my hike. But when an aftershock shudders through the building at 4:45 A.M., releasing about a cup of adrenaline into my bloodstream, I figure, Oh what the hell, I might as well leave now. Combat soldiers may be able to sleep minutes after a life-threatening experience, but I have not yet mastered that skill.

I beat the traffic easily, but when I arrive at the San Andreas rift zone and start scouting the landscape for an appropriate hike, I find none. Two continental land masses may be vying for supremacy here, but the casual observer could easily mistake the rift zone for just another far-flung suburb of L.A., full of highways, roads, houses, exurbanites, and their dogs. Not to mention cattle, barbed wire, and Joshua trees.

Thwarted, I pull into the U.S. Forest Service Ranger Station in Valyermo to seek advice. Sheltered by big cottonwoods, Valyermo is a tiny hamlet situated on land that swells up from the flat floor of the Mojave Desert. Behind the town the land keeps rising and soon crumples into the rugged San Gabriel Mountains.

Inside the station I tell the rangers I want to hike the San Andreas fault. They cock their eyebrows at me.

"You're standing on it," says an older woman who works the front desk.

"I know. Does that bother you?" I ask.

"Don't matter none to me. If it goes, I'll just ride with it. I've been riding earthquakes since 1933."

After some discussion, a ranger and I finally agree that I should start hiking at Jackson Lake. From the map on the office wall, I note that the elevation at Jackson Lake is about five thousand feet, so I ask him how much snow I will encounter on this morning in March.

"Oh, maybe a light dusting."

From Jackson Lake a path makes a short, steep ascent through big pines until it joins a jeep trail winding along the face of the sixty-five-hundred-foot-high Piñon Ridge. A few miles to the northeast rises Table Mountain, its summit a couple of thousand feet lower. In the valley between the two mountains—where two continents are crashing into each other—it's so quiet I can hear a dog barking miles away.

Up on the jeep trail I find patchy snow. In places the "light dusting of snow" the ranger predicted is a foot deep. Elsewhere the ground is clear except for a carpet of brown oak leaves and rusty-colored ponderosa pine needles. Water has ponded in ruts along the trail, and at ten o'clock this morning it's frozen hard. I tap my boot on the ice. It rattles like a loose window.

Black oak and ponderosa pine dominate the slopes of Piñon Ridge. The ponderosas grow large here; some must be a hundred feet tall. As the name of this mountain suggests, piñon pines also grow on these hillsides. Indians relished piñon pine nuts, and many of the tribes of the Great Basin founded their diets on them, just as California Indians depended on acorns. The original inhabitants of the San Gabriel Mountains must have been well fed indeed because fine dining abounds here. On these slopes they could gather both piñon pine nuts and the much-prized black oak acorn. Many Indians considered these to be the tastiest of all oak nuts. Since I have learned not to eat raw acorns, today I'll just have to trust the Indians' taste tests.

The limbs of the black oaks are bare at this time of year. These oaks are winter-deciduous, meaning they lose their leaves in the fall and winter. (In climates like Southern California, some trees are drought-deciduous; they lose their leaves during extended periods of extremely hot dry weather.) Looking up through the oak branches, I see deep blue sky.

Festooning the limbs of the black oak are large, healthy clumps of mistletoe. Hanging a sprig of mistletoe this big at your Christmas party could land your guests in jail on a morals charge. Mistletoe is a parasitic plant that sinks its roots beneath the bark of young branches. Typically it flourishes in the winter when the host tree is leafless and the sunshine unobstructed. Both the Indians of California and the Celts of pre-Christian Europe thought the spirit of the oak retreated into mistletoe during the winter. The holiday custom of hanging mistletoe in the home probably originated with our Celtic ancestors as they prepared for the rebirth of spring by bringing the spirit of the oak into their homes. Similar beliefs led some of our forebears to deck their halls with evergreens during winter.

As I keep walking, the dusting of snow grows deeper and more continuous. This will test my brand-new Gore-Tex boots. After waiting seven years for my old hiking shoes to break in, I finally gave up and banished them to Boot Hell.

Generally, the snow here is crusty. If I walk carefully, most of the time I stay on the surface. Fortunately, some unknown hiker has preceded me. During the melting that occurs every day and the freezing every night, this hiker's footsteps have widened and frozen hard, leaving me a convenient trail across the deep snow. I follow these icy stepping-stones. When I veer from them, I crash through the thin frozen crust into the powdery snow below.

The terrain here has little underbrush, so the walking is easy except for the snow. Sometimes the oaks and ponderosa pines thin enough that I can see through the trees and out over the Mojave. The desert looks as flat as a parking lot for sixty miles. Five parallel roads run straight across it, but from my perspective they all seem to be aimed at a single vanishing point, lost in a distant haze. Floating above that haze, a few dim white peaks shimmer. The Sierras.

I shift my gaze down to the valley lying at my feet. It's innocuous. Pines cascade down my side of the San Andreas fault. On the other side of this valley, over yonder on the North American plate, juniper and yucca climb the slopes of Table Mountain.

I consider the havoc that will be unleashed when Table Mountain continues its jerky march north. A slip of ten or twenty feet could release as much energy as a five-megaton nuclear explosion. (The 1906 San Francisco earthquake triggered a slip of approximately twenty feet.) Seismologists say the shaking from a movement like that could last two minutes, maybe three. The duration of the shaking reflects the length of the fault that shifts. Many geologists suggest that a section of the San Andreas from San Bernardino to San Diego could jump all at once—a distance of close to a hundred miles. Faults tend to move in sections, and no stretch along that length has shifted in recorded history. Judging from geologic evidence, we're way overdue. If that whole section goes, some experts think the shaking could last seven minutes.

I hope I'm out of town.

Unfortunately I know all too well how long a mere thirty seconds can last. The first time you live through them, they go on *forever*. And then you relive them. And relive them. Several times a night. It doesn't matter if you experience a real earthquake or a dream earthquake. Your heart beats just as fast.

Under normal circumstances there's not much I enjoy more than watching a CNN reporter attempting to describe pictures of rain blowing horizontally past the camera while he peers out at the raging force of a hurricane. Or watching news footage of houses bobbing down some rain-swollen river. Call it perverse, but I have always loved a natural disaster. But these days, in light of my newfound nervousness about earthquakes, my friends have been quick to ask if my love of disasters extends to my own. The answer is . . . yes! While I'm certainly chastened, I am not changed. I am just as fascinated by the details of our catastrophe as anyone else's.

I love seeing geologists fumble to explain why one neighborhood in L.A. looks like Sarajevo while the next stands unscathed.

I cackle with amusement when structural engineers grope to explain why steel-frame buildings sustained so much structural damage—despite those engineers' earlier assurances that these types of buildings were nearly "earthquake proof."

I feel a chill when I hear that people are vacating their homes in the San Fernando Valley not because the ground keeps moving, but because of the *sounds* it has been making. For weeks residents there swore the Earth itself was creaking and moaning. Some couldn't stand it and made arrangements with U-Haul. Chalk one up for unbridled Nature.

Up on the mountaintops a distant wind whispers through the pines. City boy that I am, when I first hear it, I think it's a jet engine. But the murmuring gathers force as the wind gusts down the slopes, then roars over me with a cold blast. Brown pine needles rain down on me.

Yes, the world spins on, unhindered by human delusions.

The dusting of snow deepens, and the snow-covered jeep road begins to blend with the snow-covered mountainsides. It grows increasingly hard to follow. Sometimes I lose the road entirely without even realizing it, and I walk beneath the trees until a thicket of underbrush blocks my progress. Then I must wander about looking for signs of the road. My predecessor on the trail, for whom I have developed enormous affection, has long since turned back, leaving me to break snow on my own. In summer, bushwhacking through open country under big oaks and pines like this would be a waltz. Today it's starting to resemble a death march.

I fall through the snow's surface and sink to my thighs. Snow crams down inside my boots. Gore-Tex can't do anything about that. What I need are snowshoes.

This wasn't the kind of San Andreas exploration I expected. I'd planned a desert hike. Come to think of it, I'm hauling nearly a gallon of water in my knapsack. When the ranger said "a dusting of snow," I figured that was manageable. Well, thanks to that dusting, my feet felt like someone spilled a pitcher of gin-and-tonic down my socks.

I try to focus on the joys of the experience. It's a spectacular, clear day. The air is infused with the smell of pine. The world smells like Christmas, and that makes me smile. The temperature is mild, except for the microclimate developing inside my boots.

Birds fill the trees: chickadees, piñon jays, sapsuckers, acorn woodpeckers. I pass a huge ponderosa pine that the woodpeckers have adopted as an acorn granary. Holes perforate the tree's bark fifty or sixty feet into the air, far up into the tree's upper branches. Plenty of other birds flit through these trees too, but I don't recognize them.

As I walk through a shadowy stretch of the forest I hear a long deep *hooo, hooo, hoooo.*

That could be a California spotted owl. Unlike most other members of their genus, spotted owls are sometimes diurnal. And the California spotted owl is more common than its controversial cousin, the northern spotted owl, the symbol for many people of everything that is bad about the environmental movement.

Personally, I'm thrilled. I feel a brush of mystery, like an unseen wing fluttering past my cheek on a dark night. I tingle with the same awe—and apprehension—humanity has felt for owls through the ages. In olden days the owl was sometimes dubbed "the constable from the dark land" because, according to many cultures around the world, it called for souls.

I hope this one isn't performing that role right now. If so, he's late. I expected him on January 17.

The hiking grows even more arduous. I trudge through a blanket of snow two feet deep. Most of the time I try to walk as though wearing snowshoes. Strike the crust of the snow as squarely as possible, exerting an even amount of weight across as broad an area as possible. That works, for a few steps. Then the ice cracks. I sink into deep powder and flail until I regain a firm footing.

What am I doing out here?

I just wanted to pay my respects to the Big One. I hoped to gain some understanding of this terrifying force, this stranger on the outskirts of town who walks softly but carries a five-megaton bomb. Unfortunately, try as I might, I can't ponder abstractions like the fate of my city when a stream of ice water is trickling through my toes.

Maybe the lesson I should be taking home today is that when it comes to Nature, I don't set the agenda. You ask for earthquakes, you get snow. The Earth has just told me, "I am not your therapist."

Nature isn't here to help us or to hinder us. Nature just is.

Thinking Nature can heal me probably shows as much folly on my part as the structural engineer who proclaims a building to be "earthquake safe." We humans may be extremely influential in controlling the shape of life on Earth, but ultimately we are merely tenants on this planet, not monarchs. Nature is not here to serve us. The system spins along with a momentum far beyond human control, or even human consciousness.

Believing that we hold enough might to rein in the Earth may well prove to be our species' fatal flaw. It's hubris. As all good literature majors know, hubris sank Oedipus, and in the end it will probably sink the human race too. Of course, ultimately Oedipus learned his lesson, and when the human race is wandering around in rags and blind (probably from overexposure to ultraviolet rays), perhaps we will have learned ours as well. Personally, I hope it's a little before then.

Walking back down Piñon Ridge is easier. My footprints have broken the snow. I just follow them. Insert the right foot into the old lefts. Insert the left foot into the old rights.

Standing again at the end of Jackson Lake, I watch a couple picnicking farther down the shore. Tethered nearby, their two dogs are barking like mad. Probably these pooches are agitated because they aren't eating, while the human couple gets first crack at the food. But what if they're yowling because of that oft-reported ability among animals to sense an imminent earthquake?

Except for that dissonant note, it's peaceful standing on the edge of the lake, listening to some ducks gabbling, smelling the pine, watching the sun flash on the rippling water, bridging two great tectonic plates with my oh-so-mortal legs.

When the time comes for the dark constable to call on me and I roll that private screening of my life story, I hope it's scenes like this that I'll be reviewing. These kinds of moments convince a mere flyspeck like myself to clutch the door frame for as long as possible.

Note

1. Some experts say a doorway isn't much of a safe haven in an earthquake. They point out that the door can slam on you. And running to the doorway—or anywhere for that matter—in a panic is dangerous. They suggest that if you're in bed, stay in bed. I don't know about the experts, but, personally, I'd like to die on my feet. I want to be ready to *move* just in case something big comes my way—like a wall unit, or the second story. Besides, I happen to know that bed isn't always so safe. On the morning of January 17 one friend of mine leapt for the door like me. When the shaking stopped, she discovered her low-slung, two-hundred-pound chest of drawers lying *on her bed.*

31

Leslie Dick is an American writer and artist who was born in Boston in 1954 and who lived in London from 1965 to 1988. She graduated from Sussex University with a degree in English and taught at Vassar before becoming co-director of the Program in Art at the California Institute for the Arts. She has published two novels, *Without Falling* (1987) and *Kicking* (1992), and one short story collection, *The Skull of Charlotte Corday and Other Stories* (1995). "Nature Near," which first appeared in the literary magazine *Granta,* makes careful use of the architect Richard Neutra's actual floorplan for the Strathmore Drive Apartments in L.A. By emphasizing the contrast between the architect's efforts to include nature and the protagonist's fear of nature, this story highlights the complexity in our culture's attitudes toward cities and nature.

Nature Near

Leslie Dick

When he got a temporary teaching job at UCLA, she didn't want to go. But it was only nine months, September to June, and he was completely broke, so she made a deal with him.

"You go first, and find us a place to live. It has to be close enough to UCLA so I don't have to drive you to work. I won't make you learn to drive if you don't want to, I'll do the driving, but I won't drive you to work. And I need a room of my own, for my work."

He went ahead, and found a place for them to live on Strathmore Drive in Westwood, near the campus. He found a Neutra apartment. The Strathmore apartments of Richard Neutra were very beautiful, and arguably theirs was the best one—it was the least changed, containing even the original "ant-proof cooler" Neutra designed.

The "ant-proof cooler" was a small larderlike cupboard in the kitchen, with a circular metal shelving unit, a series of round trays which revolved like a lazy Susan. These shelves were supported by three legs, and at the bottom, between the floor and the lowest shelf, the tubular legs were surrounded with a lip, like a little cup or frill. This served as a moat; by filling it with oil, ants were unable to pass beyond it, to attack the food kept on the shelves above. Richard Neutra's son, Dion, proudly showed it to them, explaining that all the others (there were eight apartments, of which four, on the right-hand side, were still owned by the family) had been torn out.

The front apartments in Strathmore Drive were separate, one-story houses, and theirs was at street level, and therefore the most noisy and exposed. On the other hand, it was the only one that had two floor levels, a drop of about two and a half feet, which allowed a very subtle articulation of the interior space. For example, the bedrooms were lower than the living area, and therefore had higher ceilings. Huge ready-made metal windows extended in an unbroken line across the front, yet the bedrooms were less exposed because their floors were lower. It was a classic of Los Angeles domestic architecture, built in 1937, exemplary in its minimalism. There was even an interior plan of their apartment in the big Neutra book, and proliferating myths of various famous people who'd lived there. The Eameses made their first bentwood chairs in the bathroom of one, Orson Welles's girlfriend lived in another, Fritz Lang's girlfriend too, and Luise Rainer, friend of Clifford Odets, had lived in theirs.

So she was pleased, he'd made a good choice. They bought a cheap bed, and a ten-foot 1960s Scandiwegian sofa; they bought a small red Quasar TV, with its remote in the form of an identical miniature red TV. They made two tables out of doors on trestles, and acquired four metal folding chairs. Otherwise the place was empty, full of light, showing off its complex volumes and clear lines. They moved in on October 1, and the spider bit her just before Christmas, in early December.

It had been extremely hot in late November. Unseasonably hot—one blazing day after another, exacerbating the already existing drought. It was hell crossing the parking lot to the supermarket, it was hell sitting at her desk. She hated the heat, reluctant to invest in an electric fan, and everyone was relieved when these weeks of intense heat were suddenly succeeded by an equally intense downpour. For three days, it poured with rain, sheets of water thrown down from the dark sky. Then they had dinner with an acquaintance, who suggested the 1981 Mazda GLC she'd bought was on its last legs.

"The struts are gone," he said, "like my old Honda. Does it wobble on the freeway if you're going over fifty? Then the struts are gone—there's nothing you can do when the struts are gone."

A couple of days later, Sunday morning, she woke up early, about 6 A.M., with an itchy bottom. The surface of her right buttock felt itchy, and she couldn't come up with a hypothesis to explain why. She'd been reading in the *L.A. Times* about the illnesses associated with various sporting activities—like tennis elbow, there were many others, including something called "bikini bottom," a rash particular to swimmers. As she had been swimming regularly in the UCLA Olympic pool, she surmised this could be the cause, and they lay in bed together, very romantic, making up a blues song to contain her anxieties. The refrain went like this:

I got those
struts are gone
wobblin' over fifty
bikini bottom blues

It was funny, but the itching got worse, and by late morning it had moved beyond what could be described as itching: it was beyond itching, beyond discomfort, to unspeakable pain. Rain streamed down the big windows, it was dark in the middle of the day; they turned on the lights. Nevertheless, she had to do something, so she took an umbrella and drove down to Wilshire and San Vicente, to the seven days a week pharmacy there.

Then she was lucky—there were two moments when she was lucky, and this was one of them. She was lucky because the pharmacist told her to go to the hospital. She explained.

"I thought it was a rash at first, but now I think it must be some kind of a bite. And I've got no health insurance, and I don't have a doctor, and I wonder what oral antihistamines you can give me without a prescription."

The pharmacist asked some questions; he said, "Is the area hot?"

She reached behind and slid her hand under the elastic waistband of the loose cotton skirt she was wearing; she wasn't wearing underpants because of the pain. She rested the palm of her hand flat against her buttock, and yes, it was hot, it was burning up.

"Go to the hospital," the pharmacist told her. "This could be very serious, go to the county hospital if you haven't got any money, but go."

So she did, she went home and told her boyfriend, and then she went to UCLA Emergency, and paid her eight dollars, and waited. Then she had bad luck—because she saw two doctors, then, this was on Sunday, by now late afternoon, and neither of them knew what it was. The "area" was beginning to curdle, so to speak, to suppurate, her smooth bottom skin unrecognizable. They didn't know what it was, and they gave her a prescription for antibiotics (she wanted antihistamines), and told her to go home. They said it would get better.

She went home, and it got worse. She couldn't eat, or think, she couldn't function at all. The pain was terrible, an ache and an itch so extreme it was agonizing. By Monday night she was beginning to be very frightened, and first thing on Tuesday morning she went back.

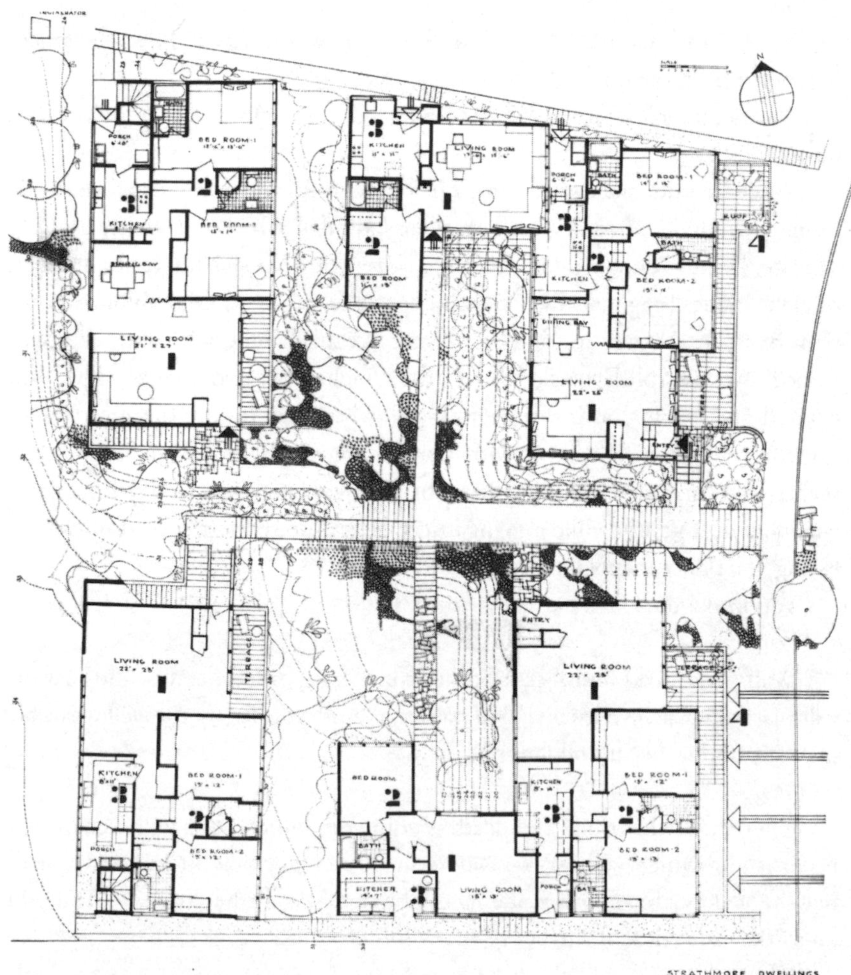

STRATHMORE DWELLINGS

Then she was lucky, again. A young male doctor looked at her bottom and said, "You've been bitten by the brown recluse spider."

"I have?"

"Excuse me for a minute," he said, and left her perched on her left buttock, sitting awry as she was forced to now, wondering what this meant. After a couple of minutes the doctor returned, and he said, "The doctors you saw on Sunday, they told you what to expect, right?"

"No, no—they didn't. I mean, they didn't know what it was."

The young doctor became tentative, as if reluctant to break it to her, to tell her what was going to happen. He looked down, as if unwilling to look her in the eye.

"So I . . ."

"You have to tell me," she said, decisively. It was terrifying, his reluctance. He took a deep breath, and looked up.

"Have you looked in the mirror? I mean, do you know what it looks like?" he asked.

"Yes," she said; she'd stood in front of the full-length mirror on the bedroom door, and craned her neck over her shoulder. The bite (she kept calling it a bite, but the doctor referred to it as "the wound") was huge, about seven or eight inches long, and five or six inches wide, a glaring oval oblong on her right buttock. At the center, there was an irregular patch where the skin had turned dark purplish black, about three inches by two inches. This was cracked and leaking, as if disintegrating slowly. Surrounding this area was an expanse of brownish yellow, with purple tinges, about six inches by four inches, and this was enclosed within a bright swollen ridge of red itching flesh, engorged and painful, like a giant insect bite. The redness spread outwards, fading. The doctor explained, carefully.

"You know the black part in the middle."

"Yes."

"Well that's dead flesh, it's dead, it's something called necrosis. So that bit will just fall away eventually." He paused. "And you know the yellowish bit that's around it, like a doughnut?"

"Yes."

"There, a battle for life and death is going on; which parts will succumb to necrosis and which will survive is unclear now. The black bit is already dead, but the yellowy bit might make it, might not." Again he paused. "And you know the red welt that surrounds the whole wound?"

"Yes."

"That's the histamine reaction, that's your immune system sending millions of white blood cells to make a wall, a barrier around this invasion, to try to contain it. The thing is with the brown recluse, you need a certain concentration of the venom for necrosis to take place. So while it makes sense to try to contain the poison, within this barrier, this moat, actually that means the area of dead flesh will be larger, and you get this other problem of a really big wound that may not heal. Do you understand?"

"Yes."

"So this is what we're going to do: we're going to give you lots of antihistamines, so the poison won't be so concentrated. There's nothing we can do about the dark bit, the black bit in the middle. As I said, it's already gone. But hopefully we can stop it getting much bigger. And we'll give you antibiotics to prevent any infection in the wound; you're already on antibiotics, but I'll give you a stronger one. Whenever there's an opening of this size, there's a real risk of secondary infection. But the problem is, by letting the poison circulate through your body, you get a systemic reaction, you get sick. We have to let it spread, to try to stop the necrosis, but it will affect your liver, and other organs, it will make you feel pretty awful."

He looked up, and saw her face. He said, "You know how I know so much about this?"

She was silent.

"It happened to me," he said, tonelessly. She looked away.

"God, how awful," she said.

"So you can expect to be sick for maybe three weeks, two or three weeks, and what I did, I just took about five showers a day. Keep the wound very, very clean, and lie down and expose it to the air, and get a lot of rest."

"Like a burn," she said.

"Yes, exactly," he said. "And come see me next week. And call if it gets much worse. You can expect it to begin to get better in the next day or two, the next two or three days."

She was too tired to say anything; she thanked him, and got the prescriptions filled at the hospital pharmacy, and paid her money, and drove home, with difficulty, trying to sit in the car with all her weight on her left hip.

She walked up the steps to the door of the apartment; it was still raining. The doctor had told her it was unusual to see a brown recluse, because you didn't feel the effects of the bite until a few hours later. She put it together: the irregular spider web in the corner beside the toilet in the other bathroom—his bathroom. She'd got up in the night to pee, it was the nearer of the two bathrooms. She hadn't turned on the light. She figured the spider had come into the house because of the rain; the frosted glass window in the bathroom was always slightly open. She walked into the apartment and went immediately to get the broom; she went directly to the bathroom and shoved the broom violently down on the spider web, over and over again.

Then she talked, she said, "We have to make a list, now, we have to go to the supermarket. They told me I'm going to be ill for two weeks, maybe three weeks, so we need to get some food in, we need to get some food." Her anxiety was overwhelming.

In retrospect, when she remembered this series of events, this was the bit that seemed hardest of all, that they didn't know anyone in L.A. well enough to be able to ask for help. Or that she was such a control freak, so omnipotent, that it never crossed her mind to ask for help. In the rain, she got behind the wheel once again, shaky, beginning to feel the shock seeping through, and they drove down to the supermarket and bought food.

Then she went to bed, she swept the floor of the bedroom, she showered, and she went to bed. It happened much as the doctor had described; she took the drugs and felt much worse, she felt very ill. The next ten days passed in a dreamy state: it was like having terrible flu, when you can't read, when you can barely manage to stare into space. Her joints ached, she stumbled on the steps in the hall. She had a fever that came and went without warning. She took four or five showers every day, letting the warm water pour down her back, over the wound. The dead flesh fell away, flaking, breaking up, and new skin began to grow back, slowly. Time passed.

The strangest symptom was the rash on her legs, all over her thighs and calves, scattered, intermittently during this time there appeared little patches of scabrous red marks, which he named "scary Hawaiis," because they looked like that, a group of irregular islands, and they were scary. First they would be red, and itchy; then they became a little rough, scaly, scabrous; and then they faded, to be replaced by dramatic deep dark bruises, blossoming up from deep under the surface of her skin. These huge dark flowers gradually faded, to be replaced by more of the scary Hawaiis, until her legs were covered with dark purple and yellow blooms, making a muted pattern on her skin.

She couldn't sit down; for a couple of months she had to sit sideways on one hip while it healed. She subsequently developed serious back problems, but never made the connection until the National Health physiotherapist in London, six months later, commented that she'd suffered some "wastage" on her right buttock, she pointed out it was smaller than the left.

"We'll have to build it up!" she said, in her Scottish accent.

"Oh no, can't we just make the other one smaller?"

"I'm surprised you haven't noticed," the physiotherapist said, laughing. "Hasn't your boyfriend noticed?"

When she got home, she ran upstairs to the room where he worked. "You're a useless boyfriend, according to my physiotherapist. You never noticed my right buttock is smaller than my left, apparently I've suffered some *wastage.*"

He was serious. "Of course I've noticed, that's where the spider bit you."

For the first time she put it together: sitting crooked for all that time, and this disc that was out of place, this broken disc, this disc that (according to the physiotherapist) would never get better.

She remembered the complicated pattern of rectangles Neutra made in the bedroom windows, the eucalyptus leaves moving outside. Silver light, long afternoons lying flat, half-conscious. She remembered the time she took a sip of white wine and almost fell over. Her liver was shot, for a few weeks, too busy processing the poison that was dispersed throughout her body. Later she'd met someone at a drinks party, a doctor who specialized in the brown recluse. He told her the venom actually attacks the immune system, and the most up-to-date treatment is to inject cortisone at the site of the wound.

Her boyfriend found a wonderful book called *Poisonous Dwellers of the Desert,* with a lurid hot red cover and a huge picture of a spider, which made things clearer still. One reason the doctors want to limit the size of the wound, the hole in your body, is because in many cases a skin graft is required, and one of the effects of the spider's poison is the skin graft doesn't take. It won't stick, it won't take.

The book said that generally, if you were for example bit on the finger, you would lose the finger, sometimes more. And if you're under two or over seventy, you die.

Possibly she'd been lucky in another way, lucky to be bit on the buttock, where there's plenty of flesh, no joint just under the surface, not like a hand or foot. Poisonous dwellers of the desert: she thought of Los Angeles as a desert, a thin veneer of greenery spread over it. Turn off the sprinklers and it's a desert, she would exclaim with disgust. People loved the desert, they spoke of going to the desert, like going to the mountains, or the country. They spoke of going to the desert with reverence, as if it were something spiritual. She thought of the desert as a place that might kill you. A glance at *Poisonous Dwellers of the Desert* would convince anyone of that. But the desert dweller had been in her bathroom, it was in her house.

Neutra believed in undoing the architectural dichotomy between inside and outside. He thought the home and the garden should interpenetrate, he thought nature should be near, nature should enter the domestic space.

Nature entered with a vengeance, rupturing the surface of her body, leaving a gaping wound, an opening to the outside. The damage to her body was catastrophic: her lower back was gone, her liver and spleen would never be the same. She understood the dark logic of Los Angeles architecture, its misleading, deceptive promise of sunshine and health. Earthquakes and the desert: Neutra's houses are flexible, they give when there's a quake. In Strathmore Drive, it sounded like tigers leaping across the flat roof, and then the shaking started. It was the night Dion came to dinner; he held her hand as the table shook, the whole house vibrating, and he said, "There's nothing to fear, my father's houses are very flexible; they *give.*"

She understood Los Angeles: under the surface it was malevolent desert and terrifying earthquakes, it was lethal. She understood it in a way she wouldn't have, without the gift of the Neutra house, the dark secret of the brown recluse.

32

Helena Maria Viramontes was born in East Los Angeles in 1954, and she now teaches at Cornell University. She has her degree in English from Immaculate Heart College with an M.F.A. from the University of California, Irvine. Her first novel, *Under the Feet of Jesus* (1995), is a powerful portrayal of the environmental and economic injustice inflicted on migrant workers in the United States. A second novel, *Their Dogs Came with Them* (1996), explores the Spanish conquest of the Americas. "The Moths," which was first published in an issue of *XhismArte Magazine* entitled *201: Homenaje a la Ciudad de Los Angeles,* is also the first short story in her collection *The Moths and Other Stories.* Nature, for the story's young narrator, is a source both of solace, when she escapes the tyranny of church and father to work in the garden with her Abuelita, and mystery, when the moths appear in the last part of the story.

The Moths

Helena Maria Viramontes

I was fourteen years old when Abuelita requested my help. And it seemed only fair. Abuelita had pulled me through the rages of scarlet fever by placing, removing, and replacing potato slices on the temples of my forehead; she had seen me through several whippings, an arm broken by a dare jump off Tío Enrique's toolshed, puberty, and my first lie. Really, I told Amá, it was only fair.

Not that I was her favorite granddaughter or anything special. I wasn't even pretty or nice like my older sisters and I just couldn't do the girl things they could do. My hands were too big to handle the fineries of crocheting or embroidery and I always pricked my fingers or knotted my colored threads time and time again while my sisters laughed and called me bull hands with their cute waterlike voices. So I began keeping a piece of jagged brick in my sock to bash my sisters or anyone who called me bull hands. Once, while we all sat in the bedroom, I hit Teresa on the forehead, right above her eyebrow, and she ran to Amá with her mouth open, her hand over her eye while blood seeped between her fingers. I was used to the whippings by then.

I wasn't respectful either. I even went so far as to doubt the power of Abuelita's slices, the slices she said absorbed my fever. "You're still alive, aren't you?" Abuelita snapped back, her pasty gray eye beaming at me and burning holes in my suspicions. Regretful that I had let secret questions drop out of my mouth, I couldn't look into her eyes. My hands began to fan out, grow like a liar's nose until they hung by my side like low weights. Abuelita made a balm out of dried moth wings and Vicks and rubbed my hands, shaped them back to size and it was the strangest feeling. Like bones melting. Like sun shining through the darkness of your eyelids. I didn't mind helping Abuelita after that, so Amá would always send me over to her.

In the early afternoon Amá would push her hair back, hand me my sweater and shoes, and tell me to go to Mama Luna's. This was to avoid another fight and another whipping, I knew. I would deliver one last direct shot on Marisela's arm and jump out of our house, the slam of the screen door burying her cries of anger, and I'd gladly go help Abuelita plant her wild lilies or jasmine or heliotrope or cilantro or hierbabuena in red Hills Brothers coffee cans. Abuelita would wait for me at the top step of her porch holding a hammer and nail and empty coffee cans. And although we hardly spoke, hardly looked at each other as we worked over root transplants, I always felt her gray eye on me. It made me feel, in a strange sort of way, safe and guarded and not alone. Like God was supposed to make you feel.

On Abuelita's porch, I would puncture holes in the bottom of the coffee cans with a nail and a precise hit of a hammer. This completed, my job was to fill them with red clay mud from beneath her rose bushes, packing it softly, then making a perfect hole, four fingers round, to nest a sprouting avocado pit, or the spidery sweet potatoes that Abuelita rooted in mayonnaise jars with toothpicks and daily water, or prickly chayotes that produced vines that twisted and wound all over her porch pillars, crawling to the roof, up and over the roof, and down the other side, making her small brick house look like it was cradled within the vines that grew pear-shaped squashes ready for the pick, really to be steamed with onions and cheese and butter. The roots would burst out of the rusted coffee cans and search for a place to connect. I would then feed the seedlings with water.

But this was a different kind of help, Amá said, because Abuelita was dying. Looking into her gray eye, then into her brown one, the doctor said it was just a matter of days. And so it seemed only fair that these hands she had melted and formed found use in rubbing her caving body with alcohol and marihuana, rubbing her arms and legs, turning her face to the window so that she could watch the Bird of Paradise blooming or smell the scent of clove in the air. I toweled her face frequently and held her hand for hours. Her gray wiry hair hung over the mattress. Since I could remember, she'd kept her long hair in braids. Her mouth was vacant and when she slept, her eyelids never closed all the way. Up close, you could see her gray eye beaming out the window, staring hard as if to remember everything. I never kissed her. I left the window open when I went to the market.

Across the street from Jay's Market there was a chapel. I never knew its denomination, but I went in just the same to search for candles. I sat down on one of the pews because there were none. After I cleaned my fingernails, I looked up at the high ceiling. I had forgotten the vastness of these places, the coolness of the marble pillars and the frozen statues with blank eyes. I was alone. I knew why I had never returned.

That was one of Apá's biggest complaints. He would pound his hands on the table, rocking the sugar dish or spilling a cup of coffee and scream that if I didn't go to mass every Sunday to save my god-damn sinning soul, then I had no reason to go out of the house, period. Punto final. He would grab my arm and dig his nails into me to make sure I understood the importance of catechism. Did he make himself clear? Then he strategically directed his anger at Amá for her lousy ways of bringing up daughters, being disrespectful and unbelieving, and my older sisters would pull me aside and tell me if I didn't get to mass right this minute, they were all going to kick the holy shit out of me. Why am I so selfish? Can't you see what it's doing to Amá, you idiot? So I would wash my feet and stuff them in my black Easter shoes that shone with Vaseline, grab a missal and veil, and wave good-bye to Amá.

I would walk slowly down Lorena to First to Evergreen, counting the cracks on the cement. On Evergreen I would turn left and walk to Abuelita's. I liked her porch because it was shielded by the vines of the chayotes and I could get a good look at the people and car traffic on Evergreen without them knowing. I would jump up the porch steps, knock on the screen door as I wiped my feet, and call Abuelita? mi Abuelita? As I opened the door and stuck my head in, I would catch the gagging scent of toasting chile on the placa. When I entered the sala, she would greet me from the kitchen, wringing her hands in her apron. I'd sit at the corner of the table to keep from being in her way. The chiles made my eyes water. Am I crying? No, Mama Luna, I'm sure not crying. I don't like going to mass, but my eyes watered anyway, the tears dropping on the tablecloth like candle wax. Abuelita lifted the burnt chiles from the fire and sprinkled water on them until the skins began to separate. Placing them in front of me, she turned to check the menudo. I peeled the skins off and put the flimsy, limp looking green and yellow chiles in the molcajete and began to crush and crush and twist and crush the heart out of the tomato, the clove of garlic, the stupid chiles that made me cry, crushed them until they turned into liquid under my bull hand. With a wooden spoon, I scraped hard to destroy the guilt, and my tears were gone. I put the bowl of chile next to a vase filled with freshly cut roses. Abuelita touched my hand and pointed to the bowl of menudo that steamed in front of me. I spooned some chile into the menudo and rolled a corn tortilla thin with the palms of my hands. As I ate, a fine Sunday breeze entered the kitchen and a rose petal calmly feathered down to the table.

I left the chapel without blessing myself and walked to Jay's. Most of the time Jay didn't have much of anything. The tomatoes were always soft and the cans of Campbell soups had rusted spots on them. There was dust on the tops of cereal boxes. I picked up what I needed: rubbing alcohol, five cans of chicken broth, a big bottle of Pine Sol. At first Jay got mad because I thought I had forgotten the money. But it was there all the time, in my back pocket.

When I returned from the market, I heard Amá crying in Abuelita's kitchen. She looked up at me with puffy eyes. I placed the bags of groceries on the table and began putting the cans of soup away. Amá sobbed quietly. I never kissed her. After a while, I patted her on the back for comfort. Finally: "¿Y mi Amá?" she asked in a whisper, then choked again and cried into her apron.

Abuelita fell off the bed twice yesterday, I said, knowing that I shouldn't have said it and wondering why I wanted to say it because it only made Amá cry harder. I guess I became angry and just so tired of the quarrels and beatings and unanswered prayers and my hands just there hanging helplessly by my side. Amá looked at me again, confused, angry, and her eyes were filled with sorrow. I went outside and sat on the porch swing and watched the people pass. I sat there until she left. I dozed off repeating the words to myself like rosary prayers: when do you stop giving when do you start giving when do you . . . and when my hands fell from my lap, I awoke to catch them. The sun was setting, an orange glow, and I knew Abuelita was hungry.

There comes a time when the sun is defiant. Just about the time when moods change, inevitable seasons of a day, transitions from one color to another, that hour or minute or second when the sun is finally defeated, finally sinks into the realization that it cannot with all its power to heal or burn, exist forever, there comes an illumination where the sun and earth meet, a final burst of burning red orange fury reminding us that although endings are inevitable, they are necessary for rebirths, and when that time came, just when I switched on the light in the kitchen to open Abuelita's can of soup, it was probably then that she died.

The room smelled of Pine Sol and vomit and Abuelita had defecated the remains of her cancerous stomach. She had turned to the window and tried to speak, but her mouth remained open and speechless. I heard you, Abuelita, I said, stroking her cheek, I heard you. I opened the windows of the house and let the soup simmer and overboil on the stove. I turned the stove off and poured the soup down the sink. From the cabinet I got a tin basin, filled it with lukewarm water and carried it carefully to the room. I went to the linen closet and took out some modest bleached white towels. With the sacredness of a priest preparing his vestments, I unfolded the towels one by one on my shoulders. I removed the sheets and blankets from her bed and peeled off her thick flannel nightgown. I toweled her puzzled face, stretching out the wrinkles, removing the coils of her neck, toweled her shoulders and breasts. Then I changed the water. I returned to towel the creases of her stretch-marked stomach, her sporadic vaginal hairs, and her sagging thighs. I removed the lint between her toes and noticed a mapped birthmark on the fold of her buttock. The scars on her back which were as thin as the life lines on the palms of her hand made me realize how little I really knew of Abuelita. I covered her with a thin blanket and went into the bathroom. I washed my hands, and turned on the tub faucets and watched the water pour into the tub with vitality and steam. When it was full, I turned off the water and undressed. Then, I went to get Abuelita.

She was not as heavy as I thought and when I carried her in my arms, her body fell into a V, and yet my legs were tired, shaky, and I felt as if the distance between the bedroom and bathroom was miles and years away. Amá, where are you?

I stepped into the bathtub one leg first, then the other. I bent my knees slowly to descend into the water slowly so I wouldn't scald her skin. There, there, Abuelita, I said, cradling her, smoothing her as we descended, I heard you. Her hair fell back and spread across the water like eagle's wings. The water in the tub overflowed and poured onto the tile of the floor. Then the moths came. Small, gray ones that came from her soul and out through her mouth fluttering to light, circling the single dull light bulb of the bathroom. Dying is lonely and I wanted to go to where the moths were, stay with her and plant chayotes whose vines would crawl up her fingers and into the clouds; I wanted to rest my head on her chest with her stroking my hair, telling me about the moths that lay within the soul and slowly eat the spirit up; I wanted to return to the waters of the womb with her so that we would never be alone again. I wanted. I wanted my Amá. I removed a few strands of hair from Abuelita's face and held her small light head within the hollow of my neck. The bathroom was filled with moths, and for the first time in a long time I cried, rocking us, crying for her, for me, for Amá, the sobs emerging from the depths of anguish, the misery of feeling half born, sobbing until finally the sobs rippled into circles and circles of sadness and relief. There, there, I said to Abuelita, rocking us gently, there, there.

33

Paulino Lim Jr. was born in the Philippines in 1935. He received his B.S. degree from the University of Manila in 1956 and his M.A. in English from the University of Santo Tomas. He and his wife now live in Los Angeles where he teaches Asian American Literature, English Literature of the Romantic Period, and Creative Writing at the University of California, Long Beach. His short story "Homecoming" won first prize in the 1985 *Asia Week* short story competition, and he has published a quartet of political novels that include *Tiger Orchards on Mount Mayon* (1990) and *Sparrows Don't Sing in the Philippines* (1994). The short story "Opossums and Thieving Pelicans" explores how individuals living in a multicultural neighborhood in Long Beach interact with various elements of urban nature—gardens, polluted waterways, and wildlife.

Opossums and Thieving Pelicans

Paulino Lim Jr.

We homeowners on our block, with a cul-de-sac on the south side of the street, are all members of Neighborhood Watch. We receive notices of meetings and monthly reports on crimes in the area from our block captain, Mrs. Rampling, a retired school teacher. With poise distilled from thousands of classroom hours, she presides at club meetings, organized to combat residential burglaries. Last summer we heard accounts of unusual thefts.

"Someone came and cleaned out my strawberry patch, darn it!" said Mrs. Sargent, who works at the McDonnell Douglas aircraft plant nearby.

Others laughed, as I recalled a letter from my mother in the Philippines. She awoke one night and surprised a thief in the kitchen, stuffing his mouth with leftover rice. He ran away carrying the pot with him.

"Let me tell you," said Dagmar, called Brunhilda behind her back by those intimidated by her six-foot stature and platinum hair, "my next-door neighbor, who's Japanese, tells me that he's missing three koi fish from his backyard pond."

"What on earth is koi?" This came from garrulous Charlie, who lives across the street from my house; he's probably never heard of koi doctors in Beverly Hills, ichthyologists who treat ailing members of a species that can cost as much as five thousand dollars each.

"Oh, it looks like a giant goldfish."

My wife, Marta, who loves everything Japanese, turned her brown face toward me with a look that said we were going to have a good laugh later. Delaying reaction or postponing laughter, I know, perpetuates the myth of inscrutable Asians, who simply fear that a spontaneous expression might offend, or making a face might mean loss of face.

"He doesn't speak English very well," Dagmar said. "The other morning he says to me, 'Missy, missy, three koi fish gone from fish pond.'" I wanted to laugh, knowing how Charlie's wife mimics the German accent of Dagmar, whose "house" speech comes out a clipped "haus."

At least there were no burglaries, break-ins, or car thefts involving the sixteen homes of our block. The meeting at the park clubhouse soon turned to chat, the mystery of the missing strawberries and koi forgotten. Tony, a fireman, told the story of a Florida burglar alarm salesman who was caught breaking into a house. Apparently, the salesman would talk to homeowners, try to sell them alarms, and help undecided customers make up their minds by burglarizing their houses.

"Dagmar," Charlie said, "I get mixed up between your neighbor and that other Asian with the ugly olive tree in his front yard. Is he Korean?"

I often see him on a ladder, a brown grocery bag for a hat, trimming the olive tree that he has shaped into two globes.

"No, he's also Japanese."

"For a Japanese he sure is a lousy gardener. I swear that tree looks like his balls."

Everyone laughed. Two worlds or two balls; the genitalia allusion was the funnier joke. We all like Charlie; he speaks his mind and drinks his Scotch with gusto. The first time our house needed painting he asked me, "Have you seen the Filipino houses on Magellan Street on the next tract?"

Who hadn't seen them and snickered? Three boldly painted houses in a lower-middle-class tract of boxlike units with single garages. Pinks, apple greens, and scarlet reds. The pink house had pink wrought iron fence, potted cactus, and two stone flamingos.

He probably wanted me to say, "Gaudy, aren't they?" Instead I blurted, "As a matter of fact, Charlie, I'm planning to strip my house of its gray and white and repaint with chartreuse and fuchsia. What do you think?"

He left in a huff. Recent Filipino immigrants gained the reputation for ostentatious exterior decor of their tract homes. I first heard about it when I worked for the U.S. Navy; I served my twenty years and applied for citizenship upon my retirement. Even my barber, who is gay, recently told me of his Filipino neighbor who painted the wood trim orange and raspberry red.

The mystery of the missing strawberries was solved two days after the meeting at the clubhouse. I was sitting at the bar watching Marta chop onions and slice potatoes and oranges—the stuffing for the two wild ducks marinating in Chablis.

"I need onions for the sauce," she said. "Could you get two more?"

Flashlight in hand, I slipped out the patio door to the vegetable garden we plant each summer in an area of about forty square feet. I pulled out two onion bulbs the size of billiard balls, stripped the outer layers from the dried leaves down to the roots.

A rustle, a hiss. I flashed the beam on the eggplants, stringbeans, and a hairy animal eating tomatoes. A pig! It had a white pointy face and naked tail, its pelage gray and dirty-looking.

"Marta," I called from the patio, "come out here quick! There's something I want you to look at."

Through the glass door I watched Marta walk from the kitchen light, a knife in her hand, until her five-foot frame became a silhouette at the doorway. I often wonder how the missionaries react, Mormons and Jehovah's Witnesses, when they knock on our door and see this long-haired petite Filipina with a kitchen knife in hand, saying, "Yes?" She once warned me that I should never surprise her at night, when I come from out of town, and showed me a cleaver she keeps under the bed.

I flashed the light on the animal, its tail wiggling in the dark like a giant earthworm. It hissed and squirmed its way through the tomato vines.

"It's an opossum."

"I thought for a moment it was a pig. I've never seen an opossum before."

"I have, at the nature center on the other side of the river. That's probably where it came from."

The river separates Los Angeles from Orange County in the suburb of Long

Beach, where we live; on the other side is Seal Beach. The water comes from the mountain, sewage lines and irrigation spills, so perhaps it can be called a river. From the country's point of view it is a flood-control canal that empties into the sea. Levees protect both sides, rising fifteen feet above the ground, leveled and asphalted at the top for joggers and cyclists.

"You know," Marta said, brandishing the knife, "we could make a stew with that opossum."

She wasn't kidding; she grew up on a farm and helped slaughter pigs and goats. I kept the light on the opossum as it grasped the cypress and pulled its stout body up the branches, with the aid of its prehensile tail.

"I had an interesting visit to the nature center with a bunch of Girl Scouts," Marta said, back in the kitchen. "We learned that about one hundred opossums live in that preserve. Many escape and look for food elsewhere."

"We should call the nature center and ask them what to do."

"How about opossum stew with potatoes, okra, and red pepper?"

"Hurry up with that wild duck. I'm getting hungry."

A woman from animal control of the city of Long Beach came with a trap, a wood frame covered with wire mesh, three feet long, sixteen inches wide, and eighteen inches high. She raised the door and showed us where to put the bait on the opposite end, a wallet-size piece of wood attached to a tripping mechanism. She left a can of catfood to use as bait.

Two weeks later, a meeting of the Neighborhood Watch of the tract was called. More than one hundred homeowners showed up. The woman chairing the meeting introduced herself as the victim of two burglaries and recited known facts. The screwdriver was the basic tool of a burglar; it took three minutes for a residence to be robbed. Two daytime robberies had occurred; thieves using trucks disguised as movers hauled away furniture, stereos, and VCRs.

The councilman representing the district took the floor; he was tall, white-haired, and prepared to listen patiently to complaints. I winced when a woman said, "There's been an influx of foreigners on our tract, coming here to fish on the river."

On sunny weekends the river becomes a play area for two kinds of sports, waterskiing and fishing. The boaters and skiers are invariably white, the fishermen members of ethnic minorities. Motorboats scatter seagulls and fishermen reel in their lines as the skiers splay the water.

African Americans cast their lines from the levees close to the Alamitos Edison plants that pour steaming water into the river; Spanish Americans stay upriver; and Asians, mostly Vietnamese, go farther up where the water is shallow and grass grows. Some bring children with them and leave trash behind, Styrofoam cups, plates, and bottles.

"It's awful, all that garbage," said Tony. "It takes a good rain to wash it down the river to the ocean."

"We should block off the street close to the freeway."

"Well, if we did that," said the councilman, "it would take longer for fire trucks and ambulances to get to this tract in an emergency."

"About two years ago, helicopters used to fly above with loudspeakers warning people not to fish in the river."

"Well, the council decided that cops had more important things to do. Besides it was costing the city two hundred dollars an hour to fly a helicopter."

"We could get the city to put up 'No Parking' and 'No Fishing' signs."

"That can be done."

"How soon can we get the signs put up?"

"We have to go through an ordinance procedure. First of all, you folks have to sign a petition."

We had quite a success with an earlier petition. An agency taking care of a group of young men and women on a drug rehabilitation program got permission to use the park and clubhouse during weekdays. The residents complained that the inmates were not properly supervised and kept their children away from the park. Tennis buffs reported that the inmates threw firecrackers that exploded on the court as they played.

The meeting broke up into small groups; our block members gathered in one corner. Mrs. Sargent reported that she had seen the opossum eating strawberries, and Dagmar said her Japanese neighbor woke up early one morning and found pelicans perched on the fence looking down on his pond.

"He thinks the pelicans are eating his koi."

It began to make sense. Pelicans and seagulls, driven from the river by water-skiers and fishermen, searched for food elsewhere and found it in people's backyards. A few nights after that meeting, we were watching television when I heard the trapdoor shut. Marta had replaced the catfood bait with a slice of corned beef we had on St. Patrick's Day.

"Marta," I said, "I think we got him."

I grabbed the flashlight and we went out to the garden. Inside the trap the opossum turned its pink nose and beady black eyes to the light, bristled the stiff hair on its face, then continued chewing on the corned beef.

"Well," Marta said, "here's our chance to experience what's considered a delicacy in some parts of the country."

Standing close to the trap, I smelled something fetid and musky, like the foul odor of a kitchen knife that was used to cut fish and left unwashed for days.

"I already found a Cajun recipe for roast opossum."

"I don't know about that—"

"God, what's that smell?" Marta cried, pinching her nose.

I waved the flashlight at the trap.

"Let's call animal control," Marta said, quickly turning away.

34

Richard Brautigan was born in Spokane in 1935, and he died in Bolinas, California, in 1984. He taught at the California Institute of Technology and Montana State University. The whimsical environmental commentary characteristic of Brautigan's work led the writer Guy Davenport to describe him as "a kind of Thoreau who cannot keep a straight face." Although he also wrote poetry, Brautigan is best known for his fiction that includes such works as *A Confederate General from Big Sur* (1964), *Trout Fishing in America* (1967), and *Revenge of the Lawn: Stories, 1962–1970* (1971). The short story below is from *Trout Fishing in America.* By using a matter of fact style to talk about segments of a "used trout stream" for sale, "The Cleveland Wrecking Yard" amplifies Brautigan's satire of society's efforts to control and commodify nature.

The Cleveland Wrecking Yard

Richard Brautigan

Until recently my knowledge about the Cleveland Wrecking Yard had come from a couple of friends who'd bought things there. One of them bought a huge window: the frame, glass, and everything for just a few dollars. It was a fine-looking window.

Then he chopped a hole in the side of his house up on Potrero Hill and put the window in. Now he has a panoramic view of the San Francisco County Hospital.

He can practically look right down into the wards and see old magazines eroded like the Grand Canyon from endless readings. He can practically hear the patients thinking about breakfast: *I hate milk,* and thinking about dinner: *I hate peas,* and then he can watch the hospital slowly drown at night, hopelessly entangled in huge bunches of brick seaweed.

He bought that window at the Cleveland Wrecking Yard.

My other friend bought an iron roof at the Cleveland Wrecking Yard and took the roof down to Big Sur in an old station wagon and then he carried the iron roof on his back up the side of a mountain. He carried up half the roof on his back. It was no picnic. Then he bought a mule, George, from Pleasanton. George carried up the other half of the roof.

The mule didn't like what was happening at all. He lost a lot of weight because of the ticks, and the smell of the wildcats up on the plateau made him too nervous to graze there. My friend said jokingly that George had lost around two hundred pounds. The good wine country around Pleasanton in the Livermore Valley probably had looked a lot better to George than the wild side of the Santa Lucia Mountains.

My friend's place was a shack right beside a huge fireplace where there had once been a great mansion during the 1920s, built by a famous movie actor. The mansion was built before there was even a road down at Big Sur. The mansion had been brought over the mountains on the backs of mules, strung out like ants, bringing visions of the good life to the poison oak, the ticks, and the salmon.

The mansion was on a promontory, high over the Pacific. Money could see farther in the 1920s, and one could look out and see whales and the Hawaiian Islands and the Kuomintang in China.

The mansion burned down years ago.

The actor died.

His mules were made into soap.

His mistresses became bird nests of wrinkles.

Now only the fireplace remains as a sort of Carthaginian homage to Hollywood.

I was down there a few weeks ago to see my friend's roof. I wouldn't have passed up the chance for a million dollars, as they say. The roof looked like a colander to me. If that roof and the rain were running against each other at Bay Meadows, I'd bet on the rain and plan to spend my winnings at the World's Fair in Seattle.

My own experience with the Cleveland Wrecking Yard began two days ago when I heard about a used trout stream they had on sale out at the Yard. So I caught the Number 15 bus on Columbus Avenue and went out there for the first time.

There were two Negro boys sitting behind me on the bus. They were talking about Chubby Checker and the Twist. They thought that Chubby

Checker was only fifteen years old because he didn't have a mustache. Then they talked about some other guy who did the twist forty-four hours in a row until he saw George Washington crossing the Delaware.

"Man, that's what I call twisting," one of the kids said.

"I don't think I could twist no forty-four hours in a row," the other kid said. "That's a lot of twisting."

I got off the bus right next to an abandoned Time Gasoline filling station and an abandoned fifty-cent self-service car wash. There was a long field on one side of the filling station. The field had once been covered with a housing project during the war, put there for the shipyard workers.

On the other side of the Time filling station was the Cleveland Wrecking Yard. I walked down there to have a look at the used trout stream. The Cleveland Wrecking Yard has a very long front window filled with signs and merchandise.

There was a sign in the window advertising a laundry marking machine for $65.00. The original cost of the machine was $175.00. Quite a saving.

There was another sign advertising new and used two- and three-ton hoists. I wondered how many hoists it would take to move a trout stream.

There was another sign that said:

THE FAMILY GIFT CENTER,

GIFT SUGGESTIONS FOR THE ENTIRE FAMILY

The window was filled with hundreds of items for the entire family. *Daddy, do you know what I want for Christmas? What, son? A bathroom. Mommy, do you know what I want for Christmas? What, Patricia? Some roofing material.*

There were jungle hammocks in the window for distant relatives and dollar-ten-cent gallons of earth-brown enamel paint for other loved ones.

There was also a big sign that said:

USED TROUT STREAM FOR SALE.

MUST BE SEEN TO BE APPRECIATED.

I went inside and looked at some ship's lanterns that were for sale next to the door. Then a salesman came up to me and said in a pleasant voice, "Can I help you?"

"Yes," I said. "I'm curious about the trout stream you have for sale. Can you tell me something about it? How are you selling it?"

"We're selling it by the foot length. You can buy as little as you want or you can buy all we've got left. A man came in here this morning and bought 563 feet. He's going to give it to his niece for a birthday present," the salesman said.

"We're selling the waterfalls separately of course, and the trees and birds, flowers, grass, and ferns we're also selling extra. The insects we're giving away free with a minimum purchase of ten feet of stream."

"How much are you selling the stream for?" I asked.

"Six dollars and fifty cents a foot," he said. "That's for the first hundred feet. After that it's five dollars a foot."

"How much are the birds?" I asked.

"Thirty-five cents apiece," he said. "But of course they're used. We can't guarantee anything."

"How wide is the stream?" I asked. "You said you were selling it by the length, didn't you?"

"Yes," he said. "We're selling it by the length. Its width runs between five and eleven feet. You don't have to pay anything extra for width. It's not a big stream, but it's very pleasant."

"What kinds of animals do you have?" I asked.

"We only have three deer left," he said.

"Oh . . . What about flowers?"

"By the dozen," he said.

"Is the stream clear?" I asked.

"Sir," the salesman said, "I wouldn't want you to think that we would ever sell a murky trout stream here. We always make sure they're running crystal clear before we even think about moving them."

"Where did the stream come from?" I asked.

"Colorado," he said. "We moved it with loving care. We've never damaged a trout stream yet. We treat them all as if they were china."

"You're probably asked this all the time, but how's fishing in the stream?" I asked.

"Very good," he said. "Mostly German browns, but there are a few rainbows."

"What do the trout cost?" I asked.

"They come with the stream," he said. "Of course it's all luck. You never know how many you're going to get or how big they are. But the fishing's very good, you might say it's excellent. Both bait and dry fly," he said smiling.

"Where's the stream at?" I asked. "I'd like to take a look at it."

"It's around in back," he said. "You go straight through that door and then turn right until you're outside. It's stacked in lengths. You can't miss it. The waterfalls are upstairs in the used plumbing department."

"What about the animals?"

"Well, what's left of the animals are straight back from the stream. You'll see a bunch of our trucks parked on a road by the railroad tracks. Turn right on the road and follow it down past the piles of lumber. The animal shed's right at the end of the lot."

"Thanks," I said. "I think I'll look at the waterfalls first. You don't have to come with me. Just tell me how to get there and I'll find my own way."

"All right," he said. "Go up those stairs. You'll see a bunch of doors and windows, turn left and you'll find the used plumbing department. Here's my card if you need any help."

"Okay," I said. "You've been a great help already. Thanks a lot. I'll take a look around."

"Good luck," he said.

I went upstairs and there were thousands of doors there. I'd never seen so many doors before in my life. You could have built an entire city out of those doors. Doorstown. And there were enough windows up there to build a little suburb entirely out of windows. Windowville.

I turned left and went back and saw the faint glow of pearl-colored light. The light got stronger and stronger as I went farther back, and then I was in the used plumbing department, surrounded by hundreds of toilets.

The toilets were stacked on shelves. They were stacked five toilets high. There was a skylight above the toilets that made them glow like the Great Taboo Pearl of the South Sea movies.

Stacked over against the wall were the waterfalls. There were about a dozen of them, ranging from a drop of a few feet to a drop of ten or fifteen feet.

There was one waterfall that was over sixty feet long. There were tags on the pieces of the big falls describing the correct order for putting the falls back together again.

The waterfalls all had price tags on them. They were more expensive than the stream. The waterfalls were selling for $19.00 a foot.

I went into another room where there were piles of sweet-smelling lumber, glowing a soft yellow from a different color skylight above the lumber. In the shadows at the edge of the room under the sloping roof of the building were many sinks and urinals covered with dust, and there was also another waterfall about seventeen feet long, lying there in two lengths and already beginning to gather dust.

I had seen all I wanted of the waterfalls, and now I was very curious about the trout stream, so I followed the salesman's directions and ended up outside the building.

O I had never in my life seen anything like that trout stream. It was stacked in piles of various lengths: ten, fifteen, twenty feet, etc. There was one pile of hundred-foot lengths. There was also a box of scraps. The scraps were in odd sizes ranging from six inches to a couple of feet.

There was a loudspeaker on the side of the building and soft music was coming out. It was a cloudy day and seagulls were circling high overhead.

Behind the stream were big bundles of trees and bushes. They were covered with sheets of patched canvas. You could see the tops and roots sticking out the ends of the bundles.

I went up close and looked at the lengths of stream. I could see some trout in them. I saw one good fish. I saw some crawdads crawling around the rocks at the bottom.

It looked like a fine stream. I put my hand in the water. It was cold and felt good.

I decided to go around to the side and look at the animals. I saw where the trucks were parked beside the railroad tracks. I followed the road down past the piles of lumber, back to the shed where the animals were.

The salesman had been right. They were practically out of animals. About the only thing they had left in any abundance were mice. There were hundreds of mice.

Beside the shed was a huge wire birdcage, maybe fifty feet high, filled with many kinds of birds. The top of the cage had a piece of canvas over it, so the birds wouldn't get wet when it rained. There were woodpeckers and wild canaries and sparrows.

On my way back to where the trout stream was piled, I found the insects. They were inside a prefabricated steel building that was selling for eighty cents a square foot. There was a sign over the door. It said

INSECTS

35

Trish Maharam was born in New York City in 1953, and she graduated from Kirkland College in New York State with a dual major in creative writing and philosophy. She now lives with her family in Seattle, Washington, where she writes nonfiction and fiction and works as a regional editor for several national magazines. She and her husband like to explore the wilderness areas of Alaska, especially the Gates of the Arctic and the Alaska National Wildlife Refuge, and she is dedicated to the joys of urban nature in Seattle. As a self-described "urban anthropologist," Maharam observes how city people yearn for nature in their lives and the ways they find to make connections with the natural world. In the powerful essay below, she chronicles how three generations of females in her family have discovered themselves through their relationships with plants.

Plantswomen

Trish Maharam

Ten years ago, when I was six months pregnant, I laid the foundation for my first garden. As I planted the first seeds on our property, it dawned on me that I was a seedpod myself.

A little more than a year later, on a rainy Seattle spring night, my husband, our new daughter, Hanae, and her grandparents dug together to plant a young Japanese snowbell tree in our garden. We piled shovelfuls of dark-brown loam in small mounds around the hollow where the young tree would be planted. I took my daughter's placenta from the freezer and settled it in the moist earth. I remembered holding it the day she was born at home, a mass of nourishment and oxygen that most women discard. When I turned the placenta inside out, it had the very defined shape of a tree. The tree of life.

Many indigenous cultures make a ritual of burying the placenta in the ground and planting a tree over it. As the child grows, so does the tree. It seemed fitting to plant Hanae's placenta under a tree so like her, graceful and gentle, with white fragrant bells that bloom in late May. We stood in the pouring rain, our heads covered in plastic rain hats, each taking a turn covering the roots, Hanae in a pack on my back. "This is your tree," I told my baby daughter; "your guardian, fed by your placenta. We will watch it grow together."

Gardening has been a tradition of the women in my family. My mother learned from her aunt Hilda Gort, who had a huge perennial garden in Lawrence, Long Island. As a child, my mother visited Hilda for a week each summer, following her through the gridded paths of pastel blossoms. Hilda wore a large hat and a billowy cotton summer dress. My mother loped behind her, carrying a woven basket, while Hilda snipped flowers with silver scissors to fill the vases that adorned each tabletop in her house.

It wasn't until my mother was in her thirties that a friend with thriving herbs and perennials invited her to learn how to make a garden. There were women in our neighborhood with whom my mother had little in common, but they became gardening friends and cultivated a language with plants that bound them, talking about the morning light on wet leaves, or bending together to admire a pink penstemon, then finding themselves a half-hour later with smudged knees and an ample pile of weeds. In this way my mother grew herself as a gardener.

Now, years later, my sister Hillary and I have our own gardens on opposite coasts. We were not born to the love of gardening. Like our mother, we learned it over time. Though I grew up with the chores of weeding and gathering berries, it wasn't until I had a home in Seattle on a large south-facing lot that I found my own relationship with plants.

I was overwhelmed by our half-acre in the city, a private dead end with a few old orchard trees, and land covered in blackberries, morning glories, and horsetails. I understood nothing of the bones of gardening, the pathways and stone walls. I'd had no formal teaching and had read few books. The only language I knew was the one my mother and I shared over the telephone about colors and simple flowers. I called her and said, "I'm not equipped to make a garden of my own."

"That's ridiculous!" she said. But then: "I remember feeling that way myself." She told me a story.

"Just the other day, I was at Home Depot. They have a huge collection of orchids. A very large woman came and stood beside me to admire them. We oohed and aahed, and then she pulled a bunch of photographs from her pocketbook. I assumed they were of her children, or grandchildren, but they were pictures of her orchid collection. There were orchids on her porch, in the house, in the garden. The same orchids I love, yet used in a completely different way. You see, we all have access to the same plants. You just have to find the ones you love, the ones that belong to you, and plant them."

Around this time, in 1987, I was offered a job as the Northwest regional editor for *Better Homes and Gardens*. It was a job my mother had learned and inherited from her dear gardening friend on the East Coast. My credentials were mostly that I was a resourceful networker with a good eye. My assignment was to find suitable houses and gardens and to arrange for them to be photographed. I didn't realize then that I would be entering people's lives through their environments.

In my second year of work I met with a Frenchman who was dying of AIDS. We walked slowly through his garden as he quietly told me about his plants. Before I left, he held in his bony hands a tiny green fava bean. "When I was a child," he said, "my mother made fava bean stew. It was my favorite dish. I have always grown them." Since meeting him I grow those long, bumpy beans, and his memory lives on in my yard.

When I was eight months pregnant with Hanae, I had an assignment to photograph a garden layered in perennials, petticoats of roses and white phlox laced in clematis and honeysuckle. For three days the homeowner brought me tea as I worked. During lunch, she invited me to lie down on her tall bed, which I reached by climbing a small ladder. When I left she gave me a fairy rose, which has grown full and abundant planted beside the gate I pass through each day going in and out of my home.

For seven years I visited and photographed the garden of a woman who looked like Audrey Hepburn. She had made her garden her lifework. There were paths of stone, each one hand-collected and carefully placed. There were birdhouses she constructed herself, and jams she made from marionberries and gooseberries, served to me on muffins fresh from the oven. We ate them seated by the small pond where the first water lilies were opening. She taught me to have a large view of the garden but to focus on one small piece at a time.

Each gardener I met gave me a list of his or her favorite gardens. That is how I found my way from one place to the next. Over the years, a number of people had mentioned a garden in Victoria, British Columbia, and finally I called to set a time for a visit.

When I opened the wooden gate, a woman in her fifties scurried toward me. She was of medium height and lean, and though she smiled, her face was hawkish.

She welcomed me into her yard, an exquisite foliage garden. A small fountain bubbled calmly in the foreground. Layered in gradations of green, symmetrical but loosely planted, the shapes and textures were carefully and thoughtfully placed. There were slender paths woven throughout. It is always a treat to come upon a garden like this one, to set up the camera in soft morning or early-evening light and compose pictures. It is the way I learn best about plants in combination. I was already looking forward to the time I would spend there.

We sat down together at a small table perched at one side of a courtyard.

"Which magazine are you working for?" she asked, her lips pulled tight into her face.

I had brought her an issue. She leafed through it quickly, barely glancing at the contents. "Well, you know, I've been in *Fine Gardening* and *Horticulture* and many other serious magazines, and this looks rather superficial."

"It's new," I countered with discretion, "but I don't believe it's superficial. It offers contemplation for gardeners, and an invitation for beginners."

Turning on me, her eyes narrowed, she said, "And what about you? Do you have a garden?"

I kept my eyes level with hers. "Yes. It's ten years old now."

"And are you a *plantswoman,*" she hissed, "or do you simply gather pretty flowers?"

She craned her neck, stretching her head up over me. The gesture reminded me of a bird puffing out its feathers to appear larger than it is.

"We all have to start somewhere." I kept my voice steady. "I have my whole life to learn about plants."

In the end, I had no desire to view her garden. It seemed tainted, like the woman. I closed the gate quietly and left, but her words had unsettled me.

Back in my own garden, I asked myself, What is a plantswoman? Was I really one? Often I felt inadequate in the presence of long-time gardeners, as though I wasn't serious enough or devoted enough. Over the years I had tried to study Latin names of plants, but I retained only the common names. I thought about my slow toil of digging out horsetail and blackberry, amending soil that was once so hard I'd had to jump on the shovel to pierce the ground. Now I could easily dig down two shovelfuls deep and find worms instead of rocks and clumps of clay.

I'd made many mistakes in the garden, such as planting whole beds with smatterings of perennials that made it spindly and unappealing. But over time I had learned to think in combinations, to use one kind of plant generously, so that it grew full and textured beside another—the loose roundness of the standard Hiroki Nishiro willow, for example, its variegated leaves and thin reddish limbs surrounded by the tall deep purple orbs of allium "Globemaster." I had learned how to choose from the nursery or others' gardens what belonged in my own. But perhaps that made me a mere gatherer of pretty flowers.

Over the next month, I contacted many women, gardeners and nurserywomen, in my quest to define what a "plantswoman" is.

"The garden," said Karen Jennings, a member of a family-owned South Carolina seed business, "is an extension of our living space, and I think that's one reason why it belongs to women. Plants have always been there at times when women didn't have many avenues for creativity. Whether it was food production or perennial gardens, it was their province."

Renee Shepherd, a seed gatherer and provider living in California, explained to me that gardening is an exchange of information. For her, "being a seed gatherer means having a link with every culture."

Jane Lappin, a grower and designer on eastern Long Island with a formal education in horticulture, has a voice to match her person, deep and gutsy. "When I began in the 1970s, I remember going to my first Long Island growers' meeting. I was one of only three women. I wanted to grow rare and unusual plants that I couldn't get anywhere else, and I wanted to grow the majority from seed. The men laughed at me. But I was driven, and excited about the growing."

When I asked for her definition of a plantswoman, she responded, "Being a plantswoman is a buildup of knowledge and experience." As an example, she mentioned a large sweep of oceanfront property in the Hamptons that she'd recently been asked to landscape. It had taken her fifteen years of planting by the sea to be able to know which plants were going to make it and which ones wouldn't. "Now I get to think about contrasting foliages, about what it's going to look like through the seasons beside another plant"—her speech quickened with enthusiasm—"the flowers, the textures, how it handles the wind. It's so exciting when you have the knowledge to put this whole picture together properly, to plant it, and stand back, and see it completed."

Each time I finished speaking with a plantswoman, I refined my own definition of the term. Over time I began to understand the language of plants and their nature. Some years are just about maintenance, other years are about change. One year, during a bout with pneumonia, I was unable to tend my plants. Instead, I sat in a chair and observed the garden. Dozing off, I woke to a quiet, uncluttered moment between sleep and waking, and there before me stood my garden. In the nearest bed, on the south-facing bank, I could see all the gradations of blues and lavenders—*Perovskia, Caryopteris, Nepeta,* and *Eryngium*—mixed with the silver-grays of *Artemisia, Santolina,* and *Achillea.*

There was a time when that bank was sandy and eroding. Now it was full, the plants mature and well blended. I let out a deep sigh of satisfaction before looking further.

In the upper bed, the *Nepeta* was making babies everywhere, crowding out the agapanthus. I watched as my nine-year-old Hanae made a path with her body through the dense foliage to smell a newly opened Heritage rose.

"Mom, there are white lilies hiding in here. You can't even see them from the house."

I had overplanted, and now I was going to have to dig out and transplant to make room for the larger plants so they could spread and drape the way they were meant to. I was going to have to go backwards. For a moment I was frustrated with this insight; then I laughed. I realized that the garden reflects my impulsive side. That's who I am. I remembered my mother telling me that if we approach gardening without the guidance of a designer or a landscape architect, it will show us what we are made of.

Recently, Hanae was helping me to prune the clematis and honeysuckle that were strangling a patch of lavender. I was using my Felco pruners, which always make me feel capable, and wearing my high rubber boots. Hanae was in her bare feet, wielding a pair of scissors. I had a sudden glimpse of her as separate from me, my seed-child growing up. In our garden I could somehow see her more clearly, her color and shape, the way her body comfortably mingled with the plants.

For Hanae, the garden is a place for observing and gathering. Unlike me, she doesn't care about tidiness; it's more important that the dogs have a place to run, that there's grass for rolling and picnicking. When we look through the gardening catalogue in the fall, she chooses the bright pinks and deep reds, colors that I avoid. She is already preparing a cutting garden with hyacinths and tulips for the spring, dahlias and peonies for the summer.

One Saturday morning we went to our favorite nursery. Hanae took her own wagon and meandered through the rows, considering, bending down to get a better look, then gathering. When she returned to me with her wagon full, I looked at the plants she had chosen. They were small mounds, little islands with delicate pink and white flowers, tiny foliage in silvery green. We read together the nature of each plant, how large it grows, whether it likes sun or shade. I saw that she was already learning to tend her own garden.

I called my mother that day and asked her, "How would you define a plantswoman?"

"You know," she said, "it doesn't matter how you're connected to the plants, it's the connection that makes you a plantswoman. If you go out into your garden and it lights up your face, or your whole body, then you're a woman who loves plants."

I walked through my yard at dusk. The oriental lilies my mother had sent had opened. I held the fullness of a pale-orange rose in my hands and finally understood why she loves roses. But I could see in the way I had planted that spring that I was shifting away from flowers toward foliage. I sat on a stone step and listened to the waterfall. I was growing and changing with my garden.

Hanae's tree had grown tall, like her, the deep-plum clematis "Niobe" climbing through her Japanese snowbell. Her placenta had become part of the earth, part of the roots of that tree.

"I am a plantswoman," I told myself. I stood over a newly planted maidenhair fern, lifted my watering can, and began to pour.